The Pincers of Death

Also by Toby Frost:

Space Captain Smith
God Emperor of Didcot
Wrath of the Lemming Men
A Game of Battleships
End of Empires

The Pincers of Death

Toby Frost

MYRMIDON

Myrmidon
Rotterdam House
116 Quayside
Newcastle upon Tyne
NE1 3DY

www.myrmidonbooks.com

First published in the United Kingdom by Myrmidon 2017

A catalogue record for this book is available from the British Library.
ISBN (Export Paperback) 978-1-910183-24-3

Set in 11/14 Sabon by Falcon Oast Graphic Art Ltd.
www.falcon.uk.com

Printed in the UK by CPI Group (UK) Ltd, Croydon, CRO 4YY

1 3 5 7 9 10 8 6 4 2

Contents

Prologue

Attention soldier! Now is the hour! Rise up for the leader!
Rise for glorious Number One!

Storm-Assault Commander 462 groaned, pulled back the covers and hit the alarm clock with his pincer. The clock fell silent.

462 sat up, yawned and stretched all four of his arms. He stumbled upright and limped into the bathroom. He rubbed his right eye and quickly buffed the lens of the bionic camera that had replaced the left one. 462 washed and spent ten minutes arranging his antennae. Today was a special day, and he had to look good.

He took his smartest leather coat-and-helmet combination from the wardrobe and admired himself in the mirror.

'Not bad,' he said. 'Not bad at all.'

Assault Unit One looked up from his basket and snarled. 462 fed him a tin of pulped minion and retreated to a safe distance to make his own breakfast. Even the officers of the Ghast Empire were feeling the effects of rationing and the food cupboard was half-empty. 462 took down a can and blew dust off the top. The label showed a snarling praetorian firing a bipod-mounted disruption cannon from the hip.

'*Vio-Lent Green,*' 462 read. '*Put a storm in your step with the Ghast Empire's favourite nutritional supplement.*'

Nutritional substitute, more like, he thought. He had once eaten a can of Vio-Lent and it had put a storm in his step and a hurricane in his hindquarters. He'd had to follow a marching band home to muffle the subversive proclamations he'd been making every few paces.

462 settled for two Ghastibix. He ate the first one whilst watching the propagandatron, his face fixed in an expression of intense loyalty in case the propagandatron was watching him back. He fed the second Ghastibix to Assault Unit One, who could chew through sheet steel, and set the video to record *The Show Trial Show* later on. Then he checked himself in the mirror again and limped to the door.

'Come on, Salty,' he rasped. 'Time to meet the Leader.'

*

The staff hovercar slid through the streets of Selenia, under rows of saluting statues. Bio-tanks and marching columns moved aside to let 462 pass. The Ministry of Accuracy was shaped like the shouting head of Number One, his antennae replaced by huge radio masts. The staff car slid into his vast, open mouth.

Four years ago, just before the Ghast Empire had begun its war against mankind, 462 had been recruited by Number Two to join the espionage department and decypher the intricacies of the British mind. Back then, he had been one of hundreds of competing underlings, analysing the political philosophy of Pancake Day and studying the military capabilities of the Girl Guides. Now he was Two's sole assistant, after all the other underlings had been mysteriously despatched to attend a rally on the far side of the M'Lak Front.

462 left Assault Unit One at the kennels, passed through the security checks and entered the main office. At the back of the room, the printer was churning out death warrants. Number Two squatted beside it with a bucket, catching the warrants as they fell out of the slot. Whilst studying Earth's scientific development, 462 had once seen a film about a diabolical genius called Frankenstein, whose ruthless intellect and mastery of twisted science had almost destroyed the human race. Number Two reminded him of Frankenstein's assistant.

'All hail to you, Departmental Manager!' 462 said, hanging up his outdoor trench coat and putting on the one he wore in the office. 'I'm looking forward to meeting Number One.'

'Yes, yes, the master!' Two replied. Light glinted on the lenses he had instead of eyes. 'And yet you look uncomfortable,' said Number Two. 'I can tell from your face that you have been eating Vio-lent again.'

So much for the expression of loyalty, 462 thought. 'I'll check the news channels,' he said.

One of 462's jobs was to prepare technical briefings for Number Two, which meant watching the BBC and telling him what was really going on. The galactic situation was not good.

The Yullian front had collapsed. The lemming men of Yullia, who didn't understand retreat, were dying in vast numbers for no real gain. On the screen, human crew climbed into an attack shuttle bound for the Yullian home-world. *'These fine fellows are going to usher in a new era for the lemming men – the Stone Age'*, said the jolly announcer.

Stupid rodents, 462 thought. The Yull had bitten off more than they could chew, or even store in their cheek pouches. Their crazed dream of murdering half the galaxy and looting it bare was beginning to look like the result of eating too much cheese before entering hibernation.

The M'Lak Front was still a brutal wasteland. On the screen, a row of Aresian deathwalkers plodded across the landscape, their tentacles drooping miserably. A group of Ghast drones trudged past, pulling a gun carriage on which sat their commanding officer. *'Morale and leadership is in decline,'* said the announcer. *'The leader-caste refuses to accept the dire reality. This political officer has not even realised that his soldiers are moving away from the enemy and towards a field canteen, and that they intend to eat him when they get there.'*

It was barely worth checking up on the human zealots of the Democratic Republic of Eden. For all the cultists' promises of holy conquest, their defences were proving more porous than pious, and the only high stakes to be fought over were the ones they used to burn each other when they lost a battle. Today, the BBC reported that something called the Former Edenite Matriarchal Military Enclave had risen up in Edenite territory: a furious woman brandished a pair of shears at the camera and loudly promised vengeance on the clergy. *'Soon, the only offensive capability left to the Edenites will be their smell,'* the voice said.

Meanwhile, the British Space Empire had designed a new

tank. '*The Compensator is able to breach the flank armour of anything up to a Tiger Prawn bio-tank,*' the announcer declared. '*These new landships will soon be rolling out of the vehicle factories on Reno V by the thousand. Equipped with the largest railgun and the biggest barrel yet seen, the Compensator has nothing to feel insecure about.*'

This, 462 thought, *is what happens when you rely on non-insects*. For all their talk of crusades and lemming spirit, the Ghast allies had no backbone. Of course, having evolved from army ants, the Ghasts didn't have backbones either, but you couldn't go wrong with a hardened carapace and unquestioning loyalty to your hive. He switched off the screen.

'Anything interesting today?' asked Number Two.

'Our allies are feeble, our leadership is corrupt and our attempt to conquer the galaxy has stalled,' 462 replied.

'Excellent, excellent. Number One will sort them out.' Number Two never seemed to take much notice of bad news. 'I've got some documents I need destroyed. I've had to correct history again.'

'Don't worry, I'll get rid of them,' 462 said. He had a stash of incriminating papers back at his apartment, just in case his superiors needed blackmailing. 'I'll feed them to my ant-hound.'

'Good. Are you all set for the meeting today?'

'Most certainly, illustrious manager. I'll just, ah, use the smallest room.'

Although the bathroom was the smallest room in the building, it could have held an armoured car. 462's entry tripped a sensor, and a loudspeaker shouted, '*Attention, visitor! Treat the officers' lavatories as you would treat the struggle for supremacy of the battlefield. Flush out corruption and aim with efficiency!'* Marching music piped in through speakers, to keep things moving.

462 straightened his antennae, did some practice salutes in the mirror, washed his hands and dried them on a fluffy banner hanging beside the sink.

'Ready?' Two said as he left. 'We're just across the courtyard.'

462 collected Assault Unit One from the kennel. The guards had fed him their weakest member, so he could be relied upon not to eat Number Two for now.

462 had never been into the conference bunker before. It was a huge lump of black marble, its massive facade held up with columns the size of rocket boosters. Outside, a stylised stone Ghast held up a lightning bolt in its pincers.

In the foyer, a praetorian soldier-ant waited behind a table loaded with surveillance equipment. These days, everyone was worried about sabotage from the British Space Empire. Of course, the British could never equal the Ghasts for tanks, marching and shouting, but their troops had a nasty unpredictability. After all, what was wrong with people who spent peacetime behaving like decadent weaklings and then became cunning maniacs when you tried to eat them all?

'Identification check,' the praetorian grunted. 'No exceptions.'

He grabbed 462's antennae, pulled his head down and shoved his face against a glass panel set into the top of the table. He pushed 462's head along the table, past a red beam.

The praetorian let him go. 'Scar-code accepted,' he said. 'The lift's over there.'

The doors rolled open and they stepped inside. The lift descended.

Number Two leaned against the wall and started to mutter to himself. Assault Unit One sat down and began to lick his own spiracles. 462 swallowed hard. He had butterflies in his stomach, caused either by fear or some ant-specific parasite.

It was important to get himself into a suitable state of mind for meeting Number One. Carrying around the glorious leader's collected speeches was impossible, since they came in a set of over thirty volumes, but 462 had a copy of Number One's *Little Book of Mindlessness* in his pocket. He slipped it out and read at random.

Today, think about your orders. Put aside all doubt and indecision and do what you are told. Try to bypass your brain entirely. Channel your aggression into more aggression. Breath in . . . breathe out . . . now shout at something.

The lift banged to a halt. 'Now,' Two said, 'you are about to witness the pinnacle of evolution. Number One is the greatest member of our great species. Destiny has chosen him to lead us to victory.'

'Right,' said 462. 'Don't show me up, Salty.'

The doors opened. 'Remember,' said Number Two. 'You are in the presence of genius.'

They walked into a huge dark room. 462 could feel the emptiness of the place on his face and antennae. Two gestured for him to stop.

With a soft, wet sound, two biocannons folded down

from above. The gun-arms twisted and pointed their barrels at the visitors. Assault Unit One growled softly.

A blue phosphorescence rose in the far side of the room. It swelled and spread, illuminating a colossal throne. 462 gazed upwards, as the swelling light revealed shoulders and then a head. The seated figure was four times his height. His antennae were like dead trees, his helmet the curved prow of a submarine.

A face loomed down at them. 462 saw the sunken eyes and square nostril-hole of a trillion posters. The mouth opened slightly. The glorious leader's voice rang through the hall like thunder.

'Is it on yet?'

Number Two shouted, 'All hail glorious Number One!'

Number One's hologram looked to the side. 'I can't hear anything,' he barked. 'Are you sure you plugged it in?' he asked, his voice rising. 'Tell me now, is it broken? I demand to know, in the name of the Ghast Empire: is it un-mit-i-ga-tedly corrupt, sickening in its wretched, dismal failure to attend the most urgent, vital, una-void-a-ble need to transmit the voice of the supreme leader?' Number One paused in mid-rant, his fist raised like a terrifying god. 'Plug it in the left side,' he said. 'Yes, the one that says *audio*. Conference calls . . . I don't know.'

Two coughed. 'I can hear your wise words, master.'

Number One looked down at them, and a thin smile crept across his face. At the sight of it, Assault Unit One drew back, his tail between his legs. 'Good, Two. Who is this?'

'My assistant, 462. He is an officer of exceptional cunning. He is the sole survivor of the Minion Purge of Zenor IX.'

One frowned. 'The sole survivor? I don't remember purging the minions of Zenor IX. Did I order that?'

'No,' 462 said. 'I did.'

'Hmm. I have a task for you, 462,' said Number One. 'Our home system is surrounded by our allied planets, much as the stony core of a Centaurian blood-peach is surrounded by its plump and squashy body. Our scum enemies believe that they can punch through our allies and enter Ghast space as if they are thrusting into the pink flesh of the peach. In my vast wisdom, I have realised that the quickest way to reach us would be to drive through the world of Radishia, here.' He opened his hands, and a map of the galaxy appeared between them like a cat's cradle, the tiny planets glistening between his palms. 'Radishia is ruled by a dictator, the Criminarch. He is a contemptible moron. However, his forces are reasonably competent – for humans.'

Number Two nodded vigorously. 'Your words are, as ever, full of wisdom and fury, glorious One.'

Assault Unit One looked up at the hologram and snarled. 462 tugged on his collar. 'Shush.'

'The British Space Empire and its decadent rabble of allies will launch an attack on Radishia, seeking to drive through and enter our territory. You, 462, will go there and bolster the Criminarch's resolve. Inform him that I will not tolerate weakness in his defences. His men must sacrifice themselves for our species. For those who accept it, there will be the honour of serving me. For those who do not, what shall await them? Death? Failure? Ignominy?' Number One shook his massive holographic fist at the roof. 'More than that, I tell you: defeat, despair and ab-sol-ute de-struction!'

'All hail Number One!' cried Two. 'All hail Number One!'

'All hail, all hail!' 462 shouted.

Assault Unit One leaped to his feet and barked.

The biocannons swung around and blew Assault Unit One to pieces.

There was an awkward pause.

'You just shot my dog,' said 462.

Number One twitched on his throne. 'Sensors detected an additional life-form in the chamber. Steps were taken to remove it to preserve secrecy. As every soldier knows, in the course of war, sacrifices must be made. It is the duty of every underling to make such sacrifices. Through my many great deeds, I have learned that it is an iron duty, a duty of will, a test of the relentless fortitude of the mighty army of the Ghast Emp—'

'That was my dog,' said 462.

'Silence! It breached security protocol. Secrecy of our meeting must be preserved at all costs.'

'Oh, of course,' said 462. 'Because I'm sure he was just about to tell the enemy everything we've said.'

The biocannons recalibrated. Number One leaned forward. 'I hope you are not being sarcastic, 462. Because sarcastic people make very good nutri-shake.'

'No,' 462 said. His own voice sounded small to him, each word carefully quietly distinct. 'You did the right thing. You always do the right thing. You are the glorious leader, right?'

Number One settled back in his chair. 'Right. You have your orders.' He looked to the side at something off-camera. 'That's enough. Yes, the third switch along.'

He vanished.

Number Two exhaled slowly. 'Well, that could have gone better.'

Above their heads, a voice yelled, 'And turn the audio off, too!'

'I think I shall return to my quarters,' 462 said. 'To wash my loyal ant-hound off my face.'

'Good idea,' said Number Two. 'You wouldn't want that muck impairing your efficiency.'

*

Back in his flat, 462 switched on the radio. At least three voices were shouting about increased tank production. It still felt quiet. 462 went to make himself some dinner, and found that he was holding a box of human-shaped biscuits. The picture on the front showed an ant-hound staring boldly into the distance.

'*For glaring eyes and a leathery coat,*' 462 read out loud. He shrugged and ate one. It wasn't bad, actually, probably because it was made out of exactly the same stuff as all other Ghast food: Ghasts.

He sat in front of the propagandatron, watching lines of troops marching and bellowing. '*These,*' the speakers proclaimed, '*are alpha-plus praetorian soldier ants, newly hatched by the division. Each one is scientifically proven to be equal to at least ten human troops. As such, they are guaranteed to bring victory to our brave forces.*'

462 ate another biscuit.

'*The alpha-plus gene-code is but one of many advances which guarantee the utter destruction of mankind. This first batch of soldiers will be joining the elite bodyguard of Number One himself: the Pincers of Death.'*

The camera panned up, past a banner with the skull-and-antennae logo of the Pincers of Death, to a balcony. The glorious leader struck poses, shook his fist at the sky.

462 reached into his coat and slid out his pistol. He turned it over and watched as Number One made gestures in the air. The pistol felt cold and solid against the scars on 462's palm.

I could do it, he thought. *I really could. Just like that.*

Part One

Radishia: Primary settled world of the Charon system
Population: 63,260,004
Alien Natives: None
Principal Land Use: Root vegetable farming – currently in decline owing to environmental decay
System of Government: Dictatorship
Principal Export: War

Notes: Under the operating protocols of Operation Garden Centre, the Joint Allied Expeditionary Council has targeted Radishia for invasion as part of the staged path to the Ghast home system. Invasion will take place by sector. British sector of invasion is graded B-14. For further information, enquire at your nearest police station.

Encyclopaedia Imperialis, Volume 39 (Pimms
– Rhododendron)

Crash and Burn

The *John Pym* was three miles above the Radishian Drylands when the storm took hold. Lightning crackled around the rusted hull. The wind hurled dirt into the viewscreens and the hurricane shook the spacecraft like an enraged child trying to get coins out of a piggy bank.

Deep within the *Pym*, Captain Isambard Smith spilled his tea and decided that enough was enough. He leaped to his feet and strode into the cockpit.

'Terrible weather we're having,' he declared.

Polly Carveth looked around from the pilot's seat. 'Don't I know it. The wind's buffeting my thrusters something awful. I just hope we won't be needing a PCH-26 comms pylon when we land.'

'Why?'

'Because it just fell off the back.'

'Hmm.' There was a light burst on the starboard wing. The ship rattled. 'Well, worse things happen at sea.'

'Do they, boss? Really?'

'Well, of course.' It was time to take charge. A captain's job was to instil his fearful crew with calm, and Carveth took a lot of instilling. He often wondered if someone at the android factory had fitted her with one too many self-preservation circuits. 'Dreadful place, the sea, even if you don't include sailors and navy rum.' Something hit the roof of the *John Pym*. 'What was that?'

Carveth consulted the sensors. 'An air kraken. Bloody hell, what next?'

'Greetings!' a voice snarled from the door. Suruk the Slayer stepped into the cockpit, spear in hand. He opened his mandibles and grinned at the storm. 'What mighty weather! Perhaps it is an omen of the hurricane we shall bring to our enemies once we land. Or perhaps we will fall out of the sky and explode. Who can say? Magnificent!'

Carveth gripped the gearstick. 'It's bloody scary, that's what.'

'Bah! Such talk shames a warrior, Piglet. Leave it to puny humans like Queen Galileo to find thunderbolts and lightning very frightening. We shall ride the storm like . . . like . . .' Something crashed in the hold behind them. 'That had better not be my skull collection,' Suruk growled, and he hurried back to his room.

'Stay on the controls,' Smith said. 'I'll be back in a moment.'

'Don't go!' Carveth cried. 'At least leave some chocolate behind.'

'I'm going to talk to Rhianna. She knows about nature.'

'Yes, but she *likes* it.'

Smith struggled down the rattling corridor and reached Rhianna's door. As he stepped in, a book entitled *Peaceful Thoughts* fell off the shelves and hit him squarely on the head.

Rhianna herself sat cross-legged on the bed. She

looked as if the electrical storm had charged her hair and blown random, tie-dyed clothes onto her body, but that was just how she was. Her expression was one of blank tranquillity.

'Hey, Isambard.'

'What ho, old girl,' he said. 'We're in a bit of a pickle.'

'Totally,' she replied. 'It's like nature's anger. I'm sensing a great force of nature, moving towards us.'

'Is that force of nature the ground, by any chance?'

'Er . . . yeah.'

'I see. Is there any chance you could use your psychic powers to get us out of this?'

'Sure.' She closed her eyes. 'Okay . . . I predict that we will be out of the storm and on the ground soon.'

'Really? How soon?'

'Well,' she said, and her face became mildly troubled, 'kind of right now, actually.'

*

The Deepspace Operations Group tore through the radish plantations in a blaze of gunfire and explosions. Their mission was to raise as much hell as possible: in their wake came the great armies of the Space Empire and its allies. Word of the Empire's attack had reached the prisoners who toiled in the Criminarch's fields, and Major Wainscott's men found themselves helping a rebellion. The country-side was in full revolt and the Minister for Agriculture, a notorious slave-driver, promptly and mysteriously fell into a legume-processing machine.

'Forward, Susan!' Major Wainscott cried, and their

armoured truck sped them out of the plantations and into the badlands.

The Criminarch did not believe there was such a thing as pollution, and so the parched, dead earth did not officially exist. Wainscott set about putting it on the map: more specifically, adding it to the growing pink part of the map that indicated the property of the British Space Empire.

By teatime, they were forty miles west of Yam Chasm. Two huge legs rose from the sand. A giant hollow torso lay beside them like the front half of a crashed missile, stripped to the metal by the desert winds.

'Thus fell Ozymandias,' Wainscott said. 'Slow down, Susan.'

Susan lowered the throttle. The lorry rolled forward. Craig covered the ruined statue with the side guns.

'So much for their glorious leader,' Susan said.

Rick Dreckitt stood up in the back. Before the war, he had worked as a robot bounty hunter in a dozen systems. He lifted his fedora and moved a toothpick to the corner of his mouth. 'That's not the Criminarch, lady. He's a muscly guy, bigger than a Mack truck and more tanned than Rodeo Roy's saddle. That there is Zipboy, the Supercola mascot.'

Wainscott looked around. 'The what?'

'Supercola. Big Radishian company. They make sports drinks. The stuff's pure fight juice. Imagine you're drinking tea before a battle, then some wise-guy slips you two fingers of rye when you're not looking. That kind of fighting.'

'Damn,' Susan said.

Wainscott frowned. 'How do you know all this, Dreckitt?'

The android shrugged. 'A good shamus keeps his ear to the ground. Obviously that's kinda hard driving round this desert – you get your speakers all fouled up with scorpions and meerkat crap – but you want to get the right guy, you need the right dirt on him. Also, I read the mission briefing.'

'I read them too,' Wainscott replied. He folded his arms and hunched down in his seat. 'This damn statue's already knackered. I'm not wasting dynamite on that. Let's find something intact so we can blow it up.'

'Well,' Susan replied, 'there should be a billboard a few miles north. How about that?'

'Splendid idea, Susan. We can test the ram on it. We'll wreck their propaganda machine and then stop for tea.' He banged on the bonnet with the flat of his hand. 'Carry on!'

*

Smith picked himself off the floor. He had been lucky. He seemed to be uninjured and a packet of crisps had fallen out of the roof and landed right next to him. He assumed they were part of one of the stashes of food that Carveth made around the spaceship when she was hiding fattening things from herself.

All in all, not bad. Not only had he found some crisps, but his capacity to think straight hadn't been impaired by the impact and also he had found some crisps. 'Crisps,' he said. Then he remembered that his spaceship, crew and girlfriend might all be badly injured.

'Bollocks.' He stumbled down the passage. Rhianna's

room was empty. He looked into the bathroom, on the very off chance that she might be washing.

Suruk lay face-down beside the shower, his legs bent back behind him. The alien groaned and stumbled upright. His mouth was red.

'God, Suruk, you're bleeding.'

Suruk shook his head. 'Ah, this is somewhat embarrassing. I had just stopped by to eat some of the little woman's cosmetics when I fell over. Now I look like the kind of idiot who cannot devour an entire lipstick without falling on his face.'

Smith left him cleaning his fangs with the large brush that he kept near the lavatory.

Acrid smoke billowed from the cockpit. Smith struggled in and headed towards a single red light that he assumed was the alarm panel. When he got closer he realised that it was the tip of Rhianna's questionable cigarette, which she was offering to Carveth.

Rhianna looked up. 'It's not good, Isambard. She's really stressed out.'

Carveth lay in her chair, surrounded by a slippery mess of magazines. She tried to rise, but her boot slid on last December's *Custom Model* and she fell back into her seat. Carveth read a range of magazines for female androids, all of which seemed to be designed to make her buy upgrades for herself. 'I was fine before your lady friend filled the room with Martian red weed,' she replied. 'The ship's buggered, though.'

The diagnostic display was largely red. That looked bad. The display said that tacheons had overloaded the warp core on Parsec Nine.

'The diagnostic computer's talking gibberish again,' Smith announced. 'Damned thing must be broken. Where are we, Carveth?'

She consulted the scanner, and then the map, and then a diagram drawn on the back of an envelope pinned to the console. 'Hard to say. I reckon we've come down in disputed territory. Looks like one of the Allied sectors. They'll have picked up the crash on their scanners. The only thing is, so will the Radishians. Typical. Less than a month to my birthday and I've crashed in a desert.'

As Smith leaned closer, one of the scanners began to beep. The sound rose and quickened. Something large was coming their way.

*

Smith took his orders – still sealed in an envelope marked *Top Secret* – his rifle and his Civiliser pistol. The others equipped themselves with water and weaponry. 'I'll see you outside,' Smith said, and he opened the airlock. The heat descended on him like a warm towel in a stuffy changing-room. He shielded his eyes.

Once, Radishia had been a free, prosperous planet, but the Criminarch had stopped all that. Now, the Radishian military called their lives Spartan and their planet unforgiving. Everyone else called them dismal and point-less. It was like New Pitcairn without the sophistication.

Burned, cracked earth stretched away from the ship as far as Smith could see, a dead ocean-floor washed by tides of fine dirt. Half a mile away, the tail of a Radishian space-ship protruded from the ground. The Royal Space Navy had made short work of the Radishian fleet, and this one had landed nose-first. By chance, an enemy armoured car and a battle-walker had been passing underneath, and they had joined the spaceship in a jumble of twisted steel.

Smith's crew emerged and Suruk slammed the airlock shut behind them. He was dressed conservatively by his usual standards and carried only his spear, half a dozen knives and the skulls of no more than eight different species about his person. Carveth wore a leather jacket and her heaviest boots. Rhianna, however, was in a trailing white garment, both voluminous and revealing. She looked rather like a Jane Austen character who had just run through a hedge. It wasn't practical, Smith thought but, on the other hand, she did look like a Jane Austen character who had just run through a hedge. He just wished she'd dressed up like that last week, when he'd specifically asked her to.

'We'll hide over by the wreckage,' Smith said, 'and see who comes along.'

Rhianna pointed to the wreckage. 'Hey, maybe Polly could get that armoured car working again.'

Carveth snorted. 'No chance. They've trashed it. These Radishians are too inbred to be any good with technology.'

'Yes, but you are, though, aren't you?'

'No, I'm not! Just because I've got a Cornish surname – oh, right, technology. Sure. I'll see what I can do when I get there. I'll just need to have a rest and a couple of biscuits first.'

Together, they set out across the sand. Suruk made good progress, using his spear as a walking stick. Smith followed. Carveth lagged behind, her legs being shorter, and Rhianna had a tendency to amble that Smith had always found rather annoying. *Still, got to give her the benefit of the doubt. Girlfriend and all that.*

'I'm worn out already!' Carveth announced.

'You've only gone fifty yards,' Smith replied.

'So? That's a long way for me. I need a drink – a *proper* drink. Did anyone bring a hip flask?'

'Sure,' Rhianna said, holding out her water bottle. Someone had painted a floral design across the side. 'Check it out.'

Carveth huffed and walked on.

They reached the ruined spaceship and rested in the shade. The battered flank rose above them like a cliff; a railgun shell had punched a hole wide enough for a train to pass straight through it.

Hurrah for the Space Navy, Smith thought. *That'll show 'em.*

He raised his rifle and scanned the shimmering horizon through its sights. A tiny speck moved towards them. It advanced in bounds, like a flea.

'Looks like a man riding something,' Smith said. 'Not a horse, though. It's got horns.'

'Is it a moose?' Suruk asked.

'What?' Carveth demanded. 'Who the hell rides a moose in the desert?'

'Lawrence of a reindeer.'

Smith shook his head. He squinted down the sights and saw that the animal had long back legs and a tail. It looked like a furry dinosaur. 'Good Lord, it's a kangaram!'

The kangaram approached them, and with each bound it became a little bigger. Soon Smith could make out the rider: his broad hat, his long coat, the rifle he held across his lap. The man looked capable, Smith thought, but he doubted that he'd be much of a shot from a bouncing steed.

Something moved to the right. Smith whipped around, and saw a figure in a gray Radishian uniform lean out from behind the armoured car. It raised a gun—

A shot rang out across the plain. The Radishian collapsed. His pistol hit the ground, slid across the sand and stopped a yard from Smith's boot.

The kangaram bounded closer. Smith stood a little way before his crew, hands at his sides but ready to grab his Civiliser.

With a final bounce, the kangaram halted ten yards away. Slowly, as if confused by its own limbs, it lowered itself onto the sand. The rider climbed down and pulled a scarf away from his face.

He walked out to the dead Radishian soldier and prodded the man's grey armour with his boot. The wind set the newcomer's coat and shorts flapping. 'Dead,' he said.

'You killed him,' Smith replied.

'Too right,' the rider said. 'This is my territory.'

Smith pointed to his spaceship. 'Well, that's my ship.'

The man peered at the *John Pym*. 'You're welcome to it,' he said.

'I am Space Captain Smith of the British Space Empire.'

'G'day,' the newcomer replied. 'I'm Bush Captain Shane of the 603rd Straalian Armoured Division. Ladies,' he added, tipping his hat. 'Person.'

'Greetings,' Suruk said. 'I admire your steed.'

'Is that so?' The kangaram snorted, and Captain Shane

leaned forward and tilted his head to one side. 'Say what, Rippy? You think they look pretty reasonable, for a bunch of Poms?' He looked back to them. 'She thinks you're okay too. Are you lost, then?'

'We were forced down in a storm,' Smith replied. 'We're meant to be meeting up with our own special forces in the British zone. We're to make contact with Major Wainscott of the Deepspace Operations Group.'

'Well, you're a bit off course, mate. This here's the Straalian sector. We're pushing forward into enemy territory right now. These radish fellas aren't so tough.'

Carveth said, 'I don't suppose you've got anything to drink? You know, proper drink.'

Shane looked rather hurt. 'As if a Straalian would carry alcohol around with him on a mission like this. Course I don't. All the tinnies get shaken up if I load Rippy with 'em. Now then, let's see where you are. Where'd I put the map, Rippy?'

The kangaram patted its stomach.

'You ate the map? Is that what you're saying?' He paused, as if listening to something. 'Oh, it's in your pouch. Good work, girl. Listen, mate . . . I'll wire up the long-range radio and put out a signal to the unit. They'll be able to give you a lift, if you don't mind pitching in.'

'We'll certainly try.'

'Great. The Wombats'll be here soon, don't worry.'

'Wombats?'

'Yeah. That's what we call the 603rd Straalian armoured. It's a new unit and all the man-eating reptiles, rabid badger-things, highly poisonous insects and spiders the size of footballs were already taken.' He looked at them, clearly expecting an objection. 'What can I say? It's a big army. We've got a lot of divisions.'

*

Smith left Carveth and Suruk with a bucket and an entrenching tool to make what Suruk described as a 'mighty citadel of sand'. He sat down in the shade of the armoured car and cracked open the seal on his orders. There was a logo at the top of the papers: a spaceship flying around a planet, flanked by a lion and unicorn. Smith saw the words *top secret*, *assassination*, *extremely dangerous* and *bit of no good* and felt that he was in home territory again.

On the next page, a gigantic man in a sort of Roman miniskirt was either wrestling or trying to have his way with a polar bear. It looked as if someone else's head had been crudely pasted onto another body.

The man was the Criminarch of Radishia. His narrow face and beady eyes made him look like the sort of creature that liked to run up trouser legs, but his massive torso, gene-spliced and muscle-grafted, was more like that of an ape than a man. The next photograph showed the Criminarch in a golden suit of servo-assisted, powered armour, saluting a gigantic mirror while a legion of minions in gaudy uniforms saluted and went weak at the knees.

Smith turned the paper over. The Criminarch was hosting some sort of morale-raising propaganda drive in the capital city. From the looks of it, he would be presiding over some sort of tacky sports event. Smith grimaced. The mention of sports reminded him of cold winters at Midwich Grammar School. You had to say one thing for the British schooling system: after a few years of 'character-building' games, galactic war didn't seem so bad.

You will locate and capture the Criminarch, the instructions said. *He will be taken via spacecraft to the Old Bailey to stand trial for inciting a war of aggression. Failing that, bag him. These orders will self-dissolve if dipped into tea.*

So, that was the target. It made sense: the Criminarch had legitimised his rule by claiming to be the heart and soul of Radishia. Take him out of the equation and the morale of the Radishians would plummet. Smith reflected that, had he been a Radishian, getting rid of a stupid tyrant would have raised his own morale considerably.

He put out his hand, instinctively expecting it to meet with a cup of tea. Instead it hit Rhianna's ankle, and the odd bits of string she inexplicably kept there.

'Hey, Isambard,' she said, sitting down beside him.

'What ho, old girl. What happened to your sandals?'

'Oh, they're around. You know. In the desert. Is that your mission?'

'*Our* mission, Rhianna. We're going to do over the Criminarch.'

'Oh,' she said. 'Is that going to be violent?'

'Well, we don't necessarily have to kill him. But probably.'

She didn't look terribly pleased about this. That was understandable. After all, Rhianna was a woman and women, being gentle creatures, didn't find villain-thrashing as inherently entertaining as men did – with the possible exceptions of Susan, Captain Felicity Fitzroy, General Young, most of the female robots he'd met, Smith's maiden aunt and of course Carveth, who could get pretty nasty once she'd had a couple of drinks and thought ponies were in danger. In fact, pretty much all the women he knew. Even Rhianna had once caused a man to be devoured by angry frogs.

Rhianna sighed. 'You know, I wish I could use my powers to make someone happy for once instead of all this violence. I worry about it, Isambard.'

She leaned forward and, studying the exposed bits of her, Smith conceived an idea how she could use her powers to make him happy right then. He decided not to mention it. Tact and all that.

Rhianna looked out across the sand dunes and sighed. 'Isambard, I'm going to have a baby.'

'*What?*'

'In about five years. I think that's a good time to have one.'

Smith paused to allow his heart and stomach to get back to normal. 'Righto. All in good time, eh? You should call it Rudyard. We should, I mean.'

'I was thinking of "Flower".'

'You can't call a baby Flower. People would laugh at him.'

'But what if it was a girl?'

'Oh, good point. Well, let's jump that hurdle when we get to it, eh?' *Preferably in about three decades*, he thought.

'Check this out,' Rhianna said. She took a thick brass disc like an oversized coin from her satchel and placed it on the sand. Rhianna tapped the top of the disc and it opened with the smoothness of clockwork. An array of mirrors unfolded and caught the sun.

'What is it?' he asked. 'Some kind of sundial?'

'Better than that,' she said. She took a tiny kettle from her bag. It looked like the sort of thing chaps used in India or somewhere like that. 'See? The mirrors heat the kettle up. All we need now is a teabag.'

'Well, as it happens, I keep one in my wallet behind the transparent plastic bit, just in case it's time for action. Gosh, Rhianna, that kettle's jolly clever. Good thinking. I think you're super.'

'Uhuh?'

'Absolutely. Much more than –' he glanced around, looking for inspiration – 'this damned desert, that's for sure. I mean, it's made of sand, for God's sake. Sand's terrible. Damned stuff goes everywhere. You don't. I mean, not like that. I mean, you *go* and everything, that's for sure, but in a localised fashion, if you see what I mean.' He paused, not entirely sure what he had just said but pretty certain that he had broadly captured the idea. Rhianna looked confused.

'Mate?'

Smith looked around guiltily, in case anyone had heard him expressing emotions. Bush Captain Shane came running across the sand.

'Mate, Rippy says the others are nearly here. Time to get moving.'

The first he saw of the 603rd Straalian Armoured Division were the outriders, bouncing along at the edge of the dustcloud. Then came the column itself, black machines hidden by the mixture of dirt and engine smoke that rose up around them.

'Do we need to make them stop?' Rhianna asked.

'Hmm,' said Smith. 'I once read a children's book where a girl stopped a train by waving her bloomers around. That seems a bit excessive, though.'

'Did they give her a ticket?' Suruk asked.

'I think they probably put her away, actually. Not the sort of carry-on one expects from a British officer.'

Suruk shrugged. 'I heard Major Wainscott once stopped a train by taking his trousers down.'

'Yes, but he was on the train at the time. They only stopped to hand him over to the police.'

The column drew closer and Smith could make out individual vehicles, as if they coalesced from the dust. A huge wagon was at the front. Had it not been rushing towards him, Smith would not have known which end of the vehicle did what. His eyes noticed details: a robot arm that ended in an oversized hedge cutter, a turret bristling with spikes, a chipped mural depicting a wombat devouring an enemy tank.

'Er,' said Carveth, 'these people are on our side, right?'

'Of course,' Smith replied. 'You have to be reasonable, Carveth. You can't expect everyone to be like us. Not only are we abroad, but these people are from abroad but in their own abroad. It stands to reason that they'll be a bit confused.'

'Well, that clears things up,' she replied.

One of the outriders pointed at them and reined in his kangaram. Flags waved on the main vehicles, and the whole strange armada slowed down. The division growled to a halt twenty yards away.

Smith saw rows of armoured figures along the side of the war machines, like very crude robots wearing long brown coats. They jumped down and fanned out. The air was full of smoke and the smell of hot oil.

Carveth sighed. 'So much sand, so many vans, and not one of them sells ice cream.'

'This here's Isambard Smith, from Britain!' Shane called out. 'He's looking for a fellow name of Scott – Wayne Scott. Anyone know where to find him?'

One of the armoured men removed his massive helmet and dumped it on the sand, like an upturned bucket. Speakers squealed into life on the largest of the vehicles. A voice boomed across the wasteland. '*Welcome, Captain Smith, and g'day to your mates. Prepare yourselves to meet the Lord of the Souped-up Ford, the Marharajah of the Turbocharger – the Ginormous Greg!*'

*

'I think of myself as ginormous of vision, really, rather than physical size.' At first glance, Ginormous Greg looked rather like Major Wainscott. However, his beard was whiter, his skin darker, and his eyes lacked Wainscott's intense, unblinking quality.

They sat in the rear of the command vehicle, surrounded by the rumble of engines. Greg was a very courteous host and had offered them beer and water. It was unfortunate, Smith thought, that they seemed to come mixed together in the same can. 'Back home, we use vehicles like these for herding genetically enlarged sheep,' the Ginormous explained. 'That's what the robot arm on the roof's for – drive-by shearing. You get a load of wool off a megasheep before it stampedes and squashes your ute.

'Now then. You're looking for a half-naked mad feller who drives around in a supercharged armoured car covered in guns and spikes, ramming things in a deranged mission to rule the wasteland, right?'

'Right,' Smith replied.

'Sorry, but I don't know anybody like that.' He shrugged. 'But there's a base about fifty miles from here you could ask at. It's got a satellite dish, a grid uplink to high command and a fortified barbecue. We'll give you a lift, if you like.'

'That's jolly good of you.'

'No problem. "Everyone deserves a fair go." That's the second law of the Straalian constitution.'

'What's the first law?'

'Drink up, everyone!' cried the intercom. 'We've got enemy coming in from the south. Looks like a Radishian armoured group. What's the plan?'

The Ginormous toggled the comm.-link. 'What do you think we should do, sit on our arses while these ant-lovers come the raw prawn with us? Get stuck in, mate!'

The engines snarled around them. On the outside monitor, Smith saw the outriders pick up speed.

'You up for this?' the Ginormous demanded.

'Bagging a few Ghastists?' Smith said, grabbing his rifle. 'Rather.'

A hatch flopped open in the roof and sunlight poured in. Smith scrambled up and Suruk gave him a shove. He clambered out into the heat and the dust, the roar of machines. Men in long coats and plate armour swarmed over the vehicles, manning turrets and ready-ing nets and harpoons. On the horizon, Smith saw dozens of grey-painted tanks flying the Radishian banner.

Suruk climbed up beside him. The alien hefted his spear and laughed. 'So much sand, Mazuran! The sun beats down pitilessly upon this arena of whirling death. Does it not remind you of the time we visited Skegness?'

Smith checked his rifle. 'I don't remember there being so much tank warfare then.'

'Really? Perhaps it was the time I went without you.'

*

'Well,' said Smith, 'I'm not sure what just happened, but I'm pretty sure that we won.'

He stood with Rhianna and Carveth on the sands beside the smoking wreckage of a Radishian half-track. A dozen enemy vehicles lay ruined around them, as if bowled along the ground by a gigantic hand. One of the tanks was still on fire and the Straalians were busy slicing chunks of metal off another. Sparks arced into the desert sky.

'Yeah,' Carveth replied. 'I followed it up the point where that lorry made out of trumpets rammed the tanks with chainsaws on the front and all those blokes dressed like mimes climbed out of the back. Were they on our side?'

Smith looked over to the far side of the battlefield. Several miserable-looking Radishians were being ushered into the back of a van like a prison block on tracks. They wore field caps and dark grey uniforms, and their faces were weary and sour.

'I think so,' Smith replied. 'The evil clowns were the ones being led by the chap who was on fire, weren't they – on the car with all the snakes?'

'No, you're thinking of the bloke in leggings on that little helicopter.'

'With an accordion?'

'That's him.'

'Guys?' Rhianna said. 'Um, aren't we missing someone?'

'Crikey,' said Smith, 'you're right. Where's Suruk?' He shielded his eyes and looked around. 'Strange. I mean, we're standing in the centre of all the destruction, so I would expect him to be here, too – causing it.'

'Hey, mate!'

Smith turned, and saw Rippy come bounding across the flat, Bush Captain Shane bouncing on her back. 'Look at this place,' he said. 'It's messed up like a madwoman's breakfast. Your alien mate went off like a frog in a sock back there. Where'd he go?'

At Rippy's feet, the ground moved. Slowly, Suruk pulled himself out of the sand and climbed upright. Something heavy had pressed him face-down into the earth: now he was covered in white dust. It rained down from his limbs and his armoured chest as he rose, turning him into a vengeful ghost. His eyes, always slightly bloodshot, blinked, and his face split into a grin too wide and toothy for any human head. 'Parp?' Suruk said.

'You're looking a bit crook there, mate,' Shane said. 'I think a truck's driven over you. How are you feeling?'

Suruk shrugged. 'Mediocre.' He walked over and prodded the wreckage of a motorbike with the toe of his boot. 'This reminds me of the time I found those gnomes in a pub. I asked one of them if he had a fishing rod. The next thing I knew, the judge said I was not to go within five hundred yards of the Satan's Soldiers Motorcycle Club.'

Carveth shielded her eyes and looked into the sky. 'Boss, is that a bird?'

Smith peered up, following the line of her finger. Like a barber-shop quartet preparing to sing, Suruk and Rhianna came in from left and right, all watching the sky.

Smith shook his head. It was hard to tell from this distance and from the harshness of the light, but it was definitely not a bird. 'It might be one of our planes.'

'Or an enemy,' Suruk growled.

Rhianna closed her eyes and lifted her face towards the sun. 'Don't worry, guys,' she said. 'I'm not sensing any intelligence there at all. It's not got a person in it at all, so it can't be an enemy plane. So that's okay.' She lowered her head, opened her eyes and blinked. 'I guess it could be a missile, though.'

Arena of Death!

Smith opened his eyes and light flooded in. A gong sounded in the back of his skull. He closed them very quickly and warily tried again.

He could hear a great roar, rising and falling. There was sand in his mouth. *Ah,* he thought, *I'm on a beach.* That would explain everything, apart from the corpse of a huge insect lying nearby.

It looked how a man would look if he had evolved from a scorpion and put on a crash helmet. *A Procturan Black Ripper,* Smith thought. What the devil was that doing on a beach? Trying to eat a shark?

Then he sat up and saw that he wasn't on a beach at all. He wasn't even outdoors. The bright light overhead came from massive floodlights. The roaring was the sound of a baying crowd.

The bodies of men and aliens were scattered around him. Blood seeped into and, in some cases, melted through, the sand.

Crew, he thought, and he staggered to his feet.

Suruk stood a few yards away, an axe in each hand. Carveth was behind him, holding a long pole. Rhianna – where was Rhianna?

A hand touched his shoulder. He spun around, and there she was, looking mildly surprised. 'Isambard, are you okay?'

Smith suddenly became aware of his body, as if it had been fine up to now. His right side was bruised, his head ached, and his moustache had been severely ruffled. 'Must'nt grumble. I'm fine, thanks. And you?'

'Um, okay, I think.'

'God, it's like a Roman amphitheatre. Look at that crowd, baying for blood—'

'No, Mazuran.' Suruk looked around. 'That is not the sound of crazed bloodlust – believe me, I know it when I hear it, especially when it's coming out of my own mouth. That is applause.'

'Huh? Applause?'

'Indeed. This puny menagerie was sent to slay us for the benefit of the crowd. One moment.' Suruk raised both axes and bellowed at the sky. 'They like it when I do that. I slew many enemies, and Rhianna the seer here used her powers to ward off some of the creatures. Even young Piglet there did her part.'

Carveth was out of breath. 'I beat off four gladiators,' she panted. She held up her stick. It was a tapered metal skewer, the end blackened and covered in ugly chunks of flesh.

'You really did someone an injury with that thing, by the looks of it.'

'This? Oh no, I grabbed it off the kebab stand.' The bravery faded from her face. 'They jumped us, threw us in a van and next thing I knew, we were here. You've been out cold. Boss, what is all this? What's going on?'

Smith looked around the arena, at the shouting crowds, the food vendors, the bodies on the sand. At the back of the arena hung rows of banners depicting a massive, heavily-tanned man with vicious little eyes: the Criminarch.

'The orders said the Criminarch was having some kind of sports day, to raise morale,' Smith replied. 'On the plus side, we've successfully infiltrated it. On the minus side, we would seem to be the sport.'

*

The Deepspace Operations Group was six miles north of the rendezvous when Major Wainscott called out from the back of the lorry. 'Look at what I've got, Susan!'

'Seen it already,' she muttered, but she glanced over and saw that the major was tapping the screen of the scanner, as if trying to get the attention of a goldfish in a tank.

'Coded beacon,' Wainscott said. 'That's the *John Pym*.'

The lorry was huge, rebuilt to Wainscott's specifications from the chassis up. Apart from the running boards, there was little to it that wasn't part of the armour, the engine or some kind of gun. Ammunition and extra battery packs had been fitted to the sides; a massive cow-catcher protected the front. Even the pintle-mounted laser cannons had been rigged for dual purpose: they could be lowered and focussed at low power on a massive kettle to brew the vast quantities of tea on which the D.O.G. survived.

Susan turned the wheel and the lorry swung out, throwing a wave of sand up behind it. Wainscott listened to the growl of the engine and smiled. In the back, Craig, Nelson and Rick Dreckitt manned the guns, scanning the waste-land for enemy vehicles.

'There,' Wainscott said.

The *John Pym* stretched along the horizon like a spine. The sand had half-covered it already.

'Big, long and brown,' Wainscott muttered. 'Like God's own pasty.'

Susan's beam gun had been clipped to a frame so it could be fired from the passenger seat. Wainscott slid his hand around the grip and pulled the stock up to his shoulder. It felt as comfortable and natural as taking his trousers off. As they rolled alongside the *Pym*, he felt the urge to bare himself for battle, but his experience of this kind of terrain told him not to. Sand tended to chafe.

'Bring us in close,' Wainscott said. Susan stopped a few yards from the ship's side airlock. She kept the engine running.

'I'm going in,' Wainscott said. 'Dreckitt, come with me.'

Dreckitt pulled down the brim of his hat. 'Let's bust the joint.'

Susan looked at the *John Pym* and grimaced. 'Don't stay in there long. You'll catch rust.'

Dreckitt and Wainscott made an odd pair as they ran up to the ship. Between them, they wore enough clothes for two people: unfortunately, Dreckitt seemed to be wear-ing most of them. He pulled his heavy pistol out from his trench coat and watched the airlock while Wainscott punched the override code into the airlock control pad. The door groaned and swung ajar.

Wainscott went in first, scowling into his beard. Dreckitt came in close behind him. Together, they moved through the ship, from the cockpit down to the cabins.

The major grunted. 'See anything?'

'Only this.' Dreckitt held out a tube like a baton. Tiny diodes flickered at one end. There was a glass panel set into one side of the tube. Wainscott saw fur behind it.

'Looks like a rat stuck in a loo roll.'

'Nix, pal. This is a cryogenic pod for a hamster. The little guy's in deep hibernation. That tells me two things. First, they knew they'd be away for a long while. My girl wouldn't leave her hamster for nothing. Second, they reckoned they'd be back.'

'No sign of your pilot girlie, then?'

Dreckitt shook his head. 'Gone like tears in rain. The joint's as empty as a Saturday night special on Sunday morning. I made her a model unicorn because she has these dreams about ponies. She keeps it in a drawer next to her bed, with some . . . electrical equipment. I hope she's okay.'

'She'll be fine. Don't get soft on me, Dreckitt. That's why I'm not married. All the women I met kept telling me I had to stay inside and not do what I wanted to do.'

'That's because all those dames were nurses,' Dreckitt said. 'Nurses at the booby hatch. Hey, you reckon Smith might have left us a message?'

Wainscott nodded. 'I saw some magazines under his bed. Old copies of *Corsetry World*, *Jane Austen Action*, that sort of thing. Maybe in there.'

Dreckitt frowned. 'Jazz books, huh? What we need is clues.'

'I have just the thing.' Wainscott pulled a wad of crumpled paper from the thigh pocket of his shorts. He opened it out, revealing a beige landscape punctuated by pencilled notes. 'There's a Straalian base north of here. Nearest allied settlement. We'll head that way.' Wainscott folded the map. 'And grab those corsetry magazines.'

'You think they'll give us a lead?'

'Clues? God no. But we'll need something to read on the way.'

*

'Bloody hell,' said Carveth, 'That's the last time I wish to be go somewhere with sand and activities. Don't these savages know that physical exertion is against my religion?'

Smith had spent the last hour examining the bars of the cell. So far, he had discovered that they were definitely metal and definitely not coming loose. 'You're an android, Carveth. You don't have a religion.'

'I'm a Pollytheist. All paths of truth lead back to me.'

'What puzzles me,' said Smith, 'is how they managed to get all of Suruk's weapons.'

The alien scowled. 'They threatened to shoot Piglet. And then they threatened to shoot you. It is strange, really . . . in theory I would have abandoned you to a meaningless and squalid death, then gone on a very brief rampage shortly before being gunned down by half a dozen guards, but instead I chose the dishonourable option. Sometimes I wonder if I am becoming human.'

Carveth snorted. 'Don't worry about it. You're still a hideous alien monster.'

Suruk parted his mandibles and smiled. 'I knew I could count on you.'

47

The corridor outside the cell was dusty and cold. To judge by the smell, it had been wiped clean with a pickled fish. Every so often, a guard would lumber past, the visor pulled down on his helmet. Smith had tried to call the man over, to use the ancient way of the Bearing to overwhelm his feeble mind, but the fellow simply hadn't heard.

'I wish Rick Dreckitt was here,' Carveth said. 'He'd know how to get out of here. Look!' She fished something out of her pocket. 'He made me an origami thing. I think it's a man with a big willy.'

'It's a unicorn,' Smith said. 'You're holding it the wrong way up. Damn it, there must be some way out of here. Rhianna, can do so some psychic stuff? Rhianna?'

She sat cross-legged on the bench, her eyes closed. 'Oh, hi guys. Are we still here?'

'Still stuck in this cell, yes. Have you got any bright ideas?'

'Yeah, totally,' she said. 'We might be locked in here, but maybe they're locked out there. Like, prisoners, but of the world?'

'Hmm,' Smith replied. 'That's not really the sort of idea I was hoping for – wait a minute. I heard someone.'

Footsteps sounded in the corridor. Smith leaned close to the bars and saw that a party of people was approaching. At the front were four bald thugs in suits and roll-neck sweaters. As they reached the bars, the heavy at the front said, 'Here they are, boss.'

A man stepped forward. He wore a suit interwoven with platinum thread. His cuffs were gold, as was his entire shirt. He was huge and ape-like, but he did not look healthy for it. His face was wrong for his body: the bone structure was too fine. It was like a weasel's head transplanted onto the body of a boar.

'Well, well,' said the man. His eyes were like a Ghast's eyes, Smith thought: small, hard and as kindly as two holes in a piece of leather.

Smith glared at him. 'You there. I demand to speak to the consulate.'

The nearest guard shouted 'Shut up! Show some respect before the father of the nation!'

'So, you're this Criminarch,' Smith said, infusing his voice with the Bearing. 'Tell your fellows to pipe down. I want to see the British ambassador.'

The Criminarch smiled. 'I am the Criminarch of Radishia. I am the one who makes Radishia strong. I smash people like you, because you are weak. Radishia is never weak! I am very manly and all the rumours are untrue. Also, I am very clever. Is it lunchtime yet?'

One of the guards leaned over to the Criminarch. 'Soon, sir.'

Smith wondered if the Criminarch had enough brains for the Bearing to take hold.

'Keeping comfortable in your cell?' The Criminarch smiled, revealing rows of suspiciously even teeth. His dentistry struck Smith as sinister and distinctly un-British.

'We'll manage,' Smith replied.

'Actually, it's crap!' Carveth called from over his shoulder. 'I want some cushions. Rhianna here needs a dream-catcher and some rugs. And Suruk—'

Suruk stood up. 'Step into this cell, fools, and I will show you how the Slayer decorates a room.'

The Criminarch snorted. 'Soft furnishings. Soft furnishings for soft people. We Radishians live in empty rooms, as suits our Spartan way of life. The majority of my palaces are furnished only in steel and gold, as a testament to my tough upbringing. On my planet, you don't tidy up a room – the room tidies you.'

'What does that mean?' Smith asked.

'Don't ask questions of me,' the Criminarch replied. 'On my planet, I ask questions of you. There will be no soft furnishings for you British. Instead, I will give you a man's death – a death any of my brave, rugged soldiers would be proud of. You will play in the arena, and there you will have the chance to prove yourselves. Not that you will win, of course, but you will at least amuse the crowd.'

'What?' Smith demanded. 'Are you saying that you want us to play *sport*?'

'Oh no, Captain. On my planet, sport plays you.'

The thugs realised that their boss had made a joke and remembered to laugh.

'We have an ancient game on our world,' the Criminarch announced, 'played by the strongest warriors, sponsored by only the manliest soft drinks corporations, where two teams fight head-to-head, face-to-face, roller-skate-to-roller-skate. But I can see that such fierce combat scares your dainty little minds. Look at that alien there. His face is covered in sweat at the thought of it.'

'It is drool, actually,' Suruk said. 'You mentioned something about fierce combat, I believe. Please continue.'

'You can find out for yourselves, in the arena. My people have been fighting hard. They're the best, the toughest.

They will enjoy the sight of you effete British runts being crushed under the boots of my players.'

Smith said, 'So your chaps don't get roller skates, then?'

'Boots *and* roller skakes. Have it your own way. Except, of course, you can have it *my* way. And on my planet, my way has you. See what I did there?'

The thugs roared with laughter. The Criminarch chuckled. Then he stopped laughing and very deliberately hooked his thumbs over his belt. He walked off, humming the Radishian national anthem, swaggering like a cowboy. Smith reckoned that he'd been practising that.

He turned to his men. 'Good lord. What a gigantic tosser.'

Carveth said, 'It's like King Kong and Liberace had a baby. And then they spoiled it.'

'The man's clearly insane. The last time I met someone that deluded was around the time my aunt's cats told her to run for Parliament. Stuff this for a game of gladiators,' Smith said. 'Not only are we the prisoners of an evil despot, but we're having to join in with some sort of sports day as well.'

'I thought you liked sport,' Carveth said. 'You know, playing the game and all that.'

'That depends an awful lot. Cricket, yes. Combat in an arena with noisy idiots, no. You see, Carveth, as a British citizen I have been a sworn enemy of tyranny since my childhood. At school I learned about the wrongness of cruelty, violence and the oppression of the weak.'

'They taught you about politics, then?'

'No, the other kids were horrible. Six years stuck in

defence on the bloody football field. It had more craters than the moon. Six years of being chosen last, time after time. The only time I wasn't in defence was when the little bastards nominated me to be a spare goalpost.' He shuddered. 'No, we're getting out.'

Rhianna raised her hand. 'Um, guys? Is this sport they want us to play competitive? Because that's really bad for childhood development, you know.'

'Of course it's competitive,' Carveth said. 'We'll be killing people out there!'

'Well then,' Rhianna said, 'we should totally escape. Like, uh, under the floorboards or something?'

'Good idea,' said Smith. 'If Suruk pulls up the toilet, we could crawl under the floor, past the toilet block and out the waste pipe.'

Carveth stared at him. 'Oh no. If you want to crawl under half a dozen lavs, on your own head be it. Not literally. Well, maybe. Anyway, no.'

Suruk coughed. 'Excuse me. There is a way of leaving here, that does not require either death or, er, pipe exploration.'

'Really?' said Smith. 'What's your plan, old chap?'

Suruk shrugged. 'Simple. We win. You three can do the sport things while I despatch the opposing team members. Then, we simply repeat the action until we have won the entire competition – or killed it – at which point this fool Criminarch will have to give us a trophy. At which point, we rip off his head and convert it. First by punting it over the crossbars and then by making it into a pleasant ornament for my mantlepiece.'

'You know,' Smith said, 'we could just jump the guards.'

'Hey, you're right,' Carveth said. 'We could pretend to be asleep and then, when we hear the door opening, we leap up and get 'em. Or you do, and I provide moral support. How about that?'

Rhianna said, 'Yeah, okay. I'd normally prefer a non-violent solution, but then we are about to enter a gladiatorial combat, so . . . cool.'

Smith said, 'Super. Everyone, pretend to be asleep, and when I give the signal, we'll leap up and overpower the guard. Now, we'll need a signal . . . what noises do I make when I'm asleep?'

Rhianna scratched her head. 'Well, sometimes you snore, and other things, and sometimes you talk about picnic rugs.'

'Picnic rugs? Do I?'

'Uhuh. And corsets and someone called Kate Bush.'

'Right. On second thoughts, I'll improvise.'

*

It was hard to tell what time it was. The lights were out, and Smith could not read the clock on the wall – which showed the Criminarch, bare-chested and smirking – because the hands were too small. He sat propped against the back wall of the cell, listening to Carveth. She had explained that her technique was to get deep into character, and if her snoring was anything to go by, she was fully immersed in her role.

Rhianna had slumped against him. Normally, he would have found this erotic, but her hair made him want to sneeze. And besides, it was hard to have rude thoughts when

Suruk was squatting on the bench opposite like an unusually featherless vulture. The alien's mandibles parted and a huge grin crawled up the side of his face like accelerated mould. Smith wondered what Suruk was dreaming about. Probably overpowering guards.

Rhianna stirred against him and put her mouth very close to his ear. 'I can sense someone,' she whispered, and Smith automatically glanced down to check that his someone wasn't visible. Then he realised what she meant and he was no longer drowsy at all.

At the far end of the corridor, the buzzer sounded and the doors rumbled softly apart. The strip-lights flickered into life outside the cell.

Heels clicked down the corridor. Louder, closer. Smith kept his eyes slightly open. The man was smaller than the Criminarch's guards and wore a hat. Smith watched as the figure walked past the bars to the door. He raised a hand, pressed the button, and the bars slid back. The man stepped into the room.

Suruk sprang at the man and bowled him down to the ground in a rush of limbs and cloth. Smith leaped up and ran over to help, but there was nothing to do except pick up the hat: Suruk had pinned the intruder to the floor. One of Suruk's long, slim hands was clamped over the man's mouth.

'Pull him into the light,' Smith said.

Suruk heaved the fellow up to the bars, where the light was strongest. 'Call out for help and I will tear off your head,' he promised, and he took his hand away.

The man was sixty at least, neat and brittle-looking. He wore a three piece suit that had been immaculate two minutes ago. His eyes were quick and bright: his skin was very pale. Two spots of colour on his cheekbones gave him a doll-like look. The intruder's mouth was small and red, as if he had been drinking wine. Smith wondered if he was an android.

'Really,' the man said. He adjusted his jacket and scowled. 'That was my second favourite cravat, you know. Do you brutalise all your guests, or am I unusually favoured?'

Smith hardly knew what to say. Anyone who could get into their cell so easily had to be either skilled or very unlucky. This person certainly didn't seem like one of the Criminarch's thugs.

'Now then,' said the visitor. 'My name is Crispin Quench. I'm here to help you win this ghastly tournament.'

'Is that so,' Smith replied. 'Are you our coach, then?'

'Goodness no. I'm your wardrobe co-ordinator. A game like this is all about image. Appealing to the oafs in the stand, the plebs, the *hoi polloi*. That's what it's really about. At the moment, you're nobodies. When you get onto the field, you need to be somebody. You need to shine.'

'But,' said Smith, 'don't we have to win the matches before we can do any of that?'

'Oh, violence?' Quench shrugged. 'I'm sure you can handle that perfectly well yourself, Captain Smith.'

Smith said, 'Who – how do you know my name?'

'We work for the same people. The Service takes care of its own.'

'You're from the Service? What happened to W? He's our master spy.'

'Ah, yes. W – or, as I call him, Eric – is rather well known around here. He's been denouncing the Criminarch for years. He's got himself on a few too many lists. I, on the other hand, am less well known. None of these apes think I could be good at our line of work. And besides, I volunteered for this.'

'God, man, why?'

Quench looked straight at Smith, and Smith sensed strength and ruthlessness behind the flippancy, like a shark under the surface of a shimmering sea. 'Because someone has to do it, don't they? Someone has to denounce the Criminarch, as Cicero denounced Verres. *O tempora!*' he declared, gesturing grandly at the ceiling. '*O mores!*'

Smith wondered what a load of fried prawns and eels had to do with anything.

'Look,' Carveth said, 'it's nice to meet you and everything, but can we go now?'

Quench turned to her. 'Go? Whyever would you want to do that?'

'Well, just call me No-Fun Nellie, but I've just got this funny feeling that I'm not going to enjoy the murderous gladiatorial combat out there. That's all.'

Quench shook his head. 'No, no. You have committed a master-stroke, all of you. Nobody has ever been positioned to wreak so much havoc on Radishia. By creating these games, the Criminarch has made himself doubly vulnerable. Not only will he suffer a massive loss of face when you beat his teams, but he will be physically close to you. Defeat his men and his armies will see just how superior they really are. Well, aren't. And take him personally out of action – well, they'll realise that there isn't a part of them we can't touch. Even without getting in a scrum.'

Smith said, 'So you want us to stay?'

'Of course! I wouldn't want to spoil your moment of glory. And think of our soldiers. Think of all the lives you'll save.'

Carveth grimaced. 'You know, I'm thinking about all those lives, and none of them look like mine.'

Smith thought. Was it that bad, really? Out there, the soldiers of the Empire were battling against the crazed lemming men and the brutal Ghasts. They were fighting the worst scum of the galaxy, often heavily outnumbered, the way they had done non-stop for four hard years. Taking on a few jumped-up humans in some kind of glorified rugger match was nothing compared to that.

'We're in,' he said.

'That's good to know,' Quench replied. 'Because you don't have another option. Orders from the top, you know. The guards will move you to the training quarters tomorrow morning. And then we can begin.'

*

The lorry tore across the flat ground. Wainscott scanned the horizon with his binoculars, squinting angrily. In the distance, things like dirty-black rocks jutted from the sand. They made Wainscott think of chunks of bone, blackened vertebrae and other biological wreckage he had seen in the course of his military career, often at the army canteen.

'Smashed vehicles ahead, Susan!' he announced. 'Let's get a better look.'

Nelson, the team's technical expert, called out from the rear of the lorry. 'Sensor grid says there's an allied beacon nearby. Straalian armoured division, apparently.'

'Hmm,' Wainscott said. 'I hope those aren't our chaps over there.' He zoomed in on the wreckage: it was burned metal, singed dirt-brown by flames and laser-fire. Susan swung them out wide to avoid traps, like a battleship manoeuvring for a broadside, and Dreckitt got on the port laser cannon, watching for movement among the broken machines.

'Nothing,' Susan said. 'I'll bring us in closer.'

Wainscott nodded and grabbed his Stanford gun. Susan slowed the lorry – not much, though – and Wainscott leaped out, rolled and ran to cover. He dropped into the shadow of a ruined Radishian tank, his bare shoulder against the warm metal.

The wreckage looked like the result of several dozen armoured vehicles ramming one another at once, because it was just that. Bodies lay strewn about: some in dark grey Radishian uniforms, others in the bushman's coats and plate armour that the Straalians called 'Ned suits'. Wainscott stepped over a lump of twisted metal. Charcoal crunched under his boots. It must have been hit with a plasma shell to produce that kind of effect. No, he realised, looking closer: the charcoal had fallen out of a roof-mounted barbecue.

An animal lay among the machines, stretched out like a sleeping Tyrannosaur. A wind came in from the south, skimming across the smashed vehicles, ruffling the creature's fur. Wainscott shook his head sadly. An animal couldn't start a war. A marsupial couldn't care if you were wearing trousers or not. A giant kangaroo couldn't shut a man away on a trumped-up charge of insanity just because he happened to blow up some stupid space dock and was laughing too hard at all the wonderful explosions to make a quick getaway. Animals were innocent, just like he had been before the authorities had certified him.

He looked down at the kangaram. 'What a waste,' he said.

It kicked him in the stomach. Wainscott flew back, crashed down onto the bonnet of a Jenkins V8 Interruptor and rolled off onto the sand. He dragged himself up, raising his gun, and as he did so, the kangaram got to its feet.

There was a man behind it, pointing a rifle. 'Who're you?' the man demanded.

'Major Arwen Wainscott, Deepspace Operations Group. Your thing kicked me. Bloody lucky half my ribs are metal, you know.'

'Bush Captain Shane, 603rd Straalian Armoured Division. You been out here for a long time? Because you look it.'

'What happened here?'

'Bastards got the jump on us. Half the column was wiped out. The others pulled back. Me and Rippy here couldn't keep up, so we played dead. She lay on the ground, and I hid like a joey. The whole operation's gone crook, mate. I need this mess like I need a third armpit.'

Wainscott grunted and walked over to the remains of a Radishian tank. 'I'm looking for friends of mine. Four British types.'

'Not Space Captain Smith's people?' Shane lowered his rifle and adjusted his hat. 'He was with us when we got hit. I reckon they must've captured him. Here, mate, are you all right?'

'Fine,' Wainscott said. He began to look at the wreckage,

grimacing at the ruins.

'It's just that, this sun and everything, it can get to a feller. Make him go troppo, you know?'

'Doo-lally, eh? No, there's nothing to worry about with me,' Wainscott said. 'The doctors never got the chance to prove anything.'

'Old Rippy here keeps me sane, don't you, Rippy?' The kangaram dipped its head. 'Say what, Rippy? This junk-yard reminds you of the theme of futility in the works of Samuel Beckett? Well, I wouldn't know much about that. Scrap dealer, is he?'

Wainscott climbed up to the burned-out cab of a Radishian scout car. The front armour had been torn open, the driver blown to dust.

'You're wasting your time, mate!' Shane called from below.

He was right, Wainscott thought. Something crackled below eye level. At first, he just thought it was static gathering in his beard. Then a voice came through from below the dashboard, human but clipped and angry, as if imitating the diction of a Ghast.

'*Spartan Squadron, report position. Report position, I repeat. Spartan Squadron, come in. You will reply immediately—*'

Wainscott reached under the dashboard and took hold of the blackened intercom. 'Where are my friends?' he demanded.

'*Who is this?*' the radio replied. '*Identify yourself. Identify yourself at once.*'

The wind stirred Wainscott's beard. 'Listen,' he said. 'I don't know who you are. I don't know what you want or where you're hiding. I'm not even certain where I am. I'm pretty sure it's Tuesday. But what I do have is a very particular set of skills. If you let my friends go now, I won't kill you. But if you don't, I *will* find you, and I *will* kill you. And then I'll kill your officers because they're probably arseholes too. And *their* officers, just in case they get any ideas. And then I'll probably find something you really like – an airfield, or a munitions factory, or something – and if somehow you've survived this far, I'll send you a picture of me blowing it up. And you know what? I'll be in the nude.'

'Well, *I'm* scared,' Shane said.

Wainscott yanked out the intercom and tossed it onto the sand. He climbed down after it. 'Thanks for your help,' he said. 'Next time you're in our territory, tell them Major Wainscott said you could stop for tea and a biscuit, and that I'll strangle anyone who says otherwise.' He turned away and started back between the ruined vehicles.

'Where're you going?' Shane demanded.

'To my team. We've got work to do.'

'Now wait a minute, mate. Come back to our base. We've got gear, tech, the lot. I'll show you the way.'

'Thanks, but no. The Deepspace Operations Group doesn't take passengers.'

'Passengers?' Shane looked appalled. 'We're partners! You need a guide, mate. Nobody understands the Wasteland as well as me.' The kangaram put its mouth to his ear. 'Say what, Rippy? Nobody except T. S. Eliot?'

*

'This is the training room,' Quench said. 'The decor's

lacking, but it should suffice.'

The room resembled the cell, except that the floor was padded and it was somewhat larger. Machinery stood against the walls. Smith reckoned that it was something to do with fitness.

Carveth looked around and scowled. 'It's like a torture chamber. And it smells like Rhianna's sandals. Now, if you good people don't object, I'm going to sit in the corner and sulk.'

'That's quite enough, Carveth,' Smith said. Carveth was right: it did remind him strongly of the changing rooms back at Midwich Grammar School. If a bigger boy had come in, turned him upside down and stuffed him into a locker, the resemblance would have been perfect. 'You know how you're supposed to play up, play up and play the game? Try missing out the playing up stage. You were saying, Mr Quench.'

'Crispin, please.' Smith suspected that Quench was about to hold a handkerchief over his nose like an aristocrat visiting the plague district. 'Now, the rules are fairly simple. Each team has two forwards, a midfield, a defence and a roller skater. To score, you place the ball behind the enemy's line. Those are the rules. Oh, and no firearms.'

'I'll have the roller skates, please,' Carveth said. 'So I can get away from things.'

'Certainly. Captain Smith, I'd suggest you take midfield, so you can command the team. Mr Slayer, how does attack sound to you?'

Suruk said, 'Right here?'

'No, on the pitch. In the game. The game you're going

to play, remember?'

'Of course,' Suruk replied. 'I am not the greatest team player, it must be confessed. But I'm sure we can thrash something out between us.'

'Which leaves you, Miss Mitchell, in defence. If that's all right with you, that is.'

Rhianna frowned. 'Um, okay. But, er, aren't we missing a player? I don't know much about sport, but if there's five of them, shouldn't there be five of us?'

'She's right,' Smith said. 'We're a man short.'

Quench smiled. 'I have it all in hand. A man will be joining us shortly.'

'It's not you, is it?'

'Heavens, no. I never engage in physical exercise, unless it's to snap someone's neck or to punch their nose into their brain. I find it terribly vulgar.' He coughed. 'What do you think about uniforms?'

'Now you're talking,' Carveth said. 'They're like ponies, but magical.'

'I think you may have misheard me.' Quench opened one of the lockers. 'I'm thinking something bold, something that makes a statement: the statement being "I am a vicious killer". And of course, comfortable and suited to the overall theme. So, voila.'

He lifted out a steel breastplate like the shell of a metal clam. It was much like a standard army chestplate, but had been polished to a near mirrored shine. 'The Imperial Ironsides,' Quench said. 'How does that sound?'

It sounded rubbish, Smith thought. Proper sports teams had place names with United, Rovers or Wednesday on the end. But then, this wasn't the Space Empire, or even any of its allies. Smith looked at the armour, and for the first time since this whole awful business had begun, he felt as if he might be able to come out on top. Quench passed him a helmet with a face-guard, and a pair of leather gauntlets. 'It's very Civil War, isn't it?'

Quench smiled. 'That's the only civil thing about it. You'll need all the armour you can get out there. Oh, and if you want to do a little chant before you start playing, it's worth remembering that "Rebellion" and "Cromwellian" rhyme.'

'Catchy,' Smith replied. 'Well, it's not the historical period I'd have chosen, but it will protect us. I say we go with the roundhead look. Just as long as we don't have to wear those thigh-length boots they had.'

Quench leaned back and studied Smith as if assessing a portrait. He shook his head. 'I don't think so. That's terribly last season.'

'All right, then. You find us a fifth man, Quench, and we'll, er, do what sport people do. Practise. That's it.'

The spy nodded. 'I'm sure we can find someone suitable,' he said, and he gave Smith a small, worrying smile.

*

Camp Uluru resembled a gigantic crown made of steel plate. It had to have been dropped in by a shuttle, Wainscott reckoned, but the wasteland had already put a red-brown patina on the metal. At the summit of each of the crown's points, an automated laser cannon scanned the wastes.

The huge gate, which was partly built out of an armoured personnel carrier, rolled back, and Rippy bounced into the courtyard. Susan brought the lorry in behind him, and several Straalian engineers approached to admire and criticise the bodywork.

Wainscott jumped down and followed Shane to the gate-house. The air was close and hot. *Too hot for shorts,* he thought. *Probably too hot for pants.*

'Major Wainscott, Deepspace Operations Group. The rest is classified.'

The gate commander frowned. 'You're from the British Space Empire, right?'

'Off the record, yes.'

'We've got one of your spies here,' the gate commander said. 'He's sitting out back – "fitting in".'

A soldier escorted Wainscott through the main buildings, to the leisure area at the back. About a dozen soldiers stood around a swimming pool, some in their smalls. The smell of charcoal hung in the air. Wainscott was surprised: there was nothing wrong with soldiers enjoying their leisure time, but sometimes he forgot that other people's idea of leisure didn't involve blowing things up.

Agent W sat awkwardly beside the pool on a sun lounger, looking like a discarded toy. He had removed his shoes, revealing two lumpy beige socks, and had put a copy of the *Daily Monolith* on his head as a sunshade. Even in full sunshine, it was hard to believe that the spy was not about to return to a damp bedsit to cook rice pudding on a portable stove.

W looked up. 'Ah, Wainscott. Good to see you.' A young woman jumped into the pool, and W frowned. 'It's like being on holiday here. Except it's not raining. Have you bagged the Criminarch yet?'

'No,' Wainscott said. 'We wrecked a few forts, freed some prisoners, that sort of stuff. But we've lost Smith and his crew.'

'Lost them?'

'We found their ship. It was intact – as intact as usual, anyhow. They must have gone on a jolly and been captured. That's what this Shane fellow says.'

'Can you verify that?'

'No, but Shane reckons his kangaram backs him up.'

W nodded. 'I see. This is bad news, Wainscott. Very bad news.' He looked no more disappointed than usual. 'If they've been captured, they'll probably have been taken into the city. It's a barbarous place, full of secret police and propaganda screens. The Criminarch's militia, the Redhats, run the place. We've got a man inside. Quench is his name.'

'Is he good?'

W nodded. 'A spy of the old school: gentlemanly, cunning, lethal where necessary and as camp as Christmas. One of the best. I'd suggest you acquire a militia uniform and infiltrate the place. Gain access to Smith's people and break them out.'

On the far side of the pool, a young woman in a vest was talking to a suntanned man in shorts nearly as large as Wainscott's. They looked almost impossibly healthy, like people in an advert for a Butlins Orbital Holiday Pod. It took Wainscott a moment to realise that they were Susan and Captain Shane. Susan looked very different without the body armour.

'Just one city, you say?' Wainscott asked. 'Shouldn't

be too hard. Do you want me to do over this Criminarch person on the way back?'

The spy paused. 'Not yet. The Service has other plans. Radishia is falling, Wainscott, but we want it to fall quickly, with as little bloodshed as possible – excluding the ruling party, of course. Think how bad it would look for the Criminarch if his private tournament went wrong. I think Radishia is ripe for revolution.'

'I like it,' Wainscott said, snarling into his beard like a pirate. 'And this revolution will be televised.'

'Exactly. Just as Waterloo was won on the playing fields of Eton, Radishia will be conquered on the playing fields of the Criminarch. Find Smith and help him. Soon Radishia will reap what it has sown – and I don't just mean root vegetables.'

*

'Right, old girl,' said Smith. 'I'm going to throw the ball at you, and you're going to catch hold of it. Ready?'

'Okay,' Rhianna said.

'Are you sure you're ready?'

'Erm . . . yeah, okay, I'm ready. Just, you know, don't hassle me.'

'I'm just a bit worried that you might not catch it. I don't want you to get hurt, you know.'

'It's cool, Isambard. I've had loads of injuries. Most of them were more, er, chemical, but still . . .'

Smith threw the ball and Rhianna closed her eyes. At the last moment, she lifted her hand. The ball seemed to hit an invisible wall and it rebounded directly back. Smith was marvelling at Rhianna's psychic abilities when the ball hit him in the face.

Rhianna helped him off the floor. 'I'm sorry,' she said. 'It's just that I totally channelled my aversion to ball games into my psychic powers. I don't know about this, Isambard. I mean, all this sport: it's just so . . . binary.'

'No, lost you there.' Smith would normally have expected that being hit on the head would make Rhianna easier to follow.

On the far side of the training room, Suruk was explaining something to Carveth. Quench watched them. He looked vaguely appalled. 'Truly,' Suruk explained, 'you are smaller, but you have a significant advantage over the other players. They have testicles, which a wise sportsman can headbutt.'

'Suruk!' Smith said. 'That is not playing the game.'

'Which game, Mazuran?'

'This one. Or any game.'

The alien frowned. 'To be honest, I have not really been studying the rules very hard. My feeling is that, once the other players are dead or incapacitated, the fine details can take care of themselves.' Suruk yawned and stretched. 'Actually, we M'Lak play quite a similar sport. The only real differences are that the sides are bigger, and there is no pitch, as such. Nor are there really any spectators. Or a ball. And you can use weapons.' He scratched his head. 'On second thoughts, that was probably a war.'

'Sounds like it. Look, we've got to win, but we've got to win *properly*. We just need to keep level-headed and approach this like sane people—'

The door flew open behind him. Smith turned. Two

sullen guards stomped into the room. The guards looked like gorillas, but the man between them was more like something from the early days of humanity: small, wiry, scowling into a beard that seemed to have been made from dirty pan scrubbers. Behind the three of them came a Radishian officer.

'We found this man out the back,' the officer announced. 'He said he knew you and you'd help him. This had better not be a trick.'

'Not at all, my good henchman. This man is a friend of ours. He's . . . fallen on hard times. He's come in here to get directions to a soup kitchen.'

Wainscott glared at Smith and made a noise in the back of his throat. 'Rubbish. I'm an elite soldier. My name's Wainscott.'

The officer frowned. 'Is this true?'

Rhianna stepped forward. 'He's delusional, too,' she added. 'It's very sad. How's it going, Uncle Wayne?'

The officer laughed. 'If it's free food you want, there'll be loads left after the game. Assuming you survive it.'

'What?' Wainscott glanced at the guards. 'You idiots had better step back or I'll holster your weapons right up your jacksie. In fact, you might as well surrender now. Smith, I'm surprised that you haven't already—'

Quench stepped forward, neatly and quickly. 'Really, everything's fine. Captain Smith's right – it's just a minor problem. We've had a slight pickle, you see . . .'

'Ah,' Wainscott said. 'Slight pickle, eh? I see.'

Smith recognised the Service code phrase for a very dangerous situation, the highest notch above *fine thanks* and *mustn't grumble.*

'Huh,' Wainscott said. 'Sports day, is it? All right, I'm in. What is it, football or something?'

The head guard laughed. 'Hardly. Football is a soft sport for weaklings. It is banned on Radishia.'

'Fair enough.' Wainscott sniffed. He looked half-feral, as if he had been surreptitiously injected with badger DNA. 'Bunch of men rolling around clutching their shins. Now, rugby – that's a proper sport. Jousting – that's also a proper sport. What's the one where all the women jump around on a beach in their smalls? That's a proper sport too. Greatly underrated game, that, whatever it is.'

'Bah!' said the officer. 'Beach volleyball is a weak sport. On Radishia, only men play beach volleyball, to make it more manly, by order of the Criminarch himself. The same with championship figure skating.'

'Look,' said Smith, 'I'm sure this is fascinating, but, if you don't mind, we have practising to do. After all, we have a game to win.'

War Without The Shooting

'It's time,' said one of the guards. 'No funny business or I'll blast you. Do what you're told and get on the pitch. Then you can die like men, fighting.'

'Actually,' Rhianna said, 'I reject your crude patriarchical stereotyping and its undercurrent of violent machismo.'

'So shove off,' Smith added. 'Let's get going, chaps,' he added, before the guard could start firing. 'Lead on.'

They left the training room and headed down a long tunnel. As they walked, the lights grew more powerful and the smell of socks less prevalent. Smith could make out a slow roar, distant at first, but undoubtedly coming from a crowd.

The corridor became a slope. Smith checked that his breastplate was securely attached. Quench took off his hat and fanned his face with it. 'Good luck,' he announced. 'Break a leg, everyone, preferably somebody else's.'

The tunnel ended in a pair of airlock doors. *This is it*, Smith thought.

The chief guard turned to them. 'Play hard,' he said, and there was not just contempt but a sort of pride in his voice. 'Fight hard. Die hard.'

He struck the panel with his gloved fist. The doors hissed and slid aside.

Light and noise washed over them. Smith gazed into a vast arena. This was not the place where he had awoken a few days before: this was the size of a spacecraft hangar, its sides crammed with stands where thousands upon thousands of Radishians cheered, shouted and gobbled fast food.

From above, a massive voice roared out of the speakers like an angry, childish god. *'Citizens of Radishia, serfs of the Criminarch, behold the elite of the enemy, taken from the puny and effete soldiers of the British Space Empire. Your master the Criminarch is proud to give you . . . the Imperial Ironsides!'*

The crowd bellowed. Smith swallowed and said, 'Well, chaps, let's go. Do the best you can, and we'll discuss tactics when they bring out the bits of orange at half time.'

'And on the other side, fresh out of maximum security accommodation, from a place where every game brings the risk of a fate so horrible it can barely be described – and that's just the post-match showers. With a total of eighty kills between them since the end of last season and the beginning of this one, put your big foam hands together for the Full Contact Felons! Warriors, come out to play!'

Five men ran onto the other end of the pitch. They wore orange overalls, reinforced with sheet metal and lengths of chain. Most of them looked desperate and vicious. Their leader, however, grinned instead of snarling, revealing teeth that would have shamed a giant rat.

The spotlights swung up to cover the commentators' box. Smith saw a young man in a white boiler suit and a bowler hat, standing next to an annoyed-looking girl of about fifteen. *'Commentating on tonight's match . . . Mr Alex Lagrande and Miss Katie Dystopia!'*

'Actually,' the girl's voice rang across the stadium, *'it's Kat. I changed it. I didn't ask to be called Katie. Nobody asks me anything. Nobody listens to anything I say—'*

'Frap up your noisings, thou whinging teenager!' Alex Lagrande interjected, *'Ladies and gentlebeings, best beloved and dear departed, have we got a frabsome box of vidding for you! Two teemies, hell-bent on grarping each other right into the naughty box. Will it be the old laurels of noble victory and all that, or a swift blow in the dangle-wanglers?'*

Smith looked at the guard. 'Do you know what he's talking about?'

The guard grunted. 'Sure. He's talking about the game. Dur.'

'Yes, but, in particular?'

'Well, it's game talk, isn't it? About the match, how it works out, stuff like that. Are you stupid or something?'

'But what's he actually *saying?'*

'I've no idea. Now get moving!'

A panel in the roof slid open and something dropped out of it. Smith jumped back, fearing a grenade, and then realised that it was the ball. A scrawny, feral-looking man grabbed the ball and raced forward.

Smith looked left and a figure shot past on roller skates, swinging out wide.

'Vinny the Shiv has possession,' Kat Dystopia said over the loudspeakers. *'Yeah, great, whatever.'*

Vinny the Shiv hurled the ball. Smith turned to see it sail overhead, unsure what one did about that. He half-expected a prefect to appear and bellow instructions at him as if sport actually mattered.

'Somebody do something with that ball—' he called, and Vinny the Shiv punched him in the arm. 'Ow!' Smith exclaimed, and a klaxon blared overhead. The crowd cheered. Smith rubbed his arm.

'*One point for the Felons!*' the speakers bellowed.

Smith was not sure how that had happened. He looked at his team: Carveth was moving about nervously, clearly expecting to dodge something; Suruk was eyeing up a hot dog stand, whose vendor was trying to discreetly drag it out of range; Rhianna was looking at the roof; Wainscott was – hopefully – adjusting his trousers. Yes, Smith could see how that had happened quite well, actually.

'Look, chaps,' he said, 'we need to get stuck in. Have you got any ideas?'

Wainscott nodded. 'I'll strangle the guards. You plant charges on the main girders, then we pull back to the ship.'

'Wainscott, are you thinking about blowing up the pitch?'

'Aren't you?'

'No. Now listen, everyone—'

He opened his mouth, and was immediately drowned out as the screens burst into life, showing a replay of a convict on roller skates neatly passing Rhianna and slamming the ball down behind the scoring line. '*Frob my williker!*' Alex Lagrande exclaimed, '*Death Row Dave's getting to work early.*'

'*Huh,*' said Kat Dystopia. '*Getting up early sucks.*'

The referee blew his whistlotron and the klaxon sounded

again. 'Looks like we're on,' Smith said. 'Has anyone got any ideas?'

Suruk nodded. 'Indeed,' he said. 'They can't throw the ball without their heads.'

The ball flew out. A man with immense pectorals grabbed it and charged forwards, head down. Smith rushed at him. The man sped up. Smith ducked low to rugby-tackle him – and Suruk stepped in neatly from the side and drove his elbow into the man's nose.

He hit the ground as if an anvil had dropped on him. '*Oh my childers!*' cried Alex Lagrande '*Knockout!*'

'*Yeah, right, whatever,*' said Kat Dystopia. '*This is really immature.*'

Smith ran forward into the enemy half. 'Throw me the ball,' he called, but Suruk was too busy bellowing and holding the ball up so his ancestors could see that he had defeated it. 'The ball, Suruk!'

Death Row Dave drove in from the left, skating furiously on a course to intercept Suruk. Smith saw metal glinting in the convict's hand. Smith threw himself on the skater.

Death Row Dave crashed onto the ground. His skate booted Smith's helmet. Smith rolled clear and scrambled upright. Something small and high-pitched sped into view from behind: Carveth. Like a pip squeezed from a fruit, she shot past into open space.

'Suruk!' Smith yelled. 'Get the ball to Carveth!'

The alien looked around as if waking from a dream.

'Carveth – ball – score!' Smith shouted over the crowd.

Suruk paused, then seemed to understand. He hurled the ball at Carveth.

It hit her in side of the head. She went over as if she'd

been tripped, skidding along the ground in a flurry of sparks. The two convict defenders rushed to intercept, their metal fists raised. Smith ran to rescue her. The ball followed Carveth over the line. She rolled over and flopped onto it.

The klaxon blared. *'That's a point!'*

As the replays sounded, they stumbled back to their places. A small fight had broken out in the crowd, and was being quelled by militiamen wielding clubs. A fanfare sounded and the ceiling-port ejected another ball.

Smith was ready this time. He ran to intercept the ball. Carveth shot forward into the opposing half of the pitch, either to get ready to score or to be as far from everyone else as possible. Smith leaped for the ball and snatched it out of the air. He landed perfectly, albeit directly in front of Death Row Dave.

Dave's punch sent Smith staggering. The convict slammed into him and Smith hit the floor. He heard the crowd cheer, but the details were hard to make out because Death Row Dave had started to beat Smith's helmet against the ground. Wainscott, or some other bearded goblin, jumped onto Dave's back. Another man grabbed at Wainscott. Suruk rushed in from the side, holding an opposing team member in one hand and a hot dog in the other.

Smith managed to crawl free. His knee was hurting. His brain seemed to have been rinsed in gin, but not in a good way. Someone in an orange costume had emerged and was yelling triumphantly.

Suruk shoved the man and he stumbled into Smith and fell over. Wainscott tried to tear the ball free. 'The legs, Mazuran, the legs!' Suruk cried. Smith ripped the man's arms open, and saw that he didn't have the ball at all – he'd been clutching his stomach. So where was it?

'Hey, guys,' Rhianna called. She was standing at the end of the pitch, in the Felons' scoring zone, gazing serenely at the chaos like someone who had just climbed a mountain and was taking in the view. She held up the ball. 'Check it out.'

Everyone on the pitch wanted it. They bellowed, cursed, pointed, clenched their fists and sprinted towards her. The players, the referee and commentators, the vendors and spectators all looked at Rhianna.

She seemed confused. Her eyes moved from player to player, clearly uncertain what to do. 'Um . . .' she said. 'I'll just leave it here, then.'

She put the ball down. The referee blew his whistlotron. The klaxons barked out a tune. In the stands, spectators ripped up their betting slips and hurled them onto the pitch in a ragged confetti of torn paper.

A second speaker system began to play a different tune. Above the arena, holographic girls danced and waved their pom-poms.

In the commentary box, Alex Lagrande was waving his arms. '*What a cronking! What a remarkabubble trickling, oh best beloved. All that scrapping and spilling of red, and just a diversion all along!*'

'*Yeah, great,*' said Kat Dystopia. '*You suck. I want to watch TV.*'

Rhianna stared at the crowd like a small child at a fireworks display. 'Wow!' she said. 'What's happening?'

Carveth skated up beside her. 'I'll tell you what's happening!' she cried. 'Not only are we not dead, but we won!'

Game, Set and Match

'You know,' said Smith as they walked off the pitch, 'that went rather well.'

'For us,' Rhianna said. 'But what about the wellbeing of the team that loses? What will their self-image be like now?'

Carveth snorted. 'Pretty bruised,' she said. She whirled on her roller skates. They gave her a speed and grace that she otherwise noticeably lacked. 'Like their heads. That's what happens when you mess with us.'

'Don't gloat, Carveth,' Smith said. 'You'll lose your moral fibre and end up brutal and vicious, like some sort of foreign tyrant, or even a PE teacher. Suruk!' he called back up the ramp. 'Come on, old chap!'

The alien jogged down to join them. At the top of the ramp, massive doors slid shut and the roar of the crowd was gone. 'Apologies, friends. I was loath to leave the roaring crowd. Always leave them wanting more, I say. In the case of the audience, more action and adventure. In the case of the opposing team, more first aid.'

Wainscott wandered past Suruk, frowning into his beard. 'Huh,' he said. 'Don't get showy.'

They reached the training rooms and the guards opened the door. In the dim light, the weights and running machines looked sinister. Smith led his men inside and the lock turned loudly behind them.

Rhianna sighed. 'Guys, really. Winning isn't everything, you know. There's taking part, and making new friends, and coming together through a shared hobby. Sport is an international language that brings people together.'

'True,' Suruk said. 'Together, at high speed! I fall upon my enemies like a drawbridge of bloody justice. I am like a door of solid oak, forged with steel—'

'Unhinged and off the handle,' Carveth added. 'Now we've won a match, will we get a sponsorship deal? There's got to be a pie shop that would like its name across my chest.'

'And it's food inside your stomach.' Suruk grabbed the chin-up bar, hooked his knees over the top and hung there like a gigantic bat.

Smith shook his head. 'There won't be a sponsorship deal. We did what we said we'd do – we won and we made the enemy look stupid. Now, we're escaping.'

'How?' Carveth demanded. 'The doors are barred.'

Suruk shrugged. 'You could pretend that the bars are made of cake. And then chew through them.'

'Listen,' Smith said. 'This whole grim business is like a gladiatorial combat. And my knowledge of Latin tells me that gladiator fights were held in the arena. And every arena had a hypocaust: a complex under-floor heating system. I knew my Classical Civilisation O-level would come in handy one day.'

Wainscott glanced up as if he had caught the scent of something tasty. 'He's right. It'll lead us out of here. Let's get going.'

Smith squatted down and looked at the floor. 'We won't need to crawl under the toilet block. We could pull up some of the lino and get through that way. We'll have to lever the floor panels open, though . . . We'll need a distraction. Carveth, get on the running machine.'

'But I hate running!'

'Exactly. The noise you produce will muffle the sound of us pulling up the floor. Rhianna, what can you do?'

She thought about it. 'Yoga?'

'Good plan. Let's get cracking.'

*

It didn't take long to pull up the floor. At one point, the viewing hatch in the door slid open, but the sight of Carveth puffing on the treadmill and Rhianna with her legs over her head seemed to satisfy the guards. 'We're ready,' Smith called, and Rhianna swung her legs down, stood up elegantly and tried to remember where she had left her shoes.

Carveth staggered off the running machine. 'You have lost – fourteen – calories,' it said.

'Fourteen?' she gasped. 'Is that all? I could lose that many opening a bar of chocolate.'

They gathered around the square of floor that they had pulled up. It lay in the shadow of a machine whose purpose Smith hadn't quite figured out yet, a mass of gears, straps and leather pads, as though for the gratification of unnatural urges.

'We ought to take Quench with us,' Smith said.

Wainscott shook his head. 'If he's Service, he'll know how to get out on his own.'

'All right, then. I'll go first. Rhianna, Wainscott, you come with me. Carveth, you're next. Suruk, would you mind watching the rear?'

Suruk looked disappointed. 'With Carveth in front of me, I will have no option but to watch the rear. Are you sure she will fit into the hole?'

Carveth scowled, but she was too worn out after her time on the running machine to reply. She was new to exercise, Smith reflected. At least she had taken the roller skates off first.

Smith climbed down into the space below the floor. It smelled of dust and something else, something chemical. He crept forward and squatted down while the others got in after him. 'Close the hatch,' he whispered.

It was almost entirely dark, save for the small lights that were standard-issue in vent shafts. They illuminated the ground about a yard before him – too little to stop something creeping up, but just enough to allow him to get a good look at what it was just before it killed him.

'Follow me, men,' he whispered.

They moved along the corridor beneath the stadium complex. A row of pipes ran across the crawl-space, and Smith clambered over them.

They hurried on. Smith looked back at his team, and counted to make sure they were all there. Suruk was smiling, no doubt remembering some other time that he had crawled through a ventilation shaft. Wainscott was all eyes, beard and grimace, like a Neanderthal who had discovered a bear in his favourite cave.

Behind them, something hissed. Carveth yelped and put her hand over her mouth a second too late. Smith stared past her, wishing that he had his weapons. 'What was that?' he demanded.

Suruk was looking back the way they had come. 'Fear not, little woman. There is nothing following us. They are probably just preparing to clean the vents with superheated steam, that is all.'

Rhianna pushed her hair away from her face. The bad light made her eyes seem huge. 'I don't know. I still sense hostility. And an equal amount of structural perfection.'

Suruk snorted. 'You are just sensing me.'

Ahead, metal glinted in the ceiling. Smith looked up: one of the panels was badly scratched. To judge from the raw metal at its edges, it seemed to have been replaced recently. He felt the panel over: it was held in place by a few screws. Smith felt his pockets, and came out with a coin. It was Radishian: instead of King Victor and Queen Kylie, like a proper British coin, it bore the image of the Criminarch, bent over like a Roman discus thrower in a very small pair of pants. Smith scowled at the image and got to work.

Very quietly, he pushed the panel up and across and set it down. The room above was almost totally dark. He pulled himself out. It smelled a bit funny, but that was to be expected from places like this. Less expected was what appeared to be a vast amount of half-chewed toffee smeared across the ceiling and the walls.

Something slid out of the darkness and bared its teeth at him. Smith wondered if it was smiling. He decided that, on balance, it probably wasn't. Like a battalion of Cheshire cats, other rows of teeth appeared in the dark. The bad light caught on fangs and saliva. The sound of hissing rose. Smith climbed back down.

'Minor problem, chaps. It's full of Procturan Black Rippers. You remember the one that we found behind the fridge that time? Like that, except bigger.'

Wainscott grunted. 'Friend of mine once had a problem like that. He was on the Upper Bridgend Peninsula, just north of the South Passage. Went to sleep, woke up surrounded by the things. He was the first man to find them there. He got his name in the paper and everything.'

'How did he escape?'

'He didn't. He was in the obituary section. Terrible business. Damned poor luck.'

Carveth whispered, 'Can't you just use the Bearing on them and tell them to sod off?'

Smith shook his head. 'They've got no ears to hear me with. And I doubt they speak English.'

'I know,' Rhianna said. 'Why don't I go up there and reason with them? I can use my psychic powers, and if that fails, what about the all-inclusive language of, er. . . interpretive dance?'

'God,' Carveth said. 'It's nearly my fourth birthday and I'm sitting under a toilet block discussing free dance with a bunch of hungry space monsters down the corridor. I'm a top-of-the-range android, for God's sake. I wasn't built for this. I was built for—'

A loud cough rang down the ventilation shaft. Smith whipped around, bashed his head against the wall and blinked as Crispin Quench crawled into view. Looming out of the darkness, the spy looked both delicate and terrifying, like the ghost of a ballerina.

'Where did you come from?' Smith demanded.

'Well, let's see . . . from further up this pipe, actually.

What in God's name are you people doing squatting in a ventilation shaft?'

'We're escaping,' Carveth said.

'Well, don't. As your Secret Service handler, that's a tactical error. As your stylist, it's an absolute disaster. Look at this filthy place. You look like a bunch of chimney sweeps. Now, come on back with me. I've got something to show you.'

*

There was a large packing case in the middle of the training room. Smith thought that he recognised the symbol on the side, which resembled a distorted banana. He'd seen it on the pitch somewhere.

'During the last match,' said Quench, as Carveth was both pushed and pulled out of the hole in the floor, 'you managed to injure three of the opposing players – a very creditable performance. But two of those incapacitations were useless. The reason why? They lacked elan.'

Smith frowned. He was not certain what elan was, although he had a feeling that it was a sort of French cake. 'How do you mean?'

Quench pointed to Suruk. 'This fellow here incapacitated one of the opposing team by hurling him face-first through a hot-dog stand. Do you know how long the cameras lingered on the hot-dog stand while the medics pulled him out? Three seconds. Long enough for sales of Unlucky Dog Foot Longs to triple. And for that, my alien friend, I am going to award you a special consignment of sausage meat.' Quench opened the box and reached inside. He stood up, brandishing a saveloy. 'Catch.'

He lobbed the hot dog across the room. Instinctively, Carveth snatched it out of the air. Quench produced another sausage from his box and jabbed the air with it to illustrate his point. 'If we are to bring the Criminarch down, we have to have the support of the masses, however unwashed and poorly-styled they may be. We need to give them something to watch. In the arena, it's not enough to be simply victorious – you must be simply marvellous as well.'

'Now wait a minute, Quench,' Smith said. 'First you ask us to play team sport, then you make us wear armour to play rugby like some sort of abroad-people, and now you want us to flounce around while we do it? Never.'

Wainscott nodded. 'He's right. Go in quick and silent, that's the Deepspace Operations Group way. Then get out before the place blows up.'

Quench spun on his heel, waving the frozen hot dog like a conductor. 'Don't you understand?' he demanded, jabbing the sausage at Smith's face. 'Can't you see that this is bigger than you?'

'That's a bit personal, isn't it?'

'The circumstances, not the sausage! Where's your verve, your fighting spirit, your urge to show the audience what you've got? You've got to get it out there on the pitch. When the spotlights come on, you can't just put on a helmet – you have to put on a show!'

Carveth raised a hand. 'This show you want us to put on – does it have to involve a hot dog? I'm not comfortable with that.'

'I know what you're asking for,' Rhianna said. She sat on

the far side of the room, her armour and boots on the floor beside her. 'You want us to perform like caged animals. You want us to become part of the system that oppresses these people, the same system that keeps the Criminarch in power. We'll become part of the state. We'll be processed like . . . like that sausage. Well, you know what, I've got two things to say to you. One, I am a free woman in my own right. And two, I'm a vegan and I totally don't eat meat.'

Quench pulled a face. 'You don't seriously think these things actually contain any meat, do you?'

'Oh,' said Rhianna. 'Well, that's okay then, I suppose.'

*

The journey out of orbit should not have taken long, but Radishian airspace was far from safe. With the Space Empire and its allies fighting their way across the planet, only one hemisphere was viable for orbital entry, and even that required careful manoeuvring. As a result, the *Systematic Destruction* touched down several hours late and, as soon as he landed, Storm-Assault Commander 462 limped to the facilities.

He spent several minutes in a cream-coloured cubicle with gold taps and a painting of the Criminarch on the wall. By the time that he reached the meeting-room and was cleared by Radishian security, the meeting had already begun.

'I will kill them all,' the Criminarch was saying. He sat at the far end of the table like a mean drunk propping up a bar, massive and brooding. 'There will be no pity, no mercy, no soft stuff. I will beat them, I will kill them, I will smash them into the ground. I will drink their tears and laugh at their misery. You think you've seen killing and smashing before? Think again. You've not seen *me*.'

Several of the Criminarch's ministers burst out in spontaneous applause. 462 slipped past several praetorian bodyguards and sat down next to Number Two. 'Who's he talking about?' 462 whispered.

'He doesn't know,' Two replied. 'None of his lackeys know, either. He does this every morning, I gather.'

'It's time to show 'em who's boss!' The Criminarch pounded the table with his fist. 'All of them – their children, their families. I'll kill 'em all! Now, what's the agenda for today? What are these ant-people doing here?'

Two hissed. 'I am Number Two of the Ghast Empire. We are here to inform you that glorious Number One is unimpressed by your failure to defend your planet. Even as we speak, your legions are being crushed by the weaklings of the British Space Empire and its contemptible allies. Are you going to defeat them or not?'

'I said I would, didn't I?' The Criminarch swallowed. 'I keep my promises. When I say I'll do something, I do it. Other people are lazy and corrupt, but I get things done. I don't just sit around all day, waiting for criminals to offer me bribes – I get off my arse and *take* bribes!'

'Interesting,' 462 added. 'Last month, you promised your generals that you would "kill the British right in the face", massacre the Space Empire's soldiers once they surrendered and personally manhandle Empress Kylie. Your followers cheered. We are not cheering.'

'Sure,' said the Criminarch, 'I said that. But if I say

something to my people, that doesn't mean that I *mean* it. You know how it is. My citizens are pig-ignorant radish-chomping peasants. So long as there are some titties on show and someone gets executed, they love it. Screw them. I can just say any old rubbish and these dopes think it's great. They love me so much three hundred and twenty percent of them voted for me at the last election.'

Two leaned forward, and the light caught on his artificial eyes. The lenses gleamed. 'You would be wise to remember that the Ghast Empire put you here, Criminarch. If it was not for our power behind your throne, it would be you in the arena – as a clown. Our master, whose antennae you are not fit to lick, demands that you double your efforts or face the consequences.'

'Well, tell him that I'm the Criminarch. I don't "double" things just because you say so. When I double something, I go big. So tell him that I will triple my efforts. Hell, I'll double the tripling and shoot anyone who disagrees. I'll . . . sextipple them.'

'You will sextipple nothing—' 462 began, but one of the Criminarch's advisors leaned forward. He was a paunchy, sickly-looking fellow with a rash of stubble across his chops.

'Don't worry,' the man said. He smiled. 'We'll get it done. We're mean. We're nasty. We're the bad guys.'

Two said, 'Bad is an understatement. "Dismal" would be more apt. Praetorian, illustrate to the Criminarch his responsibilities.'

The bodyguard grunted and heaved up its belt-fed heavy disruptor, ready to fire.

The Criminarch raised his hands. 'Hey, hey. We're on

the same side. We're both dictators. We both hate the British and their allies. Let me show you something. You'll like this.'

One of the Criminarch's minions approached and placed a large object on the table in front of them. It looked like a soft helmet with two holsters attached to the sides. 462 prodded it with a finger. Pipes ran out of the holsters.

'It's a hat,' the Criminarch said. 'You put beer in the side pockets.'

'Canisters of nutri-shake?' Two suggested.

'If you like. It's for sports. You can both have one. You'll be watching the games, right?'

'I do not think that an officer of the Ghast Empire—'

'Great! And I've had a special one made for Number One. Look at this.' The Criminarch leaned over and picked something up from the side of his chair. 'See? It's got one of those skull-and-antennae symbols on the front. And there's a matching T-shirt that says "I'm Number One so don't bother trying". How classy is that?'

'We are rendered speechless,' 462 replied.

Two frowned. 'We will take a moment to contemplate the greatness of our hats,' he rasped. 'Alone.'

In the corridor, Two lunged towards 462 as if to bite him. 'Pathetic! He considers his people to be idiots. Yet he is the worst fool of them all!' Two lowered his voice. 'Once again, we are saddled with an ally who is a violent imbecile. One would almost think that our cause attracted these sorts of degenerate low-life.'

'Agreed,' 462 said. 'But I doubt that Number One will have to deal with him for long.'

'Are you sure? I am beginning to regret signing the forms

to authorise this visit. I hope you were right to suggest it. Think how bad I would look if any harm was to come to our glorious leader.'

462 managed not to smile. 'Don't worry,' he replied. 'Number One will be taken care of. I'll make certain of that.'

*

The crowd was howling for blood, fast food and Supercola.

'Listen to those idiots,' Smith said as they walked towards the pitch. 'Bellowing like a bunch of animals.'

Rhianna said. 'They live in a miserable dictatorship, Isambard. This is the only entertainment they'll probably ever see. They just want what we take for granted.'

'Well, they can't bloody have it! They can get their own, the thieving buggers!'

'No, I mean they want democracy, the rule of law, an end to corruption and the chance to live without fear.'

'Oh, well, of course they can have those. In fact, they'd better have them – or else! If they don't stop living in fear, they'll wish they'd never been born. Look at all this . . .' With a sweep of the arm, he took in the crowd, the banners, the dancing girls and the holographic posters of the Criminarch in a pair of posing-pants, squinting and flexing his muscles. 'The galaxy dreams of proper rule,' he said. 'This is not it, Rhianna. This is not it. This is. . . well, it's bollocks, really, isn't it?'

As they walked into the stadium, the sound rose up around them like the roar of an angry ocean. Smith felt a combination of fury and contempt as he looked across the stadium, at the opposite doors. Beside him, Suruk stretched his mandibles.

'Listen,' Smith said. 'They weren't expecting us to win the last game – or survive it, for that matter. Whatever comes out of those gates, we'll have to work together to defeat it. We'll have to do this as a team. You were with me at Mothkarak. You remember what we did there?'

'Indeed,' Suruk said. 'We killed everything.'

In a gilt box at the top of the stands, the Criminarch raised his hand for silence. The crowd fell quiet, and the few who didn't stop talking soon enough were beaten unconscious by the security staff. A pair of camera-bots hovered over the crowd, holding up a huge screen between them.

The face of the Criminarch appeared on it: weasel-like, and too close to the lens. His mean, small eyes moved over the crowd as if he knew that a trick had been played on him, but hadn't worked out who should be punished yet.

'*Citizens!*' he said. '*Brave, strong, manly workers of Radishia. Today we celebrate our struggle against the tyranny of the British Space Empire. Its soldiers seek to conquer you – to force you into queues and to take away your freedom to vote for your beloved Criminarch!*

'*Their spies are among us today. Lying, deceiving, ruining everything. They are everywhere, these conspirators, so cunning that they are often impossible to see. Anyone would think that I had made them up – except there they are, in the arena!*'

The crowd howled and shrieked. Smith wondered how the war outside was going – and whether any Hellfires might be making a bombing run in the next few minutes.

'*Look at their dumb faces!*' the Criminarch cried. '*Look at the one with the moustache. He looks like – like a jerk! Yeah, a jerk. And the green monkey thing. "Duh, look at me, I'm a big green monkey." And the caveman guy and the little fat woman and the other one. What a bunch of losers! Not like me, your lord and master. I am very clever.*'

Rhianna had tried to put her hands over Suruk's ears to spare him from the Criminarch's biogtry, but the alien had dodged her. To Smith's surprise, Suruk was smiling. It was not a pretty smile.

'Listen,' Smith said. 'It doesn't matter what they see on their screens. The only damned good show will be the one we'll be putting on.'

'*Today, Radishians!*' the Criminarch declared, '*I am proud to give you the greatest show in the galaxy. The most dangerous, the most thrilling, the most nerve-racking thing you will ever see. The most brutal, fascinating, exciting, emotional, inspiring, bloodthirsty, brilliant event of your entire lives. This . . . is . . . hyperbowl!*'

Rhianna sighed. 'You mean hyperbole.'

The doors on the far end of the pitch burst open. Half a dozen people in team colours ran out, leaping and cartwheeling. The citizens cheered.

Suruk laughed. 'Is this your best, Criminarch?' he called. 'Look at these puny humans, flouncing and capering. They will cease their grinning when the Slayer takes to the field and rips them limb from limb!'

'Suruk,' Carveth said, 'those are the cheerleaders.'

Three immense figures lumbered up from the dark like

ogres. For a moment, Smith thought they were robots – eight feet tall, caked in armour – but then their leader pulled off his helmet, revealing a comparatively tiny head.

Reborn, Smith realised. They were Edenite shock troops, treated with growth serums provided by the Ghast Empire – very strong and fanatically devoted to the Edenite god, but extremely dim.

'Unbelievers!' the captain of the Reborn bellowed, and the speakers caught his voice and amplified it. 'I am Goreblast the Centurion. These are my men, Impervius the Demolisher and Jeremiad Oblitoratorius. I will crush you in the name of the Great Annihilator. I am very big and have many spikes on my armour. What do you say to that, weakling scum?'

A microphone drone lowered itself in front of Smith. He cleared his throat. 'Well, speaking as an officer of the Brit—'

Suruk grabbed the drone and pulled it over. For a moment, the alien was silent. Then he leaned in to the microphone and smiled. 'I think it is a great shame,' he said, 'that your brain is not in scale with your body.'

*

The ball dropped onto the pitch. Suruk snatched it and threw it to Smith. Smith ran forward, dodging Goreblast's huge metal fists, and tossed the ball out to Wainscott. Wainscott hurled it to Carveth and she shot into the open, eager to be as far from the action as possible. The Reborn turned, ponderous as battleships, to see her slam the ball down over the line.

Smith nodded approval – and saw light glinting in the crowd. A man ran to the front of the stand, holding an insulting placard in one hand and a huge hot dog in the other. As Suruk came close, the man reached to the end of the sausage, like a samurai drawing a sword, and pulled a long knife from the bun.

'Look out!' Smith called. The man leaned towards Suruk, but he leaned too far – in a flurry of limbs the alien grabbed his wrist, heaved him onto the pitch and ran him through with his own sign. The crowd roared and cheered.

'*Right,*' Katie Dystopia mumbled at the microphone as the medics dragged the body off the field. '*Great. Like, yeah, violence, right? Adults. Like, grow up or something? God.*'

'*Oh, spectatoids, hoist by his own placard! What fine and spurting shedding of the old reddy-red!*' Alex Lagrande cried. '*The Imperial Ironsides clomp up a pointo on the old score-fimble! Now cast your eyeballs upwards, oh my siblings and siblingettes, and viddy well the action replay!*'

'*Nobody knows what you're talking about. And, like, nobody cares.*'

'*Harsh and hurting words, little sister! But there'll be more excitement when the ball drops.*'

'*As if you'd know about balls dropping. You're such a child.*'

The ball fell down onto the pitch again, and the match burst into savage life. The Reborn wanted not so much to score as to kill, but Smith's team were ready for them. Suruk distracted Jeremiad Oblitatorius, cartwheeling neatly past him. Impervius lumbered in, grabbing at Rhianna. In one swift attack, Smith and Wainscott slammed into him with a brutal double-tackle improvised from the Advanced Commando Combat Manual and Wisden's Interplanetary Cricketing Almanac. Impervius crashed down like an upturned post box.

Smith watched as a crane rolled onto the pitch, lowered an electromagnet onto the fallen Reborn player and began to drag him off the pitch in a clatter of armour. The crowd jeered and shouted.

'Jolly good, everyone,' Smith said, as a robot hosed the worst of the damage off the galactoturf. He felt thirsty, despite the four pints of tea that he'd consumed since waking up that morning. That was the trouble with this place, he thought, looking at the yowling spectators and the propaganda screens: their tea was bloody terrible.

On the touchline, Crispin Quench was on his feet and clapping, as if at an opera. He came hurrying across the pitch, hat cocked at a jaunty angle. 'One nil! Very good, Smith. Very good. The crowd are loving it. If you're not their star player by the end, I'll eat my cravat.'

The fallen giant's shoulder-pads sparked as they scraped along the ground. 'That looked bloody painful,' Smith said.

Quench waved a hand. 'I doubt he felt a thing. The Criminarch's got all his teams pumped full of combat drugs. You didn't think he'd play fair, did you?'

'Huh.' Smith scowled. 'Damned rigged contest. I feel like a Roman gladiator.'

'We've all been there, Smith. I'll see if they can send us up a couple at half-time.'

Smith wanted to protest, but the whistle blew and he was drowned out.

Sirens blared and the ball fell from the ceiling. Suruk ran in and caught it. Goreblast belly-flopped him. Suruk dropped the ball and rolled aside, but the damage was done. Goreblast threw the ball from the ground, straight into Jeremiad's servo-assisted fist.

Jeremiad folded over the ball like an armadillo clutching an acorn. He thundered down the pitch. Rhianna ran in and tried to reason with him, but he swatted her aside. Jeremiad slammed the ball down in the Ironsides' scoring zone.

'Yeah,' said Katie Dystopia, 'that's like, one all or something?'

The ball burst onto the pitch and Smith grabbed it. Wainscott and Suruk charged and rained blows upon the nearest Reborn, Jeremiad Obliteratorius. He wasn't obliterating anything much, now: he stumbled around like an armoured toddler in mortal combat with two angry cats, flailing hopelessly.

Goreblast lumbered in. He knocked the ball from Smith's hands and hurled it up the field, then stomped after it. Legs like fire hydrants pounded the galactoturf. Rhianna closed her eyes and the ball swerved in mid-air, dropping down next to Carveth, who flinched and leaped aside as if a mouse had just fallen down her shirt.

Smith rushed to intercept, but Goreblast charged forward like an unusually rapid glacier. 'Kill the unbelievers!' he grunted. His massive hand shoved Smith away. 'Burn the pitch!'

Staggering upright, Smith saw the ogre lumber past Carveth and stoop to grab the ball. He was caked in armour: no punch that Smith could throw would stop him.

There had to be another way, some weapon Smith could use . . .

'Carveth! Stay really still!'

She turned. Smith grabbed her around the waist and lifted her off the ground. Carveth kicked and squealed. Smith judged his moment, twisted like a shotputter and brandished her at Goreblast.

Her roller skate connected with his helmet. The giant stumbled, groaned and rubbed the side of his head. Carveth slipped out of Smith's arms and landed on her backside. Smith snatched the ball and sprinted down the pitch. He saw a massive shadow chasing him, heard boots hit the ground with a sound like an elephant stamping on a kettle drum.

The touchline was in range. Smith took a huge breath, and saw the crowd yelling him on. Faces cheered. He glanced at the Criminarch's box, keen to see the dictator's anger – and froze.

The Criminarch was there, but it was the figure beside him that mattered. Small, red, wrapped in a leather coat. One eye had been replaced with a lens, where Smith had shot it out years before.

'You?' he whispered, and Goreblast the Centurion smashed into the back of him.

The impact hurled Smith into the ground. He slid, his moustache breaking his fall, the ball trapped under his body. An advert for a refreshing soft drink stopped his movement. The roar of the crowd seemed to swallow him up.

Smith blinked and staggered upright. He could hear cheering. Someone leaned out of the stands and said, in a terrible attempt at a British accent, 'Good show, sir old chap.' Smith noticed that he was still clutching the ball. He had slid over the touchline with it in his hands. It was 2-1 to the Ironsides.

'Oh my spectators,' Alex Lagrande was saying, *'Word just in, so harken well . . . that goal is disallowed. Yes, most forbidden and refused!'*

'Typical,' said Katie Dystopia. *'That is like so unfair.'*

Smith stared up at the commentary box. How could it be disallowed? He'd crossed the damned line, hadn't he?

'Best beloved, that goal was in breach of the off-side rule! You may be wondering in your heddyweds what that might be. Let Uncle Alex explain in little words. When a chelloman glunks up the pitch with the yarble clutched oh so tightly in his gromsticks, and a wibbler comes garbling in before him . . .'

It was true, Smith thought. Wherever you went in the galaxy, whatever game you played, the off-side rule made no sense. 'Suruk!' he called, 'the match is over. You can stop trying to pull that man's head off now.'

The alien let go of Jeremiad Obliteratorius. 'Stupid puny human sport,' he growled. 'We have been robbed, Mazuran! This is the worst sporting event since the last thing that stopped us British from winning any sporting events. The ref must be blind, and now he must be destroyed, too!'

Wainscott snorted. 'Reckon we'll have some more fighting to do now. The bastards'll try to do us in.'

Rhianna approached. She touched Smith's hand. 'I'm sorry, Isambard. At least we tried. Like you said, it's not whether you win or lose, but how you play the game.'

'Of course it isn't!' Smith snapped back. 'I mean, sorry, Rhianna, I didn't mean to be rude, but when I said that, I didn't really mean it. It's like . . . it's like God is supposed to make you win because you're sporting. That's what it means.'

Suruk shook his head. 'Puzzling. But not as puzzling as *that* ludicrous display.'

He pointed. On the far side of the pitch, a small figure in body armour was staggering about like a drunkard in a vaudeville routine. A camera-drone tracked her erratic progress across the field.

'Damn it, Carveth,' Smith said, 'stop making a fuss!'

'I'm dying!' she cried. 'I'm dying, boss! To lose a game – I can't take it. I'm going to drop dead right here, in front of all these cameras!'

Smith looked up. Hovercams were gathering above her like vultures, each marked with the colours of its sponsor. Scoring points was good television, but fatalities were even better.

'This is it, boss! Come closer, so I can tell you – urg – all my secrets.'

'What secrets? Stop arsing around.'

'Just play ball,' she said, and she looked straight at him.

Rhianna nudged Smith. 'She's right. Polly, how can we help?'

'Oh,' Smith said. 'Play ball, you say? Oh. Um, righto, old valued crewman, obviously we don't want you dying, do we? Suruk? Suruk, we don't want Carveth dying on the pitch, do we?'

Suruk said, 'Bah! If she was really dying, she would

shout and moan. She makes louder noises when she uses her electric toothbrush.'

Another camera swung down, but it hesitated. At the edge of the pitch, Quench was trying to hold up the security men. Smith caught Carveth's eye. She collapsed.

They ran to her side. 'What can I do, faithful friend?' Smith asked.

'I am dying of shame,' Carveth replied. Her eyes, half-closed, looked over the cameras. 'Only one thing can save me. The delicious, restoring taste of Supercola, the official sports drink of the Imperial Ironsides.'

Wainscott's eyes lit up as if he had just invented the wheel. 'Ah, I get it,' he said. 'You, medic! Bring us a case of sponsored pop or I'll punch your nose straight into your brain! And while the cameras are here,' he added, reaching to his belt, 'I might as well give the world something worth watching.'

'No,' Smith said. 'Not yet, Wainscott. Save that for the finals. Look at Carveth.'

Quench ran across the pitch, followed by a woman in a shiny bodysuit. She wore the Supercola logo down her side like stripes on a racing car. She produced a can from her belt, turned it so that the name faced the cameras and passed it to Carveth.

Carveth took a sip. She spluttered. Then she sat up. 'I'm alive,' she muttered. 'I'm alive! Oh, praise the Supercola Corporation, I live again! I feel so free. I need to find a beach and do somersaults on it. Everyone should drink this stuff!'

Rhianna hugged Smith. Wainscott said, 'It's a miracle.'

'More than that,' Carveth said, turning to the cameras, 'it's the taste of the next generation!'

Above them, the loudspeakers crackled into life. '*Well, well, my brothers and sisters. Your old friend, Alex Lagrande, has just been handed a message for you from our most beloved sponsors. And the message is. . . the goal is allowed! And that's the end of the match! The Imperial Ironsides win two points to one! And why not relax with a frabsome sipping of Supercola?*'

Carveth finished her drink. The cameras pulled back, and she gave them a final thumbs up. 'That,' she said, tossing the can away, 'is how you play the game. Before the game plays you.'

'That was quick thinking,' Smith said. 'Good work, Carveth. I see what you meant about winning the crowd, Quench.'

The spy nodded. 'Give them a reason to keep looking at you.'

Wainscott huffed. 'That's what *I* was trying to do.'

The speakers crackled, and a new voice boomed across the pitch. '*All players stand back. The Criminarch and his honoured guests will now greet the players in person!*'

'Oh no,' Carveth groaned. 'What do we do?'

Suruk's mandibles opened. He made a low noise, part purr, part croak. 'Good. They will be within striking range.'

'Great,' Carveth replied. 'And how long do you think we'll last after we murder them in the middle of a football field? There might be a few witnesses, Sherlock.'

'But think of the audience, Piglet. Could there be any greater proof of my greatness?'

Rhianna raised a hand. 'Guys, just chill. We'll be okay. They can't do anything while the cameras are watching, right?'

'Right,' Smith said, but as the doors opened and a party of armed guards trooped out onto the pitch, he wondered.

First came a group of Redhat militiamen, louts in body armour and sunglasses. They were followed by a bevy of bigger thugs with ill-fitting suits and crew-cuts. Among them walked the Criminarch, bulkier than ever and sporting a strange chemical tint. It occurred to Smith that he'd been having the same treatment as the Reborn. Only that could explain the man's sheer size.

A man of lesser moral fibre would have been intimidated, but Smith ignored the Criminarch and his riff-raff. What came behind them was far more worrying: four huge Ghasts, a third bigger than regular drones, their helmets marked with a variant of the skull-and-antennae symbol of the praetorian legions. Each carried a heavy disruptor gun normally operated by a two-ant team. In their midst was a tiny, limping creature, scrawny and large-headed. It was 462, Smith's oldest enemy. His scars were like a braile record of their earlier encounters.

462 hung back a little while his bodyguards sniffed the air. The Criminarch swaggered forward, thumbs hooked over his belt.

'You beat my team of ultimate warriors,' he growled. 'You were meant to die. All of you! How dare you refuse me this? Who the hell are you to defy the Criminarch of Radishia?'

Smith looked straight at him. He put the Bearing in his voice. 'I am Isambard Douglas Winston Smith, officer of the British Space Empire, Captain of a jolly good team, owner of a very nice spaceship, and now I will leave the pitch and have my tea, in this match or the next.'

The Criminarch's tiny eyes shrank to almost nothing. He leaned forward, so that the camera-drones would not catch his words. 'Your empire is weak. Your people are decadent and cowardly. My men are as strong and unyielding as my many muscles. They will crush your army and you will weep at your own softness.'

Smith looked the Criminarch in the eyes. 'Soon, there will come a time when you will have to stop honouring yourself,' he replied. 'Or else you'll go blind.'

The Criminarch scowled and stepped back. He muttered something about weakness and turned away. His guards flanked him.

462 lingered a moment. His remaining biological eye met Smith's gaze. 'We meet again,' he said.

'What do you want?' Smith demanded.

'You'll see,' said the Ghast, and he smiled. Then he turned and limped back towards the stands, his trench coat flapping around his protruding stercorium.

*

'Hi, and welcome to Aftermatch Aftermath with me, Chud Brockle, giving you the run-down on the scrum-down show-down. With me live tonight is Isambard Smith, captain of tonight's surprise winners, the Imperial Ironsides. That was one hell of a victory, wasn't it, Captain Smith?'

'Well, it wasn't bad.'

'That's right – it wasn't just bad, it was apocalyptic! That was some inspired play, there, especially from crowd favourite, Suruk the Slayer. How did you feel when he took out Impervius the Demolisher?'

'Feelings? You want me to talk about feelings? On camera?'

'Okay, let's discuss the rest of the season. Do you see yourself getting to the top and surviving? There's some heavy hitters to get through. What do you think about things generally? What would you say to the viewers on the network out there?'

'To the viewers? Well, crikey, that's difficult. I mean, you don't need me to tell you that things are bad. Everybody knows things are bad. There's a war on. Your planet's broke. Your radish crop has failed. You can't even get a decent cup of tea.'

'Uhuh?'

'You can't get any decent food, the militia are running wild in the streets, and there you are, sitting in front of your telly, thinking "Please, I don't want to be reminded of that. I just want to forget about it all and watch ten heavily armoured men killing one another for possession of a rugby ball". But I'm not going to let you chaps forget.'

'That's great, Captain Smith. The censors are telling me that the live broadcast session's coming to an end now—'

'Not yet. I don't know what to do to make this planet civilised again – how to stop the dictators and the army and the war and everything – but I do know that you've got to be nice. That's right. You've got to stop your non-sense right now and say "I am a human being or some similar organism, damn it! My life has value!"'

'Captain Smith . . . Captain – that's my microphone. You can't have . . . Give me that—'

'All of you viewing chaps, yes, you there: I want you to get up now, out of your chairs. I want you to go to the *windows, open them and stick your head out and say, "Hello, other viewing chaps! I am really quite ticked off, and I'm not taking this bollocks anymore!"' Then you should put the kettle on.'*

*

The next few matches came, and Smith was ready for them – not just for the opposing teams, but for the spectators. It actually wasn't too hard to win the crowd. It didn't even feel like cheating or showing off or some other devious practice from Abroad. In a lot of ways, it was enough for Smith to be himself. The worst of it was having to drink Supercola in between halves, and to look happy about it. At Smith's insistence, Quench bought tea off the black market and smuggled it into the stadium in his trousers.

'You're doing marvellously,' the spy remarked, as he tipped lapsang souchong out of his turn-ups. 'My bosses are very pleased with you all. Here, have a programme. I've got some Earl Grey sewn into my hat.'

Smith glanced through the glossy brochure, produced by Unlucky Dog hot dogs and the Supercola Corporation. Smith was praised for his fair play and stern adherence to the rules. Suruk, the brochure claimed, was an honourable master of close combat. Rhianna was a source of mystery and confusion, probably because she always seemed mystified and confused, and Carveth appeared to be regarded as a plucky mascot. The brochure claimed that Wainscott was chiefly noted for his cunning, which wasn't what most people tended to remember him for – but then, Wainscott hadn't debagged himself on the pitch yet.

'Here's a splendid English Breakfast, courtesy of my cravat,' Quench said, pulling a string of teabags from his neckline, 'and I've got a rather interesting Assam in my trousers.'

That afternoon, the Ironsides beat Los Mariachis De La Muerte 3-1, and the crowd cheered when Smith shook hands with their captain, El Luchador, at the end instead of jumping on his head. 'Jolly well played, sir!' Smith said.

'Not so bad yourself, senor,' the masked warrior replied.

The next morning, the guards came in early. 'We've got a little something to show you lot,' said the thinner of the two, a scrawny man who looked as if he had undergone a special form of liposuction to remove both fat and happiness. 'After last time, me and the boys got thinking.'

Smith stood up. Behind him, Suruk was leaning forward like a menacing shadow. The alien had been waiting for the chance to attack the guards and run amok. Perhaps, Smith thought, this was it.

'Yeah,' said the fatter guard. He pulled his jacket up, revealing his T-shirt. Across his stomach was a picture of Smith.

'Right, that's it,' Smith exclaimed. 'You will take my face off your paunch this minute, or, by God – wait a moment. What does that say next to my head?'

'*Spiffin' with the Tiffin,*' said the guard. 'It's British for "Let's kill 'em", right?'

'I don't think it's British for anything at all. But, er, yes, jolly good. Carry on.'

The guards laughed. 'That's exactly what it says on the back!' the thin one explained. 'The vendors are selling them outside the stadium.'

Carveth watched them stomp out of the room. The door closed and locked. 'We've got our own dodgy over-priced merchandise,' she said. 'We're a proper sports team now.'

The next match was tougher. The Sisters of No Mercy were taking no prisoners, but Suruk sent them to the ground in a clatter of armour, and the Ironsides won 3-2. Even Kat Dystopia had to reluctantly conclude that the match had been 'like well feminist which is good or something'. The next day, Rhianna got an offer from *Violent Sports Illustrated* to appear in their souvenir number with the star players of the Sisters, Liz de Fleur and Joan of Arcturus. To Smith's considerable disappointment, she turned it down because the corsets looked uncomfortable. 'But that's the whole point,' Smith explained.

After the next match – three goals and no fatalities against the Retro-Firing Ramjets – they walked back down the tunnel, ostentatiously holding large cans of Supercola. A man detached himself from the shadows, lowering a newspaper. He wore a raincoat and a hat.

'Look, it's Rick!' Carveth cried.

'I don't know any guy by that name,' Dreckitt said. He folded the paper and passed it to Wainscott, who immediately began rolling it into a tube. 'Toaster, gas mains,' the major muttered, out of habit.

Dreckitt walked alongside them, towards their quarters. 'I'm Dick Rocket, from the British Regulatory Institute for Ball games, Entertainment and Sport. Here to keep sport clean.'

Carveth sidled over to him, armour plates clattering. 'What if I like my sport dirty, Rick?'

'It's Dick. And I'm just doing my job, ma'am. I'm here looking for bugs.'

'Bugs?' said Smith.

'Sure,' Dreckitt said, glancing at the guards. 'You know, beetles, roaches, Carrotan Head-Chewers, that sort of thing.' He lowered his voice. 'Listen . . . we're getting everything in place to bust you guys out of this joint. All you have to do is toss the pigskin around and win the big game. Then they'll send you up to crack wise with the big cheese. You rub the Criminarch out, Radishia falls apart without the big boss running things and we all go home happier than Louie the Bum shooting craps down Tin Pan Alley. What do you say to that?'

Smith hesitated, uncertain whether Tin Pan Alley was Dreckitt's private slang for the lavatory. There was not much point in Dreckitt speaking quietly. At the best of times, he was virtually incomprehensible. That was the trouble with androids. Try as they might, their basic programming would eventually kick in.

'Look,' Smith said, 'it's all very well us bumping off the Criminarch, but how long do you think we'll survive after that? My men will be shot to pieces the moment he hits the floor. What's more, the crowd will stampede.'

Quench said, 'Actually, I think they'd probably cheer.'

'It's not a risk I can take, Dreckitt. Especially not with Carveth's fourth birthday coming up. Dreckitt, tell W and the others that I'm not game for it. We'll beat whatever the Criminarch throws at us fair and square. That'll be enough.'

Dreckitt said, 'They won't like it, Smith.'

Smith turned and leaned in close. 'Now look here . . .

Dick Rocket. If your plan goes ahead, it won't just be me taking early retirement. We'll all buy it, Carveth included. I won't condemn my men to certain death just because some private knob shows up and tells me to. Understand?'

Dreckitt sighed. 'Yeah, I hear you. What you're saying ain't so dumb. I'll let 'em know. But it's private dick.'

They reached the bottom of the slope and turned the corner. The fat guard opened the door to their training room.

Storm-Assault Commander 462 was sitting on the weights bench. Two huge praetorians stood over him like unusually determined personal trainers. 462 looked up at Smith and smiled.

The guard swallowed. 'Er . . . you've got a visitor.'

One of the praetorians growled.

Smith looked at Dreckitt. 'You said you were here to clean out the bugs.'

462 stood up. Evil had worn him down. He seemed to have shrunk since Smith had last seen him, over a year before. His thin face had become more lined and a darker red.

'Do not worry, Captain Smith,' said 462. 'I won't be here long. I find it hard to tolerate the smell of human sweat. Besides, I find sportsmanship uninteresting.' He limped forward. He was a head shorter than Smith. 'We will speak in the corridor. Guards, you will watch Captain Smith's friends. And *my* guards will watch *you*. Come,' he said, gesturing to the exit.

'Put the kettle on,' Smith said. 'I'll be back.'

They walked into the corridor and 462 closed the door.

'I didn't see you as a sports fan,' Smith said.

'I am not. To my mind, the only true contest is the endless struggle between species to dominate the galaxy. And beach volleyball with tanks. That's a good sport. And synchronised saluting. That said, I find the sports drink Supercola very satisfying.'

'I suppose sugar solution goes down well with ants.'

'Quite. Much better than your filthy Earth-drink made with hot water and leaves. I have been following your progress with interest, Smith. Your victory over our allies was of considerable interest to me. My comrades did not expect your armies to defeat the Yull. The fall of the lemming men was a matter of great gravity to us.'

'It was a matter of gravity for the lemmings, as well.'

'I have not been idle either, Smith. Since we last met, I have been climbing the chain of command. Although,' he added, an ugly smirk cracking the lower half of his face, 'you might want to imagine it more as a greasy pole. I am at a difficult stage.'

Smith had a sudden image of the greasy 462 pulling himself up a pole on a stage, while Ghast marching-music played in the background. He grimaced.

'I consider myself an ideal candidate for high command, Smith. I share many qualities with our glorious leader – cunning, ruthlessness, the will to succeed. Number One has taught me well. I like to think that there is a part of him in me.'

'Spit it out, 462.'

'How dare you! That is not the part that I meant! Such implications of decadent activity will not be tolerated – oh, I see. Right. It is about Number One that I wish to speak to you.'

'Go on.'

'You see, Smith, we are not so very different, you and I. We both want our empires to win. And . . . um . . .' 462 tried to scratch his head, but his helmet was in the way. With some satisfaction, Smith noticed that the words *Made in Sheffield* were still burned into the ant-man's palm, where he had once tried to steal Smith's sword. 'We both want the same things. Including the death of Number One.'

'Of course,' Smith replied. 'I'd bag that little bugger and have him stuffed as soon as – wait a moment. Did you just say you wanted to see Number One get killed?'

462 looked over his shoulder. He pulled up the collar of his trench coat, lowered his voice and raised his antennae. 'Yes.'

'Ah,' said Smith, 'so you've finally seen sense, eh? While that mad little insect is in charge, all you face is destruction. But with Number One out the way, you can surrender and be treated decently, within reason. You could become subjects of our empire. Perhaps there is hope for you lot, you know. Perhaps one day, it won't be just you, 462, but all of your species who realise that tyranny, murder and corruption lead only to one place . . . the spot above the mantelpiece where I hang my trophies.'

'Actually, he shot my dog.'

'Your *dog*? One of those ugly things? But they're horrible.'

'He had special skills—'

'I'm sorry, but the fact that he brought you your slippers and could reach his own stercorium with his tongue doesn't count for much. Really, 462, get it in perspective, man. There's a war on. I hate to say it, but many people have been shot over the last few years and most of them were worth much more than some scabby ant-hound. You people clone them up by the batch. They come in packs of six, I've heard.'

462 leaned forward. His voice was a quick hiss. 'What if it was one of your minions, Smith? My intelligence tells me that you have a hamster. What if it was your hamster that was gunned down? Wouldn't you want revenge? Wouldn't you want to send those who murdered your hamster to hibernate for eternity?'

'It's not my hamster. It's my pilot's.'

'What if it was your pilot who was silenced? How would you feel about that?'

'You mean "silenced" as in "killed", not as in "made to pipe down a bit"?'

462 nodded.

'Then I'd hunt the bastard down like a dirty weasel and settle his bloody hash.'

'Listen carefully, Smith. If you win this contest, the Criminarch will want to meet you in person. He is obliged to meet the victor of the games. He will expect it to be his own team, the Hunters. If your team can disappoint him, you will get the chance to assassinate him in his personal viewing-booth.'

'I see.'

'Then know this . . . the final of this moronic contest will be watched not only by the Criminarch, but by Number One, as his guest. Number One will be guarded by soldiers from his personal legion, the Pincers of Death. But when you meet the Criminarch, there will be a moment, a brief moment, when you will be close enough to attack Number One and snap his scrawny neck.'

'And then? How will I escape without being shot?'

'Well, you won't.'

'Right,' Smith said. 'I see. That's a bit of a flaw in your plan, isn't it?'

'Not really.'

'I don't know how business is done in your rubbish empire – and I don't want to – but certain death isn't a very good way of getting people to do things.'

462 shrugged. 'He dies, you die. Frankly, Smith, this is what you humans call a win-win situation.'

'Thanks.'

'Think of it, Smith. You will be remembered as a hero. There will be no greater sacrifice than yours. You will join the greatest soldiers in your history, remembered for their unceasing—'

'Deadness.'

'Glory. Think of the martial glory! Think of the heroic sacrifice! Think how big your statue will be!'

Smith thought about it. 'And then what? Some other oversized insect will take over and the war will rage on. No. I'm sorry, but the lives of my men and their hamster are worth more than getting revenge for your dog.'

462 licked his thin lips. 'We could negotiate a cease-fire. In the confusion following Number One's death, a deal would be easy to make. Especially with, er, the right insect in charge.'

'The Space Empire does not deal with monsters like you. Except when we *deal* with them, of course. This is the least convincing argument I've heard since Carveth tried to persuade me to let her keep a pony in the bathroom.'

'Think it over, Smith.' 462 looked him in the eye. For the first time, it occurred to Smith that there might be genuine intelligence there, not just low cunning. 'Our species does not believe in the greatness of individuals, other than our leader. Yours does. You could be the man who bowls out Number One. You could hit him for six.'

'I'll think about it.'

'Please do. For the sake of the galaxy, and its hamsters. Now . . .' 462 glanced back down the corridor again, 'I have been here long enough.' He hit the controls and the doors slid open. 'After you, Smith.'

They walked back inside. Wainscott and Suruk lurked at the edge of the room. Carveth was hiding. In the middle of the room, Rhianna was addressing 462's bodyguards.

'Which is like, a really interesting way to use kelp. A lot of people have heard about meat being smoked, but they've got no idea that you can totally do that in a vegan lifestyle. I've smoked loads of vegetables and I'm fine. Now, a fruitarian—'

'Storm-Assault Commander,' one of the praetorians barked, 'I urgently require orders to permit me to shoot this human. Failing that, I wish transfer to the M'Lak Front or any other battlefield free from organic produce.'

'You'd probably best go, 462,' Smith said. 'Every time I meet you, you end up getting injured.'

Suruk purred. 'Indeed. It would be sad if your head came off, little Ghast. Especially so far from my trophy room.'

462 looked at Suruk. To his credit, Smith thought, the Ghast did not seem particularly frightened by Suruk. But then, there wasn't much in it in terms of looks. Suruk

might have protruding mandibles, but the large stercorium sticking out of the back of 462's coat went a long way, quite literally.

'You should be grateful, frog-spawn,' said 462. 'I will give you a gift you will appreciate. How does death in battle sound?'

'Hmm,' Suruk replied. 'Not bad, actually.'

'Excellent,' 462 said. 'You get a heroic death, your empire gets its mission accomplished, and Number One gets to have his head torn off. That's the kind of sport I like. Everyone is a winner.'

The doors slid shut behind him. Smith stood there, looking at the doors, uncertain of what to do.

'Alright, boss!' Carveth strode into view from the sleeping area. 'Hello, everyone. Good, the Ghasts have buggered off. Did I miss anything? Rick – er, Dick Rocket – will be joining us just as soon as he's got his breath back.' She paused and looked around the room. 'Why the long faces? I mean, Suruk's face is obviously like that all the time, but what's up with the rest of you? Has anyone got any of that energy drink stuff? I think Dick Rocket might be needing it.'

The Football Field of Battle

'I know I've asked a lot from you in the past,' Smith said. 'This is obviously a very serious decision, since you'll probably be dead by the end of it. I therefore have decided to order that we decide this democratically. So, let's be clear on this.

'In the awful, wretched history of Abroad there has never been a tyrant as vicious, bloodthirsty or in need of an absolute thrashing than Ghast Number One. He has made it his life's work to conquer space and devour every living thing in it – not personally, of course. He has turned his species from something that might have been vaguely tolerable, albeit weird-looking and a bit second-rate, into a savage army of mindless insects. All right, they always have been ants, but they're particularly bad ants right now. The only thing the Ghast Empire exports is war, and the only good thing it has ever done is to provide chaps like us with ornaments for our mantelpieces and an opportunity to demonstrate our moral fibre.

'We now have a chance to destroy this evil little bugger. Defeating the Criminarch would lead to the fall of a single planet – admittedly, one that would open the way to the Ghast homeworld, but a single planet nevertheless.

Civilising Number One has the potential to overthrow the entire Ghost Empire.'

Wainscott raised his hand.

'Yes?'

'You sure about that, Smith? Say we knock his block off. What's to stop his minions from getting a clone – Number One (B) – and sticking it in number one Number One's place?'

Carveth said, 'That's right. Maybe he's got a load of identical ones frozen. You can't buy ice creams singly. The best ice cream cones come in boxes of twelve.'

Suruk thrust up his hands. 'You said they came in eights! What happened to the other four? I bet you devoured them.'

'It doesn't matter, Suruk,' Smith said.

'Yes it does. Nobody cheats the Slayer. Mazuran, you are the captain here. I demand to eat four ice creams before I die.'

Rhianna sighed. 'Guys, it's not about ice cream.'

'There are too many variables for the mission to run smoothly,' Wainscott said. 'I don't like it.'

Smith sipped his tea. 'So you're not up for it, then?'

'Rubbish. Of course I'm up for it. Since when did I want things to go smoothly? Imagine a Wainscott giving up the chance to raise hell like that! We've been causing havoc since Caesar arrived. The family motto is *Where there's a war, there's a Wainscott*. No point risking you lot, though. Tell Susan she's in charge if I don't make it back.'

Carveth nodded. 'Good idea. Wainscott can do it! He's got the, er, requirements for the job.'

'I'll do it,' Rhianna said.

Smith stared at her. 'Absolutely not, Rhianna. I forbid it.'

She twisted around in her seat. 'Hey, Isambard, I can make my own decisions. It's a free country, isn't it?'

'Not here it isn't. It's a totalitarian dictatorship, Rhianna.'

'Like, totally?'

'Yes, totally totalitarian.'

'Well, someone should do something about that.' She had changed out of her team kit into a long dress that made her look like a tie-dyed ghost. Rhianna pushed her hair out of her eyes and said, 'I'll do it. It should be okay.'

Carefully and slowly, Carveth said, 'I don't know if you've been tuning your radio in of late, but we are discussing a suicide mission.'

'That's all right, Polly. I believe in reincarnation. It'll be fine.'

'What as,' Wainscott muttered, 'a weed?'

Smith raised his hand. 'Rhianna, your sacrifice is very decent, but you should know that this will almost certainly be fatal. You'll be going up to meet Number One – and you won't be coming back down.'

'Well, that's all right. I find stairs difficult in this dress.'

Suruk had been leaning against the wall, arms folded. Now he stood up and strolled into the centre of the room. 'Mystic woman, I honestly do not know whether you are exceedingly brave or exceedingly bewildered. Your knowledge of combat is negligible. The world reveals itself to you through a haze of medication. No.' He opened his mandibles. 'This is a job for the Slayer. I shall march up the stairs and demand a prize. When puny Number One offers me a feeble cup I will take some real trophies, starting with his head. How I will laugh as I commence the severing! The Criminarch will be next in the litany of mayhem when I claim his cranium, make a sling of his posing-pouch and hurl his skull through the rafters via his jockstrap. Then I will slay his minions as the scythe reaps the corn. And then, if anyone is still standing, I will have serious words with the crowd. And after that, if the cameras want an action replay, I will start all over again.' He paused, grinning, and looked around the room. 'The question is . . . who will join me in this cavalcade of death?'

*

It was festival time in Radishia's capital city. As many tanks had been pulled off the front line as the Criminarch's men dared, and they rolled down the main street, flanked by lines of servo-armoured troopers. Trumpets blared to drown out the sound of the Space Empire's fighter ships and the sky was full of fireworks to hide the rockets.

To show his love of the common people, the Criminarch had allowed a thousand of them to pull the vast gilt wagon on which he sat. Thugs walked among them with sticks to make sure the struggling paupers hauled their beloved leader at a suitable pace. On the streets and on balconies, nervous citizens whooped and cheered and fixed their faces into smiles.

Susan stood to one side of a balcony, out of sight in the cool shadows. At her feet lay a woman in a black leather catsuit. The woman's face was hidden by heavy targeting goggles and a mask painted to resemble a skull.

'The first rule of being an assassin,' Susan said to the

body as she cleaned her knife on the curtains, 'is not to dress like one.'

Bush Captain Shane stood behind Susan, watching the window. 'Nice work.'

'I thought they'd leave a few heavies to guard the roof-tops.' Susan leaned forward to drag the body away, and her shirt parted company with her trousers.

'Gees, Susan,' Shane said, 'What happened to your back?'

'The scars?' Susan tugged her shirt down. For once, she looked less than composed. 'Oh, I got them in a bike accident, ages ago.'

'Cycling? It looks like a croc tried to eat you.'

She shrugged. 'Admittedly, the bike was rocket-powered. And I fell off quite a high bridge when it exploded. And the water under the bridge had a few sharks in it but, really, it's nothing. But thanks for asking.'

She glanced back down the corridor. Craig hurried past, carrying a guard over his shoulder. 'Just dump him with the others, eh?'

'Right you are,' Craig said, and he disappeared into a side room. 'I'll stick him on the chaise longue.'

'Classy.' Susan toggled her headset. 'Control, we're in place. We broke into a villa owned by one of the Criminarch's chums. It's full of heavies – or rather, it was.'

The voice on the other end of the line was deep and mel-ancholy. 'How is it?'

'Hideous. Nasty wallpaper.'

'I meant the mission.'

'Fine. Have you seen this parade? I've never seen so many dipsticks in one place.' She glanced at the balcony: a mini-blimp floated past, trailing banners. 'Look, are you sure you don't want us to knock off the Criminarch here and now?'

*

Two roads away, on street level, Eric Lint said, 'No. We've got bigger fish to fry. Ants to squash, anyhow. Carry on, Susan.'

Lint cut the line and pulled his collar up. He walked past a line of empty buildings, towards the shacks at the end of the road. Away from the main thoroughfare, the apartment blocks were concrete shells, the windows broken into jagged shards like the teeth of vicious beasts.

A man and a woman sat inside the nearest shack, warming their hands on a campfire. The man looked up. He was small and wore thick spectacles. The woman took her hand out of her blue coat. She looked neat and efficient.

'How goes it?' the man asked.

'Beastly, George.' Lint leaned against the wall of the shack and rubbed his hands together. He had not expected Radishia to be quite this impoverished. He'd entered the city disguised as a vagrant, but in the last hour four people had asked for the address of his tailor. 'This parade is a disgrace. Any proper parade has a fire engine for the kiddies to sit in and a place where they can get their faces painted like a tiger. Where are the tigers? Where is the fire engine?' He scowled. 'Are you ready to go?'

'Oh, of course, Eric.' George Benson wore a ragged coat and his bowler hat. He looked like someone from a terrible modern play Lint had once seen, where the lead actor hadn't even bothered to show up. 'Quench is all set. Don't worry, old boy. He's a good man. We were at university together. When you ride a fellow's punt for three years, you get the measure of him.'

Lint nodded. 'Helen?'

The woman nodded. Her smile had a slightly manic quality. 'Everything is going to be just fine. I'll take care of it just like that.' She clicked her fingers. 'Just you say the word, Mr Lint, and I'll clean the Criminarch like a sweep-bot cleans a chimney.'

Lint nodded. Helen Frampton, requisitioned android and former childcare expert, had proved herself at Mothkarak, where she had 'tidied' several dozen lemming men with a high-powered rifle, whistling all the while. 'Good,' he said. 'But no singing this time.'

'Oi!'

Lint turned. Three solid men in brown uniforms stood in the street. They wore heavy boots, leather braces and tiny red hats. The nearest one hefted a club in his hands.

'Didn't you hear the order?' he demanded. 'No trash on the streets when the ant-men are in town. And yet, what do we have here?'

Benson stood up and adjusted his bowler hat. 'These,' he declared, putting the Bearing into his voice, 'are not the spies that you are looking for.'

'Well, that's all right, I suppose.' The thug lowered his truncheon. He raised it again. 'Wait a minute. Did you say "spies"?'

'Oh no. That is not the word you are looking for, either.'

The man scratched his head. 'What is the word I'm looking for, then?'

'I believe it's "bye".'

They watched the three thugs wander off. It struck Lint as odd that, in the Space Empire, such obvious criminals would be stopped by the police. On a planet like this, such obvious criminals became the police.

'Come on,' Lint said. 'We need to get seats in the stadium. Did you bring your disguises?'

'Of course, Mr Lint!' Miss Frampton reached into her Gladstone bag and produced an enormous striped scarf. 'I've got three. They're in the appropriate colours, of course, so we'll fit in perfectly. Perhaps we can sing some sort of inspiring song between overs.'

*

It was dark in the training room. Smith sat by himself, a box of Supercola by his side. He had taken to leaving a load of cans in the training room. The stuff still tasted vile, but it was handy for greasing the exercise machines.

He turned on the television to distract himself. The Criminarch appeared, standing behind a podium.

'Once, friends, all the jobs were being taken by robots. All the hard, honest work was being done by robots. But I solved that problem. I had all the robots smashed. And then I introduced slavery. Now everybody has a job for life. Three cheers for my radish plantations!' The Criminarch beamed like a happy frog.

Smith changed the channel. Instead of the Criminarch posing with the troops, an advert for Supercola was playing. A woman in a long, black coat twirled an umbrella in a mocked-up London street. She picked up a can of

Supercola from a selection of rival brands and held it up to the camera.

'Supercola's frajulistic!' she said. 'The others are atrocious!'

The girl looked remarkably like Rhianna. The thought of Rhianna dressed in such a fashion was enough to put a spring in Smith's step, or at least to make him walk awkwardly. Clearly, the Imperial Ironsides were not just a name to be feared: more importantly, they were a name that sold fizzy drink. 'I'm like Helen of Troy,' Smith mused. 'The face that launched a thousand sips.'

He changed channel, looking for something that wasn't about the match. Suruk's face appeared on the screen, filmed from behind a glass partition.

'Personally, I prefer Bach,' the alien was saying. 'I also enjoy the music of Minnie Riperton.' Smith had forgotten how rarely Suruk seemed to blink. 'A lemming man once tried to test me in combat. I removed his skull to the sound of *Les Fleurs*.'

The interviewer, a neatly-dressed young woman, composed herself and said, 'And do you have a message for your fans?'

Suruk tipped his head back and sniffed the air. 'I can smell your perfume,' he replied. 'Or possibly your fear. Human odours confuse me.'

Good Lord, Smith thought, we're all over the television. *We are to Radishia what* Holographic Poldark *is to the over-50s*. He wondered what would happen to the local economy if they lost. Carveth had put her name to all sorts of cakes, pasties, pies and chocolate products – or perhaps she was just claiming them all for later.

'Hey, Isambard.'

Rhianna stood in the doorway. The bad light made the hem of her dress translucent: she seemed to glow around the edges. That, together with her expression, made her look like an angel who had come down to Earth to deliver glad tidings but was having trouble remembering what the tidings were about.

'What ho,' he said thoughtfully.

'Thinking?' she said.

'Yes. About tomorrow.' Smith sighed. 'It's like the eve before a battle. We had to learn a poem at school about this sort of thing.

There's a breathless hush in my clothes tonight
Ten to noon and a match to win
Half a league, half a league, half a league onwards
Play up, play up, and play the game.'

'That's really deep,' Rhianna said. She was silent for a few seconds. 'What does it mean?'

'Well, it's poetry. I don't think it really means anything. Probably something to do with Waterloo or Agincourt or something. There's probably a woman dressed as a man, too, and maybe a ghost. That sort of thing happened a lot in Shakespeare's time.'

Rhianna pulled a chair over. 'Was Shakespeare really at Waterloo?'

'Oh yes. With Napoleon and the Duke of Abba and people like that. We did it in history at school.' He saw a metal ring-pull in the light thrown by the television. He reached out and picked up the can, hoping that it was beer. 'Did you do history on New Francisco?'

'A bit. I did pretty well. The teacher said the only thing higher than my grades was me. We studied the history of spaceflight. We were going to have a field trip to see a space shuttle when I dropped out.'

'You gave up?'

'No, I fell out the airlock. I was like, concussed. I was really confused for ages, but . . . I, um . . .'

'Got better?'

'Oh, okay. That's good.'

Smith opened the can and took a swig. A second later he realised that it was not beer, but Supercola. He spluttered violently, swallowed and coughed. 'God, this stuff is foul!' He looked at the back of the can. 'Look at the ingredients . . . *drencrom, velocet, bi-carbonated rock shake* . . . no, wait, that says *rock snake*. No wonder it's such venom. Bloody hell!' He paused. 'I can't do this, Rhianna. I can't let you all buy it.'

'Isambard—'

'It's Carveth's birthday in a week's time. Four's a big age for a synthetic. I keep thinking of her little face when she sees what I've got her.'

'You've got her a present?'

'Well, no, I haven't. It's going to be an angry face, I reckon. And then there's Suruk. We've known each other for years, ever since his people stormed that fort I was defending. He let me live, Rhianna. It seems a hell of a way to pay him back, sending him on a suicide mission.'

'That was very honourable of him.'

Smith nodded. 'He said so at the time. Something about it not being worth the effort of blunting his blade on my skull. He's had such an effect on so many people's lives – a terminal effect, usually, but still . . . Do you know there's at least three Scandinavian metal bands named after him?'

'He's certainly represented his species. He's brought the issues of native alien peoples to everyone's attention.'

'True. People deserve a fair warning. And to cut that life short, after he's cut so many other people short . . . it just doesn't seem right.'

She sat cross-legged on her chair. The light from the television made her face seem almost luminous. 'I know,' she said.

'And then there's you,' Smith said. 'It's not fair to expect you to have to do this. To face Number One and all his minions—'

Rhianna reached out and touched his arm. 'Hey, Isambard. It's okay. If we win, cool. If we get shot, well, I won't feel a thing. And we'll just get, like, reincarnated as animals or something.'

'What sort of animal?'

'That kind of depends on how the great wheel of karma rolls.'

'Preferably not a hedgehog, then.'

'It's not a literal wheel. It's like a –' She made vague gestures, as though indicating the size of a fish she had caught – 'a concept.'

'Can I be a badger? Anything British. Not a Ghast.'

'We're with you, Isambard. All the way.' She pulled a tube from a fold in her skirt and held it out to him. 'Mintat? It says they freshen your mind and your breath.'

Had Smith asked his younger self, he would have found it difficult to imagine anything better than being given

Imperial Strong Mintats by a woman who looked like a morally lax Pre-Raphaelite damsel. Yet as he raised the mint to his mouth, he only wished for some peace and quiet, a respite from the coarseness and violence that surrounded him.

The belch he produced nearly knocked him off his seat. Rhianna leaped up and looked around guiltily. 'The fuzz are at the door!' she cried. 'Flush the stash!'

Smith shook his head. 'That was me, Rhianna. At least, I think it was the mints.' He took another mint and put it on the tabletop. 'I think it reacted . . .'

Very carefully, Smith tipped the can of Supercola onto its side. Three drops fell onto the Mintat, shimmering.

The sound was like a thunderclap. The table jumped.

Rhianna shook her head sadly. 'Additives,' she said.

Smith stared at the place where the mint had been. It was now just a fine brown powder, blasted apart by its reaction with the Supercola. It made sense, he thought: the combination of the toxic chemicals in the Supercola and the robust manliness of Imperial Mintats had been more than nature could take. No wonder proper food was nearly illegal on Radishia.

'You know,' he said, 'this gives me a brilliant idea of what we should do next.'

'Yes!' Rhianna whispered. 'Let's have vigorous sex while everyone else is asleep, because tomorrow we might never get the chance again.'

'Really?' said Smith. 'I was thinking that we should make some sort of secret weapon and use it to defeat our enemies and escape. But now you mention it, righto.'

*

A mass of shabby citizens surrounded the stadium gates. On a viaduct above the rabble, the plutocrats and gangsters who ran Radishia were being ushered into the stadium. Rows of luxury cars rolled overhead: Mirovs, Corvegas and Durangos.

'What's this?' Eric Lint demanded. Behind him, fans shouted and cheered at one another.

The youth who manned the refreshments booth stared at Lint as if he'd heard of such creatures, but had never believed one could really exist. 'It's what you asked for,' he said.

'No, I asked for a cup of tea. What you have made is a steaming disgrace in a polystyrene cone.'

Someone muttered something behind Lint. 'Look at this,' he said, brandishing the cup at the youth. 'I wanted Earl Grey. This is pale grey.'

'Hey,' said the boy. 'I warmed up the water properly, didn't I? That was properly lukewarm. And I didn't charge you extra for the cream, mister. So take it and go.'

At the word 'cream', Lint bared his teeth, but someone prodded him in the side. He turned and saw Benson there. 'You're not off the hook, you know,' Lint said to the boy, and he followed Benson away from the booth, to where the others were waiting to get in.

George Benson and Helen Frampton had been joined by a tall, enthusiastic-looking blonde woman and a bulky man with whiskers and a solemn, thoughtful expression.

'What are you two doing?' Lint demanded.

Benson said, 'Captain Fitzroy and Mr Khan have come to update us on the off-world situation.'

'And to watch the big game!' Felicity Fitzroy exclaimed. 'I gather it's a bit like the lacrosse I used to play back in the Imperial Ladies League, except with pads and less weaponry. But it'll do.'

'Shouldn't you be in orbit?'

Hereward Khan pushed a wad of food to one side of his mouth and said from the other side, 'We're all set to lift our chaps off-world. Just get them to a safe place and say the word. There's a Service Q-ship ready to run them out of here, with Captain Fitzroy's destroyer watching it.' He puffed out his chest and looked around slowly, like an industrialist showing off a new factory. 'To think that Smith used to work in my offices, entering data about asteroids. The boy's gone far, you know. As to whether he's done good, that remains to be seen.'

'Let's go inside,' said Lint. He looked at his cup. 'This is going to be a long day.'

*

'Well, chaps,' said Smith, 'this is it.'

They stood in their training room, bulky in their armour. It occurred to Smith that, for all the missions they had completed, they'd never had a uniform. He was surprised how ready his crew looked, how eager and unafraid. Even Carveth had set her face and gritted her teeth, like a parent on a rollercoaster who knows that there are only two minutes more to endure.

'How do we look?' he asked.

Crispin Quench lounged against the far wall. 'Hard as

nails,' he replied. 'Yet debonair and ready for the High Street. It's a good look.'

It was odd to think that they'd never be coming back here again. One way or the other, the training room was no longer needed: its exercise machines looked like siege implements abandoned outside a castle. Boxes of Supercola lay scattered across the floor.

'I'll almost miss it here,' Wainscott said. 'Those hot dogs remind me of dynamite sticks, except they're more floppy. Makes me think of home.'

Carveth said, 'You keep dynamite sticks at home?'

''Course not,' Wainscott replied. 'That would be danger-ous. I keep them outdoors, in the shed with the paraffin.'

'Come on,' said Smith. 'Let's go.'

'Best of luck, chaps,' Quench said. 'I've spoken to the rest of the Service and they wanted me to say "Carry on".'

'Not joining us, then?'

'I'll be on the touchline. I'd go out on the pitch myself,' Quench said, 'if only I had my youth back. Shame really – he was a charming fellow. Seriously, though, go out there and knock 'em dead. Perhaps literally.'

He shook their hands, working his way down the line. Then he stepped back. The door opened and the guards came in. 'Ready?' said the fat guard.

'All set,' said Smith.

They walked up the ramp for the last time. The stadium looked like a cathedral devoted to the Criminarch. Huge banners dangled from the roof. The spectators held up placards and scarves. Smith was surprised to see his own face, several times normal size, among the pictures. A fresh roar of sound rose as Smith and his team stepped into view, a thunder of stamping boots. Strangely, much of the audience seemed to be wearing false moustaches and plastic bowler hats.

'Look at it,' Smith muttered. 'A tacky festival devoted to ritual hatred of the British. It's like the Eurovision Song Contest.'

Suruk raised a hand. 'Listen, Mazuran. They are chanting something. It is, "What ho, what ho."'

'Those bastards,' Smith growled. 'They're taunting us.'

Suruk laughed. 'You could not be more wrong, Mazuran. They are *saluting* us.'

Billboards from the Unlucky Dog and Supercola corporations flashed around the edge of the arena. Trumpets blared.

'Here we go,' said Smith. 'Give 'em hell, chaps.'

Suruk nodded. 'Time to float like a butterfly and sting like a melting clock, as Muhammad Dali would say.'

Smith opened his mouth to correct him, but the speaker system drowned him out.

'*Ladies and gentlemen, boys and girls . . .*' the loudspeakers boomed. '*Tonight, the final in the championship of kings. The elite of the elite, locked in deadly battle. Are you ready?*'

The audience roared.

'*I said, are you ready?*'

The audience screamed and howled.

'*Then let the two hours of pre-match adverts begin!*'

First, there were dancing girls. They were rubbish, Smith thought, because they were not wearing enough. It wasn't half as good as that Victorian Secret catalogue he kept under his bed. Then there was a film in which the Criminarch climbed a mountain wearing boots and cycling shorts. He seemed larger than ever. More films followed: a child was brought back to life by being bathed in Supercola – 'That was my idea!' Carveth cried; workers in a tank factory smiled desperately and were made to wave at the camera; the Criminarch visited some naval cadets and gave them all hot dogs.

Much more interesting was the vast amount of contraband that Quench had been stashing about his person. 'I made this outfit myself,' he explained, removing a pack of biscuits from his waistcoat.

And then there were the interviews. Smith and his team were sitting in their dugout when two soldiers in body armour lumbered in. Behind them came a girl in the weird teenage fashions of Radishia. 'I can do it myself!' she told her guards, and a camera-bot swung in behind her, hovering over her shoulder like a steel parrot on a space pirate.

'Hi, it's like Kat Dystopia here, with a pre-match talk to these guys,' she said. 'Or whatever.'

'Hello,' said Smith.

'I've been told to interview you, but you're like not allowed to say anything subversive, which is so unfair,' she said. 'So, all ready and everything?'

'Absolutely,' said Smith. 'It's very much a game of two halves—'

'What? That is like so *old*. Are you going to play an attacking game or concentrate on an attritional approach?'

Smith frowned. 'Well, that's a difficult choice—'

Kat Dystopia nodded keenly, setting her odd haircut wobbling. 'Yeah, totally. It's like when you have to choose between two guys, and one's like really nice but really, you don't have feelings for him, but the other guy is kind of a bad boy, but really he's misunderstood but has really nice eyes, you know?'

'No,' said Smith.

'I didn't expect you to understand,' she said. The drone lowered itself to focus on her face. 'I mean, nobody really understands teenagers, especially not the government, which is like oppressive or something? I was texting my friend about it and she said . . .'

Smith looked around, stood up and slipped away to the far end of the dugout, where Wainscott was cracking his knuckles and glaring at a sausage as if it was an old enemy. 'This is going to be tough, Smith,' he said. 'It's going to be up there with that time I wiped out a praetorian shock division, or even when I had to talk to women.'

'I bet that was tricky.'

'Damned right it was. Very tough customers. One of them was Susan and the other two were psychiatric nurses. Hard buggers and no mistake.'

One of the guards nudged Kat Dystopia, and she stopped interviewing herself. 'Looks like it's time,' said Smith.

Rhianna sighed. 'At last. The sooner I can get back to normal the better. Being alert, having to wear shoes all the time . . . it's just not natural.'

They stood up.

'Right,' said Smith, 'this is it. If anyone wants to pray or hug people or otherwise make a scene, you should have done it earlier. Let's get cracking, chaps.'

They walked back onto the field.

Cameras rose up and targeted the massive gilt box at the top. The Criminarch appeared on the screens around the area. He was sitting on a vast gold throne, wearing combat trousers and army boots. Two bandoliers crossed his smooth, heavily muscled chest. There was a laurel wreath on his head.

'Friends, Radishians, countrymen,' the Criminarch began. '*It is a time of war. I am angry, friends. More angry than ever. Righteous anger boils in my veins like hot soup! My face burns with rage like the radishes of our fields! And you can be angry with me – that is, we can be angry together. If you are angry with me, I'll have you shot.*

'*We must fight. We must be strong. We must destroy the enemy outside, but also destroy the traitors within. All traitors must die! Keep talking and shouting. Tell the suckers any old crap, so long as you keep them angry and confused!*'

An aide ran up, snatched the Criminarch's notes off him and pointed to a different paragraph.

'*I didn't say that,*' the Criminarch added. '*I said . . . "Smash weak things!"*'

The crowd roared.

'*Today we have a special visitor,*' the Criminarch declared. '*Our most beloved ally, a very good friend of mine and a wise and noble leader. The uniter of the galaxy, master of all species, Ghast Number One!*'

The camera panned across the box. It stopped on an empty space. After a second, the camera lowered itself by about a metre. Number One appeared on the screen.

Smith felt a rush of energy. His limbs were flooded with anger and disgust, like a gardener finally face-to-eyestalks with a giant slug. He had seen the scrawny figure on the television screen a thousand times, and sworn to cook his goose good and proper. And now, the vile little thing was here – in the same hall, breathing the same air.

Well, not for long.

Number One stood bolt upright. His sunken eyes glared at the audience like a pair of lamps.

He screamed and thumped his narrow chest with his fist. '*Ak!*' he shrieked. '*Arak – nak – raknaknak!*'

A computer voice, weirdly calm, said, '*Hello.*'

Number One raised his fist and shook it at the sky. Smith realised that he was familiar with the little bastard's every gesture, as if he was watching the antics of one of his madder aunts. '*Rak trak hatrack,*' One yelped, punctuating his shouts with little chopping actions.

With almost religious awe, Carveth whispered, 'He is so *ugly.*'

'His vile appearance is nothing compared to his foul mind,' Smith replied.

'Look at him, all stunty and weird. His antennae are glued to his forehead with snot or something.'

Smith was going to reply, but Number One let out a screech of fury that blotted the words out of his mind.

'*What is sport?*' the translatortron asked. '*What, do we learn from sport? What, I ask you, does sport teach us gathered here today? I will tell you. Sport is a vital part of a nation's strength. In sport, the individual is subsumed into the team, the unit, the squad, the battalion. Weak individuals learn to take orders and become strong. They learn vital skills such as loyalty, obedience and the will to victory.*'

Smith had heard it a million times before. Gertie talk: the garbage these creatures seemed to spew like broken robots.

He gazed up at the screaming thing in the visitor's box and felt what Suruk must feel when he saw the lemming men; a hard, cunning determination, without fear, as if he was a bullet flying towards the great leader's little brain.

'*Victory on the sports field is equivalent to victory on the battlefield. It is for this reason, and none other, that we Ghasts enjoy many sports such as tank volleyball and synchronised shouting. But remember,*' Number One added, raising his hand and pointing at the ceiling, '*at the end of the day, what matters is that you enjoy yourselves.*'

What? Smith thought.

'*It is not really important who wins or who loses,*' said the Great Leader. '*Because, when all's said and done – all humans are equally verminous! You are all weak and pathetic! Only the Ghasts are strong, and once we are done with the tea-swilling filth of the British Space Empire, we will cleanse the galaxy of the entirety of your repellent species!*'

Number One caught his breath with difficulty. His antennae had flopped down over his right eye. His nose-hole was wet. A thin strand of drool hung from his jaws. '*Let the weeding-out begin!*'

The doors at the far end of the pitch rolled open. The Criminarch's face filled the screens.

'*Friends, I give you my Hunters: the most rugged, manly men in the whole of Radishia, gathered together to destroy the Imperial Ironsides. Each hunter is a deadly warrior, master of the skills of his calling. Together, they are unstoppable.*'

A man ran into view. He wore a stylised motorcycle policeman's uniform, bulked out and armour-plated. '*Bad Cop!*'

Bad Cop stopped on the touchline and struck a pose. A second hunter jogged out, a pistol in either hand, firing blanks into the air. The crowd roared. More of the Criminarch's hunters ran into the arena, and their master shouted out their names.

'*Six Gun . . . The Deconstructor . . . Big Chief . . . and . . . Naval Action!*'

Rhianna said, 'I'm sensing a lot of repression in this regime.'

Behind the Hunters, a broad-shouldered thug strode into the arena. He wore a black uniform cut off at the knees. Slowly, the man fixed a pair of spectacles onto a wide and broken nose.

'*Your entirely trustworthy referee,*' said the Criminarch. '*I give you . . . Mr Dougal O'Brien of the Sport Police.*'

O'Brien motioned to Smith. He walked out to the centre of the arena. Bad Cop followed.

The crowd fell silent. O'Brien leaned forward.

'All right, I want a nice brutal game. No gouging, trampling or hitting below the belt unless there's a camera watching. Bad Cop, are the hunters ready?'

Under his visor, Bad Cop smiled. 'All set.'

'Listen, it's the final, so special scoring applies. Four points for a goal, two for a long kick, one for a near-fatality. Bad Cop, you won the toss. Go!'

Smith was beginning to have serious doubts about the referee's impartiality. Unfortunately, before he could put his thoughts together, Bad Cop punched him in the head.

A Match Made in Hell

'Well,' said Smith, 'that could have been worse.'

They were in the dugout, recuperating. On the pitch, girls danced around an inflatable tank. Weirdly, half the girls were dressed as Ghasts, in long coats and clip-on antennae. Smith doubted that Number One was enjoying it.

'Have an orange,' Quench said. He quartered it with his penknife and held it out. 'You wouldn't believe the trouble I had getting this through the scanners.'

Smith took a piece of orange. It had been a savage fight. The Hunters were skilled as well as vicious. They played a fast, efficient game, always putting pressure on the ball and they had avoided contact where it was not to their advantage – at least, ever since Suruk had thrown Naval Action through a billboard, which had won the Ironsides a bonus point.

The whistle blew and half-time ended. Smith took a last suck on his piece of orange and tossed it into the bin. The players ran out into the centre of the pitch. Referee O'Brien looked them over warily, like a landlord deciding which drunkard to throw out of his pub first.

'So,' he said, 'let's recap. The Hunters have scored one

goal, giving them an impressive four points. The Imperial Ironsides have scored one goal and a near fatality, giving them an additional bonus point – which makes four points! The scores are equal!'

'Now wait a minute,' said Smith. 'You're doing it all wrong, O'Brien. That adds up to five: four for the goals and one for the near-fatality.'

Bad Cop consulted his fingers.

The referee adjusted his glasses. 'Nonsense, Smith. You're concussed. But let's consult the instant replay, shall we?' He smiled, an odd expression on his boxer's face.

Images cut to music flickered across the replay boards. Figures ducked, punched and leaped. Six Gun crashed into Carveth in slow motion. Suruk tried to bludgeon the Deconstructor with his own hard hat. Points racked up in the corners of the screen.

The music crashed into a climax, and the images were replaced with an advert for Supercola.

'You didn't put our extra point in,' Smith said. 'Suruk threw that other chap – Navy Lark or whatever he's called – through a billboard. We scored a bonus point for finesse.'

'It never happened, Smith. It was a delusion brought on by blunt force to the skull.'

Suruk strode over. 'Referee, you lie! You say these humans are concussed, and they cannot know the truth. Well, my skull is much thicker than a human's. Impacts that would slay a human being bounce off my frontal lobes. Clearly that makes me an expert in whatever this is. What is it, incidentally?'

O'Brien snorted. 'You want to argue with me? How about I just give you a red card, with a death warrant printed on the back? Your extra point didn't happen, Smith. Now go back and lose fair and square.'

Smith turned away as the loudspeakers blared above them. 'Damn it,' he muttered, 'the ref's on the take. What the hell are we going to do?' He looked up at the box where the Criminarch and Number One were waiting. It seemed as inaccessible as a mountain peak.

Cheers came from the crowd, but boos and jeers as well. The atmosphere in the stands had an ugly, vengeful feel.

'This is a travesty,' Suruk growled. 'Does the shamefulness of this place have a bottom? Honour will be satisfied only when the other team and the referee lie dead.'

'We can't,' Smith said. 'If we kill the ref, that's probably a foul. We'd lose by default. And while he's alive, he won't let us win. We're caught in a cleft stick.'

Rhianna had been listening closely. 'Whoa,' she said. 'That's like, terrible. It's, you know, the system oppressing us or something?'

'Quite,' said Smith. 'The bloody action replay footage has been cut. If only we could make him show the rest of that recording, we'd be winning. If only there was some way to make him do it . . .'

'God damn it,' Wainscott muttered. 'This game is as rigged as the tribunal that declared me criminally insane. We should find the judges and blow them all up, just like I . . . didn't.'

Carveth had been watching the cameras. She seemed hypnotised by the screens. 'Didn't you hear the crowd? They know it's rigged, too. I think I know what to do,' she said. 'But it won't be pretty—'

The ball dropped from the ceiling. 'Quickly, men,' Smith cried. 'To victory!'

The Hunters loosened their play, took their time, passed the ball back and forth without taking the risk of attacking. It was infuriating, Smith thought: if he had wanted to see nothing much happen for ninety minutes, he would have stayed at home and watched a first-division football match. The crowd began to shout: a can of Supercola arced out and burst on the pitch. Sports drink hissed on the galactoturf like acid. A group of Ironsides fans in bow ties and plastic top hats held up a sign that read 'Not on'. The audience wanted blood, and was getting nothing. That was not playing the game.

Smith's team tried as best as they could, but they were against experts. Carveth masterfully scooted in from the centre and kicked Six Gun in the shin, then pushed him over as he was hopping around. Wainscott leaped onto the Deconstructor's back and sent him staggering off the pitch, partly by striking his nerve clusters and partly by holding his hand over the man's eyes. Rhianna deflected two powerful throws from Big Chief. Smith even got hold of a piece of Naval Action but let go out of decency. There were certain types of tackle it was best to avoid.

It was Suruk who made the breakthrough. The alien had been staring at an advert for Unlucky Dog hot dogs, in the manner of a child confronted by a shiny cake, and Bad Cop made the mistake of trying to slip past him. Suruk sprang his trap. He threw himself onto the Hunter, rode him along the ground in a shower of sparks, and leaped up holding the ball. Suruk tore down the field.

The enemy closed in like missiles. Smith dashed forward

into space to catch the ball. Big Chief saw his plan and took up position between Smith and Suruk, to intercept.

Suruk turned and hurled the ball back down the field at Rhianna's head. Whether by design or instinct, she flicked her hand up and deflected it straight at Smith. He grabbed the ball and rushed down the pitch.

Smith couldn't move fast enough. He tried to weave, but the Hunters were coming in too quickly, converging on him.

Wainscott streaked in from the side. Where his undergarments had gone, Smith did not know, but the sight of the nude maniac was enough to make the Hunters check their stride. All Six Gun could do was point and cry 'Foul!'

Carveth slipped in beside Smith, skating furiously. 'Boss!' she called, and Smith offloaded the ball to her, turned and charged straight into the Deconstructor. The Hunter staggered aside and Carveth shot through the gap. She zipped to the end of the field, tried to slam the ball down dramatically, tripped over and landed flat out in the scoring zone, ball in hand.

'Disallowed,' O'Brien said.

'What?' Smith cried. 'Are you insane?'

The referee chopped his hand in the air. The crowd yelled with derision. Hot dogs flopped onto the field like beached eels.

'You heard!' the referee shouted. 'Any more trouble and I'll consult the higher powers. By which I mean the guards.'

The crowd settled down slightly.

'No,' said Smith. 'No you don't, O'Brien. That was a goal and you know it.'

The referee smiled. 'A goal? I don't remember seeing that.'

'Perhaps you should check the instant replay.'

O'Brien shook his head. 'There isn't one. And if there was, Smith, you couldn't make me replay it.'

A sense of hopelessness struck Smith. In normal circumstances, he would have grabbed O'Brien and shaken him – perhaps thrashed him – until he played ball. But now, they were playing according to the Criminarch's rules. *There are no rules,* he realised. *They call it a police state, but it's nothing of the sort. It's not policemen who run this hole, but gangsters.*

He grabbed O'Brien's shirt. 'Now you look here, my good sportsfellow –'

The guards raised their guns. Carveth cried out.

She stumbled back on her roller skates, hit the adverts at the edge of the pitch and staggered back across the pitch. 'I'm dying! Get me a glass of Supercola or else I'll die!'

A hovercam pulled in to cover her. *Yes,* Smith thought, *that's it. We need the crowd on our side.*

But the crowd didn't seem to care. Already, voices were calling for the game to continue. They wanted excitement, not justice.

'But Supercola –' Carveth called. 'It brought me back to life! I'll die if I don't get some!'

'Ah, that's old!' a man yelled from the stands. 'Get on with the game!' Other voices joined him: jeering, demanding entertainment.

Smith considered whether to snap O'Brien's neck. It would give the crowd something to look at – although it would also lose him the match. Carveth stopped, pulled herself upright and pointed in Smith's direction. 'I'll die if we lose,' she announced. 'Because I've always loved you!'

Wainscott glanced around like a sleepwalker woken from a dream. 'What? What?'

'Me?' Smith said.

Suruk retched.

The noise of the crowd died away. Smith stared at Carveth, unsure of what to do. What would work best: to deny it, or to agree with her ruse? *Please God,* he thought, *let it be a ruse.*

Something hit him on the back of the head. He turned, and saw a can of Supercola rolling away. In the stands, a voice called 'Who cares? Get fighting!'

'Yeah,' a woman yelled. 'Get back to the game!' Half a dozen voices answered, calling for blood. Smith opened his mouth, but the moment was gone. They wanted more.

Carveth seemed to be steeling herself for something. She took a huge breath and marched straight towards Smith. 'I've always loved you,' she shouted at the cameras, 'and I can't bear for us to be apart.'

'Well, gosh,' Smith said, 'that's awfully nice of you, Carveth, but –' and she walked straight past him.

Carveth grabbed Rhianna and kissed her. Rhianna, who had been looking at the ceiling, put up little resistance. For a long moment, they were locked together, and then Carveth let Rhianna go.

'I want my shorts back,' Wainscott said. 'Right now.'

Suruk leaned over and discreetly closed Smith's mouth for him. Smith blinked and turned to the referee.

'I think we'll be having our action replay, please,' he said.

O'Brien glared at him. 'There isn't anything to—'

'Replay!' a man bellowed from the audience. 'I want a replay!'

On the sidelines, Quench was feigning a coughing fit, but Smith could tell that he was grinning.

'Replay!' the crowd roared. 'Re-play, re-play!'

A large hot dog struck O'Brien on the shoulder. He glared and brushed it off. A can burst a few yards away. Smith saw flashes of blue light in the stands as the guards got to work with their shock-sticks, but that was nowhere near enough to quell the rage rising from the audience. Their chanting, the stamp of boots and the clap of hands, swelled until the stadium shook.

O'Brien swallowed. Bad Cop looked at the crowd and said, 'I think you'd better do it.'

'Show it,' O'Brien said.

The screens burst into life. The players weaved and fell. Cameras monitored them from half a dozen angles. O'Brien disallowed the goal. Then the camera went into slow motion.

'Hey, Polly,' said Rhianna, 'that looks just like you and me.'

'It is you, you dopey cow,' Carveth replied. She seized Rhianna's hand and held it up. The crowd cheered.

Klaxons sounded. The final score flashed up on the laser display board: 8-4 to the Ironsides.

Suruk tapped Smith on the shoulder. 'So, Mazuran, it seems that we have won the match and your lady friend is actually biannual. Can we get back to the fighting now?'

'Eh?' Smith blinked and looked at Suruk. 'Oh, I suppose so.'

He pushed the image out of his mind. They had won.

On the touchline, two soldiers in full body armour approached Quench. They looked like villainous knights. One took him by the arm and pulled him away.

They've got Quench. They'll come for us soon.

He looked at O'Brien. 'You owe me a trophy. And I want to shake hands with Number One.'

The referee swallowed. 'Right,' he said. 'Follow me.'

He gestured at the edge of the pitch and the two guards from the training room approached. Compared to the soldiers who had taken Quench away, they looked amateurish, like fans who had put on armour for a joke. 'Nice one,' said the fat guard.

'Take my chaps back to the practice room, would you?' said Smith. 'And, er, make sure they're all right.'

The thin guard winked. 'Will do,' he said. 'Come on.'

Smith looked at the others. 'Have a good birthday, Carveth!'

Suruk gave Smith a little bow. 'I will take care of the women,' he said. 'And Wainscott.'

Smith met Rhianna's eyes, and for once she seemed to know exactly what was going on. He tried to think of something to say, something that would let her, and his crew, know what he thought. 'Chin up, old girl,' he said, and he followed O'Brien off the pitch.

They walked up the steps, between rows of spectators, and the fans leaned over the railing and waved. A hand appeared in front of Smith and he shook it before a guard shoved the hand's owner away.

Smith reached to the side of his armour and slid a packet of Extra Strong Mintats into his left palm. He took his helmet off and pushed it under his arm, using it to hide his hand as it opened the packet. He waved with his right hand, to draw attention from his left. His stomach felt light and unsettled. It felt like school prize day.

Up ahead, in their box, the Criminarch and Number One were watching. Smith waved at them. Neither waved back. *Unsporting,* he reflected.

A cart stood on the steps, laden with cans of Supercola. 'May I?' Smith said to the vendor, and the man delightedly passed him a can. He cracked it open and pretended to take a sip.

They were near the box now. The feeling of sickness had gone; Smith felt strong and certain.

In literary works like *Robot Vixens of Mars*, villains were usually depicted as being twisted and worn down by their evil. This, Smith had found, was often not the case: a lot of the worst people in the galaxy looked pretty chuffed with the arrangement. The Ghast officer caste was an exception, however, and, even judged against his minions, Number One was a wretched specimen.

His eyes had sunk so deeply that they seemed to be trying to get out the back of his helmet. His nostrils had merged and slumped into a damp square hole in the centre of his face. His antennae had been smoothed to one side and glued down with grease that he probably secreted. He made 462 look like the Venus de Milo, except with more arms.

Smith took a deep breath and kept climbing the stairs. He was three yards away from Number One when the praetorians swung their guns up. He stopped, eye-to-eye with the would-be dictator of the galaxy, the commander of the biggest army in the history of space.

'Gosh,' Smith said, 'you're *weeny*.'

Number One twitched. His eyes flicked around like a couple of startled bugs.

Smith cleared his throat. He spoke in Ghastish, putting as much of the Bearing into his voice as the alien language would allow. 'You there, Ghast Number One. Pay attention. We have won against the Criminarch's teams through hard work and. . .' He paused, trying to think of the closest words in Ghastish for 'fair play'. 'The unceasing and merciless struggle of biological determinism,' he said.

Number One looked as if he was trying to chew a lemon. He shuddered violently and looked at the Criminarch. The Criminarch nodded.

One of the Criminarch's soldiers clanked forward in full battle armour, holding a massive trophy. It looked like a cross between a battering-ram and a church font, and was covered in gold paint.

The soldier's helmet speaker crackled. 'There you go. Now piss off.'

Smith took the trophy and held it up. The crowd cheered. He opened the can of Supercola, poured it into the top and mimed drinking from the trophy.

First, shove the mints up his nose-hole. Then, tip the Supercola over his head.

The Criminarch clapped and smiled. Between his teeth, he said, 'You can go now.'

Smith turned to go. 'Wait,' he said. 'Shouldn't we shake hands?'

The Criminarch thought about it. 'Manly hug?'

Smith put out his hand. It disappeared into the Criminarch's enormous fist. The Criminarch tried to yank

Smith off balance, but Smith was ready for that. They shook once, firmly, and then the Criminarch stepped back.

'And now it's your turn,' Smith said, and he offered his hand to Number One.

One looked down at Smith's hand.

'*Nak!*' he screeched. He flinched back, bumping against one of his bodyguards. 'I'm not touching that! Take this human away – I don't know where it's been!' Recovering some of his composure, Number One shook his fist at the ceiling. 'The unwholesome nature of Earth and all its weak creatures has been proven by Ghast science. The filthy, corrupted, unhygienic nature of the human race is in-dubit-able! And who stands above all in this parade of ignominy, this unstinting tide of garbage? None other than the so-called British Space Empire—'

'Oh, shut your cake hole,' said Smith, and he hit Number One with the trophy.

Something huge swung into Smith's back. He was instantly flat on his face. The mints rolled out of his hand. Noise surrounded him, deafening but indistinct, like being in a swimming pool while a party of toddlers was at the other end. Ghasts were snarling and barking. The Criminarch bellowed for assistance. Some kind of riot seemed to have broken out in the stands. Half a dozen soldiers were yelling into intercoms: 'Order confirmed – emergency support—'

At the edge of his vision, one of the praetorians swung up its disruptor and braced itself to fire. A soldier barged into it, perhaps on purpose, and it staggered away, screeching about protecting the leader.

'Up you get!' a voice said from behind Smith's back. He

was heaved onto his feet, a gun against his side. Another soldier ran over, grabbed his arm and hustled him towards a door at the back of the box. Smith glimpsed a huge, spiked vehicle rolling onto the pitch from the underground ramp. Music blared and girls danced on the screens. Amid the sound of wild cheering, Smith was dragged out of the arena.

*

'Once again,' shouted Number One, 'once again I am subjected to the indignity of an assassination attempt. Once again, through the superior virtue of natural selection, I have been chosen to survive. Thus it is proven – axiomatically proven – that I am the destined leader of the entire galaxy!'

He was being half-ushered, half-carried down a dim tunnel by his praetorians. Beside him, the Criminarch strode along, sweat glistening on his bare torso.

Voices came from behind. The rear praetorian stopped and fired a burst back down the corridor. Light strobed the walls. 'Scum must die,' he hissed.

'You're shooting at my men!' the Criminarch replied.

A door burst open in front of them. Grisler, the Criminarch's chief advisor, staggered into the corridor. His paunchy face was weeping sweat. 'Those bastards,' he panted. 'They're going mad. We've got to get—'

The praetorian lifted his heavy disruptor. Grisler was liquefied in a thundering blast of light. The praetorian ran his pincer along the wall. He raised the claw to its mouth and slowly licked it. 'Tastes good,' he growled.

Number One sniggered.

'You can't do that!' the Criminarch said. 'I am the Criminarch of Radishia. I rule this place. You don't touch my men. On my planet, my men touch y–'

There was a sudden burst of light, and the Criminarch felt a fist hit his abdominals. He looked down. Blood ran over his combat trousers. Number One held a little gun in his spindly hand.

'You shot me,' the Criminarch said.

'This human is slowing us down,' Number One announced. 'His men will attempt to care for him. It will be a useful distraction. Praetorian, carry me more swiftly!'

The bodyguard picked up Number One and stuffed him under his trench coat. He lumbered away, firing bursts of his disruptor to discourage pursuit.

The Criminarch listened to his guests depart. *They left me to die, the insect bastards! But I can do this,* he thought. *I am big and strong. Nobody is as big and strong as me. I am . . . dying?*

'Criminarch.'

He looked up. Two soldiers stood over him, their visors down. One opened a medical kit and slapped an emergency plaster on the Criminarch's side. The other jabbed him with a needle. Together, they hauled him upright. He stumbled along between them.

'This way,' said the soldier on the right. 'We've got a car waiting.'

The corridor opened out into a loading bay. A door slid open, and the Criminarch staggered into the back of an armoured personnel carrier. He flopped down on a seat and closed his eyes. 'Drive!' he said. 'It's all gone to hell back there.'

The intercom crackled. 'Too right, mate.'

The Criminarch looked up. Something about that voice was wrong. Sitting on the opposite bench was Isambard Smith. At the far end of the compartment, the Imperial Ironsides – or whoever they really were – waved and said hello. The door slammed and the vehicle rolled away. The smaller of the two women passed a packet of biscuits to Smith.

The soldiers removed their helmets. One was a tall, tough-looking woman. She had long pigtails that unrolled as she lifted her helmet away. The second soldier was a prim, delicate-looking man of sixty or so. A cravat poked out above the collar of his armour.

'You,' said the Criminarch.

'Us,' said Isambard Smith. 'Game, set and match. Biscuit?'

Weakly, the Criminarch reached out and took a biscuit from the packet. 'If it wasn't for that little bastard Number One, I'd have got away with this.' He looked down at his wounded side. 'You should have killed me while you had the chance.'

Space Captain Smith held out a packet of biscuits. 'We could have done, I suppose. But that wouldn't have been very sporting, would it?'

*

The armoured wagon rolled to a stop. Smith stood up and hit the button. The door swung open and the sunlight poured in. Wincing, he emerged.

They stood in a rough corral of tanks and buggies. Smith shielded his eyes and looked around. The vehicles bristled with rams, spikes and turbochargers. The Deepspace Operations Group waited by their own lorry. Rick Dreckitt sat behind the wheel, his trilby hat pulled down low.

Wainscott stepped out into the sunshine. 'It's good to be back,' he said.

'Yeah,' Dreckitt replied. 'Great.'

Quench tapped Smith's arm.

Half a dozen kangarams stood a little way back. A man stood among them in the uniform of a Straalian Ranger. As soldiers came forward to escort the Criminarch away, Bush Captain Shane pulled off his bucket-shaped helmet. 'G'day, Captain Smith. Nice to see you again, mate. The Ginormous rigged up a dish and we watched the big game. Some remarkable playing styles there, 'specially from the young lady. I bet you'll be glad to get out of those outfits.'

Smith shook his head. 'I don't have anything else. The buggers took my stuff.'

'Now, that's where you're wrong, Smith,' Susan said. 'In all the confusion back there, we did a little creative looting. Show him, Shane.'

Shane reached over to Rippy's saddlebag. 'Here's your Civiliser, and here's your rifle. Your coat's draped over the back, here, and . . . I seem to have lost your red jacket.' The kangaram lowered its snout to his ear level. 'Say what, Rippy? Of course. You've kept it in your pouch.' He reached in and produced Smith's jacket. 'To be honest, mate, it was a bit of a long journey, so you might want to give it an airing. Oh, and, ah, you probably don't want to wear it near any of the males.'

'Thanks.'

'Well, there's no point standing around. The boys are stoked for action, and I never was much of a one for long goodbyes. What's that, Rippy? Rippy here reckons that words can never truly express meaning, and that language is ultimately a flawed construct compared to thought. Well, there you go.' He paused. 'Best be off.'

They watched as he climbed into the saddle. Bush Captain Shane stashed his helmet among his swag, pulled out a broad-brimmed hat and jammed it on his head. The sound of engines rose, as the armoured division tested its superchargers. 'So long, mates! I'll see you on the road!'

The cars threw up a backwash of dust and fumes, and it seemed as if Shane and his rangers were disappearing into a wall of dirt.

Smith said, 'Congratulations, men. We are all alive and able once more to taste the sweet air of freedom.' He took a deep breath, and began coughing. 'Figuratively,' he gasped.

'Hey, Polly,' Dreckitt said. He took out the cryogenic tube containing Gerald. 'I got your hamster holster here.'

Slowly, the dust settled. On the horizon, a white plume indicated the passage of the 603rd Straalian Armoured Division.

'Well,' said Susan, 'so much for that.'

'Look,' Smith said. 'They left a load of scrap behind. That's pollution, isn't it, Rhianna?'

Rhianna shook her head. 'Actually, Isambard, I think that's our spaceship.'

Smith peered at it through the dust. 'Good lord, you're right. Well then, let's get back to business!'

It was a huge relief to see the *John Pym* again. Smith ran his hand over the steel exterior, and then surreptitiously wiped off the grime on his coat. He was back home.

He opened the door and stepped inside. The sights and smells were still there, as was the strange bundle of dangling wires that he was slightly reluctant to touch, let alone fully repair. He licked his finger and rubbed at the brasswork. It came away filthy. Not good, exactly, but business as usual.

From the cockpit, Carveth called out, 'Boss, they've repaired it – I think.'

He ducked under the lintel and entered the cockpit. He had never been entirely sure about what all the controls did, but they seemed to be in the right places again. The nosecone was back at its usual angle.

A soft croaking came from behind. He looked around and saw Suruk in the doorway. 'Mazuran, we have defeated this planet. Let us go and find another one. And this time, we shall make war, not sport.'

Smith dropped into the captain's chair. It creaked. 'Right, chaps,' he said. 'Let's go.'

'Where to, boss?' Carveth asked.

'You're all due a rest,' he replied. 'Goodness knows, you've earned it. Let's go somewhere quiet and restful, somewhere that looks nice. Take us to Didcot, Carveth.'

Part Two

Urn: 4th planet in the Didcot System – Type 72 civilised world
Population: 4,600,000
Alien Natives: None
Climate: Clement to rather sticky
Principal Land Use: 4% Urban, 96% Agricultural (plantation)
System of Government: Proper
Principal Export: Tea

Encyclopaedia Imperialis, Volume 43 (Tiffin – Vindaloo)

Carveth is Four

The sky looked huge on Didcot Prime, vast and clear and blue. It hung over the tea fields like the cleanest ocean, and the sun dragons that flew overhead made Smith think of fish.

They touched down just outside Stirwell, a town twenty miles from the capital city, Capital City. Smith, Suruk and Rhianna hired a car and headed off to equip themselves for Carveth's birthday party. They already had her main present, but Smith knew from experience that that would not be nearly enough.

Two years before, Smith had fought his way through the very streets where he now strolled. It was amazing what a couple of years of Imperial democracy did for a place: it was hard to tell that Capital City had ever been occupied by Ghasts and Edenites. Rhianna and Smith promenaded past the spot where Smith had blown up a hovertank with a plasma cannon. The place was now a knitwear shop.

But there still were signs of the invasion. Brown signs pointed to the three-tiered monument to the Heroes of the Afternoon. You could still hear rebel songs on the radio as they passed an open window; Smith heard a few lines of *Cup Killer* by Nice T.

Smith pulled a piece of paper out of his pocket. 'We'll split up and cover Carveth's birthday list. Get what you can, chaps, and rendezvous outside the card shop.'

Now that invasion of the Ghast home system was imminent, many of the military publications were feeling the touch of the censor. Smith found a copy of *Liberty Hell Yeah*, a glossy allied magazine so low on factual detail that it tended to be known as *American Vague*. The *Daily Monolith* had a picture of a slight, dark-haired man looking out of a tank turret. 'Parky Parkins Claims Sixth Tiger Prawn Biotank' the headline read. In the local news, the police were promising to fight a war on drugs.

Well, Smith thought, *it works for Rhianna.*

The people of Didcot were friendly and polite. Wherever he went, Smith asked the shop assistants 'Would this be suitable for a fourth birthday party?' He had considerable success in the card shop, but the off licence threatened to call the authorities. In the local bakery, Smith found a government pamphlet entitled *Let's Bake a Fake Cake: Transform Your Child's Birthday With Synthetic Ham*. He was unconvinced and bought the ingredients for a giant teacake instead.

Apart from a slight confusion between rolling and wrapping paper, Rhianna did pretty well. She thought that it was a shame that Carveth's birthday was going to be less of a holistic coming-of-age ceremony and more an orgy of cheap booze, but you had to let people live their lives as they wanted, and only then tell them that they were doing it wrong.

Suruk had slightly less success. The butcher's shop was open but unstaffed, and so he prowled the counter alone, fearing that his quest for chipolatas would be in vain. Suddenly, Suruk felt a sharp pain in the spine. Turning, he saw an elderly man in a striped apron, brandishing a spear not unlike his own.

'I've got him!' the old man shouted, to the empty shop. 'I've caught an alien invader!'

Suruk sighed. 'Foolish old man, I am seeking small sausages, like those hanging around your neck.'

'Sausages? Oh no you don't. The Didcot Prime Home Guard will never let alien hands sully our meat. These aren't sausages. They're tubes of HN-20 plastique, wired straight to my heartbeat. If any space-monster kills me – boom! I'll take him with me!'

'Indeed? Your fighting spirit is commendable, but—'

'Yes it is!' cried the butcher. 'We will never surrender! You can take my life but – but—' He clutched his chest. 'I – Tell my wife – No . . . Wait . . . I'm all right now.'

'I tell you what,' said Suruk, 'I shall just take some chipolatas and leave the change on the counter. And to think that they once called *me* the Mad Butcher of Didcot.'

The Last Cakestand Tea Rooms were on the far side of Sett Square. Here, the local hockey team, the Badgers, had seen off a horde of Edenite cultists in brutal combat. A statue of their fierce leader, Red Dawn, stood in the centre of the square, stick raised above her head.

The woman who owned the cafe had a brass arm, which she polished with her good hand while she waited behind the counter. Her apron bore a picture of a crashed Ghast spaceship. Below it were the words *You Want My Tea – I'll Take Your Saucer.*

'Well, Suruk,' said Smith, as the wallahbot piped

self-clotting cream onto his plate, 'I'm sorry to hear that you had trouble. Want me to go and have a word with this old fellow – before you do?'

'There is no need for that, Mazuran,' Suruk said. He began work on his third bacon sandwich. 'He was merely confused. In truth, the Empire has changed. The last time I went into a cafeteria like this, they refused to serve me. Admittedly, I did enter via the window. The proprietor called me an ignorant frog.'

'That sort of crude name-calling is completely unjustified,' Smith observed. 'You're not even slightly French.'

'So one foolish old man is no skin off my nose,' Suruk said, 'even if I had one. I am not one for holding grudges. Why waste time trying to get even when you could just get a head? The only way anyone gets to look down on me is when I put their skull on a high shelf.'

'That's decent of you, old chap,' Smith said.

'You know, I think I have been lucky. I have met many likeable humans, and all the ones I haven't liked, I have merely had to decapitate. And nobody has referred to me as a "Morlock" for some time, which I gather was somehow insulting. Something to do with George Orson Wells, I believe.'

'I'm glad to hear it,' Rhianna said. 'I mean, this is what we're fighting for, isn't it? The rights of all people to be treated fairly. That matters. People have died for the rights we enjoy today.'

'Indeed they have,' Suruk growled. 'That will teach them to get between me and my rights.'

*

On returning to the *John Pym*, Smith and Suruk retired to the hold to clean Carveth's present. Suruk kept a stack of cans of Mr Shiny in his room, to keep his skull collection pristine and gleaming. Rhianna found cleaning things puzzling, and got to work on the cake.

'Splendid,' Smith said, stepping back. The hold reeked of polish. He sighed.

Suruk tossed his duster across the room. It landed in the Hyperbowl trophy. 'You are still sad because of Number One, Mazuran.'

'Suruk, I could have killed him back there. I think I could have ended the whole war.'

'No,' said Suruk. 'You should not say that.'

'You think I'm being too hard on myself?'

'I have no idea. But that talk about ending the war . . . it makes me uncomfortable.' He shuddered. 'Everyone living in peace . . . an end to chaos . . . ugh.'

They carried the dinner table out into the tea fields and set the chairs up around it. The Deepspace Operations Group arrived in their armoured lorry, and Wainscott and his men established a perimeter with bunting and set up an automated sentry gun that fired streamers whenever it detected movement.

As they were sitting down, a staff car rolled alongside the fields, setting the plants swaying. The door opened and a tall, thin man stepped out. He made his way towards the festivities without much enthusiasm. A teapot hovered over his shoulder, buoyed up by a tiny anti-gravity engine.

'It's W from the Service!' Carveth cried.

'Happy birthday!' said the spy. 'I heard there was fun happening and as you can imagine, I couldn't stay away.'

He looked at the table, then the sky, said, 'Acceptable, I suppose,' and sat down. 'I got you a card.'

Carveth opened it. '*For the birthday girl. Congratulations on four years of not living in an unceasing tyranny. Carry on.* Thanks,' she said. 'That's encouraging.'

She put the card with the others. Carveth's friends had all sent greetings: a brightly-coloured picture of a giant robot from Yoshimi, the mech-pilot; an elegant floral card from Emily Hallsworth, an android and former attraction at the Jane Austen theme park, who seemed to have forgotten that she had once tried to murder Carveth for being a social climber; a watercolour from Celeste of the Equ'i, which was apparently hand painted – all the more impressive, since Celeste, being a small talking horse, had no hands.

'This is for all of you,' W replied. He gestured, and the hovering teapot rose up from behind his chair. It moved across the table and stopped a foot above the middle. 'The Edenites like these little anti-gravity things. We captured one when we invaded the Gilded Palace of Pious Panic, knocked the junk off the top and stuck the motor on a teapot. Thought you might find it handy in zero-gravity. If nothing else, you can take your hamster for a ride in it.'

'Great,' said Carveth. 'What's next?'

Wainscott handed her a ticking box. 'This is for your lunch. It's got a built-in time lock. You set it in the morning and it won't open until midday, to stop you scoffing your food too soon.'

Carveth looked at the picture on the front. '*Lucky Star.* I like it. Although I might like it less by elevenses-time tomorrow morning.'

Rhianna stood up. The breeze swept her hair back from her face. 'I have a gift that will be close to your heart, Polly.'

'Brill! Wait a moment. It's not going to turn out to be love or friendship or some kind of metaphor, is it?'

Wainscott leaned forward. 'I think it should be love, like in that sports match. You two ladies displayed remarkable teamwork. I've been studying the video in case there was a rematch. Never leave a job unfinished, I say— ' He grunted and slowly folded forward, grimacing. On the opposite side of the table, Susan glanced away and whistled innocently.

Rhianna reached down and came up with a large box marked SHAM. Several members of the party moved their chairs back. Nelson muttered something about leaving the washing machine on and stood up.

'Now,' Rhianna announced. 'I know what you're thinking. You see me making a cake and you immediately jump to conclusions. But chill out, it's okay. It doesn't have any sham in it because that's bad for you, but instead, I've added some of my own entirely organic ingredients. Check it out!'

Smith had bought four candles from a hardware shop in Stirwell, and he set them out on the cake. 'Those are feeble,' Wainscott announced. 'I'll show you a big red candle.'

He reached to his belt, and to the surprise of everyone didn't drop his trousers. He removed a large red candle from his pocket and brandished it.

'Stash your rod, pal,' Dreckitt said. 'That's a stick of dynamite.'

Suruk drew one of his smaller machetes. 'I shall do the honours,' he announced, and he got to work.

The birthday was going well. Tea and gin flowed and cake was carved. Smith watched a sun dragon sail lazily across the sky. When he looked around, Rhianna was standing next to him.

'Penny for your thoughts,' she said.

He smiled. 'Thanks. Rhianna. Do you think I should have killed Number One?'

She shrugged. 'You did the right thing.'

'Did I?'

'Um . . . totally. Probably totally. Look,' she added, 'would you have killed Number One if you could have done?'

'I don't know. Obviously I'd like to, but I didn't want you lot to get shot.'

'Exactly. Because you value us. A Ghast couldn't make that decision, Isambard. You know why? Because we've got something they haven't.' She pointed at his hand and raised her eyebrows.

Smith realised that she was expecting some sort of reply. He looked down at his hand, which was still holding his mug. 'Tea,' he said. 'They haven't got tea.'

'Close,' Rhianna replied.

'Biscuits?'

'Moral fibre,' she said. 'And you know what would have happened if we hadn't had moral fibre four years ago, when the Ghasts declared war on us? When we saw how big their army was?'

He nodded. 'We'd have given up. And by now we'd all be dead. Food for their praetorians.' The thought seemed to spread in his mind. 'You're right,' he said. 'Absolutely bloody right. I did the right thing. And you know what I'm going to do now?'

'Spend some quality time with your loved ones, aware of just how precious they are to you?'

'I'm going to order some more ammunition and bloody well finish the job. I've got a wall to fill with trophies and a space in the middle especially for Number One.' He paused for breath, noticed her expression, and added, 'And see all my chaps, obviously.'

'Cool,' Rhianna said. 'Let's talk to the others.'

'Wait a moment,' Smith said. 'Thanks for saying that, Rhianna. You're right. You know, maybe you've got a point about it helping to talk about things, so long as it's not about emotions and there's nobody else nearby.'

She smiled. 'Maybe we could talk some more later.'

'Great. When we do, could you say "moral fibre" in an English accent? And could *later* be *round about bedtime*?'

W strolled across the grass to join them, a paper plate in his hand. He looked strangely at ease. He was not exactly smiling, but the look of gloom had faded somewhat from his face.

'You know,' he said, 'this is much less beastly than usual. I forgot that meeting other people sometimes isn't awful. In fact, I'm glad you're not dead,' W added. 'I rather like talking to you about tyranny and how dreadful the universe is. It cheers me up.'

W was a decent chap, Smith thought, but sometimes listening to him was like being stuck in a lift with Thomas Hardy.

Glass shattered. Smith turned and saw Suruk standing on a chair. The alien held a massive knife in one hand and the remnants of a wine glass in the other.

'Friends, humans, countrymen,' Suruk announced, 'lend me your ears or I shall take your heads. We are gathered here to celebrate the life of Polly R. Carveth – pilot, warrior, malfunctioning sexbot – and to witness the union of her and cake. Now that she has somehow survived four years, I invite you to raise your glasses and other utensils and salute her with your toast. The birthday girl!'

'The birthday girl!'

'Indeed,' said Suruk. 'Many years ago – three, to be precise – I fought beside you to defend the things we held most dear. Here, in the fields of Didcot Prime, the blood of our enemies flowed like a river of exceptionally blood-like tea. And here, too, the little woman proved herself. For that, I gave her the warrior's name of Anorak, the word among my people that means "Piglet".

'We have come a long way since then. We are older, wiser people. Countless foes have fallen to our blades. The skulls of lemmings without number were heaped upon the field of battle like a huge pyramid of severed bone. Long was the slaying, hideous the gore, and from this mighty, fierce victory we learned that . . . we learned that . . . I have forgotten what I was talking about.'

'Birthday!' Carveth shouted.

'Yes, the birthday. The birthday of Anorak, she of great battles and even greater feasting. She who hunts her enemies so stealthily that she is often hiding under the table long before they have even arrived, ready to pounce upon them as the bold squirrel leaps upon the nut. Friends, the way to victory is open. With Radishia in turmoil, the fleet can strike at the black heart of the Ghast Empire.

We will take battle to Selenia, their wretched homeworld, and rip out the core of the disease of tyranny. Doom, death, destruction and birthday!'

Smith stood up. 'And now for your main present, Carveth. We know how much you like staying alive, and how keen you are on ponies, so we got you this!'

Dreckitt emerged from the hold, pushing a porter's trolley. On it stood a very small female knight.

'It's your very own suit of armour,' Smith said. 'There is an old tradition in sport that, at the end of the match, the teams swap shirts. When we defeated the Sisters of No Mercy on the sports field, Joan of Arcturus told me that it obviously wouldn't have been proper—'

'Very unsporting of her!' Wainscott interjected. 'I took mine off at the end of every match.'

'Shirts, Wainscott, not shorts. Anyway, she offered us this suit of battle armour instead. I asked Crispin Quench to smuggle it out of the arena. It's got fitted armour plates and a bit at the back to put your stuff in. And it's got an elastic waist. Quench said suits like this are very popular in Paris.' Smith wasn't certain whether the Paris in question was Paris, capital of fashion or Paris during the Hundred Years War.

Carveth stared at the armour. 'Is that for me?'

'Absolutely. It's bulletproof too.'

'That's amazing. Thank you! Wait a moment,' she added, 'didn't you say something about ponies?'

'Of course. You can wear your armour if you take up jousting.'

'Brilliant!' Carveth got up in a shower of cake crumbs and ran over to him, somewhat slower than usual. She hugged Smith awkwardly and he patted her on the head. 'Can I put it on now?'

'I suppose so,' Smith replied.

'Can I wear it to bed?'

Dreckitt lowered his whisky and stared at her. 'Hell no,' he replied. 'I may be a robot, but I don't need no dames done up like a tin can.'

*

It was dark. The night was filled with the aromatic scent of tea and Rhianna. Her herbal cigarette, made of Martian red weed, was a pinprick of light in the dark. A slightly larger light was provided by the flamethrower that Susan had rigged up to keep them warm.

Smith sat beside Rhianna, slowly drinking a gin and tonic. He felt pleasantly drunk, but slightly melancholic, as though they would not all sit together for a long time.

The flamethrower sent a belch of fire rippling up towards the sky. Rhianna raised her eyebrows. They looked slightly singed. 'Um, isn't that a bit dangerous, guys?'

'Nah,' Susan replied. 'It's a very reliable make. Keeps the insects away, and great for flushing things out the airlock.'

'Most animals retreat from fire,' Wainscott added. 'Personally, I just like staring at it.'

Suruk opened his mandibles and yawned. 'Well, good-night everyone. It has been a long day, and I must retire to my chamber of skulls to sleep off the jelly and ice cream.' He stood up and sighed. 'Early to bed and early to rise, gives a warrior the element of surprise.'

Carveth clanked past, the detailing of her suit catching the light.

'Are you okay, Polly?' Rhianna asked.

'Too much cake,' Carveth replied. 'I feel like a fat man, strangled at girth.'

A tall figure moved at the edge of the firelight. Flames illuminated tweed. 'Smith?' W stared down at him like a schoolmaster checking on a mediocre pupil.

'Sorry,' Smith said, 'I was miles away.'

'Fair enough. I'm enjoying the party atmosphere, too.' The spy took a sip of beer and scowled off into the darkness.

Rhianna and Wainscott had started to discuss psychotropic warfare. Smith said, 'W, can I have a word?'

''Course,' W replied, and he stepped back into the firelight.

'I've been thinking about what happened on Radishia. The Criminarch thought Hyperbowl was the greatest game in the galaxy. He was wrong. The greatest game in the galaxy is Number One. And I want to bag him.'

'Understood.'

'I feel as if I lost my chance back on Radishia. But if I'd killed Number One, none of this could have happened. We certainly wouldn't be celebrating Carveth's birthday. Just look at her little smiling face.'

In the distance, Carveth lurched upright, cried 'I'm gonna puke' and clattered into the bushes.

'Well, maybe just imagine it,' said Smith.

W sipped his beer. 'You needn't worry about Number One. You'll have another chance all right. The fleet's moving in on Selenia, and most of the great powers will be sending their own ships too. This will be the big one, Smith. There isn't a martial planet in the Space Empire that won't be in for this. And believe me, the Ghasts will throw everything they've got at us.'

Smith took a sip of gin. 'Let them try.'

*

Smith got up early the next morning. He walked into the kitchen, put the kettle on and was examining the controls for the hovering servopot when he saw a box beside the sofa. It was unwrapped but had been stamped with the Valdane Shipping logo, which meant that it was from the Service. He cleared some of the plates and gin bottles to one side and lifted the box onto the dining table.

Inside was a large box of teabags. Useful, he thought, but unless there was an emergency, he doubted that the *John Pym* would run out soon. Under the tea was a large tub of moustache wax. At the bottom of the box, he found a number of small wooden shields.

Smith took out one of the shields, wondering what it was supposed to do. After a moment, he raised the shield at the wall and held it there, opposite the stuffed praetorian head that he had hung there three years before.

Extra tea, moustache wax and trophy mounts. This really is it. We're going in.

In the Space Navy

'Stop here,' 462 told the limousine. It pulled up to the curb, a sleek black missile of a vehicle, gene-spliced with barracuda DNA. The door slid open. The smell of the backstreets of Selenia assaulted 462's nostril-holes. He limped down a narrow alley, coat pulled tight around him. Two worker drones loitered by a small door up ahead. 462 stopped, boosted the zoom in his artificial eye and lip-read their conversation.

'The whole entertainment industry's gone to hell, you know,' one of the drones said. It fished out a combustion-enhanced nutri-stick from its coat and lit up. 'They want fifty propaganda broadcasts a day. Fifty! How am I supposed to make art like that?'

'Oh, I know,' said the other. 'Last week, I asked the producer "What's my motivation in this scene?" He said, "Your motivation is that if you don't get on with it I'll have you shot." Ignoramus. Uh-oh, here's trouble.'

462 lurched closer. 'Is this the stage door of the Department of Light Entertainment and Heavy Indoctrination?'

The nearer of the drones lowered its nutri-stick. 'It is. But only members of the craft may enter here. Drones and punters go through the front way.'

'Subversives, eh?' 462 took out his papers and held them up. 'I read your lips from the other side of the street. I would advise you to project less well when a senior officer is present. Door.'

Once, he would have been amused to see how quickly a drone could spit out a nutri-stick and stand up straight. Now he just ignored them and walked through. He entered a narrow corridor, passed a dressing room full of trench coats – costume design in the Ghast Empire was very simple – and saw a door with a gold skull on the front. He shoved it open.

A Ghast was sitting at a dressing table in a tweed coat, smearing its face with pink paste. It was presumably playing a human in a propaganda film. 462 knew how actors worked, mainly because all the mirrors in the building were two-way, just in case the actors got too far into character and started behaving pleasantly.

'Where are the contestants kept for *The Show Trial Show*?' 462 demanded.

'Do you want the presenters, the prisoners, or the things they'll be fed to?'

'Prisoners.'

'Downstairs. We've got a load this week. They're all deserting on the M'Lak Front. It sounds hideous.'

462 took the lift. The doors opened on a murky corridor. Heavy doors opened into small cells. In each cell sat a drone. They had a miserable, battered look, their helmets scratched and their antennae drooping. As he walked by, one of the drones looked up.

'Hey.'

462 turned. 'You will address me by rank!'

The drone shrugged. 'Why? What difference does it make? I'll be dog food this evening, anyway.'

'Come here,' 462 said.

The drone stood up. Most drones didn't last long enough to accumulate anything other than injuries. This one had patched and repaired his trench coat several times, from the look of it. He wore half a dozen webbing straps, from which dangled tools, cutlery, vehicle parts, power packs, tins of food and a toothbrush. A torn orange flag had been wrapped around his right forearm as a bandage, probably torn from a M'Lak banner.

'Serial code and rank.'

The drone shrugged. 'SVN/2187, Drone-Lieutenant, Penal Legion 5937, Appended to Praetorian Division 844 – Mindless Fury. *Formerly* appended.'

'M'Lak Front?'

The drone nodded. 'We were sent out as cannon fodder. We turned out to be better at staying alive than expected. When they attached us to a praetorian regiment, we thought they wanted us for our survival skills.'

'What did they want you for?'

'Breakfast.'

'So what happened?'

SVN/2187 shrugged. 'There was an unfortunate error. Our commanding officer accidentally got shot by the entire platoon, and then happened to set himself on fire and fell down a hole. And then a bio-grenade rolled down there after him. For some reason, high command decided that we were responsible.'

'Very unfortunate,' 462 said. 'Of course, you're not

technically convicted yet. . . that happens after the General Knowledge round, I believe.'

SVN/2187 sighed. 'Nobody ever gets through the General Knowledge round. Not when they rewrite history every week.'

'Quite so. And yet, perhaps you could be released. You seem resourceful, Lieutenant. Who knows what might be possible if you agreed to do some . . . ah – special work for me.'

'This doesn't involve polishing your stercorium, does it?'

'Certainly not. But it will involve loyalty. And weeding out certain other officers who have disappointed me. But then, I'm sure you've got a taste for that by now.'

'Only to stop them getting a taste of me.'

Light flooded the corridor. From the stairwell, a voice barked, 'What is the meaning of this?'

462 turned. A Ghast in a sparkly trench coat stood in the doorway.

'How dare you barge in here and threaten to abduct my contestants?' The presenter gestured grandly at the cells. 'These drones are my stars.'

'I thought the stars were the pack of rabid ant-hounds who would be eating them,' 462 said. 'They're the only repeat performers, after all. I . . .' He displayed his insignia. '. . . am Storm-Assault Commander 462, and I am requisitioning your prisoners. Open the door.'

The presenter glared at him. 'How am I supposed to present a show trial without anyone to put on trial?'

462 scowled. 'Are you an actor?' he hissed.

'I most certainly am.'

'Well, then – improvise.'

The presenter glared at 462 for a moment, violently exhaled through his spiracles, turned on his heel and strode back up the stairs.

462 put his face against the scarcode reader. The cell door opened.

'What about my troopers?' SVN/2187 asked.

'Your loyalty is touching, but—'

'Either we all come or none of us do.'

462 stared at him. 'I am shocked by your insubordination. You clearly have no respect for your superiors. You and I are going to get along well, Penal-Drone-Lieutenant SVN/2187. Hmm. I think, for convenience, I will refer to you as Sven. How does that sound?'

'Sven, eh?' The drone smiled. 'I like it. But we need to free my adjutants, sir. They are called DIQ/4914 and ARS/7942.'

'I think I'll just address them as *Hey, you.*'

*

Space made the dreadnoughts look like pinheads on a velvet cloth.

'It makes you realise how small you are,' Smith observed as they left Didcot Prime behind and shot towards the fleet. 'I mean, we fit in the *John Pym*, the *John Pym* fits in the dreadnoughts, all the dreadnoughts make up a fleet, and all of that adds up to a bit of a headache.'

Rhianna nodded. 'That's why they call it deep space.'

'Because it's so big?'

'Because it makes you have deep thoughts. Like, the

cosmos. What is it? And what's in it? And why is it there? Where am I going in life? What day is it? Deep space.'

'You're going to a battleship,' Carveth announced. 'You're going to have your tea and invade the Ghast home-world. Your name is Rhianna. The rest is just noise.' She leaned over to Gerald's cage and adjusted his water bottle. 'Damn, it feels good to own a hamster.'

Smith gazed up at the majesty of the nearest battleship, taking in its vast splendour like a spider contemplating a bathtub. Carveth shook her head, awed. 'Just think of all the gin you could fit in there.' She switched on the radio. 'Hello fleet. This is Sheffield-class cruiser *John Pym*, asking permission to dock.'

A computerised voice replied, 'Roger, *John Pym*. This is HMS *Illustrious*. Please approach Hold Thirty-Seven—'

A woman's voice cut over the radio. 'I say, is that you, Smith? Captain Fitzroy here. Pull in to my personal docking bay. I'll have the doors opened for you. I saw you on the pitch back on Radishia. Been meaning to congratulate you in person. Especially your pilot – that girl's got spirit. Fly up to the back end and I'll have you sorted in a jiffy.'

The radio cut out.

Carveth shook her head. 'Space is infinite and we keep running into her. I'd call it karma, if I wasn't a robot. Sometimes I wonder what I was in a previous life to deserve all this.'

'A sandwich toaster?' Suruk replied. 'Or maybe a bucket full of cake.'

Docking was no problem: the hold doors were eight times higher than the *John Pym*. The ship flew into a steel canyon of a hangar and landed under a brass lion-

and-unicorn slightly shorter than a tower block. There were only two other ships in the docking bay: a M'Lak Vulture, sporting extra spikes and a fresh coat of what was hopefully red paint and a long, elegant vessel, human but from abroad, with large fins and a huge chrome bumper.

'Blimey,' Carveth said as the airlock swung shut behind them, 'look at this place. It's huge!'

'True,' Smith said, feeling slightly outdone, 'but very empty.'

The hold ramp swung down and Wainscott's converted lorry rolled out. Susan was at the wheel and Wainscott sat on the chair of the rear gun like a mad king on his throne.

The inner doors of the hangar opened and a small vehicle drove into the hold. It was a golf cart, Smith saw, and a woman was driving it. A striped Bhagparsian shelf-cat sat on her shoulder. She tooted the horn cheerfully, and Smith braced himself for the jollity to come.

'Hallo, Smitty!' Captain Fitzroy yelled. 'Almost didn't see your ship there, parked in the corner of my much larger ship. How's tricks?'

'Fine thanks,' Smith replied.

'Excellent.' Captain Fitzroy beamed. 'Major Wainscott, the map to your quarters will be uploaded to your vehicle's computer. I'll see to it that you get tickets to tonight's entertainment, at the grand theatre. Now, Smith, this . . . is HMS *Illustrious*, our first vessel in the Super-Super-Dreadnought class. It's the biggest battleship in the Royal Space Navy. It's also the biggest battleship mankind has. It's even the biggest battleship mankind has ever thought about. I've been checking science fiction books with a ruler and, believe me, their spaceships are all tiny compared to mine. The *Illustrious* is bigger than either the European dreadnought *Sternly Worded Resolution* or the American carrier *Abraham Goddam Lincoln*. It's even longer than the *Yangtze Kiang*.'

'The flagship of the Chinese space navy?' Smith said.

'No, the river.'

'Gosh.'

'Why?' Carveth said.

Captain Fitzroy stared at her. 'What?'

'Well, why? What's the point? I mean, you can only carry so many missiles before it's just a waste of metal, right?'

Fitzroy looked at Smith. '*Do* something with her, Smith, before I do. One of the reasons is to enable us to transport all the soldiers, tanks and warbots we need to invade the Ghast homeworld. The other is that, if the enemy boards it, they'll probably get lost or die of starvation before they find anyone worth fighting. Now, mounted on the wall to the left is a radio beacon. If you get lost on board, activate your nearest beacon and we'll send out a helicopter to find you. Hop onto my cart and we'll get going.'

They drove through a gigantic, empty hall. It seemed that the *Illustrious* had been designed by someone who liked cathedrals but thought that they were much too small. In five minutes, they passed two men laying phone cable, an Ordnance Survey van and a policeman on a bicycle. 'We're going to put stuff in here once the integral factory has finished making it,' Captain Fitzroy explained. 'Tanks and things.'

She turned right. A pair of massive doors slid open, and noise rushed out. The cart rolled into a vast washroom.

Rows of metal sinks stretched away as far as Smith could see, and at each sink a soldier was cleaning his or her teeth. A woman in a mechanical loader-suit lumbered past, carrying what Smith first assumed was a new kind of missile but, on second glance, was actually a colossal tube of toothpaste.

'Morning, lads!' Fitzroy yelled as they swept past. With remarkable dexterity, she snatched a towel from a rack and flicked it across the bottom of a passing commando before tossing it out behind them. 'Super chaps, every one of them. Who wants to see some warbots?'

She took a right turn, shot down a huge pipe, and swung them into a vast warehouse. 'Get a look at *this*.'

Hundreds of tubby figures dangled from the walls in rows, like the assembly line in a teddy bear factory. They were nine feet high, armour-plated, pinstriped grey for urban combat. Their legs, nearly twice the length of a man's, looked stubby compared to their massive shoulders and round bodies.

Another golf cart had stopped a little way off. A portly man in a waistcoat stood in front of an activated warbot, consulting a clipboard.

Smith tapped Fitzroy's arm. 'Pull over here, would you? I've not seen one of these up close before.'

She halted the cart and Smith got out. The waistcoated man, he realised, was Mr Chumble, android and Captain Fitzroy's second-in-command.

'This looks jolly good,' Smith said. 'Are the warbots powered up?'

'They most certainly can be, sir,' Chumble replied. 'Warbot! Please list the circumstances in which you are willing to surrender.'

The warbot let out a loud hydraulic whine. All of its limbs tightened up; it rose six inches with a loud clatter of armour plates. Its head, a tiny afterthought stuck between and in front of its shoulders, swung on its stubby neck to face Mr Chumble. 'We will *never* surrender,' it growled.

'Splendid. Let's test your tracking.' Chumble raised his hand and moved it through the air. The warbot's head followed it.

Rhianna said, 'Is that all they do, fight?'

'Indeed so, madam,' Chumble replied. 'That is their function.'

'That's terrible.' Rhianna held up two fingers in a peace sign. 'Hey, warbot. How many fingers am I holding up?'

'Victory,' the warbot replied.

'Hmm,' said Rhianna.

'Never mind,' said Smith. 'Imagine how peaceful everything will be once the Ghasts have had a damned good thrashing.'

Captain Fitzroy grinned. 'Damned right, Smitty. Just think of how these things will hit the Ghast home planet. Millions of tonnes of fully armoured fighting machine. We'll civilise the bastards until they don't know what's happened. God, the thought of it puts me in a fine mood.' She took a huge breath and exhaled towards the ceiling, the front of her jacket heaving alarmingly. Carveth took two steps back towards the cart.

It occurred to Smith that Captain Fitzroy was actually quite an attractive woman, when you came down to it.

'Well then.' Fitzroy looked at the golf cart. 'Where can I take you now?'

'On the bonnet,' Smith said. He blinked and shook his head. 'I mean, let's get on with it. The tour.'

'That's the spirit,' Fitzroy replied, and she leaped back into the cart. 'Forwards!'

'Righto,' said Smith, feeling guilty and awkward. A change of subject was required. 'So,' Smith said, 'if you are driving us around, and your first officer is checking the warbots, who's actually piloting this ship?'

'Ada,' Fitzroy replied, turning the cart under a twisting forest of brass pipes. 'A top of the range logic engine. She's the business: runs the guns, fires the engines, even sells the socks down at the NAAFI. Very clever bit of tech, that.'

Smith frowned. It sounded as if Captain Fitzroy had got herself a rather cushy option. His own duties as captain included fighting aliens, dodging asteroids and making every fourth cup of tea, which meant that he spent about two hours per day manning the kettle. 'So, if your computer runs the ship for you, what are you actually captain of?'

'Well,' said Fitzroy, 'lots of important things. The on-board lacrosse team, for one thing. Got to keep the scores up. A healthy mind in a healthy body and all that.'

The brasswork in the corridor became more ornate. Soon, wallpaper appeared between the rivets. The cart stopped before a mighty pair of doors. 'These are your quarters,' Fitzroy explained. 'Dinner's at eight.'

'Dinner?' Carveth sat up as if her power intake had been doubled.

'Of course. I'll be having you all at the Captain's table. Bet you can't wait, eh?'

*

Smith's quarters were worthy of a great space captain – which was more than could be said for his room on the *John Pym*. The *Illustrious* had space for him and, it seemed, his entire family had he been in possession of one: instead, Carveth would be getting the bunk beds, and Suruk would sleep perched on the stool next to the mini-bar.

It was, truly, an impressive ship. Carveth patched them into the internal camera system, mainly so that she could check that nobody was messing with Gerald while they were away. Smith flicked through the communal areas: a lecture hall, a rugby pitch, a pub for Space Navy personnel called The Bionic Arms – even a small bowling green. Smith flicked past CHANGING ROOM AND AFTER MATCH BATH and was both relieved and perturbed when a message appeared reading *Password Please, Captain Fitzroy.*

In gigantic barracks, whole legions from the Space Empire underwent last-minute training and briefing. In Hold 38B, guild troopers from Scarsthorpe Secundus were grimly playing football in heavy brown coats and polished armour. In 41D, under a huge banner depicting a stylised spider, the soldiers of the Dukedom of Mars were taking their protein pills and putting their helmets on.

'All set, boss?' Carveth asked, putting her head around the bedroom door. She was wearing her new armour. The plates were polished to a shine, which made her look slightly like a metal cherub.

'Pretty much,' he replied. 'You've got a bit of Brasso on your shoulder there. Is all that armour needed?'

'Oh, definitely,' she replied. 'It's got loads of pockets for keeping extra food in. And reinforced steel plates, for keeping mad captains out. Look,' she said, rummaging at the front pocket. 'I found this plastic sack. I think it's a doggy bag from a restaurant – or else for sick.'

They set out with ten minutes to spare. Eight minutes later, they arrived at an imposing set of doors. 'This looks right,' Smith said. He turned the handle and opened the door. 'After you, Rhianna.'

She looked into the room. 'Isambard, this is our room. We've moved like all things in life: mysteriously, and in a circle.'

'What about my dinner?' Carveth demanded. 'I'm bloody hungry. We need to find someone and ask for directions.'

'Certainly not!' Smith replied. 'I am not the sort of man who just asks for directions.'

'The typical sort, you mean.'

'Exactly. I am not a typical man. A British officer doesn't stop to ask people where he is. He just makes where he is into part of Britain, thus solving the problem. Captain Cook stopped to ask for directions, and look where it got him.'

'Where did it get him?'

'Well, I don't know. Nobody told him. They just killed him instead.'

'Right, sod it,' Carveth declared, 'I'm going to find out where we are.'

She stomped into their suite and activated the camera system. Her small fingers moved quickly over the keyboard. 'It's tracking Captain Fitzroy's personal signal . . . here we go. She must be in the dining room.'

The camera showed a table in what seemed to be a small music hall. In the background, two persons of uncertain gender were dancing slowly, like exhausted boxers. The camera shook violently as something struck the table and then Fitzroy herself appeared on the screen, smoking a cigar. She was wearing her fleet officer's jacket and a bra. Of her shirt, there was no sign.

'Where are you buggers?' she demanded. 'Damn it, man, we're halfway through the starters already. By the time we get to pudding—'

The room shook. The chandelier above Fitzroy's head swung like a pendulum. Dust showered down from above. 'What the hell was that?' Fitzroy demanded.

Carveth looked at Smith. 'Boss?'

Rhianna said, 'I felt something.'

On the screen, Fitzroy was on her feet, looking like a rake who had just been caught cheating at cards. The red light of the music hall began to flash.

'Damn it!' she cried, 'we're under attack. Mr Chumble, where is my shirt? Find my shirt and cat. And lock down the gin cabinet! We've got to get to the control room. Someone call a taxi!'

Smith leaned in to the microphone. 'We're on our way, Fitzroy. Tell Wainscott's men to be ready for us.'

'Righto!' Fitzroy shouted back. 'Listen, Smith, this is important. I need you to—'

With a yowl of terror the Bhagparsian shelf-cat threw itself at the camera. The screen went dead.

Carveth blinked at the screen. 'No dinner,' she said numbly. 'We were supposed to be having dinner. We can't get there. What're we going to do if we can't get to our dinner?'

'We're cut off,' Smith replied. He grabbed her shoulder and shook it. 'Damn it, woman, get a grip on yourself! We have to get to the control room. Rhianna, can you contact a vehicle? Suruk, take a look outside, see if there's a map or something.'

Something struck the ship. The floor shuddered and a low, grim rumble ran through the walls like a huge beast waking. Smith felt the urge to draw his pistol and civilise something.

He led his men into the corridor.

Rhianna stopped and pressed her fingers into her hair. Her eyes became vague and unfocused, even by their usual standard.

Smith said, 'Rhianna, are you all right?'

She frowned, concentrating. 'I'm summoning help telepathically,' she said. 'I've made contact . . . someone is coming.'

A golf cart rolled around the corner. The front of the cart seemed to have been worked over by Christopher Wren: a small shrine rose out of the bonnet, and the engine unit had been sculpted to resemble cherubs playing the exhaust pipe like a trumpet. A small woman was driving: she wore a dark robe that flapped out behind her. She stopped and looked them over. The rear of the cart was heaped with books and briefcases.

'Who are you?' Suruk demanded.

'I'm the ship's omnipadre,' the woman said. 'I heard a voice calling in the darkness, the voice of someone lost. And now, you are most certainly found.'

'Are you some kind of vicar?' Smith asked.

'Absolutely. Technically, I'm C of E, but I'm licensed to do pretty much anything.' The omnipadre opened one of her cases, revealing a bewildering array of paraphernalia.

'If it's got Abraham in it, this briefcase here will cover it. All the rest, the other case.'

'Really? Do you do agnostics?' Smith said.

She frowned. 'I'm not sure if they're covered. But on the plus side, nor are they. Get in – I'll give you a lift. Try not to sit on the cherubim.'

They climbed on board. 'We've got to get to the upper deck,' Smith said. 'There's been an attack.'

She fired the engine, and the cart sped off down the corridor. They turned left into a massive hall and accelerated. Smith felt the rush of the wind in his hair and moustache. The cart shot past vaults and archways. It was like passing through a cloister on a rollercoaster.

'Left,' he called. 'No, right, actually.'

An explosion shook the hall. Fire burst from a ceiling vent. Smith grabbed the wheel and swung them around the flames, into a side passage. Dark shapes lumbered from the edges of the hall, eyes glowing. Dozens of robot voices growled.

They weaved between the warbots. A man raced over from the side, shouting 'Here, look out!' and Smith narrowly missed him. Suruk cackled with laughter. Behind them, metal groaned. Smith glanced back and saw a joist slowly swing down from the ceiling like a falling tree.

'Slow down!' Carveth cried, 'you're going to blow the trans-axle!'

'Does a golf cart have a trans-axle?' Smith asked.

'No, but I do. I wasn't built for this!'

The floor heaved and the cart flipped onto two wheels. The omnipadre let out a stream of curses. One of the advantages with officiating for a range of gods, it seemed, was that you never ran out of blasphemous things to say. Suruk clambered across the bonnet to weigh the side down and the cart slammed back onto all four wheels.

'It should be up here!' Smith called. 'Through these doors.'

They rushed towards the end of the hall. At the last minute, the great doors slid apart and they rolled through.

'Wait a minute,' Smith said. 'This isn't right.'

They were back in the hangar.

Carveth leaped out of the cart and staggered towards the *John Pym*, weaving like a smoked bee. 'You idiot!' she said. 'We're back where we started. No, we're not even there. We're back where we started before we were back where we started the last time around!'

Smith rounded on her. 'Don't you call me an idiot. I'm the captain here, dammit. Get the ship fired up, Carveth, and open the communications.' He turned to the omnipadre. 'Madam, you are welcome to accompany us. We can protect you.'

The cleric took a long look at the *John Pym*, then Smith, then Suruk. 'I tell you what,' she said, 'I'll put my trust in God this time.'

'As you wish. Good luck.'

Smith ducked through the airlock and into the *John Pym*. He hurried into the cockpit and the ship rumbled into life around him. He dropped into the captain's chair, pulled down the portable television on its metal arm and switched it on. Quickly, he turned the knobs. The screen displayed a children's programme involving penguins. Smith swore and twiddled vehemently. The penguins disappeared and Captain Fitzroy replaced them.

Either things were going very wrong or she had taken the opportunity to party extremely hard. Something was burning behind her. Several ensigns staggered from one side of the screen to the other like a drunken backing band.

'That you, Smitty?' she yelled.

'It's me,' he replied. 'We're in the *John Pym*. We can help evacuate people.'

'Don't worry. Everything's under control.'

Sprinkler systems burst into life above her head. A wallahbot rolled past the camera, flailing its appendages. 'Danger, high voltage!' it garbled, before ploughing into the wall.

'Listen,' Smith called, 'we're going to pull off and circle. We'll come in and lift off anyone you need. We'll take the Deepspace Operations Group—'

Like some strange gopher emerging from its hole, Wainscott's head rose into view in the bottom left corner of the screen. His eyes seemed to have doubled in size. 'Everything's fine,' he growled. A cable dropped from the roof like an ambushing python. 'Mustn't grumble.'

Something large hit the *John Pym*. The whole ship rattled. Smith clutched the handrail. A bottle of gin slid along the shelf and hit a copy of the 2522 edition of *Jane's Fighting Spaceships*.

'Boss,' Carveth said, 'It's getting bloody hairy out there.'

'Pull off!' he replied. 'Captain Fitzroy, we'll come back in once the hold's stabilised. Carveth, ready the engines.' He leaned out and yelled down the corridor, 'Close the airlocks!'

He heard the airlock door swing closed. 'It's sealed!'

Rhianna called. 'Oh – actually, guys, I've shut my dress in the door.'

*

The *John Pym* flew out of the hold in a storm of decompression. Space fell over them like a curtain. The *Illustrious* shrank at alarming speed. Carveth righted the *Pym*, banked and yawed it, and at once they were in the middle of a battle.

Three Ghast cruisers lay to starboard, sleek and grey as dolphins. They hurled torpedoes at the *Illustrious*, filling the gap between them with streaks of fire. The torpedoes broadcast static to jam communications as they flew. The radio squealed and fuzzed.

Bloody hell! Smith thought. A disruptor torpedo shot past the front viewscreen, wriggling to correct its course. It looked like something bio-engineered from a void shark.

'That was too close,' he said. 'Take evasive action, pilot.'

'What do you think I'm doing?' Carveth demanded. 'I nearly evaded myself just then!'

Smith looked over his shoulder, back down the corridor. 'Rhianna? We need psychic shielding or whatever it is. Suruk?'

The alien put his head around the door. 'Indeed?'

'Could you get Rhianna to do something psychic, please?'

'Gladly. I shall start your girlfriend up at once.' He paused, and added, 'Is there a string I need to pull? A particular dreadlock?'

The radio howled as it tried to retune itself. 'Dammit,' Smith muttered. 'We can't fight these void shark things. We're going to need a bigger ship.'

'Oh, really?' Carveth called. 'Have you got one?'

'Yes.' He leaned forward and pointed to the scanner. 'There. Those output readings are human. It must be one of ours come to help. You won't be able to hail them, but maybe we can dock.'

'It's better than nothing,' Carveth replied. 'Hold on!'

She stamped on the accelerator. The *John Pym* lurched forward, throwing Smith back in his chair. They blasted forwards, through a shoal of torpedoes. A defensive laser lanced out from the *Illustrious*, nearly cutting the nose off the *Pym*, and Carveth let out a sequence of very un-robot-like words.

A pack of fighter ships appeared at one side of the windscreen and disappeared at the other a second later. Beams and bullets cut the air. The *John Pym* rushed forward like a drunk charging across a busy dance-floor as jets and weapons fired around it.

'There,' Carveth said. 'Over there!'

Smith picked up the emergency targeting system from under the screen, held it to his eyes and turned the knob to maximum zoom. He saw what she meant: behind the chaos, there was the slablike side of a human cruiser – and in the middle of it, an open hangar.

'Land us in there,' he said. He put the binoculars down and tried to get something on the radio. The *Pym* banked, synchronising itself with the cruiser. The hold opened up before them.

On the right, half of a Ghast destroyer turned lazily,

fires glowing around a huge wound in its side. It looked like a manta ray that had been bitten by a shark. A flurry of escape capsules burst from its side, seeds from a rotten fruit. They tore past the *John Pym* like squeezed pips.

'I'm coming in fast!' Carveth called. 'I'll have to land a bit hard.'

They shot into the hold. Suddenly there was metal around them, a huge roof overhead. The *Pym* slammed down, slid across the steel floor in a rush of sparks, and struck a massive broken turbine. The straps hit Smith's chest, and he flopped back in his seat. The hold doors slammed closed behind them, and the hull of the *John Pym* reverberated with the force of it.

The ship was silent.

Carveth looked around. 'Well, we're not dead,' she said. 'That's good, isn't it?'

Smith called down the corridor. 'Is everyone all right? Any broken bones?'

'Two!' Suruk replied. 'Fortunately, neither was mine.'

'Oh God!' Smith said. He unclipped his harness and staggered upright. 'Rhianna, are you hurt?'

Suruk stepped into the corridor. 'Two of my favourite trophies shattered. I spent ages getting these skulls, and now look at them. I would hold Carveth responsible, but I doubt she will be able to make amends. After all, she only has one skull with which to replace them.'

Rhianna looked out of her cabin. 'Whoa,' she said. 'That was pretty intense. Are you guys okay?'

'I think so. Suruk's hurt his skull – well, somebody else's, really—' He heard a noise behind him, and turned.

Carveth stood at the cockpit door. Her face was weirdly intense.

'What on Earth—'

'Shush.' She raised a finger to her lips. 'We've got a problem.'

'What's gone wrong now?'

'We're in the wrong ship.'

'What?'

Carveth ducked back into the cockpit. Smith glanced at Rhianna and Suruk. They both shrugged. He followed Carveth to the controls.

She crouched down and pointed through the screen. 'Look!' she hissed.

The *John Pym* faced the rear wall of the hold. The huge room was strewn with junk. Either it had been dredged in just before the battle or the crew had been planning to eject the stuff. On the wall before them was a steel relief shaped like a stylised ant, its legs outstretched like wings. Below the relief, chrome letters the height of a man read WASP.

'Workers and Soldiers' Party,' Smith said. 'That's Gertie talk. This must be a Ghastist vessel.'

'We're in the wrong ship,' Carveth hissed. 'We've landed in the wrong hold! What're we going to do?'

'Well,' said Smith, 'the first thing to do is to get out.'

'Bloody right it is!'

'And the second thing is to capture their spaceship.'

'What? You've got to be kidding. This is a warship!'

'Quite so,' Smith replied, smiling deviously, 'but I've been a space captain for long enough to know that warships have one great weakness. All the guns point outwards. And we're already in.'

Suruk chuckled. 'A worthy plan, Mazuran. We are in the belly of the beast. Now we shall strike from the inside, like a deadly curry.'

'Right,' said Smith. 'The hold doors are closed, and the sensors say that the air is breathable. So, we'll sneak out, get to the control room and take over the ship. How does that sound?'

'By sane standards, insane,' Carveth said. 'But given that our standards are already insane – it's pretty much standard.'

'Frankly,' Suruk said, 'I cannot see how it can go wrong, except for us all dying. Let's attack!'

Rhianna looked up at the ceiling. 'Yeah,' she said. 'Sure, let's do it.'

Carveth sighed. 'Don't any of you have a sense of fear?'

'Oh, totally, Polly,' Rhianna said. 'I sometimes get afraid. But then, you know, I just chill out and I forget all my troubles.'

'Do they go up in smoke, by any chance?'

Rhianna looked thoughtful.

'Oh, never mind,' Carveth said. 'It's like asking a gold-fish what happened last week. I'm in.'

She turned and put her hand into Gerald's cage. The hamster scurried out, onto the palm of her hand. She raised him like Hamlet with Yorrick's skull. 'And you, you little bugger, you're coming with me.'

Carveth powered down the *John Pym*. With any luck, it would be mistaken for part of the abandoned turbine. Hopefully, the *Pym* would not be jettisoned out of the air-lock before they had captured the Ghastist cruiser.

'Is everyone ready?' Smith asked, as he reached for the airlock door.

They nodded. Carveth had tightened her space armour and had equipped herself with as many weapons as she could find. She looked like an afterthought at the end of the Maxim cannon.

Smith turned the wheel, and the steps dropped down from the airlock.

They crept into the hold. Smith was pleased to see that the cruiser was much smaller than the *Illustrious*, but it was still massive. He led them across the great steel floor at a brisk jog, which did not help: Suruk easily outpaced him, while Rhianna was slowed by her flip-flops and Carveth clattered along under her armour and weaponry. By the time they reached the inner airlock doors on the far side of the hold, they did not resemble a team any more.

Suruk tapped Smith on the arm. 'Look up there. Am I wrong, or is that a ventilation shaft?'

'You're deeply wrong,' Carveth puffed, 'but yeah, it is.'

'Then grant me a leg up,' Suruk replied. 'While the little woman recovers from moving around, I will scout ahead. You never know what you will find in the ventilation shafts of a spaceship,' he added. 'That is why I like being in them so much. Mice, tramps, large spinning bladed things – a ventilation shaft is just an adventure waiting to happen.'

'What about man-eating aliens?'

'Give me a minute,' Suruk replied. 'I have not got in the shaft yet.'

Two minutes later, Suruk scrambled back down from the vent. 'Greetings,' he whispered. 'I have scouted ahead. Our arrival has not gone unnoticed, and even now enemies come to do battle with us.'

'Uh-oh,' Rhianna said.

'Four Ghasts and a traitorous human officer are approaching. The Ghasts are first. The human is hanging back in a cowardly fashion. We could slay them easily.'

'Righto, then.' Smith cocked his Civiliser. 'Hold on a minute. Suruk, if we sort out the Ghasts, could you deal with the human? Try not to get blood everywhere. If I can steal his uniform, I could get us to the control room that way. We could infiltrate the ship.'

'An excellent idea! I will – wait. I am sure I thought of something . . . No,' Suruk declared, 'it is gone. Let us get cracking.'

Smith crouched down and gave Suruk a leg up. The alien sprang into the vent, spear in hand, and disappeared from view.

Carveth peered at the airlock controls. 'The sensor says they're coming this way.'

'Ready, chaps?'

Carveth swallowed hard. 'Okay.'

Rhianna nodded.

Smith hit the controls. The doors hissed, gave out one loud clunk and rumbled apart. Behind them, revealed like actors on a stage, were four Ghasts – dark red, dressed in black helmets and leather coats, their second pairs of arms rising up behind them like broken wings.

Smith was struck by how alien they were, how out of place even on this traitor ship. For all that Rhianna liked to bang on about how bad it was to subject the Other to unnecessary Othering, they looked absolutely evil.

'*Ak*—' the nearest Ghast snarled, and Smith fired.

His Civiliser boomed, but it was drowned out by the roar of gunfire from the Maxim cannon to his right. Carveth swung the big gun on its support arm and the Ghasts were thrown down as if the ground had exploded beneath them. She stopped firing.

'Bloody hell!' Carveth said. 'Yeah.'

'Jolly good,' Smith said. One of the Ghasts was staring up at him, the life gone from its vicious little eyes. In death, it managed to both squint and snarl, like a pedant driven into a rage by small print – overall, an improvement to the usual expression.

'God, they're bloody ugly,' Carveth said. 'You can tell that they're vicious bastards just by looking at them.'

Rhianna said, 'I suppose you're right, Polly. But not everything that's ugly is evil. I mean . . . Suruk isn't conventionally attractive, but deep inside, his soul is . . . well . . . we'd best get moving, actually.'

The ship rumbled. Far off, an alarm was sounding.

Suruk was waiting halfway up the stairs. Behind him, a body lay in the shadows. A pair of leather boots protruded from the dark.

'Did you get the human?' Smith said.

'I snapped the traitor's neck like a biscuit,' the alien replied. 'But I have identified the problem I mentioned.'

'You got blood on the uniform? I can't wear it if it's covered in gore.'

'Not exactly.' Suruk hauled the body out and dumped it on the stairs.

Carveth said, 'That's a woman.'

'True,' the alien replied. 'But improvisation is a mighty tool in the arsenal of the hunter. If Smith here puts on her clothes and adopts a squeaky voice—'

'Certainly not,' Smith replied. 'I couldn't fit into all that leather stuff. Wait . . . Carveth, you're the right size. Maybe a bit short, but still . . .'

'I'm not dressing up like that,' Carveth said. 'I've got a reputation to keep. I didn't come halfway across space to look like some sort of sex maniac.'

'When you could do that at home,' Suruk replied.

'Exactly. Wait, what are you implying? Besides, I don't look anything like her. She's got blonde hair, but her skin's different to mine. I'm fair – she's more an olive complexion.'

'Like me,' Suruk said.

'No, not like you. She has an olive complexion. You are green, like an olive. Big difference.'

Rhianna said, 'Er, Polly—'

Carveth sighed. 'What? You're not going to tell me that comparing Suruk to an olive is speciesist, are you? Because there are other things I could compare him to—'

'I'll do it,' Rhianna said.

Smith turned to his crew. 'Look, chaps, I don't want any arguing. I'm in charge, and I'll hear any sensible suggestions, but we need to get moving.'

'Isambard, I'll do it.'

'You?' he replied. 'But you're – well, you're my girlfriend. I won't risk your life and I don't think the struggle for human liberty requires you to dress up like a traitor.'

Carveth checked the ammunition drum on the Maxim cannon. 'He's got a point, Rhianna. You'd have to pretend to be alert and competent.'

Rhianna frowned. 'I can totally pretend to be alert and – um – the other thing. You know what I think?' she added, raising her voice a little. 'I think I ought to do this. It's part of my growth as a strong and independent woman.'

'Well,' said Suruk, 'whatever you are going to do, please get on with it. Less stressing, more dressing up as a treacherous minion of an alien dictator, I say.'

'Okay,' Rhianna said. 'You can look away now. Or not. I'm totally body-confident.'

'So am I,' Suruk said. 'Hiding them, disposing of them . . . I am fine with that.'

Five minutes later, Rhianna pulled her hair back and put on her newly-acquired officer's cap. False antennae jutted from the brim of the hat. They wobbled.

Carveth looked her over. 'It's convincing,' she said. 'How do you feel?'

'Awkward and uncomfortable,' Smith replied. Something moved on the comms screen, at the edge of his vision. 'Wait – someone's coming. Rhianna, get them to take you to the bridge. We'll follow from there. Men, we'll hide down here. Rhianna, would you mind going up to see who's there?'

'Um, okay.'

'Good luck, old girl. And try to be a bit more evil and dynamic. I know it's difficult.' He paused a moment and kissed her on the cheek.

'Quick!' Suruk said. Smith ducked into cover, pulling Carveth behind him.

Boots clanged on the stairs. He heard a voice: low and brutal, but human. 'You've got to make an example, right? But you can't make too much of an example, or else there'll be nobody left to make an example to. I learned that from Ghast Number Eight.'

The voice that answered was crisp, hard, neurotic. 'Quite so. Truly our benefactors have the intellectual edge.

With this deep understanding, we cannot fail to remake mankind.'

'That's right. Only through the most ferocious struggle can the weak be weeded out, and the Ghastist officer caste will be at the forefront—'

'Hi guys!' Rhianna called.

'Who's there?' The men hurried down the stairs. Smith peeked around the corner and saw them: a thug with a beer belly and badly shaven jowls; a tall, prim youth, as thin and vicious as a whip. Both held pistols. They wore black uniforms and caps with false antennae.

As they saw Rhianna, both stiffened and saluted. 'All hail Number One!'

'Yeah, he's cool,' Rhianna said. 'How're you doing?'

The younger man stared at the heap of dead Ghasts. 'By the leader! What happened here?'

'Huh? Oh, these dead Ghasts? Well, they got totally shot.'

The big officer gaped at the bodies like a fish. 'We saw an unusual heat signature near the airlock, Over-Assault-Commander . . .' He peered at Rhianna's stolen insignia. 'I don't remember seeing you before.'

Smith cocked his Civiliser. The sound seemed incredibly loud.

Rhianna put her hands to her temples. She pressed on her forehead, and her cap fell off.

'Wait a minute,' said the younger man.

Rhianna's voice was full of a kind of dreamy certainty. 'You can see no bodies.'

The two men looked at one another.

Rhianna raised her hand towards them and made a swirling gesture. '*None.*'

The younger man took out a communicator and thumbed the button. 'Send a medical team to Airlock Alpha-Seven. The Over-Assault-Commander is concussed. Her efficiency is at risk of permanent compromise. Damn it! They must all be dealing with the torpedo strike. You just can't get the minions.'

'We'll escort you to Medical,' the big officer said. 'Follow us, Over-Assault-Commander.'

'Okay,' Rhianna said. 'Take me to your dealer – *leader*. I meant leader.'

*

Smith crept down the corridor, following the officers. Suruk was like a shadow at his side. Carveth was like a dustbin falling over some way behind. Fortunately, whatever noise she made was blotted out by the sirens, alarms and endless announcements being shouted from the ship's many loudspeakers.

They passed a big portrait of a man dressed, it seemed, like a bus conductor from a banana republic, glowering out at the viewer. Smith did not need to look at the name plaque to know the man: it was Egbert Tench, arch-traitor and former leader of the Legion of Ghastists. No doubt that felon had fled to enemy territory. The last time Smith had met him, the villain had been tying a maiden to a railway track. Just the sort of person to whom the Ghastists would dedicate a spaceship.

Rumbles came from below: partly from the ship itself, and partly from explosions. At one point, half a dozen human soldiers ran out from a side door and disappeared into one of the access passages. A Ghast ran behind them, yelping orders in its own language. Smith ducked back into cover. The thuggish officer tried to stop the soldiers, but they barely noticed him.

The younger man laughed bitterly. 'You'd be lucky. They're too busy trying to put the atoms back in the reactor from where the Space Empire shot them out.'

'Watch your mouth. If they hear you suggesting we're losing the war, it'll be bad.'

'War *is* bad, guys,' Rhianna said helpfully.

Smith grimaced.

'It's bloody terrible if you're losing,' the younger officer replied.

'Everyone loses in war,' Rhianna replied.

Except for the British Space Empire, Smith thought. *We win because we're jolly good.*

'What?' the young man said. 'God, Scrote, she's really lost it. Look, I say we should chuck her out the airlock. I don't want to be associated with someone that nuts.'

Rhianna shook her head. 'Guys, don't do that. After all, Number One's really far gone and you still like him, don't you? *We* like him, I mean.'

'Are you crazy, Brown? First we lose a squad – a Ghast squad – and then we get rid of an officer?'

'Why not? Her brain's gone. She's useless to the cause.'

Rhianna stopped. 'Hey! You can't just get rid of some-one because they're no use to you. That's like, really bad. What are you, some kind of fascist?'

There was an awkward pause. The two Ghastists looked at each other. 'Well, yes, actually,' Scrote said. 'Pretty much. Aren't you?'

Smith glanced at Suruk. He took aim with his pistol. Suruk slid a knife from his belt and raised it, ready to throw.

Brown licked his lips. 'Listen, Scrote. They'll want someone to blame this on,' he said. 'You know what'll happen. The Ghasts'll hear about this and they'll want heads to roll. But if we can point to someone who can't answer back – someone who's no use to us – and put the blame on them, it'll take the heat off us. Good plan, huh?'

Smith stepped into view and raised his Civiliser. 'Not so fast, gentlemen!'

'Yeah,' Rhianna said. 'It's confusing. And could you speak a bit clearer, too?'

'Now wait,' Brown said, and Scrote drew his pistol.

Scrote whirled – the air blurred – and he staggered into the wall. He slid to the ground with the hilt of a knife protruding from his neck. Suruk made a low purring sound.

Brown dropped to his knees and raised his hands. 'Don't shoot!'

'You are a prisoner of the British Space Empire,' said Smith. 'You will take us to the bridge at once.'

'Take you to the bridge?' Brown said.

'Yes. Now, get on up and take us to the bridge. And don't make a song and dance about it.'

'Alternatively, I could rip off your head,' Suruk said. 'Your choice.'

'Savages,' said the man, but he turned and led the way. 'You'll never get away with this, you know.'

'Then you underestimate our moral fibre,' Smith replied. 'We're British. If anyone can get away with things, it's a

British officer. Hmm . . . that doesn't sound as good as I thought it would.'

'Idiots,' Brown said. 'You sicken me, you know. All of you. Your space empire has become weak and decadent. Just look at the sort of weird-looking riff-raff you associate with.'

'If you speak about my girlfriend like that again, I'll kill you where you stand.'

Rhianna said, 'Um, Isambard, I think he means Suruk.'

'Oh. Well, any of my men.'

'None of your men *are* men,' the Ghastist said, wearily.

'So? So? My men are not men because I am enlightened and tolerant. I let robots and aliens have a go and everything. And women. So shut up or there'll be bloody trouble.'

'Hah. Typical. Your civilised values fall apart at the slightest provocation. We followers of the Ghast Empire at least are honest about taking over the galaxy. When Number One conquers the universe, we will be at the top table with the Ghasts.'

'Yeah,' Carveth said, 'because they'll be eating you.'

Smith gritted his teeth and fought down the urge to fling this supercilious idiot out the airlock. 'Quite so, Carveth – wait a moment. Your voice. It's familiar.'

Brown gave him a pitying look. 'I very much doubt we move in the same circles.'

'Yes it is – by God, you've got a British accent!'

'I suppose you're going to ask who I stole it from.'

Smith grabbed the man's collar, turned him as if steering a toddler on reins, and shoved him hard against the wall. 'You bloody traitor!' He shoved his gun against the man's ear. 'By God, to think of it! An Englishman done up like a Ghast. I've a good mind to shoot you, you flouncing turd, then bring you back to life with science and then shoot you again, just to make sure you get the message!'

For the first time, the Ghastist's composure broke. 'Get that gun away from me. You wouldn't dare—'

'I'd damned dare any day of the week!'

'All right, all right – calm down! I only said all that to get a rise out of you.'

'A rise? You'll get more than that from me.' Smith holstered his pistol and reached to his belt. His sword slid free in a hiss of oiled steel. 'Here's my pointed retort!'

'Isambard!'

He looked around. The others were staring at him. Rhianna said, 'I know you've shot a lot of people, Isambard. And hacked a lot of other people with your sword. I know you like doing that. But you can't shoot and hack someone who isn't armed. And he's a prisoner.'

Suruk said, 'She speaks truly, Mazuran. Give him your pistol, so that honour is satisfied. And then hack him really quickly, before he can shoot you with it.'

Smith sighed. 'You're right. I stand corrected. I would have killed this arsehole in a fit of righteous anger. That would have been doubly wrong. Not only would that have been murder, but it would have involved a display of excess emotion. Thank you, chaps. It's an honour to be in such honest company. Come on, you.' He yanked the man around. Smith focussed his mind in the Shau Teng style, putting the Bearing into his voice. 'Chop-chop, or I'll fix it so you never goose-step again.'

They started off down the corridor. 'Thank you for not

killing me,' Brown said crossly. 'Although it does demonstrate your inherent weakness, of course.'

Carveth nudged Smith in the side.

'What is it, Carveth?'

She held out a small leather square. 'When you shoved
him against that wall, his wallet fell out. I'm just thinking
that, you know, reparations and all that . . . He's got fifty
quid.'

Smith took it from her and passed it to the officer.
'Here.'

'Thank you so much,' the officer said. He glanced
through the wallet. 'And the rest, fatty.'

'Bollocks to that,' Carveth said. 'I'm keeping that twenty
for hurt feelings.'

They hurried up the corridor, past a sign in English and
Ghast script. 'You're nearly at the bridge,' Brown said,
pointing. 'You go hard right and don't stop.'

'I thought as much,' Smith replied. 'You're coming with
us.'

They marched up the passage. 'Ready, chaps?' Smith
asked. His crew nodded. He pressed the button and
marched straight in.

The bridge was much smaller than the control room of
a British dreadnought. There were only two seats, in fact.
In one, a man in a dark uniform was operating a bank of
controls. Behind him sat a Ghast officer.

'Left at the asteroid,' the Ghast was hissing.

'Hands up!' said Smith. 'Except for the pilot,
obviously.'

The Ghast turned and looked over its shoulder. It stood
up silently and raised all its arms.

'This ship is under British control,' Smith said. 'You will surrender command to me.'

The Ghast officer growled softly. Its antennae shuddered. Slowly, with exaggerated courtesy, it gestured to the chair. 'Feel free.'

'I always do.' Smith sat down. 'Keep driving, pilot, and there won't be any trouble. Now, Gertie, where's the radio on this thing?'

The Ghast officer pointed with its pincer. 'Just above your head.'

Smith looked up. The ceiling was covered in alien biotech, like the inside of an old nose. He grimaced.

An overhead compartment burst open and a biomask leaped out at his face. The mask's oxygen pipe whipped out and snapped around Smith's neck. He grabbed the mask, held it back with both hands while it thrashed and strained to clamp itself around his face. At the edge of his vision, figures shouted and struggled.

With a yell, Smith tore the mask free and hurled it across the room. The Ghast officer drew a shock-stick. Carveth's gun roared and the alien was hurled into a panel beside the doors. It fell in a blue cascade of sparks. Brown dropped down and pulled a dagger from his belt. Rhianna cried 'Isambard!'

Smith moved but he was too late. Brown lunged – and Suruk caught him and hurled him quiff-first into the wall.

'Freeze, scum!' The pilot was on his feet. He held an automatic pistol.

Smith turned to him. He filled his voice with the Bearing. 'Stop that nonsense this instant, traitor fellow!' he said.

'Keep back,' the pilot gasped. 'I'm warning you—'

'That's quite enough of that, thank you. Put the gun down and stop making a fuss.'

The pilot paused. 'Of course . . . I didn't mean anything, sir. . . I thought you were . . . oh.'

Smith pulled the pistol out of his hand. 'Now, power down the weapons systems. We're in charge here and there'll be no more silliness from the likes of you. I've just about had – Carveth, look out!'

Something sprang from the shadows like a striking cobra. Smith saw digits and a thrashing tail, and the biomask flew towards her.

'No!' Suruk cried. He shoved Carveth out of the way and stepped roaring into its path.

Suddenly, the biomask was gone. Smith blinked, confused. Suruk stood in the middle of the room, flexing his mandibles. He belched. 'Problem solved,' he said.

'So we're in charge now?' Rhianna said. 'Can I change back into my normal clothes? This uniform is totally chafing.'

'Feel free,' said Smith. 'And jolly good work, too. Now, what's it like outside, Carveth?'

Carveth looked over the monitors. 'Bad news. There are gun stations all through the ship firing on the *Illustrious*.'

'Power down the turrets. There'll be an override option on the controls.'

She glanced around. 'Got it. Boss, we've got some internal problems, too.'

'That is for sure,' Suruk replied. 'I need to cough a pellet.'

Smith looked over her shoulder at the row of blurry screens. Deep within the ship, figures were gathering

– humans and Ghasts in long coats. He saw guns being handed out, arms waved and orders shouted. 'Tell them to pack it in or we'll commence emergency evacuations.'

Carveth looked around, suddenly hopeful. 'You mean we're getting out of here?'

'Of course not. They'll be doing the evacuating. Give them to the count of ten and open all the airlocks.'

He climbed down into the captain's chair. 'You there, pilot. Activate communications and turn the knobs to the British Space Empire frequency. Quick march.'

The comms screen crackled, and a face appeared. Lines swung across the screen. The face vanished and was briefly replaced by the test card. Then it returned, with a second person in the background.

'What ho, traitor types!' Captain Fitzroy declared. 'Your fleet's in pieces. Are you going to come quietly, or do you want a plasma torpedo up the trash compactor, eh? Wait a moment – what's going on there?'

'It's me. Smith. I've taken command of the Ghastist ship. We've powered the guns down.'

'Smashing.' Fitzroy leaned forward, peering into the camera. She beckoned to someone off-screen. 'Hey, come and see this. You'll enjoy it.'

Wainscott's face loomed into view. 'Good lord!' he said. 'You don't see that every day.'

'Bloody right,' said Fitzroy.

Smith leaned back in the chair, feeling very pleased with himself. It wasn't often that both Fitzroy and Wainscott were looking both impressed and in his direction.

'Well I never!' Wainscott said.

'Hey guys,' Rhianna called from the back of the control

room. 'Don't mind me. I'm just putting my clothes back on.'

Smith frowned. 'Look here, Fitzroy,' said Smith, 'or rather, listen here and look away. This ship is ours. Send some chaps over at once. I have a plan. Just do it quickly.'

He deactivated the screen and turned to his comrades. Rhianna was just pulling on her dress, and looked very much like that woman who stood in a shell, or Lady Godiva or one of those types.

'Good show, everyone,' he said. 'Especially Rhianna.'

*

The orbital battle was over. The Ghast ships had been destroyed, albeit at considerable cost, and now the edge of the Didcot system was full of glowing wreckage. Already, the *Illustrious* had sent marines across on shuttles to take the prisoners into custody, and by now the *Egbert Tench* was almost deserted.

Smith and his crew were playing a quick game of cricket outside the *John Pym* when the others arrived. The inner airlock doors slid open and a small crowd of beings entered. Smith saw the Deepspace Operations Group, mercifully unharmed, Captain Fitzroy – who had put her shirt on again – and a small group of spies from the Service. An antigravity teapot hovered above them, ready to dispense.

Behind them came a deputation of M'Lak naval warriors. They wore goggles and long brown coats, with scarves thrown over their shoulders as tradition required. In their midst was a massive steel box, dwarfing them like a bread-bin among a family of mice. Doors in the tank folded back, revealing tinted water. A creature somewhere between a porpoise and a crocodile swam to the front and waved.

One of the M'Lak called out, 'Helmsman Sedderick of the Gilled, Pilot of Uncharted Space, Explorer of the Deep Void, Plumber of Unimaginable Depths.'

The speakers on the tank crackled. 'Hello,' said Sedderick. 'Is this a secret meeting?'

'Very much so,' W replied, stepping forward. 'Good to see that everyone's in good shape.'

Sedderick bobbed in his tank. 'I'm staying afloat.'

Dreckitt stepped over to Carveth. 'You okay, lady?'

'Fine, Rick.'

'No hoodlums messing with you, huh?'

Carveth patted the Maxim cannon. 'I wouldn't be much of a robot without some iron, Rick.'

'Damn,' Dreckitt said, 'that's my kind of talk.'

'I'm hard boiled and I crack wise,' Carveth replied. 'Like an egg. A sexy egg or something. Because . . . eggs get laid? God, this private eye talk is really difficult.'

'Right,' Smith said. 'That's enough emotion for now. This vessel is ours, and I propose that we make the most of it. Did any of the enemy ships get away?'

'I should damned well think not,' Fitzroy replied. 'I haven't dished out a thrashing like that since the Proxima Centuri Ladies Lacrosse final. Red arses everywhere,' she said. 'So, what's your plan? Reclaim this heap for Blighty and get back to business?'

Smith tucked his cricket bat under his arm. 'Our aim,' he said, 'is nothing short of the complete defeat of the Ghast Empire. To do that, we need to punch through the Ghast defences and knock out their HQ on Selenia. Getting Radishia out of the way cleared much of the path for our attack. But you can bet that Number One will be fielding everything he can get to stop us landing on Selenia – orbital weapons platforms, missile batteries, field lasers, the lot. But what if we could bypass all that, get in close and then strike? It would be much easier, wouldn't it?'

W looked around the hold. 'Are you suggesting flying under false colours, Smith? Because that would be a crime under international law, not to mention not cricket.'

'The boffin's right, Smith,' Wainscott said. 'It's not the done thing. I say we show 'em our colours. Run 'em up the flagpole, go straight in and say "What do you think of this, eh?" That's what I'd do.'

'Not at all,' Smith replied. 'We'd reveal the naval ensign once we got close. Then, we would drive straight through their ships, land on their planet, take out the defences, destroy their armoured divisions, capture their leader and win the war.'

W rubbed his chin. 'We've got a list of possible landing-spots on Selenia, places where we could launch a full attack. I can't tell you much, but let's just say we've given Number One a bit of false information . . . Anyway, the main thing is getting there.'

'Exactly,' Smith replied. 'We already know where to strike. After all, you have to know what you're dealing with before you wade in. Sometimes, what's on the surface isn't the real truth. There's a big difference between rescuing puppies from drowning and trying to steal the offspring of a maternally-enraged sea lion. That's just an example,' he added, instinctively scratching the scar on his right buttock. 'A theoretical one.'

W shook his head. 'You forget, Smith, that Selenia is probably the most heavily-guarded planet in the galaxy. Number One isn't just paranoid – he suffers from a full-blown military-industrial complex. We may have the Empire's finest soldiers with us, but there are at least fourteen billion Ghasts on Selenia, all of them armed and dangerous. This mission could be suicide for everyone involved.' He paused. 'I tell you what. I've often thought that the passage of life is made substantially easier with tea to lubricate it.'

'I do not like the sounds of this,' Suruk said.

'So let's put the kettle on.'

*

'Well,' said W, 'we've had our tea and a chat, and we of the Service think this plan, while somewhere between insanely dangerous and possibly suicidal, is workable. Sedderick?'

'I like it,' the helmsman replied. 'As someone who lives in a fish tank, I know thinking outside the box when I see it. I'll be right behind it.'

W sipped his tea. 'Well, then, we're decided. We'll use the *Egbert Tench* to get deep into enemy territory before launching our attack. Now, Smith, once Captain Fitzroy gets through the enemy defences, you'll take the *John Pym* and—'

'Now, wait a minute,' Smith said. 'Fitzroy?'

Fitzroy brushed dust off her left epaulette. 'Of course,

Smith. We'll need a skilled captain. One with experience of driving a battleship.'

'But you've already got a battleship. I should be the one to captain this ship. I captured it, and besides, I've never had a proper go before and it's my turn.'

W frowned. 'Those are good reasons. At least, one of them is fairly good. But I should warn you, Smith . . . this will test your competence and intelligence to the limit. You may not come back.'

A low, dirty chuckle came from above. Smith glanced up. Suruk crouched on the wing of the *John Pym* like a gremlin, holding the wooden tent peg that he used as a toothpick. 'Fear not. With the Slayer fighting beside you, you cannot lose. I will turn this "suicide mission" into murder.'

'That's for sure,' Carveth said.

'Thank you, Piglet. Ah, this will be a battle worthy of the name! We will re-equip this vessel and put the armour into Armageddon!' Suruk grinned horribly. 'And the rock, into Ragnarok.'

'Quite so,' said Smith. 'I realise that some of you might think that, while this mission is viable, I lack the leadership experience to carry it off. I therefore propose that we decide the matter with a show of hands.' He raised his hand.

Carveth put her hand up.

'Good work, Carveth. I'm proud to have you with me.'

'No,' she said, 'I've got my hand up to ask a question.'

'Oh . . . Well, all right, then. What is your question?'

'What exactly are we putting our hands up to decide?'

Smith lowered his hand. 'Listen, chaps. With the capture

of this vessel, we are poised to deliver a deadly blow to our enemies. Now is the time for Britain to strike, and in doing so to show our allies, both on alien planets and on Earth, that the Ghast Empire can be beaten.'

Fitzoy said, 'True.'

'You see,' Smith continued, gazing thoughtfully, but heroically, into the middle distance, 'I've always known that the Ghasts and their minions can be defeated. But outside the Space Empire, others may not be so sure. It is up to us to set an example, to lead the way. Some might say that the timid folk of rival, smaller, space empires are to be cast aside in our hour of struggle, but I say no! Britain must never desert its allies. You know what I think? Never turn your back on abroad.'

'Damn right,' Dreckitt replied. 'There's some crazy dames out there.'

'It may be,' Smith said, 'that Britain is not the best at everything. There are nations better than us at things like . . . like making clogs, or those little tree things they have in Japan. But now, we have a chance to do what we do best for the good of everyone. We are going to invade the Ghast Empire, shell their cities with a dreadnought, thrash their army, take their stuff, trash their mockery of a culture and make them part of our empire. Why are you looking at me like that, Rhianna? The Ghasts will thank us in the long run. Maybe in a thousand years or so.'

He looked around the room, from one face to another. 'This is it, chaps. It's time to show the world that we will never abandon our allies. Britain will always be there, fighting for what's right. We will never back away from the fight for liberty. We will never forget our duty to help and protect those less fortunate than ourselves. I say raise your hand and vote for my plan if you want to take this fight to the Ghasts and never give in, no matter what it takes. Put your hands up if you'll never surrender!

'Not like that, obviously.'

Into the Jaws of Deathly Hell

Smith stood on the bridge of his new battleship, staring into space. 'Ah,' he announced, 'this is the life.'

'No it isn't,' said Carveth. 'We've moved from a little spaceship that nobody noticed to a great big one that isn't even ours.'

'Carveth, you worry too much.'

'I don't think I do. I just want to be safe. I'm sure I don't worry too much. Oh God . . .' She looked over her shoulder. 'What if I do?'

'Really, Carveth. Do calm down. Empty your mind of worry and enjoy being British. I always find that, if I'm worried, I adopt the sort of stance that a good captain would have as he surveys the bridge – chin up, legs apart. Then, when I look down at myself, I find that I have exactly the kind of solid stance and upright bearing that I would expect a good captain to have. Which means, there-fore, that I am by definition a good captain. Like this.' He opened his legs, put his hands behind his back, raised his jaw and glowered out into the void.

'You look like a warbot that's had its power cables cut,' Carveth said. 'Or like a sword-swallower who's swallowed the whole sword and is hoping it'll work itself out.'

'I'll ignore that,' he replied. 'How close are we to enemy space?'

She consulted the scanner. The green glow of the instruments made Carveth's face look even queasier than before. 'Too close. In half an hour we'll be over the border and into disputed space. And then . . . well, it's a matter of how far we can get before they rumble us.'

Smith shook his head. His hair brushed one of the model aircraft that he had brought up from the *John Pym*, to make the cockpit more professional-looking. 'We're breaking new ground here, Carveth. Going further than anyone has ever gone. You and Gerald will be like Tereshkova and her dog, Balalaika.'

'Who and who?'

'Two space explorers, hundreds of years ago. The Russians sent a woman called Tereshkova and a dog called Balalaika into space. In the early days of space exploration, people used to experiment on primitive creatures.'

'What happened to them?'

'Tereshkova was fine, but Balalaika died. Being a dog, I suppose she stuck her head out of the window.'

'Great. Boss, could you leave me with my thoughts for a bit?'

'Of course. I'll go for a walk. Clear my mind and all that.'

'It seems pretty clear as it is,' she muttered. 'Where's Rhianna?'

'She went to look at the facilities. She mentioned something about the onboard communications.'

'She'd better not be going to put whale music over the bloody comms. It's like sitting next to a squeaky floorboard.'

Smith left Carveth to it. He headed down the hallway, past the discoloured squares where posters of Ghast Number One and various human reprobates had once been hung. A large board reading 'Vigilance! Vehemence! Violence!' lay on the floor. Someone had replaced it with a nice picture of the spaceport in Leicester.

The *Egbert Tench* had previously possessed a kiosk, from which the Ghastists had purchased propaganda pamphlets and cassettes of marching music. Now it sold shoelaces and tea. Smith queued behind two commandos and a M'Lak rifleman and was sipping from his polystyrene cup when Suruk appeared, holding a brown, wrinkled object.

'Either this pasty was excessively freeze-dried, or I am eating a handbag,' the alien announced. Together, they strolled down the corridor. 'The sooner we are on the Ghast homeworld, slaying enemies, the better.'

'I suppose so. I'm rather enjoying having my own battleship, though.' Smith reached up to one of the monitors and toggled the camera switch. The hangars appeared. 'Look at those fighters: Hellfires and Tempests and Hornets, too. And we've got a hold full of warbots.'

'Pleasing.' They started down a set of steps.

A woman with a white coat and a clipboard passed them and said, 'Captain.'

'Carry on!' Smith grinned. 'I like this,' he said to Suruk.

'Indeed.' Suruk's voice dropped to a low growl. 'Listen, Mazuran . . . I overheard two soldiers of the M'Lak Rifles. One of them had heard a rumour that, now that the Ghasts are pulling back from the M'Lak Front, the outer worlds of my species are arming for total war. They have been sharpening their bladed utensils, constructing spacecraft from tractors and the like, and plan to strike at the Ghast Empire – specifically, Selenia. Although I suspect that anywhere with Ghasts in it would do.'

'That's a good thing, isn't it?'

'Truly, it would help to have them at our side. After the fighting on the M'Lak Front, they will be full of rage. I only hope that their wild fury does not inspire the space navy of my people to try to ram the sun again.' He paused, as if at a sad memory. 'But, ah, I believe your Service would want the Space Empire itself to be the cause of Number One's destruction.'

Smith paused. 'I see,' he said. 'You'd rather we did it?'

Suruk nodded. 'Between you and I, I would prefer that the victory was ours. More specifically, *mine*.'

'Well, I don't see that this changes much. I mean, we've always got to prove ourselves to our allies. Not that we have anything to prove to them, but although we don't, we may need to show them that.'

'There is wisdom in your words,' Suruk replied. 'Somewhere.'

On the wall, the intercom buzzed. Smith glanced around, surprised. On the *John Pym*, the standard method of communication was to shout down the corridor or to bang a spoon on a teacup: if something buzzed that meant that it was likely to explode.

'Hey, Isambard,' said Rhianna on the intercom. 'I've detected something big. You'd better come up and see.'

'Righto. Where are you?'

'Um . . . it's a square room, with scanners on the walls . . .'

'Sounds like Communications. I'll be there in a moment.'

Smith opened the door to the communications department and ducked under a bundle of cables that dangled from the ceiling. It was just like the *John Pym*. The engineers had done a good job of making him feel at home, or else they had finished work early.

The room was tinted green by the lidar screens on the walls. Rhianna sat in the command chair in the centre of the chamber like a queen on a throne. In place of a crown, she wore a sort of upturned colander. Wires stretched from it into the ceiling. The smell of red weed hung around the corners of the room.

So, he thought, this was what a psychic amplification rig looked like.

Rhianna opened her eyes. Slowly, as if bringing a cannon to bear, she looked in his direction and focussed upon him. 'Hi,' she said. 'I sensed something. It was like a disturbance in nature. As if a million voices all cried out at once.'

'What did they say?'

'Ak.'

'We must be getting close, then.' He turned to the scanners. 'We'll power down as much as possible, pretend that we've been too badly damaged to talk to them. If you sense anything else, buzz us on the intercom.'

'Okay,' she replied. 'Um . . . Isambard?'

'Yes?'

'Have you seen my rolling papers anywhere?'

Suruk had joined Carveth in the cockpit. As the doors hissed closed behind Smith's back, Carveth slipped something into her waistcoat.

'Carveth,' Smith said, 'is that a hip flask in your pocket?'

She shook her head. 'No, I'm just happy to see you.'

'Nonsense. You've been at the booze.'

She sighed. 'Just a little bit. I do my best flying with extra fuel on board. I always say that genius is sixty percent inspiration and forty percent proof.'

'Well, just remember to stop when you reach the planet. Actually, just before.'

'Interesting,' Suruk said. 'Truly, that is remarkable.'

Smith looked around. Suruk stood by a bank of monitors. He appeared to be consulting a small computer screen. On closer inspection, Smith realised that it was a mirror.

The radio crackled. Suruk looked up and raised his eyebrows.

'It's them,' Carveth said. Her voice was low and frightened. 'The Ghasts.'

'Put them on speaker, but leave the camera off,' he replied. 'And Suruk, when I nod, initiate the audio disruption programme. Two nods, and I want complete phase-out on the comms.'

'It shall be so.'

Tentatively, Carveth flicked the switch. A raucous, screechy voice tore out of the speakers. 'Attention minion vessel *Egbert Tench*! You have diverted from your allotted task of defeating the enemy. Explain this criminal deviation from your orders or suffer the consequences!'

Smith leaned in to the microphone. 'Hello. All hail Number One and all that. We have suffered severe damage in our battle with the British space navy. We have decided to seek repair rather than to, er . . . sacrifice ourselves in an inefficient manner.'

Carveth nodded at Smith.

The Ghast barked, 'Understood. What were the reasons for your failure to achieve victory?'

'The British ships were better, of course. Obviously. That is to say, they treacherously . . . er . . . deployed a new weapon against us.'

'And the name of this weapon?'

Smith felt his scalp begin to prickle. 'Moral fibre.'

'Explain how this "moral fibre" operates.'

'You wouldn't understand.'

'What did you say?'

Smith gestured to Suruk. Suruk took his spear from the overhead locker and dealt the radio a swift blow with the butt end.

'Sorry,' Smith said, 'you're breaking up there. Could you speak up, please?'

'We ask the questions here!' the intercom yelped.

'Alright then, what do you want to know?'

'Did you hear what I just said?'

'Not very well. We need repairs. We are coming in to get them.'

'It is not for you to make demands of your superiors. Silence!'

'Whatever you say,' Smith replied.

Suruk pulled the radio off the wall.

'Nicely done, old chap.' Smith exhaled. His heart was pounding. Talking to the enemy traffic control was almost as difficult as talking to girls. 'I think we fooled them – at least, enough for now. Are we in the Ghast Empire yet, Carveth?'

'We're in it all right,' she replied. 'Up to our necks. We've got an orbital dock coming up.'

'Is that a good thing?'

'Not really. From the scanners, I'd say it's like a service station from hell. It's exactly the kind of place where we'd be pulling up for repairs if we were on their side.'

She pressed a button and an image appeared on a monitor next to Smith's head. A space station turned slowly, displaying rows of cannons and hangar doors. A huge frieze depicting a stylised ant was plastered across the front of it, like a scarab in an Egyptian tomb.

'They'll expect us to stop here, not go on to land on Selenia,' Carveth said.

'You're right. Change our course to the orbital dock, Carveth.'

'What?' Alarm spread across her face like a rash. 'You're not seriously planning to land on that thing, are you?'

'Of course not. We're going to ram it.'

Suruk chuckled. 'An excellent plan, Mazuran. Doom comes for you, service station of evil! Their overpriced food will be paid for in blood. Long will they lament as their air fresheners and plastic sandwiches are cast into the endless void!'

Carveth appeared to be trying to swallow a snooker ball. 'Right,' she said. 'Whatever you say, boss.'

'Jolly good.' Smith looked at the image on the monitor, with its guns and insignia. 'This enemy battlestation is about to get a good deal less fully operational. Carveth . . . ramming speed!'

He leaned back in the captain's chair. It was an order that he had always wanted to give but had never had the opportunity; the *John Pym* had rammed plenty of things over the last few years, but never quite on purpose. He pulled the microphone close and opened the ship's public address system.

'Hello, everyone! This is your captain speaking.' On the internal cameras, soldiers froze and listened. A Jovian Dragoon stood still at a row of sinks, toothbrush half-raised to his mouth. One of the New Farringdon Hussars paused midway through waxing his moustache. In the mess, a Ravnavari Lancer and a Charybdian Battle-Queen stood motionless at either end of the ping-pong table, still clutching bats in their hands and tentacles. 'We're going to have a spot of turbulence up ahead, because I've set a course to ram an enemy spaceport. I hope that's not too much of a nuisance for you. All of you commando chaps, you might want to hold on to your little hats. And make sure the warbots' heads are screwed on tightly. And if you've got anything fragile out, get it stowed away. That means you, Major Wainscott. We may be in for some chop, and the last thing anyone wants is a chopped chap.'

'Not as much chop as the Ghasts,' Suruk growled. 'Soon, the hacking will be without limit. But now, let us imitate the action of the tiger, especially a metal, space-ship-shaped tiger that drives straight into things!'

Smith picked the radio up from the floor and plugged it back in. At least half a dozen voices were shouting in Ghastish. It was hard to make out individual words, but the tone was clear. They had realised that the *Egbert Tench* was coming in much too fast. 'You will cease your approach!' a voice screeched from the babble. 'That is an order from High Command!'

Smith activated the visual link. A snarling red face appeared on the comms screen: a naval-storm-colonel, by the look of his insignia. 'You said your visuals were broken,' he rasped. 'You will explain your actions immediately!'

'Very well,' Smith replied. 'Here's your explanation. I will not be changing my approach because I intend to ram you. And I will not be following any of your orders because I take no orders from an alien tyrant. I am an officer of the British Space Empire and this vessel is part of our navy. It is no longer the *Egbert Tench*, because Tench was a traitor and a coward. It is now the *Horatio Nelson*. Colours up, Carveth!'

She flicked a switch. Red, white and blue spotlights burst into life along the bow and flanks of what had been the *Egbert Tench*. The comms link played *Rule Britannia*. The aethernet projector broadcasted a visual file displaying a bulldog sitting on the back of a lion, superimposed on the Naval Ensign.

The effect was pleasing. It made a refreshing change to see a Ghast displaying something other than low cunning or mindless rage, especially because the officer's bionic eye nearly fell out of its face in shock.

Suruk leaned forward in his seat, eyes gleaming. 'It's a trap!' he cried. 'And you are in it, fools!'

'Fire torpedoes,' Smith said.

Like a shoal of piranhas preceding a shark, torpedoes burst from the front of the *Horatio Nelson*. They crashed into the front of the station as its defences flickered into life.

The station burst into spinning chunks of biotech. A second later, the *Horatio Nelson* ploughed through the debris. The radio fell onto the carpet. Pieces of whirling detritus bounced off the hull. Several praetorians spun past. A lemming man, presumably a member of some liaison team, twirled with remarkable elegance and hit the windscreen with a battleaxe. Carveth winced, but the blow had no effect. A second later, the rodent flew off to the side, and was gone.

Smith glanced at the monitor. Before them, spinning slowly, were the planets of the Ghast home system: factory worlds, garrisons, entire moons devoted to the making of those weird films where the ant-people stood in lines and shouted at things, which Smith was pretty sure were the Ghast equivalent of the copies of *Corsetry World* that he had stashed under his bed. The planets were almost perfectly aligned with the system's sun – perfectly aligned for his attack. It was like a diagram of how to do snooker tricks. One push and they would bypass the remaining defences and drive straight into Selenia.

The intercom crackled. 'Hey, Isambard. Is everything okay there? I'm sensing a lot of anger here.'

'You certainly are. We rammed the enemy defences and destroyed their space station.'

'Oh, okay. That would explain the anger.' She sounded sad. 'You know, anger can ruin your life.'

'So can getting rammed by a spaceship,' Carveth observed.

Smith raised his hand. 'Shush, pilot. This is a momentous occasion. We are the first people to break into the Ghast home-system who are neither traitors nor already dead. Men, this is not the end of the Ghast Empire—'

'Yes it is,' Suruk said. He pointed. 'We are at the end and the middle is that way.'

'No, it's a figure of speech. Let me finish and it will all make sense. You see, today is not the end of the Ghast Empire. It is not the end of the beginning. But it is the end of the beginning of the end, and now we've finished the beginning we can really get on with ending it. Any questions? I didn't think so. Carry on!'

*

'You know,' said Captain Fitzroy, 'I could have captained two battleships at once.'

She was sprawled in a massive leather armchair, her boots up on the table. The captain's private lounge seemed to have been lifted wholesale from the Folies Bergere, stopping only to steal a drinks cabinet from the Hellfire Club. The various members of the Service deputation hung back in the shadows, waiting for news from the *Horatio Nelson*.

'Nonsense,' W replied. 'Nobody could captain two dreadnoughts at the same time.' He sat bolt upright in his chair, slowly sipping a pint of Stalwart Mild and trying to fight down the nervousness he felt. Not only did the fate of the galaxy turn on Smith's mission, but the only way to get to Fitzroy's lounge was through her bedroom. He had seen the number of marks on her bedpost, which had so many notches that it looked as if it had been assailed by a gang of lumberjacks. Either Fitzroy had a vigorous private life or she had been to bed with Suruk the Slayer, which was saying much the same thing.

Fitzroy refilled her glass with gin. 'Oh, I could take it on easily. I'd be happy to have two crews under me, provided they were up to it.' She paused and leaned forward. She lowered her voice as much as she ever did. 'Look, do you ever think your trust in Smith is misplaced?'

W glared at her over his pint. 'Not at all. I have every confidence in him. One day, when this is all over, we will tell the story of our secret war against the enemies of decency: how the common people stood firm against the bastards, arseholes and idiots of the galaxy. Smith's name will be up there with the greatest of them.'

*

Lieutenant Sven ran into the Ministry of Accuracy, rifle in hand. 462 lurched in behind him as quickly as his bad leg would allow. 'What's this?' the nearest guard snarled.

'This,' 462 said, 'is a crisis. Get me Number Two at once.'

The guard's vicious eyes narrowed. 'He gives the orders round here, not you.'

'Well, tell him to get here immediately and give me some.'

The guard frowned, aware that he was somehow being deceived but unable to process the details. He prodded the intercom sulkily with a pincer.

462's soldiers entered the foyer like an invading army. They looked nothing like the huge, smart praetorians that guarded Two, sleek in their polished leather coats. The drones of Penal Legion 5937 were filthy and battered, more like robbers than soldier ants.

A heavy door swung open at the side of the room and Two hurried out. He saw his deputy and his lenses widened.

'462? What are you doing here? You're supposed to be in the comms tower, monitoring enemy broadcasts.'

'I was. Our sensors have picked up multiple battleships entering Sector One of Ghast space. The orbital barricade has been breached. Space Station Thirty-Seven, *Antennae of Vigilance*, has ceased transmitting. It has almost certainly been destroyed.'

Two nodded. 'I thought this would happen.'

'You did? Then why in the leader's name didn't you do anything about it?'

Two smiled. 'Oh, I have done. Number One, in his flaw-less genius, warned me about the possibility of a full-scale invasion when Radishia fell. So I took a little... precaution. Come, minion. We need to discuss this in the cellars. Just the two of us.'

The cellars? Is this it? 462 wondered. Had Two found out about his efforts to kill Number One and been instructed to dispose of him? *Just what I need,* he thought: *ignomini-ously polished off in the car park, chewed up and quickly spat out like an unusually large ration bar.* He made him-self smile. 'I'd be delighted. Wait here, Sven. If I don't come back soon, you know what to do.'

They stepped into the lift. The doors slid shut, and the dark little cabin began to descend.

A screen lit up beside the doors. The face of a Ghast drone appeared. As the camera pulled back, it began to sing.

> *Which is the greatest beast of them all?*
> *Chimpanzee, man, elephant?*
> *All of these mammals are destined to fall—*
> *For tomorrow belongs to the ants!*

More voices joined in.

Why bother thinking when you can obey?
Find strength in ignorance
Sharpen your pincers and get ready to slay—
For tomorrow belongs to the ants!

Who needs a culture when you have a gun
And a record of Number One's rants?
The age of the insect has just begun—
For tomorrow belongs to the ants!

'Off,' said Number Two, and the screen went black. He addressed the ceiling, as if having a religious awakening. 'You see, 462, Number One anticipated that this would happen. He has been planning this all along. Our allies have revealed themselves as weaklings. The Republic of Eden is collapsing. The Aresian tripods are tripping over themselves in their hurry to surrender. Even the lemming men have been driven back to Yullia with their tails between their legs. But nobody will be invading Selenia. Our war-fleet will take care of those idiots. And I have made a little plan of my own . . . Do you remember Batrachia Four?'

'An Anglo-M'Lak world. We annexed it six months ago, to strip the swamps for minerals.'

'Exactly. During the invasion, I captured about four hundred of the offspring of the enemy. All of them are under a year old. In the event of a human invasion, I will issue an ultimatum . . . *stand down or I start shooting.*'

462 swallowed. 'I am not sure that is a good idea.'

'Does that trouble your conscience?'

'Of course not. I would not insult our leader with such a display of weakness. But it will make the humans very angry.'

Two adjusted his helmet. 'This is a war of annihilation, 462. We must hit the enemy where it hurts. When they know that we have their young, they will hesitate long enough for us to strike a deadly counter-blow.'

The lift slid to a halt and the doors opened.

Noise greeted them: growls and yelps that made 462 wonder if a pack of ant-hounds was being kennelled down here. The ceiling was low, the walls bare biocrete. A terrible alien smell wafted up from a huge pit in the floor.

'Look,' said Two.

462 walked closer to the edge of the pit – but not too close. He glanced down, and saw chubby figures at the bottom of the hole, dozens of them. Dirty faces stared up at him: small hands were raised up.

'There's one small problem with your human shield,' 462 said. 'It's not made of humans. Those are infant M'Lak.'

Two shrugged. 'One type of enemy is much like another. Weak, all of them.'

Hundreds of tiny yellow eyes fixed on 462. Long tongues licked wide lips. Thousands of wicked little teeth gleamed. He was not sure whether they were croaking or growling.

One of the M'Lak spawn leaped at him. It couldn't jump high enough – *Not yet*, he thought – and it hit the wall and slid back down.

'My guards toss them the odd minion,' Two explained. 'They really are disgusting little creatures. They'll eat anything.'

Sometimes, 462 realised, the most complex plans weren't

the best. Sometimes, for all your scheming, you just had to accept that rising in the Ghast Empire was about seizing the moment. If you took the right action at the right time, everything would just drop into place. Literally.

'*Anything?*' he said.

'Oh yes,' said Two. 'Their lack of discrimination is indicative of their inferiority. That's what Number One would say. In fact—'

462 gave him a good shove. Two fell straight into the pit.

Two let out a single wail of terror, and then he was drowned out by the belching of the spawn. Scraps of leather coat flew up from the pit. It was a horrible death, 462 reflected, but not a lingering one. At least, the spawn in the pit didn't linger about it.

How times change, he thought. *Once, I served you obediently. And then I served you to a horde of frogs.* He grinned.

On balance, it served you right.

*

The *Horatio Nelson* rushed on further into Ghast space, closer to the enemy homeworld. But it was no longer alone: behind it, like hounds on the same scent, came the battleships of the Imperial Navy.

'Status update, pilot!' Smith called.

'Still bloody terrified,' Carveth said.

'I meant the ship.'

'Well, it's holding together, isn't it? On the good side, the rest of the fleet is following us. On the bad side, they're not following us as closely as I'd like and the entire Ghast Empire probably wants us dead by now.'

'They always did, Carveth.' Smith felt curiously content about everything. It was probably because they were finally taking the war to the enemy, he reflected. The fact that he'd broken out the navy rum probably didn't hurt either.

He glanced at the monitor. In the hold, boarding parties were arming themselves. They moved as quickly and efficiently as any Ghast, and with much less shouting. The warbots stood grim and silent, ready to be activated. In the hangars, rows of Hellfires and Tempests were being fuelled. Pilots, marines and engineers took up their positions.

'Look at them,' said Smith. 'These are the people that Number One considers weak. These are the citizens who the Ghasts plan to reap like so much corn. Well, here's a stone in your mower, Gertie. You face the elite of the Space Empire. By God, it's like a convention for circus strongmen down there. I've not seen so many large men with moustaches since that parade on New Francisco that Rhianna took us to.'

'Indeed,' said Suruk, from behind his chair. 'An imposing display of manliness. Frederick of Mercury would be impressed. And the M'Lak Rifles will be doing their share of slaying, too. Long have you hungered to kick the enlarged arse of Number One, Mazuran. I, too, have a dreadful hunger for his end. Now, Ghasts, you will reap what you have sown, assuming that you sowed some kind of enormous decapitating scythe. And who buries a scythe in the ground? An imbecile! For soon you will learn the cost of your imbecility, ant-scum, when we render your minions into tiny pieces and smother your homeworld in a vast pile of your wretched, shameful, puny skulls!'

'Ahem,' said Carveth. 'I hate to spoil the fun, but we've got incoming fighters. And missiles. And battleships.'

'How many?' said Smith.

'All of them, by the look of it.'

She flicked a switch on the keyboard.

The monitor showed the fleet's progress into Ghast space: a single arrow in the colours of the Union Jack, punching deep into enemy territory. Other arrows closed in on it from all directions, decorated with the insignia of the Workers And Soldiers Party, turning and crossing over one another, creeping across the screen towards the Imperial fleet.

'Looks like Number One thinks he can stop us,' Carveth said.

'Who does he think he's kidding?' Smith replied. He pulled down the intercom. 'Attention fighter wing. This is the captain speaking. We have bandits incoming from all sides. Scramble all fighters – I repeat, scramble all fighters. Give them hell, chaps!'

*

462 hurried back upstairs. In the office, he tore a length of string from one of the spare banners and attached it to an empty can of Vio-Lent Green. His hands were shaking. He didn't have long.

He returned to the basement. With great care, he sank down onto one knee, his bad leg sticking out to the side. Leaning out, 462 lowered the can into the pit. The M'Lak spawn seemed to be resting. The can bumped gently on the sludge at the bottom.

Very carefully, 462 moved the can around. Two metal objects glinted in the gunk. The can swallowed them up. He reeled it back in and tipped the items into his palm. They were the mechanical eyes of Number Two. He left the string hanging down into the pit, so that the spawn could climb out. For a moment he wondered why, and then he realised that their fangs and their savage hunger reminded him of Assault Unit One.

Two's office safe had an iris lock. The artificial eyes opened it. 462 pulled out a wad of documents, including a file with his own picture on the front. He opened it, saw the words 'Questionable loyalty' and stuffed it into his coat. Then he grabbed Two's identity cards and hurried outside.

Sven drove the staff hovercar while 462 barked directions from the back. The car swung into the outer confines of the Leaderhive, and half a dozen praetorians ran out to meet it. 462 wound down the window and held out his credentials. 'I need Number One. I'm on urgent business from Number Two.'

An honour guard of bio-tanks flanked the hovercar, shoving and occasionally shooting other traffic off the road. They stopped outside a bio-engineered fortress. It looked like a cross between the Collosseum and a whelk shell. The praetorians hurried 462 up the stairs, under the gaze of rows of massive statues, and into a rear chamber. His gun was pulled out of its holster, his face pushed against a scarcode reader and he was shoved through a doorway, into a tiny room.

There was a desk, a chair and a big mirror. Half a dozen officers stood around the desk, trying not to be noticed. A sign on the desk read, in Ghastish script, *You don't have to be mad to work here, but it helps.* The creature behind the desk was eating cake.

'All hail glorious Number One!' 462 exclaimed.

Number One looked up. 'Who are you?' he croaked. 'Who are you to interrupt me? Who, I demand, dares to interrupt the cake of the lord and master of the entire galaxy?' He shook his fork at 462. Bits of semi-chewed sponge spattered 462's lapels.

I could kill him now. A pincer to the throat would do it. But I would be dead before he hit the ground. 'I'm 462.'

'Oh, you. Where is your master?'

'There was an accident concerning Number Two. It was messy.'

The officers drew back against the wall until they resembled a row of coats on hooks. Number One put his fork down. In the frightened silence of the little room, it sounded like a gong being struck. He shuddered violently, lifted his hand and pushed his antennae across his scalp. '462 stays. The rest of you leave.'

The minor stampede nearly pushed 462 straight back out the doors. The flurry of bootsteps died away down the corridor. A troll-like praetorian leaned in and closed the door. Only 462 and the glorious leader remained.

Number One smiled through a thick rime of icing. It looked as if his face was cracking in the sun. 'Did you kill Number Two?'

'Of course not, great leader. He was—'

'Do not lie to me, 462! I see through you. I see right to the centre of you.'

Deep in Number One's face, two bitter little eyes glared out at 462. They had all the kindness and pity of candle-flames, as if a rat was driving the leader from inside his skull.

'You do?' 462 swallowed hard. 'I – really?'

'Oh yes.'

The game was up. It didn't matter that the guards outside the door would kill him the moment he took his revenge. 'You shot my dog.'

'Yes,' said One. 'I did. And it clearly was a good lesson to you. Let the strong survive, and the weak fall by the wayside, eh? You murdered Two to get close to me. And do you know why? I will tell you. Because you wanted to admire my genius, my perfection, my un-mit-i-gated bril-li-ance from up close!'

'Oh,' said 462. He blinked, confused, all thoughts of murder gone. 'I mean yes, of course. Look, we've got a problem. The British fleet has entered this solar system.'

Number One gave a tiny nod. 'Good. Then my plan is working. We will bring them close, and destroy them.'

'Listen to me, please.' 462 leaned close. 'They have punched through our outer defences. They are coming with an armada of dreadnoughts to destroy us.'

Number One twitched. His shoulders shook. A smirk crept across his face. 'Those things? Human beings? You are talking about our new source of nutrition, 462. Does one fear one's dinner? Or, I ask you, does one consume it?'

'No! No. Listen, please.' 462 wanted to yell, to slap this

idiot in the face: for once, he forced his voice down. 'These are the people who destroyed the lemming men. Remember the lemming men, who take no prisoners and never give in, who had no word for "retreat"? Them. We're facing the same people who destroyed the Edenites and assassinated Number Eight, the pinnacle of the praetorian breeding programme. And they hate us, Number One. They absolutely despise us. They won't ever stop.'

'You worry too much,' said Number One. 'This fear, this timidity, this unreasoning terror is un-be-coming of an officer of the Ghast Empire. Come. Let me put your fears to rest. Praetorian!'

A guard opened the door. Numbly, 462 realised that his chance to assassinate One had gone.

He followed the glorious leader down the corridor. They crammed themselves into a lift with two immense bodyguards, and sank into the earth.

Doors slid open. They were in a laboratory. Half a dozen white-coated drones from the Science Division jerked to attention.

A huge metal figure lay on a table. It was humanoid but misshapen, even by the wretched standards of mankind.

'This is a robot,' One said helpfully. 'A soldier constructed artificially, like a primitive attempt to emulate the tanks in which we grow our own fearsome battalions.'

'I know, great leader.'

'Observe.' Number One gestured to a Science Division officer. The officer stepped forward and leaned over the robot's chest. Its gloved fingers worked quickly. The scientist emitted an evil snigger and lifted the robot's front armour away. The armour plate clattered onto the floor.

A piece of paper lay wedged behind the armour. One reached in and pulled it out. 'Three weeks ago, 462, this robot was found near a crashed British shuttlecraft. It had clearly failed to land correctly and thus destroyed itself. We inspected the wreckage and found this message on its body.'

He unfolded the paper. 462 saw writing, but could not make out the individual words. Number One held it up to the light.

'*Dear wife,*' One read. '*I am writing to you in secret. I have been forbidden to say anything, but I know that to fight the Ghasts is certain death, so I must tell you the truth.*' One lowered the paper. 'You see, 462? To fight us is certain death. You can tell that this robot knew what it was talking about.'

'Right . . .' said 462.

'Ahem. *Beloved mecha-spouse, I have been entrusted with a mission that we hope may even outwit Ghast Number One. He is a genius and the greatest leader in galactic history, so our chances are slim. We will land a ship on the ash plains of Selenia as a distraction. When the enemy detects our landing, he will send his forces in such numbers that the Ghast cities on the far side of the planet will be unprotected. Then we will make our attempt to invade, while Number One's mighty armies are distracted by our decoy landing. Please destroy this letter so it cannot fall into the pincers of that terrifying mastermind Number One. Farewell, robot wife, and bid our children goodbye.*'

462 looked away. He looked across the room at the technicians, who had drawn back out of range. He took a deep breath.

'Speechless, eh?' said Number One.

'I don't know where to start. Truly, I don't.' 462 swallowed. 'Just one small thing, glorious leader. I have studied the enemy very closely, to better understand how to defeat them, and I don't honestly recall any robots having wives before.'

'Oh really? Then, if the letter was not truly written to the robot's wife, why did the robot keep a picture of her in its wallet?' One unclipped a small photograph from the back of the letter and held it out. 'Note the wife's multiple legs and dual upper slots, presumably for communication.'

462 took the picture. 'Not that I would dream of questioning your obviously flawless judgment, but this looks suspiciously like a toaster on a metal trolley. It is a machine for warming bread, not a wife. Glorious leader, have you shown this letter to anyone else?'

One shuddered. 'Of course not. Why would I need to?'

They knew you wouldn't. You're too arrogant. 'I need to go and instruct my minions to follow your brilliant plan,' 462 said.

'Naturally.' Number One smiled. 'You've got potential, 462. You could make a very good minion for me.'

Sven drove 462 back to the Ministry of Accuracy. 462 rummaged through Number Two's files on the way. He hurried to the communications suite and dialled a coded number.

A voice at the end of the line said, 'What is it?'

'This is High Command. You'll have received an order from Number One telling you to deploy on the far side of Selenia. Cancel that. Redeploy our forces to the ash plains. Tell them to expect an invasion.'

The voice said, 'That will take a while. I hope you realise what you're asking for.'

'Of course I do. I'll take full personal responsibility. It's Five, Number Five.' He hung up.

*

The *Horatio Nelson* ploughed through Ghast Space like a drill through muck, followed by a pack of Imperial fighters. A cloud of bio-missiles rushed in and were cut down by the *Nelson's* defence lasers or sent spinning into the ether, bewildered by chaff ejected by the ship's new counter-measures boxes. They saw their first enemy warship, a Ghast light cruiser, appear at the edge of the viewscreen, arming itself to attack. Moments later a squadron of Tempest fighters blew it apart.

In the middle of the screen, Selenia was growing. It looked like the Moon, only much bigger, and the grey colour came not from rock but dirt. The sensors picked up a Selenian transmission: on the screen, Number One waved his arms at a map of Earth and screamed some evil gibberish about monthly calorie yields.

Lasers and missiles flared around them. The fighters did rapid and deadly work. The ruins of enemy space-craft rolled like dead whales, little bursts of flame showing where they had been torn open. Something's engines burst on the right and the shockwave rocked the hull. Carveth pulled her goggles down and they drove onwards.

A voice came over the radio. '*Human scum!*' it screeched, '*you will surrender immediately or*—'

Smith reached for the intercom, but Suruk got there

first. 'Wrong!' the alien shouted. 'We are coming for you, insect. Now it is *your* empire that will be hunted – your planets, your cities, your soldiers and your heads! I believe that covers it,' he added.

'I think that's about right,' Smith said.

'Tell them that they're dickheads, too,' Carveth said.

Smith got up and put his hand on the back of his chair. 'Look at it, chaps. Ours for the taking. Only several trillion ant-people between us and certain victory.'

'The head of the beast,' Suruk observed.

'True,' Smith replied, 'and we will have the privilege of mounting it. Are we within missile range, Carveth? Because I want to be the first person to blow a hole in their rotten planet.'

'Soon,' she said. 'We're about to hit their atmosphere.'

The screen glowed. Fire lapped around the nose of the ship. The *Horatio Nelson* started to rattle.

Smith toggled the intercom. 'Two minutes, landing party.'

'Roger!' Wainscott barked back. 'Two minutes, Susan. Someone crank up the warbots.'

Carveth said, 'You do realise that a warship of this size isn't designed for landing on planets, don't you?'

'Of course,' Smith replied. 'But the Ghasts don't. Element of surprise and all that.'

The flames raged around the cockpit – then they parted suddenly. The windscreen looked over a landscape stripped and ruined by industry, lit by a sickly red sun. Spindly towers dotted the horizon. Smoke poured from holes in the ground. Bio-chimneys like calcified windpipes belched green fire into the polluted air. Smith had expected more cities: the surface of Selenia was as much a wasteland as a fortress.

'Mordor,' Rhianna said.

Smith glanced around. He hadn't heard her come in. She still wore her psychic amplification gear, which made her look like a ghost in a tin helmet. 'What ho,' Smith said. 'Shouldn't you be plugged in?'

'I'm trailing an extension lead,' she explained. 'What a negative place. I expect us to see the eye of Sauron any minute.'

'I hope we do,' Smith said, 'because we'll be putting the fist of civilisation right into it. Carveth, we need to set down. How about next to that mountain?'

'That's not a mountain,' she replied. 'That's a statue.'

Good God, he thought. Carveth was right. A gigantic statue of Number One loomed out of the dirty clouds like a giant coming to fight them. Number One had been rendered in absurdly heroic proportions, his sloping shoulders squared off and his beady, vicious eyes fixed on the horizon. He shook his fist at the heavens, his pincer-arms rising behind his back like the spindly wings of a demon.

'Right, you little bugger,' Smith said. 'Carveth, blow his head off and ram whatever's left.'

She pulled a lever, and half a dozen rockets burst from the front array.

'Keep close behind,' Smith ordered. 'I want to see them hit him in his arrogant chops.'

'I'll try,' she said, wrestling with the joystick, 'but manoeuvring this thing isn't easy.'

The rockets smashed into the statue's head. A cloud of

dust billowed from the point of impact. 'There's one in the eye for you, Gertie!' Smith exclaimed.

'I can't see—' Carveth cried. 'Oh my God – brace, brace!'

The statue's snarling face broke through the dust as if to swallow them whole. The *Horatio Nelson* slammed into the middle of it. The impact hurled Smith onto the ground. Carveth flopped back in her chair. Rhianna landed beside Smith. Slowly, she righted herself and adjusted her colander.

Smith heaved himself upright. He stumbled to the monitor and toggled the controls. Down below, the commando teams were still strapped in. Wainscott leaned into the monitor and gave him a thumbs up. Smith brought up the ship's status on the screen.

The *Horatio Nelson* stuck out of the front of Number One's head like a monstrous nose. Number One had the distinction of being the only person in galactic history who looked better after having a spaceship crash into their face.

'We're stuck,' Smith said. 'That's not good.'

'It's about to get much worse,' Carveth replied. 'There's serious seismic activity going on directly beneath us.'

'Good God. You don't mean that Number One's nostrils are about to blow?'

'Polly's right,' Rhianna said. 'Can you sense that? Something's coming from below. That's a statue, but it's full of lava.'

The cockpit shuddered. Slowly, Smith heard what Rhianna had sensed: cracking. Outside the hull, the monstrous head of the statue was falling apart.

'Thrusters,' he cried, 'now!'

The *Horatio Nelson* roared. The decking shook under Smith's boots. A terrible shrieking of metal came from the walls, as though an army of spirits was trying to scratch its way in. The ship rumbled – and tore free. Below it, Number One's head fell apart. The statue had been hollow; it must have served as some kind of venting for the facilities below ground. The snarling face cracked and collapsed, and superheated steam blasted up from within.

'He always was full of hot air,' Smith observed. 'See what I did th—'

The ship lurched. Smith staggered.

'Hah!' Suruk cried. 'His pestilential face bursts like a craven zit. Let the fingers of our rage close around the bulging head of – actually, I am not entirely happy with this metaphor. Let's just attack.'

Pieces of rock crashed and broke on the plain below. The ground fell in beneath them. Great caverns were exposed: Smith glimpsed rows of tanks, growth pods and personnel carriers lined up by the hundred.

'My God,' he gasped, 'they were underground! The Ghasts have been living underground all this time, like – oh, like ants. I suppose I shouldn't be surprised, really, but, well – bugger it, let's get 'em!' He toggled the intercom. 'Release the attack pods! Drop the warbots! The invasion starts here!'

*

The landing barges hit the surface of Selenia. Several punched straight through, down into the catecombs below.

Ramps flopped open and the Empire's finest rushed out.

The drawbridge fell down and Wainscott bellowed 'Forward, Susan!' She hit the accelerator and the battle-wagon tore out of the landing craft. They rolled over a slope of rubble, down into an underground hangar. Alien ships loomed out of the darkness like missiles in a launcher. Wainscott grinned and fired up the bonnet-mounted laser. The beam sliced the landing gear off a fighter and bisected several maintenance Ghasts. A hose thrashed like a wounded snake. Sparks raged across the nosecone of a subspace attack shuttle. Wainscott cheered.

'Faster, Susan! More lasers! More explosions! More nudity!'

*

'Let's go, chaps,' Smith said. The *Horatio Nelson* lay on a shelf of rock, swathed in a cloud of swirling dirt. It seemed to have come to a standstill – at least, for now.

'We're getting out of this awful ship?' Carveth said. 'Thank God for that.' She glanced at the window as she climbed out of her chair. 'I've not experienced a drop that rough since—'

Smith raised a hand. 'Is this going to involve curry, Carveth?'

'Beans, actually.'

'Well, don't. I don't want our landing soiled by your dirty bean stories. If I wanted to hear lavatorial anecdotes, I'd have – well, I'd have lived on the same spaceship as you for four years. That said, your enthusiasm to get cracking does you credit. Let's go!'

'Wait a minute! We're not going *outside*, are we? I thought we were getting back in the *John Pym*!'

'Of course we're going outside. This planet is ours now. It's time to civilise its wretched inhabitants.'

He opened the weapons locker and took out his rifle. Suruk collected his spear. Rhianna helped Carveth into the Maxim cannon and looked for her shoes.

Smith led his men into the corridor. 'I can't go out there!' Carveth protested. 'I don't have my lunchbox. I'm allergic to gunfire. Can't someone else storm this horrible planet full of monsters?'

At the airlock, a dozen warbots were readying themselves to disembark. The nearest warbot swung its head towards Smith. Its lower jaw jutted out like a battering ram. It raised one of its metal hands and saluted. 'Outside terrain has been recognised as Category 1B – landing ground. All surrender protocols deleted.' Its voice was a low growl, at once calm and menacing. The warbot slapped a magazine the size of a manhole cover into the underside of its gun. 'Commencing victory acquisition.'

'Jolly good,' said Smith. 'Warbots, your fighting spirit and emotionless demeanour is an example to us all.' Smith reached to the door controls. 'Anyone want to say anything?'

'Next year,' Carveth replied, 'let's just go to Benidorm Prime instead.'

Smith pulled the lever.

Part Three

Selenia: Homeworld of the Ghasts and capital planet of the Ghast Empire
Population: Unknown, estimated in the trillions and rising
Alien Natives: Many
Principal Land Use: Barracks, defences, statues of Number One
System of Government: Dictatorship
Principal Export: Tyranny and evil

Encyclopaedia Imperialis, Volume 39 (Rhubarb
– Spiffing)

Abducted by Humans!

The first few hours had been fine, if you liked that sort of thing – which Carveth didn't. Ships began to land to reinforce the beachhead captured by the *Horatio Nelson*. Vehicles dropped out of loading-ramps and whole regiments jogged out from their shuttles. Commando units, led by the Deepspace Operations Group, finished securing the area. 'Securing' a location, Carveth now knew, meant trashing it to the point where the Ghasts not only wouldn't be able to recapture it, but probably wouldn't have wanted to, either. A huge machine rolled around the perimeter of the landing zone like a cross between a robot lawnmower and an incontinent rabbit, and a long sausage of grey putty, six feet across fell out of the back of it. The putty hardened into ferrocrete. It was clever, but Carveth didn't want to touch the stuff.

And then, just as she was reaching for the biscuit tin, the counter-attack came. Ghasts swarmed up from below. Bio-tanks rose up on their hover-jets, and the air was thick with fighter ships and gunfire. As the battle raged overhead, Carveth fired up the engines of the *John Pym*, which Smith and Suruk thought was very brave until they realised that she intended to fly away rather than join in. A legion of praetorians called Murder All Humans hurled itself at the barricades and the soldier ants were thrown back by the thousand, except where the barricades hadn't quite dried and they just stuck there, as if on giant flypaper.

At last it finished, and Carveth emerged from under the table and took the biscuit tin off her head. The ground around the landing zone was littered with dead aliens and smouldering lumps of biotech. The prisoners were rounded up or peeled off the wall, as appropriate, and sent up to orbit. Sector Command retained a few Ghast drones and put them to work flattening the ground to make a cricket pitch. Carveth found herself wishing that she was an earlier model android, and could just wipe the last few hours from her memory banks. Instead, she made herself a large gin and tonic. With any luck, that would have much the same effect.

*

Everything was going rather well, Smith thought.

Rhianna had crossed to the other side of the compound to talk to the psychic division – strangely, she seemed to have to be standing next to them to do it. Sedderik the Helmsman had been joined by a deputation from the Vorl; ghostly, insubstantial beings made of pure mental energy. Earlier that evening, Smith had tried to strike up a friendly conversation with one of the Vorl while it was crossing the perimeter, but it had turned out to be a large piece of tumbleweed.

Suruk was indoors, boxing up some of the lesser skulls in his collection to make room for the vast ossuary that he had planned to bring back from the Ghast homeworld, and Smith and Carveth sat on deckchairs outside the *John Pym*, watching a platoon of Martian Highlanders setting up camp.

Smith leaned back in his deckchair and sipped his gin and tonic. 'Funny things, kilts,' Smith observed. 'I don't see why they wear them over their spacesuits like that.'

Carveth sipped her gin. 'They probably don't fit down the legs. Spacesuits really don't go well with highland dress. I suppose it helps with identification, too. If I saw a chap in a spacesuit with a multi-limbed blob stuck to his face, making horrible noises, I'd assume it was some kind of a parasite. But it there's tartan involved, you know it's just the bagpipes.'

'True,' said Smith. 'Funny, isn't it? I've never thought that the war would end. But now we're on the Ghast home-world, victory may be in sight. What will you do when the war's over?'

'If I survive? I don't know. Peace frightens me almost as much as war. I worry that by the time I've sobered up after celebrating the end of this war, the next one will have started and I'll miss the good stuff in between. But we could go out on the town, all of us. How about the cinema? There's a film with ponies in it. It's called *Animal Farm 2 – All Animals Are Sequel*.'

'Carveth, what is it with ponies and you? You're virtually obsessed with the things. Your pen-pal is a talking space horse. I don't really understand what you see in all this pony stuff.'

She shrugged. 'Well, either you like ponies or you don't. There's no sitting on the fence. Except in dressage, of course. You get bonus points for that.'

Suruk appeared at the door of the *John Pym*, brandishing a feather duster and wearing the apron that he favoured when polishing his skull collection. 'Mazuran, the phone is calling for you.'

'Ah,' Smith said, getting up. 'That'll be High Command to congratulate us for being the first ship on Selenia.'

'Actually, it is the curry house,' Suruk replied.

Puzzled, Smith hurried up the steps. His memory, and his stomach, told him that he hadn't eaten strong curry for a long time, at least three days. He ducked into the cockpit and picked up the intercom. 'Hello?'

'Smith.' A pinched, hard voice rasped out of the speaker, at once soft and unpleasant on the ear. 'We meet again.'

Smith frowned. It was not the accent that he had expected. 'Who is this? The line's terrible: it's making you sound like a Ghast.'

'I am a Ghast. I am 462.'

'You? What the devil do you want? And why are you in a curry house? I thought it was poisonous to you lot?'

'I am not in some weak human eating establishment. That was a cunning ruse. You disappointed me on Radishia, Smith. Both you and Number One are still alive.'

The telephone hissed. 462 faded out, and a new, human, voice inquired 'Hello? Did you want a starter?' It faded out, and 462's ugly voice replaced it.

'Smith? Do you hear me?'

'I hear you, 462. How did you get this number?'

'It was easy. When you departed from Radishia, you left several items in your locker at the stadium. They included the business card for something called A Taste of India. I rang them and used a bio-scanner to hack their list of frequent contacts. Then it was simply a matter of telephoning everyone they had ever served called Smith.'

'That can't have been quick.'

'Your name was at the top of their list.'

'That figures, I suppose.'

'Hello?' the third voice said. 'Can I take your order?'

'Silence!' 462 barked. 'You will receive orders when your commanding officer permits it! Leave this line at once! Now, where was I? Ah yes. Things are coming to a head, Smith. You failed to kill Number One, but he could still be yours. But I need your full co-operation. Either you will have the full glory of destroying Number One, or you will have none.'

'Plain or garlic, sir?'

'Not you! I'm talking to Smith. Now, listen. Number One is well-defended. He is always accompanied by his personal bodyguards, the Pincers of Death. They are heavily armed, with access to the new AV-943 and 945 tanks, which you humans call Ant Lions and King Prawns—'

'Rice with that, sir?'

462 made an inarticulate scraping sound. 'How do you humans tolerate such gross inefficiency?'

Smith raised his voice. 'Look here, 462. Just speak your piece and get off the line. The signal is terrible and this whole business is making me hungry.'

'Listen,' said 462. 'Meet me tomorrow, at noon local time in Formican Square. Bring nobody with you and tell no one about this. You will be able to recognise me because I will be carrying a rolled-up copy of The Daily Informer in my left pincer.'

'And you'll be a giant ant with a limp and a metal eye. Where is this square?'

'You will come to co-ordinates 60, 48, Continent Four.'

'Sorry, sir,' said the voice. 'We don't deliver there.'

462 hung up.

'What a rude bloke,' said the man. 'You'd think he was one of those ant-people, carrying on like that.'

*

Smith strode out of the *John Pym* and across the landing pad. A wing of Hellfires roared overhead, followed by a trio of assault ships, taking the fight to the enemy. He stopped to put ten pence into the slot on the front of a wallahbot, and looked away politely while it dispensed him a cup of tea and deposited two biscuits on a paper plate. Then he headed to the large shuttle parked on the far side of the base.

A sign over the door read *Unimportant Bureaucracy*. Smith hurried up the steps.

The hold was large and echoing. Sedderik's tank was parked against the side wall. The shutters were closed. Presumably Sedderik was elsewhere.

In one corner of the metal cavern, from the look of it, a merchant had set up an 'exotic' bazaar: swathes of coloured cloth adorned the walls and the floor was strewn with cushions. Rhianna was stretched out on the cushions in something that seemed to have started off as a skirt and become trousers at the last minute. Her eyes were closed.

'Hullo there,' Smith announced. 'Doing psychic stuff?'

Her eyes opened. 'Hey, Isambard. I was just doing my mental exercises. My powers will be needed soon. They say that a beginning is a very delicate time.'

'Ah, I see. Best not cock it up, eh?'

'Yeah. Why don't you sit down?'

Smith lowered himself onto the ground. Being male, he threw the cushions out of the way, and ended up sitting on the bare floor. He had once been to a restaurant where you had to sit on the floor, but that was only because Suruk had smashed the chairs following a dispute about the starter.

'So,' he said, 'how's things in the psychic world?'

Rhianna shrugged. 'Better than you might think. Better than you *do* think, now I come to think about it.'

Smith's head began to hurt. He assumed that this was part of her powers.

'I'm just glad that people are taking my abilities seriously,' she said. 'I get so sick of being asked if I can bend spoons. It's really oppressive.'

'Can you see the future yet?'

She frowned. 'Mmm,' she said, 'I know that something good is going to happen. I don't know when. But I'm getting better at controlling my abilities. I'll be able to look into the future soon. At least, I think so. I'm not sure . . . because I can't look into the future yet. Trying gives me a migrane.'

'Me too. Look, Rhianna, I'm aware that I've not seen much of you recently, or not as much of you as I'd like. When the war is over, would you like to stay with me, er, permanently?'

She thought about it. 'Um, okay.'

'Great.' He sat there, confronted by the familiar problem of wanting to initiate physical contact but not knowing how to do it. Simply lunging at her would be wrong, and anything else would make manoeuvring a dreadnought through an asteroid belt look natural and effortless. He reached out and put his hand over hers, then whipped it back as a sharp pain ran through his palm.

'Sorry,' Rhianna said, transferring her roll-up to her other hand.

'I know you're not supposed to say that women look good because it makes them seem stupid or something,' he said, aware of Rhianna's knowledge of feminism, 'but you're looking jolly super in those trousers or whatever they are. Like Sinbad. No, the other chap. Scheherazade.'

'Well,' Rhianna said, 'normally, you look like a colonialist oppressor, but in the right conditions I tend to think you look like a spare member of Sergeant Pepper's band.' She took a long drag on her roll-up, and kissed him.

Clearly, Smith thought, these were the right conditions. Unfortunately, she had forgotten to exhale first, and so the next few seconds were rather confused, but Smith had never known a coughing fit to be so erotic. She really was very lovely, he thought, as they got down to business. He just hoped that he was good enough for her. He even remembered not to say 'Boobs!' when they appeared. It was jolly good.

*

Smith got up early the next day – or at least the clock said that he had. Selenia always looked the same, no matter the time of day: a worn out ashtray of a planet, swathed in orange fog. On the horizon something – hopefully a Ghast stronghold – was on fire. It was strange how almost every planet ruled by a dictator ended up as a polluted dump. After eating all the plant and animal life on their home planet, the Ghasts had turned their homeworld into a wasteland. Rhianna would have called it a callous attack on Gaia, spirit of nature; to Smith, it was more like not bothering to differentiate between your lavatory and your kitchen sink.

He washed and dressed, then took a piece of paper and wrote on it:

Going to top-secret rendezvous with No.462 to find out how to bag No.1. If betrayed and killed, carry on. Carveth, I hid the custard creams on top of the wardrobe. Ask Suruk to help you up.
Smith.

He paused, feeling that something was missing.

X

He took one of Suruk's drawings from the fridge door and used the magnets to attach his note. Then he buckled on his sword and Civiliser, threw on his coat and crept to the airlock, impressed by his ability not to wake his crew.

He opened the door, climbed down the steps and sat down to fasten his boots.

Looking up, Smith saw that Suruk, Rhianna and Carveth were standing in front of him. 'Hello,' he said. 'What're you doing here?'

'You said you were going alone to this rendezvous,' Rhianna said. 'We thought you might need some help.'

He stood up. 'It's good of you to offer, but I've got to go alone.'

Carveth shook her head. 'Don't worry. If we see any trouble, I'll make myself scarce.'

Suruk chuckled. 'The fools will never see us coming.'

'Look,' Smith said, 'I really don't need any help, chaps. In fact, I don't know where you've got the idea that I do.'

'I read your mind when we were together,' Rhianna said. 'And you've tucked your coat into the back of your trousers.'

'You read my mind?' he said, pulling his coat free. He decided not to mention the trousers. 'That's not on. You can't go around reading people's minds.'

'It was hard not to,' she replied. 'You were scared, and it was all in big letters.'

'I'm not scared,' he replied. 'A British officer never is – especially not in front of his crew. At Space Fleet Academy they taught me that emotion is like disease – get it in the open and it'll probably spread. Nevertheless, thanks, chaps.'

'Fig roll, Mazuran?' Suruk asked, holding out a carton.

'Excellent.' Far off to the west, veiled by a swirling cloud of orange crud, a gigantic propaganda screen flickered into life. For three seconds Number One shook his little fists at the sky. A rocket hit the middle of the screen, and the image died. Strange, Smith thought, that even with the biggest army in the galaxy, Number One still seemed runty and neurotic. He made Carveth look like Lancelot.

'Well,' Smith said, 'let's get cracking.'

*

They walked all morning. Smith could tell that his crew

meant business: Carveth went for several hours before asking if they were there yet and Rhianna was wearing shoes. She even read the map.

They began to see traces of the enemy. Suruk slashed through a roll of biowire and they slipped through the gap. The fingers of a metal hand stuck up through the ground. Smith crouched down and pushed at the dead earth. Beneath the surface, a hideous face gurned up at him like an iron skull.

'What is it?' Carveth asked.

'A statue of a Ghast. I don't recognise him. It must be a minion who fell out of favour. They hide all their statues when that happens.'

'He fell from disgrace,' Suruk observed.

Carveth squinted into the distance. 'Very funny. You should be a wit like Coward or Wilde.'

Suruk shielded his eyes with his hand. 'Wilde sounds good. Coward, less so.'

'Those are names, not titles.'

'Hmm. Are you sure?'

'As in certain, or George Bernard? And where are we, by the way?'

'We're going over there,' Rhianna said. She pointed.

'All right,' Smith said. 'That looks like the spot. Radio silence from here on, chaps, even when it's time for *The Archers*.'

Twenty yards on, and Suruk made a quick chopping gesture with his hand. Smith stopped and ducked down. Carveth followed suit in a clatter of armour and, seeing that Rhianna hadn't noticed, Smith caught her eye and gestured. She dropped neatly into the lotus position.

Smith crept over to Suruk's side. Further up, the skeletons of two Ghasts lay on the bare earth, washed by the sand.

'Stay here,' Smith said. 'I'll go and look. And keep out of sight.'

'Understood, Mazuran. If I see any enemy, I shall hoot like an owl.'

'Right,' Carveth said, 'because I'm sure this place is just full of them.'

Suruk glared at her. 'Can you think of a more suitable bird, then?'

'How about a vulture?'

Smith crept forward. The ground opened up before him and he found himself crouching on the steep edge of a pit. The pit was about fifty yards across and ten deep. It contained the ruins of a small military base: rooms had been dug into the rock and sandbags thrown up around disruptor guns. In the centre stood a massive, semibiological thing that could have been a gun emplacement or a wad of chimneys, but which looked like four enormous black candles glued together and allowed to melt.

The Royal Space Fleet had bombed the emplacement; the ground was charred and strewn with broken alien technology. Half a banner dangled from one of the walls and the propaganda posters were striped with soot, as if Number One was behind the bars of a prison cell. A few dead Ghasts lay at the bottom of the pit. Smith crept to the ramp at the edge and descended.

It looked deserted. It could have been packed with enemy, just out of view. He wondered if Suruk had the same feeling of being watched.

Smith walked across the floor of the pit, to the machine in the centre.

'Smith,' a voice rasped. 'Is that you?'

'It's me, 462.' He walked around the edge of the machine. The Ghast sat on a ridge protruding from the main bodywork, his coat pulled around him like the wings of a damaged bat. A Ghast newspaper was jammed under his arm. He held what looked like a cross between a doner kebab and a shoelace. He was chewing.

'So,' said 462. 'Here we are. Enjoying the view?'

'It probably looked worse before the Royal Space Force blew it up.'

462 held up the strip. 'Minion jerky? I hear it ranks about equal with your own tinned Sham. You can start on the end I haven't chewed yet.'

'No, thank you. Let's get down to business.'

'As you wish. Number One is an idiot. He claims to have a grand plan to defeat the British Space Empire. Having seen the quality of his other grand plans, I anticipate that it will be about as much use as an anvil in a parachute jump.

'I have pulled some useful information out of Number Two's archive. As you would expect, Number One fears for his miserable life. In order to reduce the risk to himself, he moves around, giving his orders via bioscreens. He travels via a network of underground railways. In two days' time, he will be at Hive 21, approximately a hundred miles from here.' 462 raised a pincer and pointed. 'That way. He will give orders from there for around a day, local time, then he will move on to the next zone. Even I don't know where he will go after that. His schedule is irregular.'

Smith looked down at his old enemy. 'So how do you know he's going there at all?'

462 smiled and rubbed his antennae together. 'We Ghasts have a fondness for sugar. Most of us have to make do with sucrose solution, but Number One is particularly fond of icing. He has been known to have all the calendars in the Ghast Empire rewritten just so he can eat his birthday cake a month early. Three days ago, a department of the Catering Corps took up occupation in the bunker under Hive 21. They brought with them the equipment to make a very sizeable cake, along with a high-ranking human advisor.'

'A chef?'

'Oh no. The advisor went into the cake.'

'Like a showgirl, you mean?'

'Like an ingredient.' 462 grinned.

'I see. So, in two days, we break into this train line and find Number One in it. And then we bag him.'

'Exactly.' 462 put the strip of jerky into his mouth, clamped his teeth shut and shook his head like a terrier killing a rat. A length tore free. 462 looked up and swallowed it like a gannet. 'Sure you don't want some?'

A shot rang out. The top of the jerky burst.

Smith grabbed 462, hurled him to the ground and dragged him behind the broken machinery. Smith drew the Civiliser and pressed it to 462's scarred jaw. They crouched in the shadow, surrounded by silence.

'You set me up,' said Smith.

'No I didn't. If wanted you killed, Smith, you would be dead by now.'

'No, if I wanted you killed, it would be *you* who would be dead.'

'You are both dead!' a voice roared. Smith whipped around. It came from above the rim of the pit: an amplified growl like the wrath of God. 462 lurched upright and drew his pistol.

The voice bellowed, 'British meat-thing Isambard Smith, Storm-Assault-Commander 462, you are enemies of the Ghast Empire and are to be destroyed. You are surrounded. 462, you are hereby charged and convicted with treason against glorious Number One. The sentence is death. You may now amuse us by pleading for mercy.'

Nobody said anything. On the edge of the crater, just out of view, there came the clatter and rattle of Ghasts preparing to fight: engines, running feet, weapons being checked and loaded.

'When I give the word, 462, run to the ramp,' Smith said. 'My people are up top.'

'You brought your minions with you? I told you to come alone! On the other hand, I also brought mine. Sven!' 462 barked. 'Prepare to defend us.'

Slowly, almost shyly, faces appeared at the windows: red, noseless, ugly faces under dented helmets. They were drones, Smith saw, but meaner and tougher-looking than most, their coats patched and weighed down with extra pockets and stitched-on slabs of armour.

'Remember, 462,' Smith said, 'one false move and you'll regret the day you came out of some weird machine's arse. Ready? Then let's go!'

They stepped into the open. Smith saw a massive figure at the edge of the pit. It snarled and pulled up a disruptor rifle. Smith fired, and the praetorian froze, folded over and toppled into the hole.

As if at a signal, chaos broke loose. A dozen praetorians ran into view, heading towards the ramp. 462's penal squad stepped out of cover and let rip. Ghasts were everywhere, firing wildly and screeching like angry ducks. Smith half-led, half-dragged 462 to the ramp, blasting the praetorians as they charged.

A bio-grenade scuttled over the lip of the pit and dropped onto four of the penal squad. The explosion blew dirt and bits of drone into the air and knocked Smith stumbling. He blinked, righted himself and saw 462 lurching up the ramp. Smith ran up behind him, pulling his rifle into his hands.

'Strength in obedience,' a soldier ant screamed from the left. Smith turned and lifted his rifle. 462's pistol cracked out. The praetorian staggered, buffeted by pistol shots, and Smith finished it with a single bullet.

They reached the top of the slope. Two open-backed troop carriers stood nearby, their hatches down. Huge Ghasts swarmed out of them, roaring slogans. Smith grimaced with disgust and opened fire.

Something slammed into his side and he fell. 462 crashed on top of him. White disruptor-fire tore overhead. 462 fired twice, ejected a charge pack and reached into his coat for another. Smith shot from prone. The shot threw a huge Over-Attack-Lieutenant onto its back. It thrashed like an upturned beetle.

Gunfire raked the side of the nearer troop-carrier, tossing praetorians against the vehicle in a shower of sparks. The other vehicle rocked furiously. The window burst and a head sailed out. It stopped moving. Suruk climbed out after it.

Everywhere was silent. The absence of gunfire seemed almost as loud as the shooting itself. Carveth and Rhianna stepped into view: one covered in armour and strap-on artillery, the other etherial in her long dress and untidy hair.

Rhianna looked at 462. 'Aren't you a little short for a praetorian?'

'I am not one,' he replied. 'I am the acting Number Two.'

'So who's the real Number Two, if you're just acting?'

'There isn't one. He had an accident. Frogs were involved.'

Suruk chuckled nastily.

One of 462's soldiers approached. The drone took a long look at Suruk and shuddered. 'You were betrayed, 462.'

462 nodded. 'Rumours of my promotion were clearly exaggerated.'

Carveth stood over one of the dead praetorians. 'Look at this, boss. He's got a funny mask on.'

The alien wore a biomask over its mouth and nostrils. The tail-pipe of the mask stretched into the back of its rifle. In place of a telescopic sight, a large fleshy wedge had been mounted. The thing had two large holes at its widest end.

'Scent-hunters,' 462 hissed. 'They have been tracking us.'

'Nobody tracks the Slayer,' Suruk replied. 'Ghasts, lemming men, the Inland Revenue – nobody. Not even my own offspring can find me.' He glanced around. 'What is that on the horizon?'

In the distance, vehicles moved under a column of dust. Smith peered at them and saw a tiny Union Jack fluttering above them. 'Landships,' he said.

'Ah,' said 462. 'I would advise you to send your men away, Smith. My soldiers here are hand-picked veterans of the M'Lak Front. They are fanatically loyal to me.'

A loud thud came from behind him. Smith glanced over and saw that Sven had dropped his rifle and raised all his hands. 'I give up.'

'What?' said 462. 'What do you mean, you give up?'

'I mean,' Sven replied, 'Screw this for a game of bio-engineered soldiers. Don't get me wrong, 462, you're not the worst by a long way, but I'm done with fighting. I've spent three years being used as cannon fodder, freezing my stercorium off, trying not to get my head taken as a trophy by maniacs like this savage –'

Suruk cleared his throat. 'Noble savage, thank you.'

'– and standing a mile in front of the army, jumping up and down in case there's a minefield nearby. Three years I've spent trying to keep my head on my shoulders. And then they threw me to the dogs – literally. I'm sick of being bossed around by violent idiots, and that's why I'm surrendering to the British Space Empire.'

'Think you might be in for a surprise there,' Carveth said.

'Shut up, pilot,' Smith replied. 'Congratulations, Ghasts. You are now our prisoners. Your first lesson in conducting yourselves decently will be to form a queue, so we can arrest you properly.'

462 sighed. 'Wonderful. I now seem to have joined a third army consisting solely of me. Well, if nobody objects, I am ordering myself to retreat. Goodbye.' He turned and limped away, still holding his pistol but letting it hang

down by his side. His stercorium bobbed with each lurching step.

Suruk turned to Smith and raised first his eyebrows, and then his spear. 'Shall I?'

Smith shook his head. '462! Come back here at once. I am taking you prisoner in the name of the British Space Empire. You will be treated in accordance with your rights under the Geneva and, um, what's the other convention?'

'Fairport,' Rhianna said.

'That one too. Your convention rights will be treated as is, well, conventional. Stop this instant, damn it! You don't think you'll get anywhere, do you? You're a wanted man now, an ant on the run. If they catch you, they'll shoot you down, 462. *Like a dog.*'

462 stopped. Slowly, almost mockingly, he raised all of his hands. 'Well, then. For me, Captain Smith, the war is over.'

Suruk chuckled. 'After all this time, all this fighting, and now you are defective.'

'Defecting,' 462 replied.

'I know what I mean.'

'Not by a long way,' Smith replied. 'But look on the bright side.'

The Ghast turned around. 'And the bright side is what, exactly?'

'Us,' said Smith. 'Welcome to civilisation.'

Plans for Victory

'I still find it puzzling,' 462 said. He sat in the living room of the *John Pym*, on one end of the battered sofa, a plastic cup of orange squash in his pincers. Carveth sat in the armchair opposite, watching him closely. Smith leaned against the wall, slowly drinking a mug of tea. 'The shire horse is larger than the Shetland horse, yes?'

'Pony,' said Carveth.

'Pony, then. The Shetland pony is weaker. So why don't the shire horses eat all the ponies?'

'You people are really sick,' she replied. 'Even for insects, you're disgusting.'

'But we are survivors. Unclouded by conscience, remorse or delusions of gymkhana. This "orange squash" is excellent, by the way. You will have to give me the recipe. Puny and weak, too,' he added quickly. 'That goes without saying.'

'You could put some more cordial in if you want it stronger.'

'Additional sucrose solution? I'd better not, not before midday.'

462 might have been a prisoner, but it felt wrong to see the Ghast here, of all places, sitting down in Smith's living

room as if there was nothing unusual going on. It was like opening a box of eggs to find a tarantula holding up a sign that read *Don't mind me*.

462 sipped his drink. 'I see you have a trophy up there.'

Smith glanced at the far wall. He had forgotten about the stuffed praetorian head mounted there. 462 seemed to have taken it pretty well, considering.

The Ghast crossed his legs. 'It doesn't bother me, if you are wondering. A commander is entitled to keep a momento of his victories, surely. In fact, this entire ship seems to be full of artifacts looted from crude and primitive cultures, such as this settee and your pony-obsessed android.' He shifted in his seat. 'I am impressed by this vessel, Smith.'

'Thank you.'

'The fact that it can actually fly without the wings dropping off is close to awe-inspiring.'

'We must be doing something right, 462. After all, you're in it. Not that I especially want you here . . .'

462 nodded. 'For a long time, I have assumed that our best leaders had been posted to the M'Lak Front, or that there had been some terrible mistake at the High Command annual dinner and they had ended up on the menu, leaving us only with the idiots. But I have come to suspect that my superiors were *all* idiots, especially compared to me. Our commanders are deluded, Smith. Number One, for all his claims of genius, is beginning to look less and less stable.'

Smith said, 'The only "stable" thing about Number One is that he's full of horse crap.'

'You know, Smith, I have studied Earth culture, but it still confuses me. The Ancient Greeks had a concept called Nemesis, the idea that there was one person meant to oppose another. I think of you like that. Sometimes at night, when the propagandatron has gone off for the evening, I mull over the two of us, locked together in struggle.'

'Yuck,' said Smith. 'I don't know what the Ancient Greeks get up to, but you can mull over someone else, thank you. When I'm in bed I think about the Queen. In an entirely proper way, of course.'

'I meant that there is one person who brings doom to another individual.'

'Rubbish,' Suruk said from the doorway. 'I bring doom to *everybody*.'

Rhianna slipped past him, crossed the room and put the kettle on. She gave 462 a long, thoughtful look, then shook her head. 'No offence,' she said, 'but you're really spoiling the vibe.'

'You know, Smith, it is not your achievements as a society that impress me,' 462 said. 'Although there have been events that even we Ghasts found remarkable. . . the Trans-Galactic postal system . . . the Anglo-M'Lak military agreements . . . the universe's largest Cornish pasty factory . . . all of these are considerable feats. But what strikes me is that you have accomplished them so *quietly*. In the Ghast Empire it is hard to even get the post delivered without having to shout orders and threaten to have somebody shot. And even then all your letters have already been read. If something is not obligatory, it is forbidden. There is a constant background of angry noise. The propagandatron is on so loudly that I can scarcely hear myself not think. And then there's the whole denial of objective truth. We rewrite history so often that you barely know what's going to happen from one day to the previous. Our entire society is crippled by suspicion.'

'Well,' Smith said, 'you know what they say about paranoia . . .'

'No,' 462 replied. 'What do they say about paranoia? Who is saying that? Is it about me? I demand to know!'

'Hey, chill,' Rhianna said. 'You think you're getting freaked out? Think about us. We've got a giant talking ant in our living room. That's the craziest thing I've seen for, oh, almost a fortnight.'

'Right,' Carveth added. 'Keep your antennae on.'

462 took a deep breath. 'And then there is this creature,' 462 added, pointing to Suruk. 'I always assumed that it was some kind of attack dog. Yet you treat it like one of your own.'

Rhianna frowned. 'You should say *he*, not *it*. Although he technically is an *it*, except kind of both *its* at once. Actually, Suruk, what is your preferred form of address?'

'*Sir*,' Suruk replied, although I would settle for *Grand Warlord*.'

Rhianna stood up. 'We live in harmony on this spaceship, 462. Our relationship is based on mutual understanding. Through tolerance and togetherness we come together as one and celebrate our unity.'

462 smiled weakly. 'How absolutely repellent. All the same, I think I will remain on board. For all your claims of kindness, I doubt I would last long wandering around this dock.'

Smith met his eye. 'It's not the dock you should worry about. It's the jury. You'll have to face trial, you know.'

'Ah,' said the Ghast. 'I thought I might be able to arrange

275

some sort of . . . what is the word? Plea bargain. Turn Queen's evidence.'

Suruk snorted. 'Bah! A warrior never pleads. Nor does he leave evidence. As I have told several members of the judiciary, over the years, the best defence is attack!'

462 looked at Smith. 'Would you mind if I activated your propagandatron? This "BBC" thing of yours intrigues me. When humans say that it reports the truth, do you mean your truth or the Ghast Empire's truth?'

Smith flicked the switch and the television came on. A reporter was interviewing a foreign officer in green body armour and a little hat. The armour had chrome fins.

'You mentioned shock and awe, General Carnby,' the interviewer said.

'Hell, yeah!' General Carnby replied. 'Aw, we shocked 'em good. Right now it's about commanding the battle-field. We're looking at tactical spec recon ghost ops in the north, black deniable strategic protocols in the south and, out west, we're just kicking asses. That's the key to our strategy . . . asses.'

'This man is from abroad,' Smith explained.

462 nodded thoughtfully.

General Carnby adjusted his hat. 'Victory. Victory is like an ass. Everyone wants a piece of it. Some people, though, can't tell victory from their own ass. Me, I can. I like the smell of victory in the morning, but as for my – say, what the hell was that?'

Both men looked to look at something out of view. A dark filter fell over the screen.

'Goodness, I believe that might be an enemy attack,' the interviewer said.

'Attack? Not on my goddam watch! Saddle up, people—'

The screen went dark. The image cut to the newsroom.

Carveth said, 'Where's that happening?'

Smith replied, 'Allied Command has been organising people by similar languages. That sounded quite like English, so I suppose they're not too far from us . . . oh. Chaps, we may have a problem.'

462 said, 'It would appear that my comrades – my former comrades – have decided to launch a counter-assault. But then, did you think that Number One would take your invasion lying down?'

'He won't be taking anything, lying down or standing up,' Smith replied. 'Except surgical bruise lotion for the bloody good thrashing I'm going to give him. Men, we need to strike and strike fast. The hour is at hand. Suruk: fetch Wainscott and the Deepspace Operations Group.'

'Ugh,' Carveth said, 'can we not? I'm sick of him running about in the nude.'

'Sorry, but we need Wainscott. Besides, you can't judge a man by his eccentricities. I know he likes getting his old chap out but, when push comes to shove, it's inconsequential.'

'I know. I've seen it. Inconsequential isn't the word for it.'

Suruk walked to the door. 'Enough talking. I shall fetch our allies.' He paused, and looked from face to face. 'We must act fast. The time of war is already at hand, and my hands are ready for war. Admittedly, war was at hand before, but now it is most definitely handy, which I find convenient. I shall gather our forces and then we shall fall upon our enemies like a big collapsing thing!'

462 looked at Smith. 'If I may ask, Smith . . . how do you stay sane?'

Smith shrugged. 'I drink a lot of tea, I stay calm, and I crack on with things. And I remember what Kipling said . . . "If you can keep your head when all about you are losing theirs—"'

'Then you are almost certainly me!' Suruk said, helpfully.

*

The kettle had boiled and the biscuits had been handed out. Smith's closest comrades stood around the dining table, ready to hear his plan.

'Gentlemen,' Smith began, 'also ladies and indeterminate things, I have called you here to propose a plan that may cripple the Ghast Empire. Let me begin by saying that what I propose is both daring and extremely dangerous.'

'Well,' said Wainscott, 'you've got my vote.'

'As you know, the surrender of Storm-Assault Commander 462 brings us a large amount of information about the workings of the enemy.'

Dreckitt took the cigarette out of the corner of his mouth. 'How do we know that he's on the level? You've only got to look at the guy to know he's a cheap punk who can't even wear a trench coat right. For that matter, where is he?'

'Safely locked up. Carveth, you shut him in the brig, didn't you?'

At the far end of the table, Carveth hesitated. 'The where?'

'The brig.'

'What's a brig?'

'It's the ship's prison.'

'Boss, we don't have one of those. It's not in the Haines manual.'

'Don't tell me you've lost him.'

'No, I know exactly where he is. When you said "brig", I thought you meant "bridge". So that's where I left him.'

'Well,' said Smith, 'that's all right, then – wait, the bridge is where the controls are.'

Carveth shook her head wearily. 'Don't worry, he's not on the loose. I shut him in the weapons locker so he can't cause any trouble . . . Actually, that doesn't sound so clever when I say it out loud.'

Smith said, 'So long as he can't get out. Besides, I think for now he'll work with us. Number One shot his dog, and that's enough to send any man on a quest for revenge. Just think of what happened to Carveth here when the Yull threatened to eat her ponies.'

There was a rumble of agreement around the room. Nelson, who had been standing near Carveth, took a step back from her, presumably in case the memories brought on a relapse.

Smith cleared his throat. 'Anyway – look here, chaps. You know what really gets my goat?'

Suruk said, 'Goat thieves?'

'The thought of Number One hiding away, thinking he can wage his war against us with impunity. But now, we know where to find him. Pay attention, everyone. On the table before you, I have mocked up the route that will lead us to Number One himself, deep within City 21. Take him out of the equation and the Ghast Empire will fall to its knees or whatever monstrous equivalent these ant-men possess.' He gestured along the tabletop. 'These cereal boxes represent large governmental structures within the city. The toaster is the Ministry of Law, which appears to be a blasphemous parody of our Parliament.'

'Blow it up,' Wainscott said.

'The toy soldiers, which by chance happened to be lying around and aren't the sort of thing that I might purchase, represent the larger statues of Number One, which would be used as way points in our attack. We would approach the city by air, flying just over ground level at high speed. We are represented here by this model aeroplane. Carveth, demonstrate the approach.'

She picked up the ship's broom and used it to push the model down the length of the table, between the cereal boxes. 'Eeeeow.'

'Don't do the noise,' Smith whispered. 'It makes it look silly.' Raising his voice, he said, 'Once air insertion is complete, we will leave the ship and begin inserting on the ground. Gertie won't like that. The enemy will have access to heavy weaponry, including force-fielded heavy tanks.'

W loomed over the tabletop. 'I can arrange fighter support,' he said. 'That shouldn't be too difficult, provided you go in quickly.'

Smith said, 'Thanks. It's likely that the immediate area will be unsafe for flying. Therefore, we will complete the approach by vehicle.'

On the far side of the table, Susan said, 'We can deal with any tanks.'

'Easily done,' Wainscott said. 'If we hit them hard enough, we'll just cut straight through. If anything gets in our way—' He blew a raspberry. 'Like bugs on a windscreen.'

Carveth said, 'In that lorry thing you've got? I don't think it's big enough. There won't be enough room for everyone. Some of us will have to stay behind.'

W looked down at the table. He rubbed his chin. 'We're using every tank we've got to fight off the Ghast counter-attack. But we could probably borrow a spare one . . . yes, I can get one brought in from the allied sector. Don't look like that. It'll be fine. It'll even drive on the left. Actually, when you're a tank, you can drive on whatever side you like, really.'

'Excellent,' said Smith. 'So, Phase One of the attack will be to fly in. The second phase will be to complete the approach by road. Phase Three will be to defeat Number One's guards. Then, we'll move to Phase Four – capturing Number One. On the intelligence I have received, in the vicinity is an entrance to a system of tunnels that will lead to Number One's hiding place. He only spends a couple of days in each location, so we need to move fast.'

Suruk grinned. 'Our prey lurks below, thinking himself safe. We shall track this beast to his hideout and spear him in his watering-hole!'

'Ouch,' said Carveth.

'Erm, guys?'

They looked around. Rhianna approached the table, hair and dress wafting out around her like a ghost about to identify its murderer. 'I just had a thought.'

'Good work,' Smith replied. 'What is it?'

'Well, what about this regiment of praetorians that follows Number One around? The, um, Pincers of Death?'

'They'll be there, too,' Smith said. 'And we'll beat them.'

'Oh, okay.'

'Wait,' Carveth said. 'Not okay. There's a whole load of them, right? And they're Number One's poster boys, yes? So they'll be really big and have lots of guns. I know our standards are . . . different, but really, there will be several hundred of them and about twelve of us. We'll be lucky if we get past the cereal box towers here, let alone the Ministry of Toaster. Couldn't we fight someone smaller and less violent, like, say, Genghis Khan's Mongol horde?'

Suruk laughed. 'Puny dogs!'

For a moment, nobody spoke. Carveth glanced around. 'I'm just saying.'

Smith said, 'But we have the element of surprise.'

'That's for sure. They'll be bloody astonished when they see that there's only a dozen of us.'

*

The vehicle hangar was a huge green building that had been dropped out of orbit as part of a sectional deployment shuttle. It looked somewhat like the Crystalline Palace of Billingsgate Prime, its sloping sides held up by immense scrollworked girders. Leviathan landships and Caratacus tanks were parked in orderly queues along its length. Mechanical arms stretched down from the ceiling, spot-welding the hulls. Engineers in goggles and heavy coats scrambled over the tanks, directing the robot arms. The hangar rang with the growl of engines and the sudden hiss of sparks.

A woman in a yellow servo-suit lumbered towards the door as Smith and his crew walked in, a packing crate held in the suit's pincers. 'What're you looking for?' she called.

'Bay Twelve, please,' Smith replied. 'I'm with the Service.'

The woman took out her cigarette. The suit's arm followed her movement, swinging out alarmingly. It did not seem to bother her. 'In the far corner,' she said. 'Your engineer brought it up earlier today.'

Smith glanced at Carveth. '*This* is my engineer,' he replied.

The woman shrugged, and her suit's shoulder pistons lurched up and down. 'A bloke came by this morning with a modified Bloodhound armoured car,' she said. 'Said he was paying back a mate and they deserved a fair go.'

'A "fair go", eh? Did he have a funny accent, by some chance?'

'Well, this is space. It's relative. But yeah, he had an accent. It was hard to tell, though, what with that bucket on his head.'

'A bucket? A sort of metal helmet? And a long brown coat?'

'I think so.'

'And was he riding a giant kangaroo, by any chance?'

She moved to rub her chin thoughtfully and decided against it before her suit could punch her out. 'You know, now you mention it, he was.'

'I see. Thanks.'

Their vehicle was waiting for them. It sat on four huge, armoured tyres like a bunker on wheels, slab-sided and ominous. It had looked deadly before it had been upgraded;

now, the cow-catcher at the front and the engine intake gave it an air of specialised menace. The Bloodhound's main armament, a tank-quality railgun, jutted overhead like the arm of a crane.

'Blimey,' said Carveth. 'I think I'd quite like to drive that.'

*

W was waiting at the *John Pym* when they returned. The spy stood in the shadow of a warbot, smoking. Carveth slowed the Bloodhound to a halt and Smith climbed out of the turret hatch.

W approached, and the warbot lumbered after him. 'Thought you might need this,' he said.

Smith clambered down the side of the armoured car. 'Warbot, can you give us supporting fire?'

The robot's head swung to look at him. Its jaw moved forward. 'I have nothing to offer but blood, sweat, oil and gears,' it growled.

'What's your programming?'

'Line Ten – go to war. Line Twenty – fight. Line Thirty – go on to – end.'

'Sounds good. We can attach the warbot to the back of the Bloodhound, but it's going to be a tight squeeze.' Smith looked into the back of the ship: the Deepspace Operations Group's battle-wagon was already in place. 'We might have to keep the back door open. We've got some rope to tie it shut somewhere. All right, Carveth! Back the armoured car up the ramp and try not to squash Wainscott's lorry. Well,' he added, turning to W, 'see you back at base, eh?'

The spy shook his head. 'Certainly not, Smith. I'm coming with you. I've put my ravnaphant gun inside already.'

'Is that a good idea, sir? You seem to get damaged whenever you have to fight. First there was that time you got a piece of metal through your neck in that space battle, and then that giant mouse savaged you on Ravnavar. No offence, sir, but the only person I've known to get hurt more often is 462, and that's because I'm usually shooting at him.'

'No. I'm in. I've always wanted to be there to see tyranny defeated by the common people of the Space Empire. And there is no tyrant worse than Number One.'

A loud metallic clang came from the ramp. Carveth shouted 'Bollocks!'

'And no people more common than yours.'

'Very well, sir. You can keep an eye on 462. Let's get going.'

The Deepspace Operations Group installed themselves in the sitting room. The battered furnishings and grim faces reminded Smith of the waiting room at the dentist's. He ducked into the cockpit.

Suruk and Rhianna were already sitting on the fold-down seats. He took his own place in the captain's chair.

Carveth struggled in and sat down in the pilot's seat. She reached out and turned the ignition key. The *John Pym*'s engines began to come alive.

'Will the hold door be all right?' Smith asked.

'It's fine. We had to hold the door shut with string.' Seeing his expression, Carveth added, 'Don't worry. It's tactical string. We'll be able to deploy much quicker. Just out of interest, what's my insurance situation here?'

The engines rose up around them, as if they sat atop a massive, snarling beast. 'Fine,' Smith replied. 'The ship's insured for meteors, comets, man-eating aliens, giant monsters, acts of Godzilla and fully operational battle stations.'

'Not the ship – us. I'm an android, so don't I get a ten-year guarantee or something? Because every time I fly this bloody ship I feel as if I'm about to void my warranty.' She sighed. 'I suppose it's too late. Let's get going.'

'Well said. Pilot, take off and set a course for victory.'

Carveth paused. 'Right you are, boss.'

She hit the throttle. The engines roared. In Suruk's room, the rows of skulls shook and jiggled as if with crazed laughter. In the cockpit, the model aeroplanes swung on their bits of string. A blizzard raged within the paper-weight on the dashboard. The *John Pym* tore loose from the ground and burst into the sky.

All Against One

The intercom crackled. 'This is 644 Squadron, out of Percival Base Camp. We have orders to escort you into enemy territory.'

Smith opened communications. He raised his voice over the growl of the engines. 'That's correct.'

'We have no orders to escort you back. Can you confirm that?'

'I can. We won't be coming back.'

'Then be aware that your sacrifice will not be forgotten, sir. With that kind of bravery, we'll win this bloody war if it takes a million years.'

'It won't take that long,' Smith said. 'We're going to win it this afternoon.'

A Hellfire fighter swung down on the port side, a sleek, deadly shark of a machine, and matched their speed. In the cockpit, a man raised his hand and gave them the thumbs up. Smith waved back.

The Hellfire rocked its wings and sped forward. Other fighters dropped in beside it: Hellfires, Tempests and a single Cranefly, almost the size of the *Pym* itself.

'A fine sight, Mazuran,' Suruk said. 'A spearhead to drive deep into the enemy.'

Smith twisted around in his seat. 'Chaps,' he said, 'we're going in. This is it. Once he knows what's coming, Gertie will throw everything he's got at us. Whatever happens down there, it's been a pleasure, and an honour.'

'Yeah,' Rhianna replied. 'It's been cool.'

'This may well be a suicide mission. We may never fly together again. We may die horribly. But I'm bloody glad you're here with me.'

'Gosh, I'm glad to be flying into this deathtrap with you,' Carveth said. 'Ah, what the hell. I'm glad to be with you lot. I don't have any other friends. I just wish we could go somewhere nice.'

Smith turned to her. 'Pilot, if we come out of this, I give you my word that we will indeed go somewhere nice. How does Bognor Regis sound to you? In summer, no less?'

'Could we stretch to the Bahamas?'

'Cardiff Dinosaur Park? It has a petting zoo.'

'Hold on tight. We're going in.'

The city opened up before them, a black, sprawling chitinous mass like the back of a beetle enlarged a million times. Smoke spewed from chimneys of misshapen black bone. Flames belched from refineries. Insignia glinted on the tops of buildings: wherever there was flat space, the ant-symbol had been drawn. And massive statues rose out of the buildings like giants striding through a dark river, huge snarling images of Number One pointing, saluting, shaking his fists and pincers at Heaven. Spotlights shone up from the ground, swinging their columns of light through the air as they hunted for enemies.

'God,' said Smith, 'what a place!'

'Boss,' Carveth said, 'We're picking up some unusual

readings. Heat signatures, but there's nothing there—'

White light burst on the starboard flank. Smith winced, and the light was gone. It its place, a tiny, moving speck.

'Enemy fighter!' he called. 'Where the hell did that come from? Men, we've got a bandit at two o'clock.'

The radio crackled. 'I see him,' the squadron leader replied.

More white flares exploded in the orange sky. They vanished as soon as they appeared, and left fighter ships behind them. 'What the hell is that?' Smith demanded.

'Teleporter, *John Pym*. Gertie's pulling out all the stops now. Don't worry, we'll get him. Let's get stuck in, chaps. This is where we part company, *John Pym*. Cranefly, open up the way for these fellows. Press on regardless, Smith, and bloody good luck to you.'

'Much appreciated. You too.'

The fighters twisted away from the *Pym*, swinging out to meet the enemy. Smith felt as if a layer of armour had been pulled off the ship. Only the Cranefly remained, a massive high-speed attack shuttle. It drew ahead, and a voice said, 'Going in.'

The Cranefly dropped so rapidly that Smith thought it would slam into the ground. It pulled up at the last moment, flying just above the rows of blue street-lamps that lit the avenue below. Smith craned his neck and made out road-blocks, lines of bio-tanks and mobile gun emplacements.

'Follow,' he said, and Carveth swung the nose down.

Light burst from below. Carveth toggled the chaff button and released a wad of countermeasures. The Cranefly opened fire down the length of the street, and suddenly the ground was a stripe of searing flame. Tanks rolled and blew apart; scraps of armour sailed into the air like cinders.

'There you go,' the Cranefly announced. 'The way's open. Bag one for me.'

It pulled up, twisting perilously close to the antennae of a colossal statue, and slipped off the edge of the windscreen.

Now it's just us, Smith thought. 'Take us in, Carveth.'

The *John Pym* was not built for low-level manoeuvring. Carveth fought the controls as if strangling an enemy. The cockpit rocked. 'Scanners say there's a lot of AA up ahead!' she called.

'Rhianna?' Smith looked over his shoulder. 'Psychic time.'

'Sure.' She closed her eyes and hummed.

Carveth levelled the ship. They rushed on. In the centre of the screen, a vast, ugly dome rose above the statues and habitation-blocks. 'That's it,' Carveth said. 'The Ministry of Law. One minute 'til we land.'

Smith unbuckled himself from his seat and strode to the cockpit door. 'Is everyone all right back there?' he called.

A long, weary face stared back at him. 'This is a disaster,' W said. 'I just dropped my cigarette into my teacup. By God, war is a beastly business.'

'Ready to throw lead, pal,' Dreckitt called back from the lounge.

Smith ducked back into the cockpit. He felt the *John Pym* dip, felt his stomach tense as they swung in for the kill.

He opened the weapons locker. 462 was wedged inside like a vampire in a badly-measured coffin. He could not have used any of the guns, Smith saw: it was too tight a fit.

Sourly, the Ghast said, 'Are we nearly there yet?'

Smith tugged him out of the locker. 'Thirty seconds. You'd better be right about this. Everyone, we're disembarking the moment the ship lands.'

'But what about all my things?' Carveth cried. 'The Ghasts will steal them.'

Suruk snorted. 'I doubt they require eight bottles of hair dye and a stack of magazines about cellulite. But fear not. I have booby-trapped your room.'

The ground swelled up beneath them. Smith saw details of the road. For a moment, he looked into the windows of a Ghast apartment block. A hundred screens displayed the same line of marching ants.

The *John Pym* touched down. The ship creaked, the hydraulics let out a despairing wheeze, and then it was still. 'Everybody out,' Smith called. 'Let's go!'

'Not without my hamster,' Carveth replied, snatching Gerald's cryogenic tube. 'Or my lunch.'

Rhianna adjusted the psychic amplifier on her head and helped Carveth pull the Maxim cannon out of the weapons locker. Carveth struggled through the door and down the corridor.

They hurried into the hold. The Deepspace Operations Group were on their battlewagon and checking the guns. Suruk half-pushed, half-threw Carveth onto the Bloodhound and she scrambled inside. The warbot was clamped to the back, inert.

Suruk and Rhianna climbed aboard. Smith followed. As he swung himself into the commander's chair, the huge engines of the armoured car growled into action.

W unfastened the ropes and hit the switch. The hold

door flopped down with a clang that ran through the hull. Smith felt queasy with anticipation. 'Forwards!' he cried.

The Bloodhound rolled down the ramp. Wainscott's lorry followed it, W scrambling on board at the last minute. Smith pressed the button on his keys and the hold door swung shut. The vehicles sped out into the night.

Smith settled down into his seat. He pulled the hatch closed above him and looked over the turret controls. It all seemed fairly simple. The brasswork was very shiny.

From just below his boots, Carveth called, 'I'm going test the railgun. I'll just take control for a moment.'

Servos whined around Smith's chair. The turret rose and his seat swung back as if he was about to be launched into space. The railgun boomed.

Four hundred yards away, an armour-piercing plasma shell slammed into the crotch of a statue of Number One. 'Good shot, Carveth. No wonder he looks so angry.'

'I've been waiting four years for that,' she replied, and the Bloodhound tore down the avenue.

Smith toggled the radio. 'Wainscott, are you with me?'

'Damned right I am!' the speaker called. 'It's a fine night for a drive, eh? Very fresh out here. I can feel the wind in my beard. Faster, Susan! My shorts are rippling!'

Rhianna and Suruk were sitting at the back, where the extra supplies and tea-making facilities were stashed. 'Guys,' Rhianna called, 'I'm sensing a lot of hostility here.'

'That'll be me, old girl,' Smith replied. 'Let's get the buggers!'

'I mean the enemy. They're really angry. And they're on jetbikes, coming from behind.'

'Dammit. Wainscott, we've got company. Carveth, full ahead. I'll handle this.'

Smith pushed the left pedal and the turret rotated. Strung out along the road behind, three Ghast attack bikes were approaching rapidly. Smith pulled the targeting screen down on its metal arm and zoomed in. The front armour and handlebars of the nearest bike had been sculpted to resemble a skull with antennae: a goggled, snarling face glared at him over them. In the sidecar, a praetorian pulled a hornet-launcher onto its shoulder. Smith wrapped his fingers around the controls, eased the targeter over the jet-bike and pulled the trigger.

The jetbike and its sidecar disappeared in a burst of flame. The remaining bikes swerved; so too did Wainscott's lorry. The cannon on the back of the lorry rotated, and fire blared from the barrel. A bike shot across the road and ploughed straight through a propaganda billboard.

A bio-rocket burst from the remaining bike. It sailed up, gaining height to slam down on the upper armour. 'Cool, that's mine,' Rhianna said. The rocket reached the top of its arc, shot downwards – and burst fifty feet above them.

'Nice work,' Smith said.

The radio crackled. 'Smith?' Wainscott called. 'Scanners have two tanks coming in. You've got the big gun there.'

'Righto,' Smith said. 'Battle stations, everyone.'

Suruk drew a large knife.

'Ah, hell,' Carveth called. 'I've got two bloody great bio-tanks on screen – a Tiger Prawn and a King Lobster-Tank. Both're showing up as belonging to the Pincers of Death.'

'Excellent,' Smith replied. 'Then we're in the right place.' He peered at the computer. The image of a Ghast heavy tank turned slowly on the screen; he saw the thrusters, the immense gun jutting from the front and the segmented rear engine. A skull-and-antennae had been stencilled on the side of the turret, surrounded by a mass of kill markings.

'Mazuran.' Suruk's voice came over his shoulder like a tempting devil in a cartoon. 'It will be my pleasure to slay one of these monsters, if you want the second kill.'

Smith toggled the ammunition from high explosive to armour piercing. 'I don't think that'll work, old chap.'

'You wish me to slay them both, then?'

Smith opened his mouth, and the sound was drowned out by an explosion. The Bloodhound rocked and he was thrown against the seat padding as Carveth swerved. 'We're hit!' he cried.

'That was a *miss!*' she shouted.

'Isambard . . .' He twisted around. Rhianna stared up at him like a ghost at the bottom of a well. A thin trickle of blood ran from her left nostril. 'I can't block them. Not a shell like that. I can slow it, but—'

'Righto,' he said grimly. 'Carveth, evasive manoeuvres.'

She veered right. Smith pushed the pedal and the turret turned to the left. Cross-hairs appeared on the targeting screen, converging on the Tiger Prawn. 'Steady, pilot . . .'

The crosshairs flashed. Smith pulled the trigger, felt the turret shake from the force of the main gun. The shell streaked out.

Twenty feet from the tank's hull, it exploded. Smith saw the flicker of an energy shield. It was strange to see them deployed on anything smaller than an Aresian death-walker; the Ghast tanks were so big that they could carry the necessary projectors.

'Damn it! I didn't even scratch the bloody thing!'

He flicked to the King Lobster. It was blazing away at Wainscott's lorry. Wainscott was returning fire more to hold its attention than to damage it. Cannon shells burst on the bio-tank's front shield like raindrops on a sheet of glass.

'Ram them,' Suruk said. 'Do it!'

'Carveth! Can we ram them?'

'Well, yeah, but why?' she demanded. 'I mean, we could drive in under the shield . . . but then what?'

Suruk snarled. 'Boarding action.'

Smith glanced at him. 'Are you sure?'

'With prey like this? I am certain!'

'Bring us in,' Smith said.

Carveth took a very deep breath. 'Here goes.'

The Tiger Prawn fired again. The Bloodhound shook as if to rip itself apart. For a hideous second the armoured car rose up onto two wheels, and then slammed back down. Metal squealed; so did Carveth.

Suruk scrambled over the command chair like a spider. He reached down and grabbed a metal box from behind the driver's seat. A red light winked on the front.

'That's my lunch!' Carveth cried.

The Bloodhound swerved, and what Suruk had instead of a backside nearly made violent contact with Smith's nose. The computers fuzzed with static. Smith felt a strange pressure pushing against the armoured car, as if it was passing through a sheet of glue, and the ram on its front hit the back of the Tiger Prawn.

Smith pulled the handle and the hatch swung open. Suruk leaped out. Smith turned the turret so that the railgun pointed straight at the Ghast tank.

Suruk raced down the length of the gun and jumped. Smith saw the alien land on the Tiger Prawn and run along its back, waving Carveth's lunchbox over his head. The red light flickered at the corner of the lunchbox's time lock. 'With this nuclear bomb I shall destroy you!' he cried.

On the right, the King Lobster pulled closer. The top hatch opened and a Ghast poked his head out. Grinning, he swung the turret's disruptor gun to rake the back of the Tiger Prawn. 'Careful!' Smith called. The Bloodhound dropped back, and the two tanks drew close, their fields overlapping as the Ghast crewman aimed at Suruk.

Suruk threw his spear. It hit the Ghast square in the chest. He flopped forward, dead, and the hatch dropped onto it, unable to close.

'He's wide open!' Carveth cried.

With a roar, Suruk leaped from the Tiger Prawn to the King Lobster. He landed beside the hatch, heaved the dead crewman out over the side and slipped down the hole like a stoat into a rabbit warren.

The King Lobster swung around and slewed into a building. Smith could only guess at the mayhem going on inside it. The bio-tank spun on its thrusters and clipped the Tiger Prawn, shoving the Tiger Prawn's front into the air, revealing its underside.

Smith flipped the targeting computer in front of his eye. A puzzling little graphic appeared. It looked like a cross between a trigonometry problem and the internal workings of a toaster. It flashed red as Smith linked the railgun up with the Tiger Prawn's belly.

He fired. The shell slipped under the Tiger Prawn's armour and detonated. For a second, it seemed as if nothing had happened. Then the bio-tank crashed down onto the road. The thing burst from within. The turret was hurled across the road, spinning end over end like a thrown hammer. Flames poured from the Tiger Prawn's orifices. It struck the King Lobster, scraped across the road and came to a halt.

'Slow down,' Smith commanded, and Carveth hit the brakes. 'Let's get Suruk.'

They pulled up level with the wreckage. On the far side of the road, a figure waved a spear above its head. Smith grinned and looked out of the hatch. 'Well done, old chap.'

'A mighty fight!' the alien replied. 'Too bad this turret will not fit on my trophy-rack!'

Carveth sniffed. 'But what about my lunchbox, eh?'

'Right here,' Suruk replied. 'I dented a corner bludgeoning the tank commander to death, but otherwise your sandwiches are intact. Tonight, we dine on cheese, pickle and victory!'

'Let's get moving,' Smith said. 'Wainscott, the route is clear.'

The enemy were making a roadblock up ahead. The Bloodhound's railgun blasted it open, and Wainscott's men made short work of the defenders. Then they were speeding through, with a few shots rattling after them, and Wainscott's fierce, jaunty voice crackling over the radio.

Smith checked the targeter. 'There it is!'

A black building loomed up ahead, straddling the road. It was a marbled slab, hundreds of feet tall: Smith thought of a tombstone. Stylised statues of ant-men flanked the huge doors, flexing their limbs and grimacing at the sky.

Banners hung from the walls; spotlights swept the night air around them.

'Tasteful,' Carveth said. 'Even the stuff it's made from looks gross.'

'It's some sort of secreted resin,' Rhianna said.

'Yeah, but secreted from where?'

'This is it, chaps,' Smith said. 'The nerve centre of the heart of darkness. Within those walls beats the brains of the enemy – Number One, head of the Workers And Soldiers Party. Today, men, we will break the backbone of the Ghast Empire and bring it to its knees.'

'Kind of like a pretzel,' Rhianna said.

'Quite so, Rhianna. A pretzel of tyranny, devoured by our hunger for justice. Full speed ahead, Carveth!'

'Oh God,' she replied, and the Bloodhound's engines roared.

A row of steps ran up to the massive doors. Figures in long coats ran out and took up positions. 'Rhianna, can you shield us?'

'Yes,' she said. 'But seeing that we're going in – group hug?'

Carveth didn't look back. 'We are in a tank, you stupid woman.'

'Hey,' Rhianna replied. 'You're totally distressing me here—'

'Enough talk!' Suruk snarled. 'Their soldiers are lined up on the stairs, like in the *Battleship Pumpkin*. Bring us in close, robot girl. I wish to slice them with my spear.'

Smith looked into the targeter and fired the railgun. The steps were lost in a blaze of fire. He swung the coaxial laser cannon across the stairs, bisecting several praetorians.

Three armour-breaker rockets streaked out from the infantry line. Rhianna made a low noise of concentration. Two bioshells burst in the air, the third skewed off and was lost to view. Small-arms fire popped against the Bloodhound's front armour. Wainscott's lorry appeared on the right, glowing in a halo of gunfire. Smith felt a kind of furious exultation, a mixture of anger and righteousness. He fired the main gun again, tossing masonry and Ghasts into the air.

The ground burst under them. The Bloodhound lurched, then crashed down lower than the wheels ought to have allowed. A terrible screeching ran through the hull. 'Landmine!' Carveth called. 'The axle's buggered!'

'Steer us towards them,' Smith shouted. 'Brace yourselves!'

The Bloodhound crashed through the enemy defences in a flurry of sparks. It broke through the nearest barricade and slid up the steps like a ship beaching itself. The armoured car hit the doors of the Ministry of Law, slid back, and stopped.

A warning light flashed in the turret. Something hissed loudly. Smith blinked and found that the air was full of smoke. 'Come on, chaps!' he called. 'I can smell burning. This crate may blow up at any moment.'

'Um, that's me,' Rhianna said. She held out her cigarette. 'It all got pretty stressful. Anyone?'

'We need less smoke and more firing.' Smith grabbed his rifle. 'Let's go!' He pulled the lever on the hatch and it burst open. He was first out.

The Bloodhound lay in the middle of a firefight. The Deepspace Operations Group had dismounted and were tearing into the remaining Ghasts. Only Wainscott remained on the lorry, manning one of the mounted guns.

Smith scrambled free, firing his rifle and cocking the next shot. A massive praetorian swung a hornet-launcher onto its shoulder, and Smith put a bullet between its eyes. The monster fell, and Smith fired again. A second Ghast flopped onto its back, one of Suruk's knives jutting from its scrawny throat.

'Fire up the warbot!' Smith called, and he ducked back behind the wrecked Bloodhound as a team of Ghasts raked the metal with a bipod-mounted distortion gun.

Carveth hit the switch, and the combat robot unfolded from its position at the rear of the Bloodhound. It stood up, all ten feet of armoured steel, and its little head surveyed the area. 'Perverted science,' it growled, and it cocked its gun.

A tremendous low boom came from Smith's right. He glanced around and saw W, the ravnaphant gun smoking in his thin hands. He looked mad with determination. By his side – but slightly behind him – stood 462. The alien's expression was hard to read, beyond its usual ugliness.

The last few praetorians put up a fierce resistance. Wainscott's men cut them down and, suddenly, for the first time in what felt like days, there was nobody left to shoot. Apart from the explosions in the distance, it was quiet.

'Good to see you, Smith,' W said. 'Quite an interesting journey, wasn't it?'

'It got a bit rough,' Smith replied, 'but our moral fibre held out, even if our tank didn't.'

Wainscott strode up the steps, fearsome in his big shorts.

'Craig . . . Nelson! Set the charges and blow the doors open. The rest of you, get ready to go in.'

Rhianna raised her hand. 'Wait.' She walked up to the doors. She reached out and put her hand on the metal, then closed her eyes as if listening to a message tapped out on the far side. 'It's full of them,' she said, and there was an unusual level of clarity in her voice. 'Hundreds of the Pincers of Death, all watching the doors. But it's the only way in. Whoever goes in there first won't last a second. Which is, like, kind of bad,' she added, reverting to normal.

At the bottom of the steps, 462 raised a pincer. 'She is right,' he rasped. 'They will be awaiting you. Us, that is. I would offer to bargain with them, but I am *insecta non grata* here. As far as Number One is concerned, my serial number is mud.'

'Send in the robot,' Wainscott said.

Carveth moved rapidly backwards. 'Oh no you don't. I'm not getting shot full of holes. These are my best trousers. Why don't you do it?'

'I meant the warbot,' the major said.

Smith stared off into the sky. Far away, a battle was raging: fighter-ships looped and turned like flies around a lamp. The beams of spotlights tried to follow them, swinging ponderously through the warm air.

Something moved in front of his face. It was Suruk's hand. 'You appear to have entered Dreamland, Mazuran. Do you return enlightened?'

'Sorry?'

'Are you enlightened?'

'Enlightened? Hmm . . . yes, actually, yes I am! Jolly

good work, Suruk. Men, I have a plan. It's quite light out here, isn't it?'

Carveth sighed. 'Where is this going?'

'And it's going to be pretty dark in there, yes?'

'Yeah, almost as dim as—'

'So we'll bring up one of those searchlights and shine it in there. It'll dazzle them. While they're blinking, we can get inside.'

Wainscott laughed. 'I like it. Susan, what do you think of that? We burst open the doors, get inside, and then I'll show them a bit of no good.'

'I'd rather you just shot them,' she replied. 'I've seen your bit of no good already.'

*

The warbot pushed the searchlight up to the door. Like all Ghast technology, the lamp had an unpleasantly biological look. It made Carveth think of a single leering eye on little stumpy legs. A hand touched her shoulder.

'Hey, lady.'

'Hi, Rick.'

Dreckitt looked more rugged than usual. 'Look out there,' he said. 'The city, alive with danger. Down these dark streets, somebody has to go. Tonight, doll, it's us.'

'Rick, I'm scared,' she said.

He turned to her. 'Hey, I thought Battle Girl didn't get frightened, eh? That's what you said when *Freedom Hell Yeah* interviewed you.'

'Rick, I also said that I was a nuclear scientist and sixth in line to the throne.'

'I know,' he replied. 'I kept the article. Especially the picture of you sitting astride a tank gun. It's on my locker. Back in the desert, when we were fighting the Radishians and all there was was dirt and tanks, the thought of you kept me out the nuthouse.' He glanced back at the Deepspace Operations Group. 'Whenever it seemed like this outfit was going to get me screwed, I'd think of you.'

Carveth grabbed him by the trench coat and pulled him close. 'Ooh, what's this?' She drew a flask out of his pocket. 'You really *are* happy to see me.'

He nodded. 'I figured you'd appreciate two fingers of the hard stuff.'

'Damned right.' Carveth undid the top and took a deep swig. 'Here.'

Dreckitt took a swig. 'Thanks.'

Suruk approached. 'Friends, the time for war is upon us. Less yakking, more hacking. You look troubled, Piglet. Fear not. Tomorrow, we will stand among the heroes of the Space Empire. And if you die, which is reasonably likely, think of the welcome your ancestors will give you in the afterlife.'

'I'm a robot, Suruk. My ancestors were typewriters and word processors.'

'Then think of the words they will process about you – *blood*, *mayhem* and *doom*! Your deeds will be burned into every memory card. Typewriters will garland you with their ribbons. Floppy disks will stand to attention at your name.'

'Loony.'

'Piglet,' Suruk said, 'I would be proud to have you fighting by my side. And even prouder to have your skull on my shelf.'

'That's . . . almost nice.'

Smith clapped his hands. 'Chaps, we're all set. Anyone got anything they'd like to say?' He looked around. 'Good. Let's get cracking. See you on the other side.'

*

The bombs tore the left door off its hinges and tossed it end over end down the stairs. It crashed down beside the spotlight, twisted as if half-chewed.

In the depths of the Ministry of Law, voices roared and snarled.

'Lights!' Smith called.

The spotlight thumped into life. Smith turned away, but he still felt the blast of brilliant light behind his eyelids. Screeches came from inside the Ministry.

'Move!'

Susan and Nelson tossed grenades inside. Clouds of smoke billowed out, together with a smell somewhere between wet dog and cheese.

'The scent-hunters won't be able to snipe us!,' Wainscott called. 'Let's go!'

'With me!' Smith bellowed. 'For the Space Empire!'

He rushed into the doorway, into the darkness and the reeking smoke. Four steps on and the smoke cleared. 'Bloody hell,' he said.

The Ministry was a single vast room, like a concert hall. The war in the sky had blasted four massive holes through the roof, and shafts of weak light stretched down from the dome. Across the back wall, a gigantic stylised ant made of hammered bronze hung above a podium, eighty feet from the tip of its pincers to its stercorium.

The stone seats had been piled up into barricades before it. Behind the barricades, the light caught on banners, portraits and hundreds of helmets.

Smith hesitated a second, appalled by the scale of the thing. This was the heart of the Ghast Empire, a blasphemous affront to civilisation and moral fibre. For a moment he stood there, shaking with rage and disgust. Then a deep voice beside him roared 'Friends, this is the hour! Slay *everything!*'

Gunfire burst from the rear of the hall. Smith ducked behind a statue. He pulled up his rifle, looked down the sights and saw bobbing helmets, each one marked with the insignia of the Pincers of Death. He fired. An armour-piercing bullet blew through metal and a praetorian dropped.

'One.'

To his left, Carveth scrambled into cover. The plaster-work burst around her and she threw herself down. She fired the Maxim cannon from prone, raking the defences, filling the air with chips of stone. Smith tried to give her covering fire.

A beam of searing light cut across the hall, slicing helmets and leather coats. Susan strode forward, shooting from the hip. Nelson worked the grenade launcher fixed to his Stanford gun, and Ghasts were thrown out of their defences by the force of the blast. The warbot lumbered forward like a man struggling through a hailstorm, disruptor-fire pattering against its armour. The sound of shooting was a steady, constant roar, as if Smith stood in the bowels of a machine.

Shadows moved further up; Smith saw a pack of praetorians creeping along the west edge of the hall. 'They're trying to flank us!' he called. He couldn't tell if anyone had heard.

One of the advancing soldiers had a cylinder strapped to its back. Sludge dripped from a tube it carried. *Acidthrower.* Smith lined up the sights with its chest, then moved them back a little. The shot hit the pressurised canister and it burst with very satisfying results.

'Eight,' he said.

Carveth was up and firing, Dreckitt by her side. Rhianna stood among the Deepspace Operations Group, both hands pressed to her temples, shielding them with her powers. Wainscott needed shielding because he had removed his shorts and climbed onto a heap of rubble, firing with one hand and gesticulating in an apelike fashion with the other. Something burst from the warbot's shoulders and a ripple of explosions ran along the Ghast barricades.

Where was Suruk, though? Smith glanced across the hall. He could see nothing: the far side of the room was dust, shadow and the flash of alien weapons. Smith fired, catching a massive praetorian by surprise and sending it spinning to the floor. He was out of ammunition. He ducked down and reloaded.

Wild motion and flames from the left. The warbot staggered like a drunken dancer and crashed flailing through the enemy defences. 'Tomorrow, I will be repaired!' it bellowed, 'and you'll still be screwed!' It raised its hand in a vulgar gesture, shouted 'Victory!' and exploded.

*

Suruk dashed between the pillars, quick as a shark. Gunfire rang around him. He slipped behind a column and a volley of alien fire blew chunks out of the stone. The air was full of dust. He dropped down and rolled across the floor, through the smoke. A praetorian appeared before him, an assault cannon clutched in its pincers. It swung the gun up, but Suruk was on it in a second. He cut the Ghast across the shins and lopped off his head before he could finish falling over.

Suruk felt very angry – and very pleased. This wasn't like the second-rate fighting in the Criminarch's arena: this was like Andor, where he had piled dead lemming men twelve-deep into an enormous heap of dishonour and fluff. This was proper battle.

He wondered if his noble ancestors were watching him from beyond. He closed his eyes for a second and asked them humbly to turn the volume up, then sprang back into the fray. A Ghast lumbered out and jabbed at him with a skull-headed shock baton. Lightning crackled between the skull's antennae. Suruk laughed at the idea of this lurching brute besting the Slayer. He tossed one of his smaller knives into its chest, grabbed the front of its helmet and yanked it back the way human commandos did, to snap the monster's neck.

Its head came off. Suruk shrugged and hurled the head at another praetorian, knocking it flat. His ancestors and his spear were pleased by this.

A Ghast leaned around the edge of a pillar and shot at him. Suruk's shoulder was hit, which was annoying. Half a dozen ant-men ran into view, no doubt planning to saturate the area with gunfire.

Suruk jumped, landed boots-first on the nearest enemy, ran up the Ghast's front, kicked it in the eye and leaped onto the nearest pillar. He snatched the top of a banner and tore it loose. As the Ghasts raised their weapons, Suruk tossed the banner over their heads. They flailed about underneath it, trying to pull themselves free. Suruk whirled his spear like a majorette and waded in.

*

The gunfire faded for a moment. Smith saw the others readying their weapons. His eyes met Susan's. She looked grim.

Carveth scurried up beside him. 'Oh God,' she said. 'There's too many of them.'

A voice screamed out from the Ghast defences. 'This is ranking Over-Storm-Major 637. You cannot defeat the Pincers of Death. You are outnumbered by twenty to one. Surrender now and we will eat you quickly!'

'Oh, bollocks,' Carveth muttered.

'You hear that?' Smith shouted. 'Battle Girl says "Bollocks". And so do we all!'

'You scum!' the Ghast screeched. 'When we are done with your weak planet, no one will know you ever existed!'

'They'll know *you* existed, matey-boy,' Smith called back, 'because I'm going to have you stuffed.'

Under the metal ant, the praetorians were yelling and braying. Smith tried to make out voices, but the racket was too jumbled. He looked back, past Dreckitt and Carveth. 'What's happening?'

W stood near the doors, leaning against the wall. He

said something to Craig. 'They're getting ready to attack,' Craig said. 'All of them.'

'Where's Suruk?'

Craig shrugged.

Smith looked at the rubble at the far end of the hall, the alien bodies scattered around it, half-covered in dust. Surely Suruk couldn't be among them. Surely.

He looked up. Something was moving across the roof. It clung to the upraised pincers of statues, the bumpy frames of official portraits, the dangling cloth of the banners. It was working its way to the enemy lines. It was Suruk.

Smith looked from Suruk to the back of the hall, to the two massive chains that held up the metal ant. 'Dreckitt, do we have a plasma gun?'

'We've got every type of gat short of a Chicago piano, pal.'

'Get it. I'll need a satchel charge, too. And Rhianna?'

She glanced around. She looked mildly perturbed by the firefight. 'Hey, Isambard.'

'I'm going to need you to shield me. Can you do that?'

'Sure.'

'Thanks. And your psychic colander thing's a bit skewiff.'

She shrugged. 'That's just how I wear it, man.'

'Wainscott, can your chaps cover me?'

The major nodded. The gear was tossed down the line, from one soldier to another. Smith slung the satchel charge and the plasma gun over his shoulder and readied his rifle.

'Then let's go. Follow me, men!'

He stepped out and ran forward. Rhianna ran beside

him, surprisingly nimble in her sandals, one hand pressed to her temple. Smith fired, more to keep the Ghasts back than out of accuracy. A great wave of gunfire washed out behind him as his comrades gave him support.

His rifle ran out and he tossed it down and drew his Civiliser. Smith zigzagged from one statue to the next, hearing the marble burst behind him. He ducked behind one and a startled praetorian glared back at him. The praetorian turned, hefting a bipod-mounted heavy disruptor, but Smith was too quick, and civilised him twice before he could shoot back.

Suruk caught his breath. Beside him, Rhianna took out her cigarette and looked at the glowing end. 'This place is really ugly,' she said. 'It's like, seriously uptight. And some-one could trip over this rubble, too.'

Carveth simply shook her head.

Smith looked up. Suruk was almost directly above the metal ant. Smith caught his eye and pointed to the satchel charge. Suruk burst out laughing, clamped his hand over his mouth to silence the noise, and nearly fell off the ceiling.

'Righto,' Smith said. 'Cover me, chaps!'

He ran out of cover, tore across the ground, reached the barricade and raced up a heap of rubble. Suddenly, there were Ghasts below him and they raised their guns. Bullets and disruptor shots tore the air around him, pattering against Rhianna's psychic shielding. A scrap of rubble cut his thigh as he raised the satchel charge over his head and threw it.

Suruk snatched it out of the air. Smith turned and sprinted back the way he had come, the marble floor bursting around his boots. He ducked behind a statue, back beside Rhianna and Carveth. Quickly, Smith swung the plasma gun onto his shoulder.

He leaned out. Suruk was nowhere to be seen. The satchel charge sat wedged into the links of the right-hand chain, warning light blinking. Smith sighted the left chain and pulled the trigger.

A plasma shell burst from the end of the tube. Smith saw it streak across the chamber into the chain. The satchel charge detonated as it struck home.

Both chains burst. Below the ant, a shadow fell over the Pincers of Death. The shadow spread and, slowly, with a sound like the yawning of a metal god, the ant fell off the wall and onto its front. It was like watching a drawbridge drop down, without the chains to slow it.

The Pincers of Death were either very loyal or very stupid. They kept on firing, manning their posts and defending the hall as they had been ordered to do. Only at the last moment did panic break out as the huge metal ant fell onto them like a paving slab onto a colony of woodlice, and by then it was much too late. In one deafening second, the whole unit was squashed by its own insignia.

*

Smith staggered through the dust and the quiet like a man who had walked out of a spaceship crash. 'Rhianna?' he called. 'Carveth? Suruk?'

Carveth lay on her back. Rhianna crouched beside her, in the middle of a perfect circle free from rubble. She looked up and gave Smith the peace sign.

'You're alive,' Smith said. 'Thank God. And you're – you're cleaner than everything around you.'

'It's a miracle,' Carveth croaked.

Other figures appeared from the detritus. Susan walked out, professional as ever. Dreckitt ran to Carveth's side, hip flask at the ready. Craig and Nelson emerged, brushing dirt off their armour. W was last, coughing horribly. He looked at Smith and wiped dust off his pencil moustache. 'Tyranny – nil,' he said. 'The common people of the British Space Empire – one.'

'Wait,' Carveth said. 'Where's Suruk?'

A figure stumbled from the dust. Suruk was bent over, clutching his side. He staggered forward, shaking, doubled over and slumped to the ground.

'Suruk!' Smith raced to his friend. 'Are you all right?'

The alien looked up. He stared at Smith for a moment, and only then seemed to recognise him. His mandibles parted in a thin smile. 'Mazuran, I have hurt myself.'

'Oh God. What is it?'

'I . . . I was too close when the great ant fell upon the Pincers of Death.'

'God – the debris—'

Suruk shook his head. 'I saw it fall. I saw their evil faces as the sheet of metal dropped on them like a scythe of doom, when they knew for sure that their damnation was at hand. I should not have got so close. When I witnessed their destruction, I laughed so hard that I pulled something in my groin.'

Carveth snorted. 'I didn't know you had anything to pull down there.'

Smith helped Suruk to his feet. 'Come on, old chap.

Let's go. Oh – you've got a nasty cut just above your ear.'

'It is nothing. A mere head wound cannot stop me. I shall just shrug it off.'

'I'm not sure that's a good idea.'

'The wound, Mazuran, not my head.'

'I knew that, Suruk.' Smith paused. 'Wait. Someone's missing.'

Carveth checked her pack. 'Don't worry. Gerald's fine.'

'No. Where's Wainscott?'

W moved forward. 'Smith, old chap—'

'He's gone,' Susan said.

Smith stared at her. 'What? Gone? But – but he's an escaped lunatic. We have to get him back!'

Susan shook her head. 'He's dead. One of the statues fell on him.' She looked around the group. 'As the acting head of the Deepspace Operations Group, I want this place secured until we can call up reinforcements. Smith, get up on the roof and radio in that we've taken the Ministry of Law. Come, on, get cracking.'

'Right,' he said. 'Right.'

Even the back stairs were large and sinister. They looked as if there should have been a ghost waiting at the top. Smith hurried up, found an access door and shouldered it open. He walked out into the warm, polluted air.

Suruk had the unit's collapsible flag. He drove it into the ground and the Union Jack unfolded. The building was theirs. Carveth set up the communications rig and dialled the number for high command.

'You know, guys,' Rhianna said, 'Major Wainscott would have been proud of you.'

'Thanks,' Smith replied. 'He died with his boots on – just a bit of a shame that was all.'

Carveth said, 'I've typed our co-ordinates into the network. They'll come and secure the building soon.'

Suruk walked to the edge of the roof and stared out into the night. 'And yet no Number One,' he said. 'I had expected to take his head by now. In fact, I have not been so disappointed since I went swimming with sharks and they made me stand in a stupid cage.'

Nobody replied. On the far side of the city, a jet of flame rose up and shrank away, like the blooming and wilting of a flower viewed in high speed.

'So,' Carveth said, 'this is victory, then. I don't know about you lot, but it's rubbish. I'm going inside. We can use Susan's laser to heat the kettle up.'

They trooped back down the stairs. They were near the bottom when Nelson shouted, 'We've found it!'

Smith ran into the hall. Craig knelt beside a hole in the centre of the floor. 462 stood beside him, and W stood warily next to 462. 'Get over here!' Susan called. 'We've found it.'

'*I* found it,' 462 rasped. 'It was under this.' He tapped a metal disk a yard wide. It had been painted to resemble marble, with the WASP logo drawn across the centre.

'It looks like a manhole,' Smith said. 'But then, I expect Number One feels at home down the sewers.'

Susan shook her head. 'Anything could be down there. And the hell we've been raising will have got every Ghast within ten miles swarming here. This room is the most defensible spot. We need to hold position.'

'No,' Smith said. 'After all the fighting, Number One

will know the game is up. He'll try to escape. I'll go down and catch him.'

'It's too dangerous alone, Smith.'

'That's all right, Susan. I'll take my crew with me. Don't look at me like that, Carveth. You'll go down in history.'

'So did the *Hindenberg*,' Carveth replied. 'Somebody's got to do it, I suppose. What the hell. Let's go.'

Suruk went first. He slid down the ladder, a torch on his belt, and dropped the last thirty feet. Next went Smith, his boots clanging on the rungs. Then 462, kept in the middle for safety's sake, with Carveth above him. Rhianna was last of all.

'Hurry up, 462!' Smith ordered.

'It is difficult,' the Ghast replied. 'My stiff leg is no good on these rungs. Normally I would order one of my underlings to do the climbing for me. And it is hard to see. Were it not for your fat minion blotting out the light from above—'

'You're lucky I don't stamp on your antennae!' Carveth snapped. 'I'd kick you off, but your big red arse would just bounce you straight back up the shaft.'

'Your insubordination is disgraceful,' 462 said, puffing as he descended. 'Strange, how mankind has mastered space travel but has yet to equip its androids with a mute button. *Ak!* That was my pincer! Mind where your boot is going!'

'Shush!' Smith said. 'We're nearly there.'

Suruk was waiting at the bottom of the shaft. He helped Smith off the rungs and the pair of them lifted 462 down. Carveth dropped down and hefted her shotgun. 'I see why you Ghasts build everything so big,' she said. 'Your bums wouldn't fit otherwise.'

The shaft ended in a small square room, featureless except for a single door. It smelled of dust.

'An iris lock,' 462 said. 'And I have just the thing to open it.' He took something from his coat pocket. It was a bionic eye. 462 pressed it to the scanner. 'Thank you, Number Two. Shall we, Smith?'

Smith nodded. 462 pressed the button, and the door slid open.

They looked into a long, white chamber, like a drained swimming-pool. Pieces of Ghast machinery stood in rows, humming. The way they were spaced made Smith think of bookshelves in a library. There was a faint smell, both clean and unpleasant, like cheap detergent.

Very carefully, Smith crept into the room. He scurried to one of the machines and dropped behind it. He peeked out of cover, down the length of the chamber. It seemed empty, as far as he could tell. He gestured for the others to follow.

'What is this place?' Rhianna whispered.

462 nodded at the machinery. Each device had a mis-shapen tube at its centre, about six feet long and covered in wires like vines. 'Cloning tanks,' he said. For a Ghast, he was getting good at speaking quietly. 'They say Number One copies himself to live longer, then transfers his memories into his new body. He is surprisingly cunning.'

Smith said, 'If he's that clever, he ought to copy himself into a body that doesn't look like the last prawn in the cocktail. Come on.'

There were consoles on the walls. Lights blinked and

flickered. Screens displayed maps of Selenia and the galaxy. On one, an image of the British Isles appeared. Text scrolled across the top: SECTOR ONE . . . DEVON AND CORNWALL . . . ESTIMATED MONTHLY CALORIE YIELD . . .'

'Let's get this little bugger,' Smith said.

'*Not so fast.*' The voice was huge and cracked, the words spoken carefully. It seemed to come from the air itself. Smith glanced around, checking the corners of the room with the Civiliser, and saw speaker grilles mounted high on the walls. 'When this facility was first built, I had loud-speakers fitted so that I could hear my own voice at any time. Now you too have that privilege. I am waiting for you at the end of the room. I have no gun.'

Suruk opened his mandibles and mouthed, *Trap.*

Smith nodded. 'Fan out,' he whispered.

They split. Carveth and Rhianna took the left flank, Suruk the right. Smith stayed beside 462. 'Have you got a gun?'

'Your people removed the ammunition pack. But I con-cealed a spare. Look away, please.'

Smith glanced down the hall. When he looked back, 462 held an officer's pistol in his hand, and was push-ing a magazine into its unwholesome underside. 'You are too trusting, Smith. I could have had anything stashed up there.'

'That's exactly why I didn't look.'

462 frowned. 'Admittedly, it took a lot of pushing to keep it out of sight. And getting it back out again was uncomfortable.' He grimaced. 'It is fortunate that I always keep a spare magazine under my helmet.'

'Your helmet?'

'Of course. Where did you think it was? A wise ant is always forearmed,' 462 said. 'Unless he is using his middle arms as legs.' He cocked the gun with a wet click. 'It's time to see a man about a dog.'

They advanced. Smith drew back the hammer on his Civiliser. With every step, the low droning of machinery became louder. It seemed to numb his brain.

A board had been attached to the wall. It was nearly covered in a strange collage of pictures cut from books and magazines. At the bottom was the Great Pyramid and heaped upon it were the Empire State Building, the Eiffel Tower, the Taj Mahal, Big Ben and the Brandenburg Gate. On top of the whole thing stood a picture of Number One. The whole construction was labelled *Monument to My Conquest of Earth*.

The Ghasts might build big, Smith reflected, but they thought small.

The rear of the chamber was overrun with bio-machinery. It swarmed up the wall like mutant ivy: pipes reached up to the ceiling like spines, encrusted with glowing nodes. Two long objects hung down from the ceiling, somewhere between robot arms and scorpion tails.

Number One stood beneath them. His hands were raised: a red LED winked in his little right fist.

'That's close enough,' One said. His English was harsher and more measured than 462's: it sounded as if he was quoting an evil phrase book. 'First – if you stop my pulse, or if I let go of this device, this whole laboratory will explode. Second – well, well, well. If it isn't the man from the sport centre. Captain British or whatever you are called. And you brought your team with you. Did you expect a rematch?'

'I wouldn't expect anything sporting from you,' Smith replied.

'A despicable bevy of scum!' One yelled. 'You and your pathetic moustache – a degenerate frog-thing that should be hopping in a swamp. And two women – one a psychic freak, the other. . . I don't know . . . fat or something. And the arch-traitor himself, 462.'

462 hissed, 'You shot my dog.'

'You know, this is conclusive proof that you just can't bio-engineer the staff these days. Always, I am telling my minions to work harder. Always, I stand ready to scream "You are failing!" at them. Always, but always they betray me.' He seemed to draw into himself, as if absorbing malice from the air. 'The Edenites, the Ghastists, the Criminarch, the lemming men and even my own servants – they all betrayed me! I give them the opportunity for certain death in my name and this is how they repay me! It is un-reason-a-ble!'

He moved forward, the detonator still flickering in his grip, as if daring them to take it from him. 'You have landed on my planet. You have punched through my defences. You have destroyed the Pincers of Death, the very pinnacle of mil-i-tary efficiency! You think that makes you tough, do you?'

Smith said, 'Yes, actually.'

Horribly, Number One began to smile. On a face wizened by hatred, it looked appalling. He wore the smile like a hat covered in rotting fruit. 'You are weak. Your species is weak. I have known this ever since our Science Division first made contact with mankind. Let me show you something.'

A screen flickered into life beside him. Smith saw a scene from Earth. A small man in a battered coat stood behind an easel. In the background, a man was playing the tuba, and people were waltzing around it.

'Six hundred years ago I sent a ship to your wretched planet, to acquire a specimen for investigation. It was then that I learned just how imperfect your species are.'

'Is,' said Smith.

The man stepped back from his watercolour. His back was to the camera. He seemed to be angrily addressing the easel, in a matter not wholly unlike Number One. The bushes burst open behind him, and two huge praetorians grabbed him and dragged him into the shrubbery.

The scene switched to the inside of a Ghast spaceship, festooned with insignia. The little man was being forcibly debagged under an enormous red banner. The man twisted and thrashed, and his face turned to the camera. Smith saw his wild eyes and square moustache.

'My God,' Smith said. 'I'd know that little moustache anywhere. It all makes sense now – the shouting, the banners, everything. You abducted Charlie Chaplin!'

'I didn't bother to ask his name. You humans are all so alike. I just probed him and threw him out the door. Of course, this puny specimen was terrified,' One continued. 'But when he saw my strength, my legions, my banners and my many, many portraits, what this human felt was envy – envy at my greatness! The first word he said was "Awe"! Although, given that we were probing him at the time, it might have been "Aargh".'

'Good Lord. It all makes sense now. No wonder Chaplin had such a funny walk.'

'It does not matter. We dumped the test specimen back where we found him. I doubt he amounted to anything. But from then on, I knew that your weak species was ripe for conquest. All I had to do was sit back and wait for you to come to me.'

Smith looked him in the eye. 'Your overconfidence is your weakness.'

'Overconfident? How could I be overconfident when I am already invincible? Your wretched planets will supply us with food for centuries to come.'

Suruk laughed. 'Stupid little creature. I am Suruk the Slayer, not Suruk the Supper. The only thing of mine you taste will be the blade of Gan Uteki, Spear of the Ancients.'

Number One raised his hand. 'I knew you would come for me, so I laid a trap for you. And you walked straight into it. This planet's ecosystem was ruined years ago, when my minions ate it dry. We have no resources except the heat of the planet's core. For years, Selenia has been kept running by a sequence of reactors, all tapping into the core. I have rigged them to explode.'

'What?' cried Smith. 'The whole lot?'

'When they go, the entire planet goes too. All the major cities – wiped out, extinguished, anni-hil-ated! This planet will burst like a hand grenade. And your armies will die with it. Of course, a few billion of my underlings will be destroyed, but you can't order the execution of an omelette without breaking a few eggs. And I can replenish my forces far quicker than you.'

Carveth said, 'But you'll be dead, right?'

'Wrong. Our scientists have built teleporters: imperfect,

but sufficient. They will be used to carry me to a safe location directly above this installation. And then I will leave this planet and conquer the galaxy while the cream of your army is in-cin-erated below!'

Number One shuddered violently, and for a happy moment Smith thought the glorious leader had somehow wired himself to the mains. When the twitching had subsided, Number One gestured at the machinery around him. 'This is the teleporter. It is coded to my DNA. So are the controls that can stop the detonation – and without them, you are helpless. I invite you to remain here and watch as the world ends. In fact, you have no other option.'

'Good God,' Smith said. 'You really are a little arsehole, aren't you?'

'I am not little!'

'True. My pilot here is little. You're miniscule. Suruk, you take the machine.'

Suruk purred.

Number One slicked his antennae down with a pincer. 'As they used to say in the puny Roman Empire – Hail and farewell.'

'As they say in the British Space Empire – bollocks to you, Gertie.'

Smith whipped up the Civiliser and fired – not at Number One, but at the teleporter itself. Sparks burst from the bio-machinery. Suruk's spear flew into the workings. Light burst from the machine, swallowing Number One. He vanished.

'Now,' said Smith. 'Let's catch the little bugger. 462, get over here and tell me how I follow him.'

The Ghast limped over. He leaned over the controls. 'Let

us see. This is not my area of expertise, but . . . it seems that you could follow him to wherever he has gone.'

'Excellent. Let's get cracking.'

'Wait.' 462 raised his hand. 'You would have to go one at a time. This sign here warns the user not to activate the teleporter when there is an insect in the teleportation area. Any trace could result in genetic splicing. It's not safe.'

'How long have we got?'

'Until the first detonations? Four minutes.'

'Right. Stay here, everyone. If I can catch him, I can make him turn it off.'

Smith stepped onto the pad, under the two prongs of the projector. He readied his rifle. 'Follow me through, chaps,' he said. 'See you on the other side.'

462 hit the switch. Light flared from the teleporter. Smith covered his eyes and disappeared, as if blown to dust by an explosion. Then he was gone.

462 turned to the others. 'He seems to have been vapourised,' he said. 'Who's next?'

The teleporter roared. A great blast of light blew out from the centre. Electricity crackled at the edge of the room.

Smith crouched in the centre of the teleporter. Slowly, he stood up. 'Ow,' he said. 'Oh. I'm back here. Strange. We must have got it on the wrong setting.' He turned towards the machine. 'I feel . . . odd. Chaps,' he announced, 'I'm feeling a bit under the weather. I think you should all go back upstairs.'

Rhianna moved forward. 'Isambard, your aura. . . it's turning red.'

'I'm fine,' he said. 'Just a bit peaky. There's nothing to be worried about, minions.'

'Minions?'

'Just go,' said Smith. 'Go back and help Susan.'

'You're ill,' Rhianna said.

He whipped around. 'No. I am strong. Mustn't grumble. Because grumbling is for the weak, and the weak *must – be – destroyed!*'

For a moment, nobody said anything. Smith's voice echoed through the room.

462 bent over and ran his pincer along the floor of the teleporter. He held it up. 'Smith,' he said, 'is this – one of your secretions?'

'Of course not. It looks like the sort of dribble that comes out of Number One –'

'Genetic matter,' said the Ghast.

'Oh, no,' Carveth said. The sound seemed to come from deep within her. 'You can't have – not with him . . . What're we going to do?'

'Go,' Smith said. 'All of you. That's an order. And orders must be obeyed – obeyed without hesitation! No – wait – not yet. Chaps, before you go, I just want to say that I couldn't have had a better crew. You have been smashing . . .' He pointed at them. 'Top-notch.' He made a fist. 'In-valu-a-ble! Now go, dammit, before it's too late!'

'We must leave,' said 462. 'Our orders say—'

'Mazuran,' Suruk said, 'One day, we will dine in the halls of my ancestors and smash the crockery together. I will leave my spear here with you. It has given me company many times.'

Carveth opened her mouth and a high, rising wail came out. Suruk turned her around, gently but firmly, and propelled her towards the door.

'Rhianna,' said Smith, 'I – ah – well, you know. I'm not much good at, er, speaking to girls, and I've never been good at emotion – except rage and hatred to all puny vertebrates—'

'Shush, Isambard,' she replied. She stepped close. 'There's no need to make a fuss. And anyway, I'm psychic. I *know*.'

She turned and left, not looking back. Smith heard the door close. He raised his hands. The skin was starting to turn red. He ran his fingers through his hair. It was thickening at two places on his temples, clumping together as if making horns.

Antennae. Well, this is it, then.

He turned back to the machine. Smith reached out and put his palm against the reader. There was a jab of pain in his hand, and a voice said, in Ghastish, 'Genetic sequence accepted. What are your orders, Number One?'

'Shut it down,' he replied.

*

The kettle whistled. Susan turned off the beam gun and Craig poured the water into the collapsible pot. He stirred it with his commando knife.

'Well,' Nelson said, 'we've not exploded yet. He must have turned the bomb off. Which means . . .'

'He's dead,' Susan said.

462 sat on the ground, his bad leg stuck out in front of him. He had taken off his helmet. 'Or worse,' he said.

Carveth blew her nose.

Dreckitt stepped over with a cup of tea and passed it

to her. 'A long time ago,' he said, 'I had to hunt down an android who'd gone crazy. It was a tough case to crack. The guy was one jump ahead of the nut factory. He chased me up onto the roof, took his shirt off, waved a dead bird in my face and started quoting poetry. And all I could think of was, *you're a man*. Okay, a crazy robot man with no shirt holding a pigeon and making jaw like some kind of hophead, but a man. Same with Smith.'

W stepped forward to take his tea like a mourner accepting an order of service. 'Smith certainly died like a man,' he said. 'Even if it was some kind of bizarre half-man, half-insect hybrid. I always thought teleporters were a bad business,' he added. 'Science fiction nonsense.'

Very quietly, Rhianna said, 'What if . . . guys, what if he's . . . not dead? I mean, worse.'

'Don't worry about that,' W said. 'I'll shoot him.'

'No you won't!' Carveth cried. She stepped forward. 'You won't shoot the captain.' She caught her breath. 'Because if he had to – he'd have done it himself.'

Suruk sighed. 'It is going to be strange without him. And without my spear. My two best friends, gone. Who will talk to me about war and violence? And what will I do without Isambard Smith?'

'Don't worry about me,' a voice said.

They turned. Smith stood in the doorway, barely upright. His coat was battered and torn. His eyes were bloodshot. He staggered forwards.

Rhianna and Suruk ran to his side. Together, they helped him into the room. Smith stood there, head drooping.

'Boss?' Carveth ventured, as if afraid that the sound of her voice would shatter him. 'Boss, are you all right?'

Smith licked his lips. 'Been worse.' He pulled aside, as if to be sick. Carveth gasped. Smith put his hands to his forehead. He tore at his hair, and cried out. When he looked back at them, there was blood on his hairline.

He tossed two things onto the ground. Antennae.

'Thought I was turning Gertie there,' he said. 'Turns out I've got a bit too much moral fibre in my blood.'

W held out a cup. 'Have a bit more, Smith.'

'Cheers.' He took a deep swig of tea. 'That's better.'

Carveth stared at him. 'So you're not turning into a Ghast?'

'I don't think so. I think I sweated it out.' He looked down and pulled his coat to one side. 'You're the expert here, Carveth. Tell me: does my arse look big in this?'

'About normal.'

'Good. God, I do feel rough, though. No wonder the Ghasts are so bad-tempered.'

'Damn,' Dreckitt said, 'it's good to see you, pal. Now, I'm about done with this dive. Would you look at this place? There's so many pincers lying around, it's like the dumpster out back of a lobster chow-house.' He lit a cigarette and drew deeply on it. 'Since we've blipped out Number One's chopper squad, I say we cheese it back to the ship and nibble one. The joint's busted. All that's left is to pour out the hooch and write up the report. What do you say, Susan?'

'As long as it's not you writing the report, that sounds good to me.' She paused for a moment. 'Poor old Wainscott, buying it like that.'

They murmured their agreement.

'Wait,' Smith said. He looked at his watch. 'Just a couple of minutes more. There.'

He pointed. A pin-prick of white light hung six feet above the ground. It grew, swelled, and they looked away as it threw hard shadows across the rubble-strewn floor. There was a rush of light, a sudden flooding of the chamber, and it was gone.

A single Ghast of the officer class stood where the light had been. It was unusually small, the eyes sunk deep within its head.

'That took too long!' Number One shouted. 'Minion, get my things. My safety is – oh . . .'

'Fancy seeing you here,' Smith said. 'You're just in time for tea.'

'Keep away from me! I am the commander of the greatest army—'

'What you are,' Smith said, 'is under arrest.'

One shuddered. His little eyes flicked left and right, suddenly desperate.

Carveth pointed her shotgun at him. 'You're nicked,' she said. 'Apprehended. In-dub-it-ably in-car-cerated.'

Number One stared at her. His mouth opened and closed. At last he said, 'How?'

Smith cleared his throat. 'I took the liberty of adjusting the settings on the teleporter. Welcome to Selenia, Number One – the newest province of the British Space Empire.'

Debriefing

The next few days passed strangely, not least because Smith was recovering from turning into a giant ant. Number One was passed to the security services, who ushered him into a shuttle with darkened portholes at the far side of the base. A camera crew from the BBC came, took some footage, and disappeared.

Many Ghasts were too angry – or too stupid, to want to give up. Several legions of praetorians were destroyed over the next few days, along with rump forces of human traitors, who knew what they had coming, and lemming men determined to go down in a blaze of gravity. The 634th Free M'Lak Assault Army captured the parliament of Selenia and, having nobody else to fight, declared war on the 635th Free M'Lak Assault Army.

The fleet was joined by enormous cargo vessels, converted into prison ships to take the captives off-world. The drones of the Ghast Empire would be slowly introduced to basic decency. The praetorians were to be taken to the far side of the galaxy, to help terraform new worlds for the Space Empire by breaking moon-rocks.

Smith made a model of a space dreadnought and hung it from the roof of his room.

Number One was a prisoner, and Number Two had been eaten by frogs. In their absence, the acting Number Two took over: namely, 462. The Service arranged for 462 to make a broadcast in which he called upon his species to surrender. It went quite well until he started cackling and shouting 'I am the leader now!'

Two days later, a shuttle touched down a hundred yards from the *John Pym*. Four warbots and half a dozen policemen with very large moustaches trooped out. Smith stood by the airlock, watching. They were followed by a fat man, who stomped out of the shuttle, tearing off his jacket and rolling up his sleeves as he went.

Three policemen grabbed the fat man and pulled him back. 'Just one,' the fat man shouted, shaking his fist at the ship where Number One was being kept. 'Just one on the jaw, dammit.'

'No, Prime Minister,' one of the detectives called. 'Think of your constituents!'

'Oh,' said the Prime Minister, shaking his fists, 'do they want a piece of this too?'

Later that day, when the Prime Minister had been escorted off the premises, Susan and Dreckitt knocked on the door of the *John Pym*. 'How are you?' Susan asked, over tea and cake. 'Fully recovered yet?'

'Fine, thanks,' Smith replied. 'I've got a bit of stiffness in my upper lip, but I don't want to make a fuss, so I'll carry on regardless. How about you?'

'It's different, not having Wainscott,' she replied. 'Shame he didn't make it. I don't think he would have enjoyed victory, though.'

'I doubt civilian life would have suited him.'

She nodded. 'I reckon he would have stayed in uniform – in theory. Does a straitjacket count as a uniform?'

Rhianna opened the biscuit box. 'Perhaps he's looking down on us right now.'

Suruk shook his head. 'I doubt it. Heaven would not be ready for Wainscott. I expect he will have used his powers of infiltration to creep into the afterlife of my species and is probably destroying things with the greatest of our warriors.'

'Well,' Susan said, 'I'd love to sit and chat, but I've got special forces things to do. I'm on the Anglo-Straalian liaison committee now. There's me, Shane and Rippy, but Rippy's just in an advisory role.' She hesitated, before adding, 'He's a nice guy, Shane. He sent me flowers. Not only are they pretty, but they're the only form of plant life from his homeworld that isn't deadly poisonous.'

'Considerate,' Smith replied.

'Anyhow, W wanted to know if you'd like to see Number One. They're debriefing him right now.'

They headed out to the unmarked shuttle on the far side of the base. A dozen people waited in the hold. The mood was like a drinks reception at an accountant's wedding: pleasant, but serious. Smith and his crew were congratulated by Khan and Benson of the Service, Seddrick the Helmsman from the M'Lak, a multi-limbed brass drone sent by the Space Empire's logic engines, and even by Captain Fitzroy, who had demanded the honour of piloting the shuttle down to collect Number One. Smith shook hands with all of them, except Seddrick. He settled with knocking respectfully on the side of the Gilled Helmsman's tank.

'You'd better come through,' Khan said. 'You've yet to see our special guest.'

The rear of the hold was partitioned off with a single piece of glass. Behind the glass was a table, and either side of it sat W and Number One.

Seeing the great leader, Carveth made a gesture. 'It's two-way glass,' Khan said.

Smith reached out and took Rhianna's hand. 'I suppose you're sensing hostility from him,' he said.

'No,' she replied. 'I'm sensing defeat.'

W made a note on a clipboard. Number One swung his legs. His feet did not quite reach the floor.

'Funny to think he was their leader,' Carveth said. 'He doesn't look like much.'

'Nor do you,' Suruk replied, 'and yet you are Battle Girl.'

W crossed his legs. 'So,' he said, 'when exactly did you first realise that you wanted to take over the galaxy?'

Number One glared at him. 'I demand a lawyer and the immediate suspension of the entire legal system.'

'All right then, let's try something else. Tell me only the good things that come into your mind when I mention . . . moral fibre.'

One screeched and drew back like a vampire confronted with a crucifix. 'I have human rights!' he yelped. 'When I speak to humans, I am always right!'

W sipped his tea. One paused, looked awkward, and relaxed.

Smith said, 'What's going to happen to him?'

Khan ran a hand over his whiskers. 'He'll be taken far away, where he can't harm anyone again. 'We'll exile him, the way we did the Prince of France – a little planet, all alone, with a flower for company. The galaxy may not be entirely civilised yet, Smith, but it's a lot closer.'

Smith nodded. 'Good-oh.' He didn't know what exactly to feel. But that was always the way with emotions.

*

Suruk spent Friday morning squatting on the roof of the *John Pym*, sharpening the tail fin with a whetstone in case they flew very close to an enemy vessel. As he brushed away some of the shavings, a magnificent shuttle dropped out of orbit and landed at the base. It was vintage, beautifully kept, with polished brass around the airlocks and gold scrollwork on the observation dome. A squad of Ravnavari Lancers emerged, their tunics and sashes bright against the drab colours of Selenia. A slim M'Lak officer in a white jacket followed them across the landing pad. As he approached the *John Pym*, he smiled and waved.

Suruk looked up and grinned. He dropped down from the ship. 'Morgar,' he said. 'What brings you here, brother? Have you come to fight?'

'Goodness, no. We've been busy enough with the lemming men, thanks. We've been polishing off what's left of them. It's been a tough fight. Hand-to-paw combat, by and large. But the end is in sight. Actually, I've come to take custody of your prisoner, Commander 462.'

'You are welcome to him,' Suruk replied. 'He is too puny to bother killing, and he doesn't even seem to want to face me in battle at all. And the amount of orange squash he consumes! He barely dilutes it, like a savage. Truly, the Ghast Empire is based on barbarism.'

Together, they walked into the ship. Isambard Smith was sitting in an armchair, drinking a cup of tea. 462 sat on the settee, holding a book.

'I still find it puzzling,' 462 said. 'If Miss Marple simply shot all the suspects, she would not have to waste time establishing which one was the criminal. It seems very inefficient. With the power she wields, she could easily crush her enemies and seize control of the entire St Marymead Women's Institute. And this other book you gave me . . . is the very hungry caterpillar's commander aware of his over-consumption of supplies? Why is his officer allowing this gluttony?'

'Ahem,' said Morgar. 'I'm here to collect 462.'

The Ghast looked up. 'Excellent,' he replied, and he rubbed his pincers together.

Suruk said, 'You accept your incarceration cheerfully?'

'It will not be for long. Someone will have to run the Ghast Empire, after all.'

Smith lowered his cup. 'I think you'll find that's us, old chap.'

'Perhaps . . . and perhaps not, Smith. Take this officer here,' 462 said, pointing at Morgar. 'His world, Ravnavar, is almost wholly run by his species.'

'Yes,' Smith replied, 'but the M'Lak haven't tried to conquer the galaxy and eat everyone.'

'Not recently,' Suruk said.

462 shrugged. 'My people need proper leadership. They need someone to look up to.'

'And you think they'll look up to you?'

'Of course. I'll be on a podium. I will make them stand tall again, preferably in rows. With me as their president, we will grasp the future with both pincers and march towards progress as one – in an entirely unthreatening way, of course.'

'Hmm,' said Smith.

'Even once the praetorian legions have been sent into penal servitude, there will still be huge numbers of Ghasts left leaderless. This is a very difficult situation for an ant-person to find himself in. But in me, they will have found a leader, in the nick of time.'

'Emphasis on *in the nick*.'

462 put the books down beside the sofa. 'I am sure that this imprisonment is a mere formality. My species needs me – and so does yours. If we are to join the modern world, elements still intent on destroying Earth will have to be weeded out. Once I am in charge, there will be a certain amount of purging.'

'I think the only purging you'll be doing is when it's time to slop out. You realise that you're going to be doing a lot of porridge, as they say?'

'Rather porridge than pulped minion,' 462 replied. He stood up and limped towards Morgar. 'Which pair of limbs do you want to handcuff?' He paused and looked back. 'Goodbye, Smith. And good luck.'

*

The crowd poured out of the concert hall and into the chilly evening street. Students in long scarves talked earnestly. Wealthy patrons of the arts claimed to have understood what they had just endured. Normal people decided to go to the pub.

Eric Lint, journalist and spy, followed them with his hands in his pockets, enjoying the sounds of the street. There was a new note in people's voices, a sense that not only would they doggedly carry on with life, but they might actually enjoy it. The auto-dirigibles still floated above the Space Empire's cities, the emergency services robots still lumbered in the background, but there was optimism as well as defiance now. Victory was a matter of when, not if.

The lights of the shop windows made Lint think of Christmas. A sign in a tailor's said *Tweed for All Occasions and Species – 10% Discount for Servicebeings*. A robot was offering a waistcoat to a thing that looked like a combination of a dinosaur and a plucked vulture.

''Scuse me, mate.'

Lint glanced around.

A small man sat on a bench beside the street, an old coat draped over his shoulders. 'Spare some change for an old soldier?'

Lint sat down on the bench and crossed his long legs. 'It is terrible to think,' he said, 'that a veteran should be on the streets.'

'Better than back in the loony bin,' the man replied. 'Or in that concert, from the look on your face. How was it?'

'Beastly. It was called *Fairy Bells* – a medley of folk songs by some oaf called Peter Peason. It was like the carpet bombing of a piano factory. Peason himself sounded as if he'd been gargling soap just before the performance and most of the way through it, too. There used to be a good show where two girls dressed up as chaps and sang rude songs. That was much better.'

'I liked that one too. Modern music is a con, if you ask me. I once paid good money to go to a jazz concert and it turned out the buggers were making most of it up as they went along.'

'Well done on faking your death, by the way.'

'Thanks,' Wainscott said. 'It wasn't easy. I did consider leaving my clothes on a beach and swimming to safety, but I reckon people are pretty used to me getting my kit off. Sorry to cause distress, but I couldn't take the risk of anything slipping out in front of the men. How's Susan doing? Has she found anybody to replace me yet?'

'I heard they were interviewing someone called Timmy.'

'What outfit is he from?'

'Search and Rescue. He's a border collie.'

Wainscott sniffed. 'What're you going to do now?'

W lit one of his roll-ups. 'I think I'm going to have a rest,' he said. 'There's a planet they've just finished terraforming near Signus Nine. It's got good views, no human inhabitants and an automated whisky distillery. I thought I might leave the Service and have some fun.'

'Is that possible?'

'Of course. I have lots of fun. I just do it while there's nobody else around to depress me.'

'I meant leaving the Service.'

'Extended holiday. The top brass are going out for a curry next week to celebrate catching Number One. I'd invite you along, but I'd have to kill you afterwards.'

'Thanks for thinking of me.' They sat there for a

moment. 'Hard to know what to do without anything to blow up,' Wainscott said. 'Perhaps I'll visit my sister, see if she's caught herself a man yet. Check the traps.'

'There'll always be work, Wainscott.' W took a long drag on his cigarette. 'If it's not one sort of tyranny, it's another. One of the Logic Engines has gone rogue. It chartered a ship into deep space and is calling itself Steelor, Lord of Machines. We'll need someone to pull its plug out.'

Wainscott grinned. 'I'm in. The show must go on.'

'That's the spirit,' said W. 'Welcome back.'

*

'A British officer always keeps his word,' Smith said as he finished hammering the nail into the sitting room wall. 'I told this bugger I'd have him stuffed, and by God, I did.' He reached down and picked up the head of the captain of the Pincers of Death. It was mounted on a polished wooden shield with brass edging, the antennae wired at a jaunty angle. The eyes glared madly across the room.

'Left a bit, Mazuran,' said Suruk the Slayer.

Smith stepped back to admire his work. 'Excellent. It complements the one we got back on Drogon, when the war was starting. We've done well. Now the galaxy can be at peace. Are you pulling a face, Suruk, or is that just . . . you know, normal?'

'All this peace,' Suruk said. 'It feels a little disappointing. I was hoping that the war wouldn't end like this. Actually, I was hoping that the war wouldn't end at all. You don't think there is going to be another one, by any chance?'

'I doubt it.'

'If, ah, one just happened to start somehow . . . if there was to be some sort of international incident . . .'

'Don't even think about it, old chap.'

Rhianna came in. 'Guys? Is anything going on?'

'I wasn't planning a war,' Suruk said. 'Honestly.'

Rhianna looked at the stuffed praetorian and shook her head. 'Isambard, Polly's not good. She's kind of . . . you know, down.'

'Oh dear. Do you want me to buck her up?'

'No. Just talk to her, Isambard. Empathise.'

'Righto. I'll get her to snap out of it, don't worry. You chaps stay back. This calls for an expert.'

Smith walked into the cockpit. Carveth was standing beside the pilot's seat, gazing into the void. Smith felt oddly nervous. In a film, she would have turned around to reveal that she was actually a monster. When she heard him and turned, he felt quite relieved that she had the face of a small android who looked about thirty.

'Hallo there,' he said. 'Everything all right?'

'I was just looking out the window,' she replied. 'That's the best thing about this job – they pay you for staring into space.'

In his cage, Gerald's wheel began to rattle.

Carveth reached down and picked up a paper cup. The words *Now You Are Four* were printed around the top. 'Funny, really,' she said. 'I met you here first, all those years ago. We've come so far, and yet here I am, still in this little room with you.'

'True.'

'I've never really known anything except war,' she said. 'I've seen so much of the stuff you'd almost think I liked it.

And now – well.' She took a drink and winced. The liquid in the paper cup was clearly not suitable for a four-year-old. When she lowered the cup, Carveth looked almost frightened. 'Boss, what's going to happen now?'

'Well, it's gone six, so it's probably time for gin—'

'I mean, to me. To the ship. It's not going to be scrapped, is it? For that matter, I'm not going to be scrapped either, am I?'

'Of course not. You're protected by law as a synthetic person. As for the ship, well, it could do with a bit of work, but I'm sure we can afford that. Suruk's got so many trophies from the Pincers of Death, he could open his bedroom to the public as a museum.'

'But – we'll still stay here, won't we? You and Rhianna and – okay, Suruk, I suppose. You're all the family I've got.'

Smith decided not to mention the fact that neither he nor Rhianna – and certainly not Suruk – were related to Carveth by descent. As an android, she probably had a closer lineage with the fridge than any of her crewmates. He thought of the pale, lumpy refrigerator, and the huge amount of food and drink that had gone into it over the years, and said, 'You're worried, aren't you?'

'Weird, isn't it? I've spent four years trying not to get shot and now I'm frightened because nobody's shooting at me anymore.'

'Ah,' said Smith. 'I've been thinking about this.' He felt pleased to be able to suggest something positive instead of having to express empathy. 'Suruk! Rhianna! Can you come in, please?'

They entered. The cabin felt almost cosy with everyone aboard.

'Now,' said Smith, 'I've been thinking. Obviously, we've been kept quite busy, what with the galactic war and everything. But we're going to need something new to do. I have it on good authority that the Service will need transport and so on, but we'll need a day job.

'Obviously, there's been a lot of destruction across the Space Empire – and the new territories we've captured from the enemy are in a bad way, as you'd imagine. A lot of the galaxy's most exotic creatures have been reduced almost to destruction, which isn't any good. And obviously we've all got rather . . . specific talents, which it seems a shame to let go to waste.

'So here's what I propose we do. We are going to apply for a grant from the Galactic Wildlife Fund to open a nature reserve on some large planet – Ravnavar, perhaps, or Urn. We will convert the hold into a holding environment – a big cage or tupperware box, as appropriate – and use the *John Pym* to transport all sorts of endangered creatures to suitable land where they can be bred before re-release into the wild.'

'Hey,' said Rhianna. 'That sounds kind of like conservation.'

'Exactly. Of course, this won't be easy. Most of these creatures will be large and extremely dangerous. Capturing them alive will probably be even harder than killing them.'

Suruk flexed his mandibles. 'Dangerous, eh?'

'Quite so. An expert hunter would be needed. While there wouldn't much opportunity for trophies – if they've got heads to start with, they'd need them by the end – you'd get your name in the paper quite a lot.'

'Hmm. The newspaper, you say? I like it, Mazuran. Indeed, for too long the regional news of the galaxy has been ruled by cats being taken out of trees. But how can a cat being removed from nature compare to a Procturan Black Ripper being introduced to it? This plan has legs, and claws, too. Now we have saved the galaxy from tyranny, let us save it from boredom by collecting a menagerie of death! And to think that I worried that peace would be boring. Can one be bored where every spaceship, every escape pod, every ventilation shaft holds the prospect of adventure? Did not Shakespeare or someone like that say that if you loved something, you should set it free? I love really large dangerous animals, and—'

'We'll iron out the details as we go,' Smith said.

Carveth sipped her drink. 'Well, leaving aside the whole carnage thing, I do have one question. Do all these animals have to be dangerous?'

'Not necessarily,' Smith replied, before Suruk could say anything.

'So, is there any chance—'

'We could fit a few Shetlands in, I reckon. We'd need something for the petting zoo.'

'I'm in.'

'Jolly good,' Smith said. 'I shall put together a proposal and put it to the authorities. I'm sure our determination and combined skills will do the trick. And if that doesn't work, being friends with the secret service ought to tip the balance. Carveth?'

'Yes?'

'Put the gin down for a minute and programme us a new destination.'

'I can do better than that,' she replied. 'I can programme the computer with one hand and drink gin with the other!'

'Excellent. And I think I'll dish out the ration for the rest of us.' He reached over and broke the seal on the emergency cabinet. Smith opened the bottle and poured out three glasses. 'Victory is ours, chaps. The Space Empire is safe and even bigger than before. Soon, the whole universe will know civilisation and enlightenment, whether it likes it or not. Someone once observed that the past is a foreign country, which is why I say we must never go back. We have only one place left to conquer.' He raised his glass. 'To the future, men!'

Epilogue

462 opened his eye and looked at the ceiling. The last thing he remembered was entering a cryogenic pod for the voyage to His Majesty's Penal Colonies. He sat up cautiously.

He was lying on some kind of bed. It was soft and smelled very clean. The room was bright and cheerful. There were no propaganda pictures and not a single screen to tell him what time it was. His coat and helmet were nowhere to be seen.

Warily, 462 got to his feet. He felt bad, but not terrible, as if he'd indulged in a few pints of mid-strength sucrose solution the previous night. He needed to use the facilities in order to increase his efficiency.

There was a door on the far side of the bedroom. It led to a small room with a shower and lavatory. 462 sat down and closed the door. He was part-way through his business when he noticed a large poster on the back of the toilet door. It showed a man with a moustache covering his eyes with one hand. The message read NOBODY IS WATCHING YOU.

Perturbed, he returned to the bedroom. His coat, or one very much like it, was hanging in a cupboard. Some fool had sewn white piping to the hem. His helmet and pistol had gone.

'Good morning!'

He whipped around. It was a woman's voice, coming from outside the room. 462 pulled on the coat and emerged.

She wore a blue overcoat, a little hat and a long striped scarf. She was sitting on the sofa in a neat, pleasant living room, smiling at him. 'What a lovely day it is today!'

'Where am I?' 462 said.

'You are in the Colony,' she said.

'Who are you? The secret police?'

She stood up. 'Nonsense. I'm here to look after you. It's your first day here, isn't it?'

'What are your orders?'

'I don't really have any. Neither do you. That's the whole point – you can decide what to do for yourself now. Like a grown-up. My name's Helen,' said the woman. 'Shall we look outside?'

He frowned. 'Is that an order?'

She gestured towards the door. 'Knock yourself out.'

'Is *that* an order?'

She opened the front door and light flooded in. 462 winced, partly at the sunshine, but mainly in disgust at the green, tranquil little town before him. Water bubbled merrily out of a fountain. A robot policeman was strolling slowly around a square of thick green grass. He could hear a brass band in the distance.

Helen walked through the door and 462 followed warily, as if afraid that the ground might give way.

They crossed the little square.

'This settlement is primitive,' 462 said, feeling that small talk was necessary. 'In any developed society, it would be demolished and its inhabitants pulped for nutritional purposes.'

345

'That's quite unnecessary,' Helen replied. 'Here, we are nice to one another. We say nice, helpful things.'

She pointed at a piece of cloth hanging from a building. It was like a banner, except with less insignia and no picture of Number One. Instead, it showed a man with the moustache. He was holding up a cup. *WHY NOT STOP FOR TEA?* It said. *IT'S YOUR CHOICE!*

462 looked away. He paused, feeling the sunlight, and tilted his antennae. The music was getting louder: trumpets, punctuated by the thump of a bass drum.

A Ghast drone appeared. It was wearing a hideous striped blazer and a straw hat and waving a striped stick in the air. A second drone came around the corner, wielding a trumpet. More Ghasts followed them, waving pennants.

'This is the worst parade I have ever seen,' 462 said. 'Where are the tanks? I bet some of those flags are not even state-approved.'

The whole noisy group moved slowly past the bench, failing to march in step. One of the drones saw him, waved, and beckoned him over.

'Where are you going?' 462 demanded. 'Is there a rally somewhere?'

'Oh no.' The drone wore a badge that said *Rod*. The one next to it had a lilac jumper and a badge that read *Freddy*. 'We're just taking the air. We've passed the basic pleasantness test, and soon we'll be able to go to places on our own.'

'What? You must cease this conduct at once!'

One of the drones looked straight at him. 'We don't say *must* or *mustn't* anymore.'

Another leaned in from 462's left. Her badge said *Jane*. '*Mustn't* is a bad word.'

'This is absurd.' 462 glared at Helen. 'You! You have indoctrinated them!'

'De-indoctrinated, actually,' she said. 'Do come along.'

Stunned, he followed her away from the parade. The band passed by in a stream of colour, pennants and parasols spinning and fluttering above it. The drones waved him goodbye. 'Knock yourself out!' they called.

'This level of free thought is intolerable,' 462 declared. 'This is what happens when you don't have a leader.' He glared at Helen. 'Where can I find someone capable of taking orders?'

'In the tea rooms? The service is very good.'

462 felt as if he was going to pop. 'I need the lavatory,' he said.

'Jolly good,' said Helen. 'Knock yourself out!'

462 locked himself in the public convenience on the far side of the square. Quickly and awkwardly, he clambered up onto the toilet bowl, reached up to the window and smashed it with his pincer.

It was difficult to pull himself through the gap. He dropped down on the other side in a mass of limbs and leather and picked a few pieces of glass out of his stercorium.

The road ahead was empty. He smirked and hurried on his way.

It was amazing how humans could bear to live in such small, unstandardised buildings. He scanned the horizon, with its weird blue sky and complete lack of statues, and wondered where exactly he was going. Somewhere, he'd find other Ghasts, or at least someone he could boss around. He'd have some order here.

Some fool had propped a two-wheeled machine against the back of the map-board. With difficulty, 462 climbed onto the device and pedalled it down the road, experiencing the inefficiency of each cobblestone as he rode over it.

Voices spilled out of a long, white building. *A rally*, he thought. Perhaps he could address it and take command, figure out how to get away from here. 462 stopped the bicycle, climbed down and crept to the window.

Rows of robed men sat at desks, looking at a screen. *Edenites*. That was better than nothing. A horde of stupid, enraged cultists could be quite useful.

A photograph of a woman appeared on the screen. A female voice said, 'Who's this?'

'A whore of Babylon!' one of the Edenites screamed. 'Burn her, burn her!'

There was a loud buzzing sound and the Edenite leaped about three feet into the air. He sat down slowly, rubbing his behind. 'A . . . nice . . . lady?' he said.

'Well done,' the voice replied. 'Your desk will now dispense a biscuit.'

'*There* you are,' a woman said. 462 turned: Helen was standing in the road, looking amiable.

'This is where we teach the Edenites to be pleasant,' she said. 'By, er, giving them biscuits.'

'*I* am not an Edenite.' 462 pulled away. He lurched past her, down a sun-drenched alleyway. He saw water at the end of it.

'There's no need to be rude!' Helen called. 'Not when you can be civilised.'

462 strode to the end of the alley. His breathing was hard. He emerged onto a beach. Gulls shrieked above him. Further down the beach, a large white ball was bouncing up and down. No doubt the humans wanted him to play some idiotic game, where the taking part was what mattered instead of crushing the opposition.

A Ghast was sitting on a bench a little way forward, looking out to sea. It turned around as he approached.

'Sven?' said 462. 'Is that you? We've got to get out of here.'

'Hello there!' Sven replied. 'Here, have a seat. It's a lovely day. You can just take your time, relax . . .'

'They got to you too,' he said. Fear rose in 462: they were going to keep him here, make him like them – make him nice. He stumbled back across the sand. Helen emerged from the alleyway. She raised her umbrella like a parasol. He backed away from her.

'No,' he cried. 'Get away from me! I will not be *civilised*! I will not be reasonable, or pleasant, or nice. I will not stand in queues, or talk about the weather or eat biscuits. I should be running the Ghast Empire – what's left of it – not being exiled to this wretched hive of mildness.'

'Well,' said Helen, 'we'll begin the civilising process whenever you're ready. Take your time. You're a free man now.'

'No!' cried 462. He raised his pincers and shook them at the heavens. 'I am not a free man, I am a number!'

'*Really*,' Helen replied. 'Do stop making a fuss.'

Acknowledgements

Writing a novel is a rather solitary business, so it's nice to have someone to tell you that you're not doing it wrong. I'd like to thank Myrmidon for publishing this novel, to John and Ed for all their help in making it presentable, and to Owen and Ian for their comments and suggestions (including That Joke). Thanks are also due to, as ever, my parents, whose stock of tea has been greatly diminished during the writing of this book, and the various readers who kindly asked for more. The Space Empire sends its thanks, chaps!